Blandings' Way

BY
ERIC HODGINS

"The spirit of liberty is the spirit
which is not too sure that it is right."
—Judge Learned Hand

19 50

SIMON AND SCHUSTER

MANUFACTURED IN THE UNITED STATES OF AMERICA
BY HADDON CRAFTSMEN, SCRANTON, PA.

In Memoriam

William McCreery Strong

· 1 ·

OUTSIDE THE HOUSE it was so cold that the earth rang like slag. All day long the skies had been sunny, but the thermometer had begun dropping from the middle twenties a little after noonday, and with dusk it stood at Fahrenheit twelve. The sun had been silver-colored in a sky that was a deep blue void, and the moment it vanished the blue became incredible, and the stars punctured it with sharp dagger points from zenith to horizon, and it was too cold for them to wink. The thermometer on the porch sank as you looked at it: its red column dropped to eight, to four. It reached the zero mark, and did not pause. A light breath of wind was stirring, but the frigid trees stood stolid as castings.

Mr. Blandings opened his front door a quarter of an inch to get a better look at the thermometer on the outer jamb, and a scimitar of icy air slashed at him through the crack. His nostrils stung with it; his lungs gave a spasm as he took a breath. He slammed shut the heavy door and snapped the double lock to underline his purpose. The warm air of the living room re-enveloped him.

"Close the door, for heaven's sake," said Mrs. Blandings looking critically at the closed door.

"I have closed the door," said Mr. Blandings. "I just opened it to get a better look at the—"

"We'll catch our death of cold," said Mrs. Blandings, grooved in the tense of her choosing.

Mr. Blandings held the back of his hand to the edge of the door-frame. Despite an impressive system of weather stripping, an edge of cold stung the backs of his fingers where the air leaked through. He returned thoughtfully to the fireplace, rubbing his hands, and settled down again in his upholstered chair. It would be nice to go out and study the enigma of the solid, star-punctured darkness but it was too cold, just too damn cold even if you bundled up with everything you had and left only your eyes and nose exposed. It was better to sit by the fire and think about the enigma. Heavy crystals of frost, exquisitely arranged, were forming on the window-lights; in another few minutes the glass would be as bafflingly opaque as the windows in a Pullman toilet.

Now that was a fine simile to occur to a man, Mr. Blandings thought; a fine, poetic simile. Tennyson had called frost "ice ferns" once, but when it came *his* turn he thought of a toilet window. Well, everyone couldn't be a poet. There had been a time, years ago, when he had been a mild sort of aesthete on the Yale campus and belonged to the Elizabethan Club. The Professors Chauncey Tinker, Johnny Berdan, and Billy Phelps, whose courses he had taken, had at one time or another all made mild allusions to the success in letters that might someday be achieved by the young man he once had been. Events had taken a different turn, that was all. "Having contracted early in life the unfortunate habit of requiring three square meals per day," he had written for the memoirs of his five-year reunion, "I shortly after graduation accepted employment with the firm of Banton & Dascomb, Advertising, and cut my eyeteeth as a junior copywriter. I am now in more or less complete charge of such accounts as. . . ."

Which side of the window was the frost on, Mr. Blandings wondered. It must be on the outside; that was the side exposed to the elements. He got up and scratched a pane with his index fingertip. The frost was on the inside.

Mr. Blandings sighed, came back to his chair and picked up his book. "On the other hand," said his author, "we must not overlook those cases of compulsion where the dominant symptom-formation appears to have its genesis in a trauma due more fundamentally to cathexis than to a struggle between *id* and *super-ego*."

"What went click?" said Mrs. Blandings.

"What?" said Mr. Blandings.

"What went click?" said Mrs. Blandings.

"I didn't hear anything go click," said Mr. Blandings.

"I did," said Mrs. Blandings. "I distinctly heard something go—"

"You're always hearing something go click," said Mr. Blandings.

2

"I'm not always doing anything of the sort," said Mrs. Blandings.

At that instant Mr. Blandings heard something go click. He braced himself for a triumphant rejoinder from his wife, but to his surprise she gave no sign, and her eyes did not rise from the sweater on which she was sewing a name tape. There was a silence.

"Metal contracts in the cold," said Mr. Blandings after a little, anxious to re-establish in his own mind the principles of physics that had eluded him in the condensation of water vapor on cold surfaces. "Maybe it was a pipe or a duct somewhere."

"Maybe what was a pipe or a duct?" said Mrs. Blandings.

"Whatever went click," said Mr. Blandings.

"I gathered from you that nothing went click," said Mrs. Blandings.

"I didn't say nothing went click," said Mr. Blandings. "I merely said that—"

"You're always telling me I'm imagining things," said Mrs. Blandings. "You'd think I was living in a world of complete delusion."

Mr. Blandings put his book down on his knees.

"Muriel," he said, "do we have to peck at one another this way all the time?"

Mrs. Blandings sighed a deep sigh. "I wish we didn't," she said. "We didn't used to."

Husband and wife looked at one another for a long moment.

"I guess I'm sort of keyed up these days," said Mr. Blandings. "If I'm short with you I'm sorry. I don't mean to be."

"That's all right," said Mrs. Blandings. "I guess I'm short with you, too. I guess it's. . . ."

Whatever had gone click before now went snap.

Mr. Blandings sprang up, eager to translate his apology into action. "I'll find out what that is," he said, in the spirit of St. George, and made for the wing of the house that contained the kitchen, service quarters, and access to the cellar. He gave his wife a little pat on the top of the head as he went by her chair.

In the dark of the wing, Mr. Blandings fumbled for the electric switches. He snapped one, and the garage was flooded with light. He twitched his head in irritation and tried the next. Far down

3

the driveway, a brilliant bulb on a poletop spread its sudden radiance on the graveled driveway. A third switch produced a vague sense of a change in illumination somewhere overhead. In a burst of impatience Mr. Blandings snapped all the switches within reach of his arm and one of them—he could not tell which, in his haste—produced a pale pinpoint of light at the bottom of the cellar stairs. "God damn it," said Mr. Blandings. It was his way of saying "At last."

He clumped down the eighteen gently spaced treads that brought him to the smooth cellar floor. When his house was built, so shortly ago, somebody had mismeasured something, so that the cellar doorframe and the bottom step were too close together; Mr. Blandings had always to make a conscious decision whether to stoop forward or bend backward to ease the top of his skull past the top of the frame, before both his feet could rest on the concrete. This time he stooped forward, but not enough, and found himself momentarily wedged in the frame, like a brace for a box kite. He unsprung himself, rounded the turn at the bottom of the stairs, and with some force kicked a carton of empty fruit jars that lay against the wall. Then he made for the oil burner.

He did not know why, but he was sure he would gather wisdom at the oil burner. It was, so the salesman had once assured him, the Heart of the Home, without which even the finest dwelling was a cold, lifeless shell. Obviously then it was a place to begin looking for clicks and snaps, or other slight but important evidences of misfunction. He could see it in the distance, the beautiful thing, lacquered a stylish light brown with a blue carriage-stripe trim simulating dainty bowknots at the corners, as if it were a great Christmas package artfully corded by the gift-wrap section of a fussy department store. But before he could approach it more closely he encountered a distraction. At his left was a door that should be closed but was ajar, and a room that should be dark but was alight.

Mr. Blandings peered inside. In the bright beauty of the room he forgot his householder's vexation at the burning light. Here was the canned-goods storage room, and from ceiling to floor its walls were lined with peas and beans and tomatoes and corn, all encased in gleaming, hermetic cylinders of glass: the products of

4

a home-canning activity into which Mrs. Blandings had flung herself with an almost intolerable zeal last autumn. She had been new to it; in the absence of a garden she had practiced on boughten vegetables. At the time this had produced smells and burns and violent lashing bad tempers, but now the end results lay in layers and rows and files, serene and beautiful.

Serene and beautiful also were some well-disposed wooden cases on the floor. There, to the left, were four cases of France's dearest wines. Along with the elaborate flourish of the Château, branded into the wood, were such mundane remarks, in English, as the assurance "Bottle casings all new straw," and the injunction "Stow away from boilers." Ah, it was good to know wines a little and to be able—

To the right was a profusion of whiskies and gins, plus other miscellaneous colored and flavored alcohols for numerous imagined but so far unconsummated social occasions. It was to the whisky cases that Mr. Blandings' eye went, and instantly discovered something amiss. One bottle had not the settled look of its fellows. Mr. Blandings looked at it more closely and saw that its elaborate cellophane seal was broken. He grasped it and held it up to the light. A third of it was gone.

Mr. Blandings could think of half-a-dozen despoilers among the workmen still drifting at random in and out of his house in the endless business of finishing the last one per cent of the job: a man to plane a binding door one day; a man to unstick a jammed Venetian blind; a man to replace the glass broken by the man who fixed the blind. The process could go on forever, and after a while it would be time to repaint the whole house, which would in turn call for a whole new series of plumbing and hardware and other adjustments, which in turn . . .

Mr. Blandings picked up his ravished whisky bottle and studied it with deep distaste. On its lithographed label was the picture of an aged and gently crumbling structure about which were entwined, in elaborate script composed of ivy, the words *Old Supine: A Blend of the Superfine*. Mr. Blandings knew it well; it was a Banton & Dascomb account, and he wrote the copy for it. It was 75 per cent straight grain alcohol, plus some caramel solution for color, plus a dollop of somebody else's whisky to make it taste

5

like whisky. Somehow it managed also to taste slightly and disgustingly of chocolate. Mr. Blandings had a practically unlimited supply of it, renewed for him gratis every month by Old Supine Blenders, Inc. "You can't write the copy unless you know the product," was Apothegm One of the advertising profession. As a client, Old Supine Blenders knew it well—and Mr. Blandings had come to know Old Supine well. "Too well," Mrs. Blandings would remark on some occasion that seemed appropriate to her woman's mind.

Mr. Blandings' life, he had long ago decided, was ruled, dominated, enkindled, extinguished, made a bliss or made a hell, and in every way manipulated by Coincidence. There had been something in *Moby Dick* that Mr. Blandings vaguely remembered about the great malign Ruling Force of Coincidence: Melville had certainly been right, whatever it was he'd said. But at this moment only the most minor of coincidences overtook Mr. Blandings. It was merely that as he examined the unlawfully opened bottle of Old Supine his eye by chance also lit on a jelly glass. It rested on a narrow shelf, and was heavily coated with dust. A small insect, dead and desiccated, lay feet upward in its bottom. But it was a glass. The coincidence of a bottle and a glass was too obvious to escape anyone but a clod.

When Mr. Blandings finished scrounging around inside the glass with a small piece of old paper bag, it neither gleamed nor was sterile, but it would do. It belonged to one of the families of smaller jelly glasses, so Mr. Blandings allowed for this by filling it a little more than half full of Old Supine. He poised himself and then with a practiced gesture flung the glass and his head backward in perfect co-ordination. The Old Supine, as it flashed past his glottis, shook his entire frame from neck to ankles. He breathed cautiously through rounded lips for a moment; then daring to resume normal respiration he squared his shoulders and made for the oil burner. In a moment, he knew, the nagging cares of life would soften and melt a little and he would be what he wanted to be: a man competent and calm and unafraid; a man who could grapple with clicks and snaps in his own home and conquer them, and slay them, and lay them at the feet of his mate and say, "There now."

6

By the time he reached the oil burner he felt precisely like this, except a little more so.

Mr. Blandings stood in front of the oil burner and gave it a man-to-man appraising look. It issued a remote-sounding roar of vast controlled power and through a small round window of some high-fusing plastic he could see the shimmering flames of Hohm-heet oil in happy vaporization. Everything about the oil burner was as trim and tidy and high-functioning as a battle cruiser waiting an admiral's inspection. With a total lack of fuss it was pouring thousands of cubic feet of heated air into the upstairs of the Blandings house. Yet it itself was cool, almost chill, to the touch, so efficacious was the Kozy-Dozy Sana-Kuhl Best-Oss insulation with which, so a delicate brass plaque testified, its walls were packed.

Instantly Mr. Blandings realized that he had started on a false scent. He had begun a prowl for something that had gone click; that, gathering strength and ferocity, had then gone snap, and might, any instant now, go whack or boom unless dealt with decisively. But the oil burner was not the answer. The oil burner was guaranteed, so another plaque expressly stated, to function perfectly without any human attention for the next quarter century—and nothing about its present conduct seemed to indicate any slightest lapse. The plaque made clear that the guarantee was void "in the event of a direct hit by any shell, bomb, rocket, or other missile, whether atomic or non-atomic," but this would not happen tonight; Mr. Blandings, the slug of Old Supine expanding his capillaries everywhere, was certain of that.

Moreover, there was nothing on or about the oil burner that could be in any way manipulated; it was a masterpiece of that sort of streamlining which particularly characterized those things designed to be immobile completely; its only protuberances were a couple of glossy chromium swellings, obviously designed for ornamentation and not to be pushed, pulled, twisted, or in any way fooled with. Mr. Blandings dismissed the oil burner with a cordial wave of the hand; he must turn his attention elsewhere.

In a corner of the cellar ten feet from the oil burner there was a room, half closed in. The studding for partitions had been jammed

7

and hammered into place, and rough wallboard would someday completely enclose a rich miscellany of activities. The room had begun as a tinkering space for Mr. Blandings and a heavy oak-topped workbench was already built into it. Realism had over-taken the Blandings during its construction, however; it had been admitted that Mr. Blandings had never so far shown himself the type to create full-rigged sailing vessels inside bottles, and other subsidiary purposes had thus been assigned to the room-to-be: for only a small addition to the contractor's bill the space had been made to serve as the laundry as well as Mr. Blandings' sanctum. A two-burner portable electric stove had also converted it into the canning center where Mrs. Blandings would preserve the vege-tables from her kitchen garden-to-be. But Mr. Blandings still held some theoretical jurisdiction over these quarters, and thus it was that on the portable stove there rested a filing cabinet: the kind made of heavy cardboard with metal squares clasping the corners. The filing cabinet had not made a happy journey from New York to the new Blandings country home: somewhere along the route it had been subjected to a heavy torsion stress and now looked like a model of an early unsuccessful aeroplane. Its drawer was half open and a disorderly bulge of papers protruded from the top. Mr. Blandings strolled over to it mellowly, and pulled out a wrinkled sheet.

"Dear U.S. Citizen," he read. "Will you accept, absolutely free, a full half year's subscription to *Zounds*? *Zounds* is a new kind of weekly magazine, designed for people precisely like yourself who, with everpressing duties, are everywhere voicing greater and greater need for a publication which, stripped of excess verbiage, will bring you the facts of every week, fresh, free, and fertile. To launch *Zounds*, the publishers have authorized me. . . ."

Oh God, thought Mr. Blandings. He had written that. Poor old *Zounds*. Poor old Jerry Lucas, who had conceived *Zounds*, and then never been able to give it birth. There had been so many difficulties; so baffling, so completely unexpected. Chief among them had been an absence of working capital. A letter to Marshall Field, flawless in logic and irresistible in emotional appeal, had brought a prompt answer beginning "I shall be most happy—" but the instant of bliss enkindled by these five words was, the next instant, doused unutterably when it became apparent that Mr. Field was answering a $500,000 proposal with the firm promise of a year's subscription at the Founder's Rate of $3.75, once *Zounds'* actual first publication date was assured.

That had been pretty nearly the end of it; soon thereafter a dream had died in Mr. Blandings' bosom. It had looked so easy and, what was more, so essential to create a new, vital magazine whose function would be . . . whose function . . . of course that might have been one of the troubles with the damn thing: its function had been so easy to think of, yet somehow so difficult to put into words. Mr. Blandings was to have been an associate editor, but his pre-publication job had been to devise the initial circulation promotion plan, and write the letters that would bring subscribers flocking to its standard: for this Jerry Lucas had promised him five hundred shares of capital stock once the vision was incorporated—and Mr. Blandings had slaved on nights and Sundays and holidays at this extracurricular job. For a while he had seen freedom forever from the thralldom of a highly paid job with Banton & Dascomb, Advertising, and a throne in the kingdom of publishing. . . .

Ah well, thought Mr. Blandings, what the hell. Was there anything sadder than the contents of an old filing cabinet? A scrapbook, a diary, were much less sad; into the scrapbook went things that *had* turned out right; into the diary—well, Mr. Blandings had never kept a diary, and spent a moment in grateful thanks. But an old filing cabinet contained things that were *going* to turn out right, except that when you looked at them again, none of them had. What had been enthusiasm five years ago was in retrospect mere fatuousness; what had seemed like wisdom turned out to be the purest sort of miscalculation; events had paid no attention to the wisdom, had not made it wrong so much as ludicrously off the point—the wisdom was a dam built to contain a river that had then shifted its course and left a huge barrier of piled-up thoughts crumbling in a desert; a monument to miscalculation and inacuity.

Apparently this busted filing cabinet was Mr. Blandings' major repository of dreams come untrue. He rooted slowly and with a sort of dejected fascination in its contents. The thing to do with it,

9

he said to himself, rising and set for action, was to cast it instantly into the flames. He seized it by the corners, pressed it to his belly, and lifted it clear of its resting place. Only then did the disadvantages of sealed-in, no-human-hands, guaranteed-forever oil burners occur to him: there was no firebox door to be opened, no naked flames available into which to consign the past, no way of watching that past scorch, shrivel, curl at the corners, and convert itself in one bright flash to indiscernible, lightly broken, fluttering gray wafers.

Just as this frustration made itself clear to Mr. Blandings the filing cabinet collapsed. Most of the papers fell with a leaden thump at his feet, but a few dipped and swirled gaily before they came to rest. Mr. Blandings stood up, his fists on his hips, and said a hideous word. It was of no avail. After a moment of contemplation he made a violent gesture and walked resolutely back to the canned-goods storage room, where was the bottle of Old Supine and the now germproof jelly glass.

"Well!" said Mr. Blandings. In the last ten minutes his mood had undergone a miraculous transformation. He was sitting on his workbench, his legs dangling happily in the air. By his side stood the jelly glass, well and darkly filled; through his hands was passing a procession of papers. There was the inevitable novel, unfinished; the inevitable play, unfinished. There was something called *The Theory of Publishing*, by James H. Blandings, written when the excitement about *Zounds* was at its height. There were notes and sketches for stories and articles of every sort. Most of them were over ten years old, and until this moment totally forgotten. But they were all full of adroit invention and graceful phrase as Mr. Blandings saw them now, and there was scarcely a thing that could not be dusted off and touched up for the benefit of this or that literary market. The whole business of the busted filing cabinet was one of those lucky accidents, those blessings in disguise, and Mr. Blandings sat happily upon his workbench, the Old Supine making a song within him, and felt that he had not hitherto realized the potential richness of his life or the singularity of his gifts.

MRS. BLANDINGS sat in the mellow pool of light, sewing and thinking female thoughts as she sewed. From below came an occasional
light scuffling that seemed to indicate her husband was postur-
ing as a man about the house. She wondered if he was taking
an occasional slug of whisky as he roved the cellar, and decided
he was.

Oh well, thought Mrs. Blandings. The deep attraction alcohol
seemed to offer almost all men of her acquaintance was a strange
thing to her; she felt that men intended it, whether they knew it
or not, as a criticism of their wives. A flock of drinks would more
than likely incline a man to dalliance with some woman he had
only just met, but whatever alcohol did to a husband it did not
make him amorous toward his wife; anything but. Wives got
pushed around; as Mrs. Blandings viewed matters this evening,
it was an open question whether it was worth while being a wife
or not. It was a terribly disloyal thought to Mr. Blandings, but she
couldn't help wondering if she mightn't have been happier as a
businesswoman—a brisk creation of tweeds and lightning deci-
sions and high professional competence by day; by night a crea-
ture of soft and fatal feminine allure decked in lascivious marabou
and chiffons who would have a passionate affair with a new man
every six months, casting away the old one, his heart broken, his
best forever given beyond recall.

"Mother?"

Mrs. Blandings jumped. "Joan," she said, "*what* are you doing
downstairs and *what* will Dr. MacLaren say?"

"Mother," said Joan, "I can hear Father."

"You couldn't possibly hear your father," said Mrs. Blandings;

11

"he's in the cellar. Girls who are just getting over the mumps don't hop up and run around without being properly covered up." She began making preparations to do something maternal.

"I took my temperature and it's totally normal and I can hear Father as if he were right beside me," said Joan.

"Come here and let me see your throat," said Mrs. Blandings.

"Neither you nor Father realize," said Joan, "that when you're in that cellar room next to the oil burner I can hear every word you say. It comes straight up the laundry chute into my bathroom and right into my ear. Father's been reviewing his past life and saying 'Oh Christ.'"

"Joan," said Mrs. Blandings.

"Speak to Father," said Joan.

"If you'll cuddle up warmly by the fire I'll let you stay for fifteen minutes," said Mrs. Blandings, giving up on one topic and covering her defeat by opening another. "Otherwise you won't be getting back to Barleydew until Winter Term is half over, and all the other girls will be ahead of you."

"I don't want to go back to Barleydew," said Joan. "Not ever again. What's Father doing in the cellar?"

"I never heard of anything so ridiculous as not going back to Barleydew," said Mrs. Blandings. "He's looking for something that's going click."

From a tailor's cross-legged position on the floor Joan rose to her tiptoes like a ballerina, all in one graceful movement of her thirteen-year-old body.

"Come away from that window," said Mrs. Blandings.

"I am away," said Joan. "I was fixing your click."

Mrs. Blandings looked at Joan.

"What I can't understand about you and Father," said Joan, "is why you always make things as complex as possible and look in the farthest-off places for the most difficult explanations, when all the time the cause is right in front of your noses."

"What was it?" Mrs. Blandings asked with a certain deference.

"The wooden tassel on the Venetian blind," said Joan; "there's a little air stirring around the window frame and it was knocking the tassel against the glass. Mother, I truly don't want to go back to Barleydew."

12

"We won't discuss it at ten o'clock on a Sunday night," said Mrs. Blandings.

"Barleydew's just fine for Betsy," said Joan. "Betsy has no brains."

"That is not the way to speak of one's elder sister," said Mrs. Blandings.

"And even if she had brains she wouldn't know what they were for," said Joan, "with those boys from St. Clarence's swarming around all the time. What I know about *her!*"

"We don't talk about our own sister behind her back," said Mrs. Blandings. "There's a lot of difference between being thirteen and being sixteen, as you may begin to find out soon for yourself, and it's only natural—"

"I didn't say it wasn't natural," said Joan. "I said—"

"Joan," said Mrs. Blandings. "You can march yourself straight upstairs."

"And listen to Father saying those things up the laundry chute?" said Joan.

The life of a businesswoman-harlot seemed overwhelmingly attractive to Mrs. Blandings.

"At Barleydew," said Joan, "they don't teach you anything, except dancing and horses. Mother, you *know* that's not going to be my life."

Mrs. Blandings did know that. She knew that something more than the span of three years separated her two daughters. Betsy had been the fractious first child, Joan the serene second. Yet Betsy's life so far had taken a course of complete conventionality, and Joan's had not. Betsy's childhood had been lived in a welter of dolls from rag to bisque; she had mothered a family of twenty with an overflowing maternal zeal. Now that Betsy was sixteen her mind and her body were both conspicuously feminine, and Mrs. Blandings felt no doubt that she would be married at twenty —which would be "in time, pray God," thought Mrs. Blandings, without fully examining what she meant. Joan, on the other hand, had let her dolls gather dust in a neglected, neck-broken heap in the nursery of the New York apartment where the Blandings had lived when their children were little; she had instead poured out

13

her four-year-old love on dump trucks and toy airplanes and spring-driven model tractors. None of these was permitted to function as if in the hands of a little boy; they were not to be wound or sailed or scooted but instead existed to be fed when Joan was fed and perpetually put to bed in their hangars and garages, and perpetually gotten up again. By the time Joan was ten the words proton isotope were commonplaces in the daily press; Joan had determined on a life of science and had kept this image before her with such unshakable firmness that her parents were now being forced to take it seriously. At thirteen she had begun to plump up a little but her heroine remained Madame Curie. That all this was noncongruous with Barleydew, Mrs. Blandings was becoming more and more aware.

Damn Barleydew, thought Mrs. Blandings. When she and her husband had made the great decision that converted them from city-dwellers to country-dwellers, that took them out of a New York apartment in the East 70's and into a gleaming new house near the summit of Bald Mountain, seven miles out from the center of Lansdale Town, something new had to be done about the children's education; Barleydew had seemed the best substitute for the progressive school on New York's upper East Side, close by an asphalt works. Mrs. Blandings, Bryn Mawr graduate though she was, had never been overenthusiastic about the effects of progressive education on her children, but now she was wondering if perhaps in picking Barleydew, nestling beautifully in southern New England, she and her husband had not gone from one extreme to another. If so, Mrs. Blandings reflected, it was like them. Anyway, the trouble with a boarding school was that you simply couldn't begin to tell what it was really like. Your children's talk was baffling: so elliptical, foreign, and presumptive that there seemed no facts to be winnowed from it at all. To Betsy, Barleydew was everything the catalog said and more; but here was Joan, whose evidence ran just the other way.

"I could go to public school right here in Lansdale and not learn any less than I learn in Barleydew," said Joan. "There's nobody there who knows what the word *fissile* means, and if you were to ask a question about gaseous diffusion you'd just get a blank stare."

"The schools here aren't very nice," said Mrs. Blandings. She was searching the first years of her own teens for some recollection of what she and her world had been like. She could remember Rudolph Valentino and Heywood Broun; the strangeness of this pairing put her further memories out of kilter. Were there airplanes? Of course there were airplanes; how silly. But when had she first heard of an atom? Whenever it was, it had certainly been a bore. A deadly bore. *There* was an accidental perfect choice of words if ever there was one. The bore was so deadly now that the rocks could any day vanish in one subliming flash, and there would be no more planet Earth, nor anyone to know that there was not. Yet children looked full at this horror, and saw no horror there, but only a fascination one step higher than the jet-powered rocket.

"There's a lot of fine talk in this family that doesn't come to much," said Joan in an even voice that broke in on her mother's thoughts.

"What fine talk?" said Mrs. Blandings.

"Yours and Father's," said Joan. "You're always pouring it on to Betsy and me about equality and democracy, but I notice that when it comes to picking a school for your children you're governed entirely by the most conventional bourgeois snobbery-stencils."

It was going to be a long time before the influence of Miss Stellwagon at the progressive school was forgotten, Mrs. Blandings reflected. Who was the more confused: herself or her daughter? If her daughter thought that somehow a rural public school would satisfy her yearnings to experience democracy and at the same time cultivate her unique intellect, maybe the idea should be put to the test, if only to show how hopeless it was. But this could not be said aloud.

"We want our children to have the best," said Mrs. Blandings.

"In that case," said Joan, "why not give up all the hypocritical democracy-equality talk?"

"Joan," said Mrs. Blandings.

"The greatest unmet obligation in American life," Joan intoned, "is the obligation of the superior individual toward something greater than his own individual way of making money. That's what

15

Miss Stellwagon used to say. If the schools here aren't very nice why don't you and Father do something about them?"

"Joan," said Mrs. Blandings, "Mother's had a headache all day and she's afraid it's getting worse, and I've already said that this is not an appropriate time for all this discussion."

"Meeting the child's inquiries with evasions blockades the normal channels of healthy curiosities," said Joan, in a voice she intended to resemble that of Dr. Lispetha Suellity Worplin, author of *Toward the Emergent Sibling*, to whom the sentiment belonged. She rose. "Very well," she said, "when *will* there be an appropriate time?"

"Next week," said Mrs. Blandings, "when you're all better, and Father isn't busy and we're all in the mood. Then we'll talk about it."

"In *general*," she added hastily.

"So that means I have to go back to Barleydew anyway?" said Joan.

"Most certainly," said Mrs. Blandings, faintly, and without heart for her answer.

At the staircase foot Joan turned and leveled a glance at her mother. "Lifelong neuroses get formed right around my age," she said, and disappeared like a slow neutron up the carpeted stairs.

Mr. and Mrs. Blandings were disrobing in the master bedroom, and Mrs. Blandings felt cool toward Mr. Blandings. She had had to summon him from the cellar, and when he came up he smelled rather strongly of Old Supine. He was not at all out of focus, as he sometimes got, but he seemed more jaunty than was appropriate to a late hour on Sunday night. He had obviously lost all trace of recollection why he had gone down into the cellar in the first place. Lost in abstraction, he had his right arm behind his back, and was scratching his left shoulder blade grossly, like a lemur.

"Joan came downstairs," said Mrs. Blandings.

"Good," said Mr. Blandings.

"I let her stay for a while," said Mrs. Blandings.

"Fine," said Mr. Blandings.

"She doesn't want to go back to Barleydew," said Mrs. Blandings.

16

Mr. Blandings stopped whistling. "Well, well," he said.

"It just makes me all confused and upset," said Mrs. Blandings. "We no sooner try to get our lives as a family reorganized than things start coming to pieces again."

There was too much truth in this to face. "Nonsense," said Mr. Blandings.

"Sometimes," said Mrs. Blandings, "I wonder how I keep going. I worry about Betsy and boys, and I have this house to manage without any help, and when I feel as if I'd go crazy that's the very time you telephone and say you'll have to stay in the city all night, so I have no one to talk to, no one to lean on, no one—"

"That'll all be different when we've lived here long enough to have some friends," said Mr. Blandings.

"Will it?" said Mrs. Blandings. "We don't seem to have made very much progress yet. It's been—"

"It's high time we hired a couple, too," said Mr. Blandings. "You can't go on doing all the housework yourself, and when it gets to be spring there's certainly going to be enough work to keep a man busy full time out of doors."

"I can't make up my mind whether it's worse without servants or with them," said Mrs. Blandings. She sighed a deep sigh and went into the bathroom, and Mr. Blandings could hear her making little strangled sounds as she brushed her teeth. Was she right, he wondered, that things were coming to pieces again? It had not been so long ago that a home in the country, and the abandonment of city life, was to be a cure for every tension and distress the Blandings felt in daily life and living. Might the panacea be proving a little less powerful than they had first supposed? No, said Mr. Blandings. No. He wondered if a small final shot of Old Supine would banish the lingering doubt, but at that moment his wife emerged from the bathroom.

"Joan wants to stay home and go to school right here in Lansdale," she said. "And I must say she said several things that struck home. She said there was a lot of fine talk about democracy in this home but that we just acted like snobs when it came to the actual business of sending our children to school."

"She's at the superior age," said Mr. Blandings.

"She also said you and I liked to make things as complex as pos-

17

sible," said Mrs. Blandings. "She said we looked in the farthest-off places for the most difficult explanations instead of right in front of our noses."

"What brought all that up?" asked Mr. Blandings.

"You did," said Mrs. Blandings. "By going down into the cellar looking for something going click, and staying down there two hours, and forgetting what you went there for in the first place."

Mr. Blandings' euphoria broke, and he was in a harsh, granular world, full of craggy, unscalable problems. With the Old Supine wearing off, his visit to the cellar was now seeming to become only a miniature, frighteningly exact, of the process by which he lived his life.

"As things turned out," said Mrs. Blandings, "Joan found what was going click. It was just a tassel in the living room."

"What was Joan doing downstairs anyway?" said Mr. Blandings.

"You woke her up," said Mrs. Blandings.

"*I?*" said Mr. Blandings.

His bewilderment was so genuine that Mrs. Blandings put a drop of oil on her épée.

"Jim," she said, "I'm sure I don't know *exactly* what you were doing in the cellar, but you got to the point of holding a dialogue with yourself, and it was right in front of the laundry chute. It couldn't have piped everything up to the girls' bathroom more perfectly if it had been a speaking tube, and it woke Joan up, and after she'd listened I don't know how long, and heard I don't know what, she came downstairs. I'm just telling you this for your own protection."

There was a silence. Mr. Blandings, having considered several refuges, chose dignity.

"It so happens," he said, "that I found a number of things I'd written long ago," he said. "Before I was married." It was his intention that this remark should have edge.

"And I got interested in them," he went on. "And it so happens that I'm going to bring them out and do some work on them, and maybe get a little relaxation and sense of achievement from them. That's what I need in my life—*if* I can get a little privacy around here."

"You needn't raise your voice," said Mrs. Blandings. She

18

climbed into her bed and switched off her side of the dual bed lamp. "You have all the privacy in the world here provided you just don't stand and yell up a laundry chute."

"Well, all right," said Mr. Blandings. He switched off his half of the light, and ground his ear into the pillow. The weekend was over.

3

You COULD HEAR the train whistle far up the valley eight minutes
before it swerved around the bend and bore down on the Lansdale
station. The Wintinock River had sought out the easiest way
through the bases of the blue green mountains a good many thousands of years ago, and when the railroad was laid out in the 1850's
the surveyors could find nothing better, for the long stretch of
miles through the Lansdale Hills, than to parallel the riverbed
with their right-of-way. So although Train No. 173, which bore
Mr. Blandings to New York every morning, was in general heading
south, it writhed as it pounded as it clanked and for short local
stretches it might head east or west or even north for a while, on
the way to its eventual discovery of 125th Street and Grand Central Station.

This morning the train was only about ten minutes late, which
was not bad.

Mr. Blandings stood on the platform and waited. The platform
was of cinders loosely constrained by boards; in the summertime
the cinders were springy but now in the dead of a cold snowless
winter they were frozen into a monolithic slab that felt harder than
steel. When Mr. Blandings' heels struck the frozen cinders they
gave out a hollow clinkery sound as if a little cracked bell had
been tapped with a brittle stick. The air was still so cold that Mr.
Blandings could feel no sensation in his feet; his hands, encased
in heavy gloves, would answer only the simplest commands. His
nose and ears felt incandescent and his every exhaled breath was
a blast of steam. He could, of course, go inside the station except
that it smelled too horribly to be endured by a man who was never
at his best or strongest in the early mornings.

The heavy mountain locomotive rushed in, dragging with it five noisome cars and an intolerable breeze of newspaper scraps, dead leaves, and stinging dust.

"G'bye," Mr. Blandings shouted. He kissed his wife's cheek and could not hear some injunction she was shouting at him.

"I'll try to," he bellowed. Years of marriage had revealed this as a response that rarely went wrong.

The railroad was doing well this morning: the coach in which Mr. Blandings disposed himself was heated to the temperature of a hayfield just before an August thunderstorm. For five minutes it felt wonderful; then it became oppressive; then it became unbearable. After ten minutes of active sweating Mr. Blandings discovered it had become merely oppressive again. He turned his gaze out the window and watched Lansdale County jounce slowly by.

How beautiful it was, he thought; how deeply he wished he need never leave it for the city. His mind took up again the fancies it had held last night. He was conscious that he might have had one drink too many and that perhaps the manuscripts he had rediscovered were not quite the glowing pearls they had seemed as he sat sipping and reading on the workbench. But his thoughts had gone in the right direction just the same, Old Supine or no Old Supine. The reason he and his wife had bought and built in the country was because city life had become unendurable. If country life was not yet an idyll that was only because its rhythms and routines were still new or undiscovered. "A period of transition—that's what I'm in," Mr. Blandings said to himself, and felt pleasure at the exactness of his thought.

Remember, Blandings, said Mr. Blandings to himself, that you have a violently unstable system of emotions. You have the same knowledge of normality that an English lecturer has of Omaha; you have never dwelt there but only whizzed through it on a journey from one extreme to another. Your new life in the country is expressly planned to give you the materials to overcome this; a means of slowing yourself down to loaf and invite your soul, and nurture what comes forth from it. Don't forget that.

Slow and steady; easy does it; those were to be the watchwords of the future. It was easy to identify some of the sources of the irritation and impatience that he felt with his home in the country so

21

far. The lovely house lacked any landscaping; there were no new, young trees, no shrubs or garden paths about it to cradle and protect it, give it softness and warmth and a feeling of belonging to the earth about it. What grew on the Blandings' acres grew more or less at random or had been totally without care for twenty years. No impatience, no amount of bullying arrogance, no "executive decision" however arbitrary could wrench the dislocated ground of his country acres into shape overnight; time, time, that alone could help him. Time and patience. Time and ease. Time and the conscious cultivation of serenity. Time and a constant reverie on what the ultimate beauty must be. What had Henry Simms, his architect, once said to him? "It takes fifteen years to achieve peace and solvency in a country home." Remember, Blandings.

Now we're on the track again, thought Mr. Blandings. An elm-shaded lawn of English beauty; rugged but perfectly kept forest; model orchards; rock gardens; cascading waterfalls artfully made from streams; a wildlife sanctuary carpeted with moss and fringed with laurel; those would be the Blandings' acres of the future. The raw materials for everything lay at his hand; there was no unreality in thinking of this peace-drenched setting for the balance of the Blandings' family life. Someday, of course, he would retire from the city altogether; a turn of economic good fortune, left blank in his thoughts for the moment, would make it possible that he give himself up wholly to the bucolic enchantment of caring for a herd of sleek, chestnut-coated cows who would gaze at him with exquisite frankness out of their limpid, beautiful brown eyes. . . .

Mr. Blandings recognized a forbidden thought, and canceled the cows. Simultaneously, he canceled the White Wyandottes and the Poland China hogs that had been taking rapid substance out of a white mist in the back of his mind. What a fool a man could make of himself in the country if his imagination were unchecked by a firm self-discipline. The Lintleys had gone in for livestock, even to the extent of raising sheep for wool to make their own blankets; it was a matter of laughter, in which the sobered Lintleys could now themselves join, that so far as money could be counted, the blankets had cost them $475 a pair, and had not been very good.

However, there was no sense living in the country and behaving as if you lived in the East 70's, Manhattan, with a foot-thick crust of concrete and asphalt smothering the earth through which a tangle of pipes and sewers and cables periodically burst, backed up, or short circuited. Perhaps he and his wife might sow a country acre or so to clover or buckwheat and become apiarists, walking without fear through an atmosphere thick with bees to extract the combs of honey which connoisseurs would insist upon in preference to all others. Perhaps the old Dutch oven would inspire Mrs. Blandings to search out some great-grandmother's lost secret for the honest baking of a perfect loaf of bread. No, that one was no good; there was a Mrs. Rudkin, not very far away, either, who had done just that, and the inhabitants of dozens of states had rushed in such concert to her ovens that no matter how much she baked she could not bake enough. So that wouldn't do for Mrs. Blandings, and besides, come to think of it, the Dutch oven was torn down. But it just went to show: country enterprise could be more than a hobby, more than subsistence; it could make contentment and security bloom side by side.

Furthermore, with adequate income assured, there was another whole aspect of things to be considered: the cultivation of the intellect. City life gave the intellect no opportunity, but the country could provide a very different story. Mr. Blandings would someday have plenty of time to spend in his book-lined study on some work of scholarship, field yet to be determined. Perhaps at the outset he might write a volume of mildly iconoclastic observations on advertising. Perhaps in a later phase he would consent to give four or five lectures a year at the Harvard Business School or the Yale Institute of Human Relations; lectures remarkable for their combination of informed scholarship, gentle wit, and penetrating insight. Later on he might even discover the neglected works of some local John Burroughs or Henry Thoreau; these he would edit with an introduction and a set of illuminating footnotes and cause to be privately printed in a design made by Bruce Rogers and exquisitely impressed on a handmade, all-rag paper——"Of this edition, numbered and signed by the Annotator, twelve hundred and fifty copies have been struck off, and the type distributed. This copy is No.____."

Of course, mere library research would not suffice for this sort of thing; there must be a scholarship that struck its roots into the humanity about it. And that meant a wide acquaintance with the families that lived in Lansdale Town, and particularly in that section of the township designated on the maps as Bald Mountain, atop which stood the Blandings home. Mr. Blandings had not yet made any worth-while progress in this direction, he was bound to confess. Mr. Ephemus Hackett, out of whose family acres Mr. Blandings had acquired his own, was an acquaintance but not exactly a friend; having bilked Mr. Blandings in the matter of land purchase he had thereafter taken on a manner of truculent grievance toward him, and was unlikely ever to be the man to haul down from an old barn any treasured records of the long ago. But he was not the only resource. The roads leading from the top of Bald Mountain to the heart of Lansdale Town were dotted every few miles with the farmhouses of dairymen; a tough, accordion-necked breed of men engaged in a convulsive struggle with the boulder-strewn land to make it yield them a living. In time Mr. Blandings would get to know them, and understand them, and neighborliness would flower. . . .

Mr. Blandings glanced out the window. The train had left the Lansdale Branch and was rattling through country that would, any moment now, become overbarbered suburbia. A host of members of his profession would soon begin to board it, and one of them, inescapably, would sit down beside him. With a sigh, Mr. Blandings put away his thoughts of the shining future and constrained his mind to deal with present reality.

But nowhere that he looked in present reality could he find anything but a combination of depression and anxiety. A familiar little singsong began in his mind: *"Today's the day they're going to find me out."* It was silly; it was ridiculous; but there it was. Who were "they," and what were they going to discover? He had worked for Banton & Dascomb long and loyally, and almost every year, save the black depression ones of the early thirties, his responsibilities and rewards had increased. Yet he never began a week's work without this same thrill of alarm. So far as he could analyze what his inner being was saying to him it went like this: Blandings, you are an incompetent. You know nothing, you have no gifts, you

24

have no background of solid accomplishment whatever. But you belong in the classification of *lucky* incompetents: that is to say, whenever you have been at your incompetent worst, people have been looking the other way. This persistent, inexplicable luck has operated in your favor for more than twenty years now. It cannot endure much longer.

Usually, at this point, some small battalion of emotional troops loyal to Blandings would rise up and make a stand. Sir, they would say to their beleaguered commander, we will fight for you to the end. Are the likes of you going to give in to the likes of Lorbet Neen, Banton & Dascomb Vice President in Charge of Media? Are you to admit that you are his inferior? Why are the two of you enemies? Is it not because he is a tough and cynical bastard, where you are a man of sensitivity and a becoming capacity for honest doubts? Surely you are not going to give up the battle because you enjoy the enmity of a man whose principal assets are a bass voice and an unshakable belief in his wormy thoughts.

Having come this far in his introspections, Mr. Blandings would release the desperate remaining handful of troops still loyal. You have done all that is possible, men; find your way back to safety as best you can. For there is one more thing about me you should know. It is not just that I am an incompetent, or even that I am a lucky incompetent. It is that I cannot bear to think of the success of my deceits. When somebody listens to Lorbet Neen and nods sagely, it must be that Lorbet takes this agreement with quiet satisfaction. Well, every now and then someone nods sagely when *I* say something—but this has a very different effect on me: it merely makes me feel overwhelmed with guilt, shame, and alarm. Somebody has taken seriously something I said. I said it with a confidence I did not feel—instantly ready to modify it, take it back, reverse it, or re-explain it in such terms that nobody would know what I was originally talking about. That I should have caused agreement among a group of grown men to some proposition in which I myself felt no solid faith—this is the worst of all, the hardest to bear. I am paid $25,000 a year and bonuses—and these rewards belong only to people who are sure of themselves. They are not for the likes of me.

God, thought Mr. Blandings, his thoughts on a long reach, in the whole roll call of business enterprise is there no one else like my-self? There are the ruthless and successful, the bitter and success-ful, the proud and successful. Am I the only example of the *fright-ened* and successful?

Suppose I went to some psychoanalyst and told him my fears and worries? He'd say, "You're crazy." *Yes, that's exactly what the son-of-a-bitch would say:* "YOU'RE CRAZY!" I can hear him. You have said you enjoy a good salary? Yes, doctor. You have been con-tinuously employed by one firm since your graduation from col-lege? Yes, doctor. And your financial rewards have increased more or less steadily since then? Yes, doctor. Are you suggesting that this firm has for some reason been paying you increasing sums of money which you do not legitimately earn? Not exactly that, doc-tor, but——

How was an advertising man ever to suggest to a man of medi-cine the particular, minute insanities that were his daily tasks? Mr. Blandings thought of the accounts that made up his professional life. Old Supine, A Blend. Mr. Blandings' task on this account was to find ten thousand different ways of evading the true issue. Old Supine, unlike some other products, had a true, definite function, which it would unfailingly perform. This function was to get the consumer into a hyper-normal state: buzzed, crocked, looping, fried, boiled, plastered, or stinko, according to the amount in-gested and the psycho-physiology of the consumer. Could this delightful truth be as much as hinted? Even if there were no Fed-eral Trade Commission, the American mores would revolt at the slightest suggestion. In "building" ads for Old Supine, it was Mr. Blandings' task to take such notions as aroma, flavor, body, color, bouquet, mildness, more mildness, more body, less body, and play with them like an eighteen-month infant in a playpen until some combination satisfying to the client emerged. Good fellowship, gracious living, liberty, equality, fraternity, snobbery, professional success, breadth of experience might also be used in advocacy. But the joys of getting more or less drunk? No.

Then there was the Hair Removal Institute of America. Mr. Blandings tried to imagine describing his efforts on its behalf to a fully mature diplomate in psychiatry, and gave up instantly, a pulse beating dully in his stomach. Between the Hair Removal Institute

26

and its deadly rival for ladies' favor, the World Depilatory Foundation, a struggle had been raging in and out of the women's magazines for the last fifteen years. Grown men were deeply involved in it, and so desperate became the battle on some occasions that the proprietors of the American press would refuse to let some of the deeper and more terrible issues be fought out in their pages. But the Hair Removal Institute of America could not be explained to a psychiatrist.

Mr. Blandings dismissed the psychiatrist altogether, on the grounds that he wouldn't understand anything of Mr. Blandings' life or problems. One of Mr. Blandings' problems, this very day, as soon as he reached his office, was to begin drafting a whole set of Middle Commercials for the Queeze radio show that would go on the air Wednesday night. . . . "Have *you* tried the new Queeze? Queeze, the new modern luncheon spread, is at *your* grocer's *now*. Fortified and irradiated, Queeze contains more Vitamin C than two pounds of *thick*, juicy sirloin. So . . . why not buy the economy tube *today*, and give the *whole* family a treat? For Queeze is *better* for you. Um-*yum*. You see, Queeze is never sold in jars, boxes, or in bulk. Queeze comes only in the handy collapsible tube that you'll find in three *scientific* sizes: large, super, and economy. So for the best in cheese, squeeze Queeze, and give the whole family—"

A coarse tremor swept Mr. Blandings. There had been some talk of the client wanting to switch over to a singing commercial with a future eye on television, and now that he thought of it, one of his first jobs must be to turn out a sheaf of preliminary jingles that the radio department could examine for later conversion into song. . . .

There was also Arf, the dog food. This was less his concern than the concern of his young assistant, Mr. Dward Wayburn, although it was up to Mr. Blandings to keep an alert supervisory eye peeled. Arf came close to being Mr. Blandings' favorite account. He had no notion what was in it, but it came in Three Balanced Odors: Meat Odor, Fish Odor, and Cheese Odor. Whatever the hell it was made of, Mr. Blandings reflected, the pups certainly went for it: he had observed an extraordinary variety of breeds, from mastiffs to Pekingese, attack its sawdust-like substance with snarling fe-

27

rocity, clean up two boxes of the stuff in less than a minute and look up pleadingly for more.

There you were. Arf, whatever it was, could only be an honest product, eagerly consumed by those for whom intended. He could explain Arf to a psychiatrist, he thought, given a little time. It was the thing in his professional life that most nearly corresponded to his yearnings to be an honest purveyor to other people's honest needs. That's it, doctor; that's what I want; that's all I ask. Simplicity; honesty; a return to the virtues by which the nation lived before the jukebox. Before the 4-color spread, the Hooperating, the guaranteed readership of 37,000,000. Before fingertip control of buzzbomb power under your hood. Before you could get Plato's Republic absolutely free by merely. Before scientists agreed impartial tests convincingly proved.

"A Hunna'n Twenny-fih Street," roared the trainman.

Mr. Blandings glanced about him in surprise. The theory was that his hour and a half commuting trip every morning would give him the opportunity for a good deal of uninterrupted work, but today the bulldog edition of the *Herald Tribune* still lay unopened by his side on the seat which, through some good fortune, no one had asked to share. In the ten remaining minutes before Grand Central he would now address himself to the state of today's world. Without unfolding the paper, he knew it stank.

4

THE OFFICES of Banton & Dascomb were on Madison Avenue and gave Mr. Blandings, every morning, a five-minute northward walk from Grand Central. As he swung into the dim lobby of the Post-humous Guarantees and Trust Building he cast a glance at the bronze clock above him. The décor of the building was "modern," which was to say contemporaneous with the year 1926, and extrusions of flat, glittering steel poked themselves at various angles from slabs of polished chocolate and clam-colored stones. The modernism of the clock lay in merging its dial numbers into small round buttons and reducing the two hands to vestigial stumps of indistinguishable size. By focusing hard Mr. Blandings gained the impression that it was 10:10. That was maybe fifteen minutes later than his accustomed arrival hour in the days when he had merely taken a Madison Avenue bus for a twelve-minute south-bound ride. Now, getting in at 10:10 meant arising in his Lansdale bedroom in the freezing gray of 6:45 A.M. instead of at a languorous and steam-heated 8:30 in his onetime apartment in Manhattan's East 70's. Ah, but think of the self-discipline. . . .

"Thirty-one," said Mr. Blandings, thinking of the self-discipline, but without relish. The uniformed oaf at the elevator controls smote a button with a crooked knuckle. "Steptida rearada kaa," he said, in a voice of quiet uninflected hate as a whole troop of riders jammed Mr. Blandings into a fixed position from which he fought his way when the car doors opened on the Banton & Dascomb reception room.

"Goodmorning Mr. Jackerd of Hair Removal has been trying to get you for an hour Mr. Blandings he says it's important and there's a Mr. Schoonladle in reception," said Miss Willersley. Miss Willersley was his secretary; a short, slim, blond girl with a worried

expression and a soul of infinite goodness. The one fault Mr. Blandings could find with her was this damnable habit of dumping the
coal scuttle on him every morning before he could hang up his
overcoat. She got to the office never later than 8:47, and by the
time her employer arrived she was usually panting with problems.

"All right," said Mr. Blandings.

"Mr. Dascomb has advanced the hour of the Plans Board Meeting to 10:45, and Mr. Wayburn hopes he may have a moment with
you before then on a personal matter," said Miss Willersley, con-
cluding the morning report.

"All right," said Mr. Blandings. "Call Jackerd and hold everything else." Before he could finish his sentence Miss Willersley was
dialing a number with a pencil fitted for the purpose with a chromium ball on its eraser end.

"Mr. Jackerd on top," said Miss Willersley. Mr. Blandings shifted
the telephone key under his desk to the *up* position and turned on
his business voice.

"Hello there Jack," he said richly.

"The Old Man is fit to be tied," said Mr. Jackerd; "absolutely fit
to be tied."

He certainly is, said Mr. Blandings to himself; how I would love
to be the one to tie him; to connect a stout cord to something vital
and then yank. That goes for you too, Jackerd.

"What's up?" Mr. Blandings inquired with solicitude.

"They put it on a left-hand page and they *guttered* it," said Mr.
Jackerd. "It's so far back it's practically in the next issue. I told the
Old Man, I said don't blame Blandings I said, it's an insult to him
and the agency as much as it is to you and me I said to him, but
he's not in any mood to listen to reason."

Mr. Blandings had discovered that there are people who discuss
a subject without first announcing what it is. Mr. Jackerd belonged
to this group. The thing to do was to play the same game.

"Which one is it?" he asked.

"April," said Mr. Jackerd.

Alert to every nuance of her business, Miss Willersley instantly
laid the April issue of *Woman's Way* on Mr. Blandings' desk, open
to the area of disaster. The end of January being near, the new
issues of the women's magazines were heralding the vernal equi-

30

nox; the *Woman's Way* cover was a pretty thing of jonquil yellows. Mr. Blandings gazed at the advertisement that he had sweated over in the heat of last year's Indian summer. "A Springtime Message to Women in a World of Tension," said the headline. "By Auvergne du Bois, *Dipl. en Dep.*, Chief Director, the Hair Removal Institute of——" The pulse in Mr. Blandings' stomach resumed beating.

"To begin with," said Mr. Jackerd. The receiver at Mr. Blandings' ear settled into a singsong of complaint. In a little while Miss Willersley crept into the office and placed on Mr. Blandings' desk a small blue piece of paper on which she had neatly typed:

> The Plans Board Meeting will begin in
> the Chart Room in five minutes and Mr.
> Schoonladle is still waiting in reception.

Mr. Blandings made an incomprehensible gesture with one hand and straightened up out of a slump that had his chin on the desktop. "All right, Jack," he said. "Tell the Old Man we're right beside him, shoulder to shoulder, to fight this evil thing through to the end." He hung up, rubbed the aching cartilage of his left ear, and rooted around in the mound of mail on his desk. "Dear Mr. Blandings," said a letter on the starchy bond of an insurance broker. "At this time of world uncertainty are you and your loved ones adequately protected against Dismemberment?"

The buzzer on Mr. Blandings' desk sounded twice. "Mr. Wayburn knows how busy you are," said Miss Willersley's voice on the intercommunicator, "but he wonders if he might have just one word with you before you get involved."

Mr. Blandings hesitated, and saw the handle of his door begin to turn. "All right," he said.

The door opened and admitted Mr. Blandings' assistant. He was a handsome young man from Mississippi, with dark velvet hair and dark velvet eyes.

"Hello, Dward," said Mr. Blandings.

"Hello," said Mr. Wayburn.

It unsettled Mr. Blandings that his young assistant never called him by name. Never "Mr. Blandings" during the days of his apprenticeship, never "Jim" in all the time since Mr. Blandings had

31

told him his job was secure, and invited him into confidence and familiarity. If only Dward Wayburn would ever smile things would be a great deal less constrained, but smile he never would. This was all the more peculiar in that Mr. Wayburn was capable of deep emotion: scorn, rage, contempt, pity, ennui—he had wave-lengths for all of these, but he had none for mirth and he had none, either, for self-doubt. Or so it seemed to his employer.

This morning it was hard to see what the wave-length might be. Mr. Wayburn must have known, Miss Willersley must have told him if it had slipped his mind, that Mr. Blandings was due now at the Plans Board Meeting, but the way Dward Wayburn took out a glossy pipe and began scrabbling with it in an oiled silk tobacco pouch suggested unlimited leisure on both sides of the desk. He never really *smoked* the wretched pipe, Mr. Blandings reflected; he was always stuffing it or lighting or relighting it with a dozen matches, but the ultimate gesture was always knocking the mass of partly scorched tobacco out on his heel into the wastebasket and then scraping around inside the bowl with some sort of warty conical ream he kept on the end of a key chain. Once the process with the pipe had begun there was no shutting it off until the cycle was complete.

"How's everything this morning?" Mr. Blandings asked, fatuously.

"Fine," a man of normal social reaction would have responded.

Mr. Wayburn was not a man of normal social reaction. "I feel I must place my resignation on your desk," he said.

He emitted a thin puff of smoke, which instantly perfumed the room with the sicksweet odor of Latakia.

Mr. Blandings felt sand flowing through a puncture in his aorta. He could not lose Mr. Wayburn, not possibly. He had spent a long, painful time in training him, and now he could handle the Arf account almost unaided. Old Supine was full of plans for a summer campaign to suggest that it had been the choice of an assortment of Civil War Confederate Generals for The Mint Julep Whose Memory is an Unforgettable Fragrance Under the Southern Cross, and Mr. Wayburn seemed a heaven-sent blessing in this desperate situation. He was developing a way with laxative copy, too, and all by himself he had recently evolved a small mortician's

32

account into daily three-inch space in all the New York newspapers with the phrase, "The Last Sad Farewell Is Not of Stygian Gloom Under Our Conductance." Mr. Wayburn was difficult to steer, but just now life without him was worse to contemplate than life with him.

Mr. Blandings put his feet on the desk, as he always did when he was disturbed and needed to conceal it.

"Tell me all about it," he said. "Just come over you, or have you been brooding?"

"Neither one," said Mr. Wayburn. He began poking vent holes in his pipe tobacco, and retamping it with the bottom of a matchbox. He did not seem to feel the need for saying anything further.

"Dward," said Mr. Blandings, "I know advertising is never going to be your career, but you owe it to yourself to stick with it at least until you're thirty. I've put a lot into training you, and I'm going to be selfish about reaping my reward."

Mr. Wayburn removed the pipestem from his pipe and blew through it professionally, like a woodwind player during a rest passage.

"I have the greatest respect for you, and all that sort of thing," he said in his quiet, somber, candied-yams voice, "but the general situation here is such that I don't feel in justice to myself I can go on."

There it was, that peculiar mixture of deference and contempt that Mr. Blandings felt as a constant emanation from his assistant. "I have the greatest respect for you" was spoken in what seemed to be open sincerity, and then "and all that sort of thing" made the whole sentence a mockery. Or did it? Maybe "all that sort of thing" was only a kind of verbal tic. This was precisely what you could never tell in sounding the deeps of Mr. Wayburn.

Mr. Blandings muffled these thoughts. "Suppose you did quit. What would you do?"

"Devote myself to my book," said Mr. Wayburn. "I don't reckon I'd starve."

Oh God, thought Mr. Blandings, Dward Wayburn and his book. It was obvious that Mr. Wayburn thought of himself as the man who would someday pick up the torch when the hand of William Faulkner should at last drop it. To that end he was engaged in a

33

monumentally incomprehensible novel of Southern degeneracy entitled *Tandem Two, Ring Down, Bezonian* of which he had once shown Mr. Blandings half-a-dozen fat chapters. Mr. Blandings had been unable to make anything of them, and therefore in returning them had referred to them as "provocative." Mr. Wayburn had listened to Mr. Blandings' confused comments for three minutes, until they ran down, and had then said with no inflection whatever, "Thank you for your criticism," and withdrawn from the office, his shoulders expressing the quiet scorn of the creative artist for the bourgeois patron of the Womrath Rental Libraries. An over-polite constraint between Mr. Blandings and his assistant had begun then.

Mr. Blandings' buzzer sounded again. "The Plans Board Meeting has been going on for fifteen minutes and Mr. Dascomb is inquiring," said Miss Willersley. "And I'm worried sick about Mr. Schoonladle; he's still in reception."

"Tell Mr. Dascomb I have a situation," said Mr. Blandings, "and I'll join the meeting in just a few minutes. And tell Mr. Schoonladle I have nothing to do with media selection."

Mr. Wayburn, his pipestem rigid in his pursed lips, showed obvious satisfaction when his compressed breath suddenly expelled something as from a blowgun.

"Look, Dward," said Mr. Blandings; "I must be remiss, somehow. I've probably been too tied up in my own problems to tell you what a swell job you've been doing, but you certainly must have noticed how I've been pushing responsibilities your way during the last few months."

"Yes," said Mr. Wayburn, "I have noticed."

"Well," said Mr. Blandings, "you'd be very wrong if you thought I was doing that without making plans to ask the Merit and Morale Board to give you Midyear Consideration."

Mr. Wayburn had reassembled his pipe but on taking a puff found something unsuitable and began flailing downward with it.

"Not a question of money," he said.

"Then what is it a question of?" said Mr. Blandings.

From under his caterpillar eyebrows Mr. Wayburn shot a look at Mr. Blandings. "I thought you might be the one person around here who wouldn't need to ask," he said.

34

There it was again: reproach with contempt in it. Mr. Blandings knew perfectly well what was corroding Mr. Wayburn, and Mr. Wayburn knew he knew it. Mr. Wayburn loathed advertising with a dark rancorous loathing. He loathed it in theory and he loathed it in practice. He had come to New York after an education at Blackmuck College, one of those enlightened hew-your-own-wood-and-draw-your-own-water institutions in the Ozarks, and who at Banton & Dascomb had hired him was a mystery lost in the personnel records. But it was apparent he had entered advertising only as a young physician might have entered a feversome jungle —for experience of a unique and terrible sort that would serve him in some totally different later life. Mr. Blandings had found this out during the first year of his association with Mr. Wayburn but had kept his discovery to himself. For young Mr. Wayburn did have gifts: given a piece of Mr. Blandings' "pattern copy" he could ring changes on its theme so that lo, a campaign emerged from it. This was artisan's work, but for some unfathomable reason Mr. Wayburn while despising it could do it better than any of half-a-dozen eager young disciples who burned to succeed at it. In a most important way, therefore, he was too good to lose.

Naturally Mr. Wayburn had to be kept away from almost everybody. He had to be kept away from Horace Dascomb with particular care; although Mr. Wayburn was a taciturn young man there was something about Mr. Dascomb that drove Mr. Wayburn dangerously close to speech, and speech would not have done. He had to be kept away from clients, too; there was even less likelihood here that Mr. Wayburn would say anything, his contempt going too deep for utterance—yet you never could tell. If Mr. Wayburn were to be taken to lunch with a client and permitted a cocktail there was no telling what might burst forth. "Down to our most junior member, this Agency's personnel is steeped in its client's problems, and sedulously cultivates the client's point of view," Mr. Dascomb was fond of asserting; it would not do to have young Mr. Wayburn loose in the same arena with this thought.

"Dward," said Mr. Blandings, "you know I sympathize with a great part of your point of view. You just go too far with it, that's all. I don't believe any more than you do that advertising's what

35

Horace Dascomb says it is, but you have to credit Horace with absolute sincerity. You can admire him or you can make fun of him, but you have to hand it to him that he believes heart and soul in everything he does."

"That's all I ask for myself," said Mr. Wayburn with an ominous slowness. "But I can't have it here." He began knocking the rim of his pipe bowl gently against the heel of a scuffed tan moccasin held over Mr. Blandings' wastebasket.

Mr. Blandings turned a troubled gaze out the window and stared at the enormous Knapp's Laxative sign suspended over Broadway to the west. The three words on it were his own creation; they were responsible for the first gold medal award he had received to mark him as a leader in his profession. They had made an incredible success; he was completely identified with them and they would no doubt go on his tombstone. He did not think he wanted them there. The sight of them did not make easy a response to Mr. Wayburn.

"Maybe you can't," he said, after a thick sort of pause. "And I'm not urging you to keep on trying all your life. All I'm saying is I don't think you should chuck a job right in the midst of everything. You may think you've taken as much of this as you can stand, but it's good practice and good discipline, and if you were to stay on here until you'd had five years of experience why *then* I think you could pull out and devote yourself to something else."

Mr. Wayburn had now reached the delicate stage with his pipe where its bowl needed to be scraped and reamed without damaging the quarter-inch char built up inside it. Intent on this process, he said nothing.

"You can consider I'm not accepting your resignation," said Mr. Blandings. "It's only fair to both of us that we ought to have a couple of long talks—about it, and you, and me, and everything."

"Give me five years here and I'd be in *your* fix," said Mr. Wayburn.

"What fix is that?" asked Mr. Blandings. He began to feel anger rising inside him, but anger had to be suppressed: it made his face flush and his hands tremble, and it was uncomfortably like fear.

"All fouled up," said Mr. Wayburn, placing his pipe in a shaped case lined with purple velvet. "Good writer, honorable man, best

36

of intentions toward everybody, and all fouled up because he doesn't know which to believe—what he's paid to write, or what he can't help thinking."

So it was *that* transparent; even his assistant knew.

Mr. Blandings' buzzer sounded a loud, hornet-like note. "All right," he said into his telephone mouthpiece, "I'm on my way to the Plans Board Meeting right this minute."

5

MR. BLANDINGS strode past Miss Willersley and down the hall. His week was getting off to a rotten start. Young Mr. Wayburn was not popular in the Banton & Dascomb agency, and on any occasion that found him criticized Mr. Blandings had always assumed the role of his defender. Now, for his pains, the young gentleman he championed had just told him that he was a confused and lily-livered pimp in the service of a great prostitution. It was disturbing. It would not be disturbing unless it was true, would it? This question was so much more disturbing that Mr. Blandings put it behind him entirely. He took a preparatory breath and opened the door of the Chart Room to squeeze into his seat at the massive pickled-oak table in the soft-carpeted room.

"—the greatest challenge and opportunity that could come to this or any other agency."

It was Mr. Dascomb's mild, thin voice. "Hello Jim," it said patiently, and with no reproach for Mr. Blandings' lateness. "I was just beginning to give The Group my thinking in regards to the situation with International Screw."

Mr. Dascomb was tall, pink-cheeked, and silver-haired. In defiance of every stencil that was supposed to mark an advertising man he was gentle, quiet, and full of dignity. No one had ever seen him lose his temper. No one had ever seen him consume anything more devilish than one glass of pale sherry. And no one had ever been able to pierce his geniality. Everyone in the agency was afraid of him, to one degree or another, but no one was able to explain why. If a wrong thought were uttered, a wrong emotion expressed, Mr. Dascomb found it unnecessary to take refuge in any emotion as crass as indignation; a mildly incredulous surprise was all he needed. "Surely you're not asking us to believe that's what you *really* think, Jim," was the strongest note of rebuke Mr. Blandings ever remembered receiving from Mr. Dascomb in his years of employment, but Mr. Dascomb's even tone and faintly depreciating smile always seemed to rally public opinion to Mr. Dascomb's side. If Mr. Dascomb had chosen the Church as his career he would have been a bishop, and a bishop among bishops, Mr. Blandings was quite sure; he had a bishop's overwhelming advantage that although his human frailties might be intermittently evident, it was obvious that he was nevertheless in constant two-way communication with the Holy Ghost. Where others had to rely on feeling, or, at best, on facts, Mr. Dascomb had the higher advantage of Revelation. But he had much too much good taste to boast of this advantage or even allude to it. He merely let it be manifest in everything he said and did.

There was, however, a widespread opinion throughout advertising circles in the United States that Mr. Dascomb was a bastard.

"I claim no personal credit for what is coming about with International Screw," said Mr. Dascomb; "I think they just felt that the time was finally ripe, and if I did play any part in it it was just to emphasize to them that their own selfish interests happened to coincide with a great World public service. And when I parted with Mr. Heffingwell after a long weekend he and his wife spent with Mrs. Dascomb and I in Pelham it was on his expressed intention to spend two million dollars with us during the next twelve months."

Nobody in Banton & Dascomb called Mr. Dascomb "chief" or "H.D." or "boss." They called him Mr. Dascomb; those who could, never corrected him in an occasional lapse of grammar, which was always on the genteel side and in no way reflected upon Yale University, from which he had graduated in 1909.

"That's a lot of money, Mr. Dascomb," said Lorbet Neen.

There was a general murmur of assent. Lorbet Neen had the knack of stating simple truths simply.

"It *is* a lot of money," said Mr. Dascomb, looking up from the pencil he had been modestly twirling in his lean, strong-looking fingers. "Let's none of us lose sight of that point Lorbet's made. Of course Mr. Heffingwell will have to bring his Directors along

with him on any such appropriation, but knowing Heff as I do"—
Mr. Dascomb paused and lighted his features with a smile—"I
don't think there'll be any particular complications there."

Mr. Blandings wrote on the memorandum pad in front of him
"What's up?" and passed it to George Stout, who sat on his left.
George Stout scrawled something on the pad that looked like
exquisitely written Greek and passed it back to Mr. Blandings:
"He just got going as you came in. Who can tell?"

Mr. Dascomb coughed gently into his fist and looked up. "*Someone*," he said, "has got to do something about Russia."

The room rustled, and became still.

"One American businessman who thinks on a scale large enough
to see the problem straight is Royal Heffingwell," said Mr. Dascomb. "The situation is beyond the scope of our present State Department. I grant it's not an easy job for anyone to bring the Russians around, but the idea that developed between Royal and I
over the weekend, and that the Board of International Screw is
considering right this moment, is one of those ideas that's so
simple it's startling."

In doodling on the yellow pad in front of him Mr. Blandings
pressed too hard with his pencil point, which snapped. He looked
up guiltily and saw Lorbet Neen glaring at him from across the
table.

"The whole idea," said Mr. Dascomb, "is describable by the
series' headline: 'An Open Letter to Joseph Stalin.' Full pages once
a week in twenty to thirty key newspapers from coast to coast. A
page or a spread in every weekly worthy of the name, and every
monthly on the best list that Lorbet's department can work up
for us. The strongest copy that the best minds in this agency can
produce—and when I say strong I mean strong in logic and per-
suasion, not name calling. If Joseph Stalin himself had any idea of
what we really have in this country, he'd change his whole line
tomorrow. But he simply doesn't know. International Screw is in a
unique position to be able to tell him. This agency has worked
with them for years on the problem of international accord on
screw-thread standardization, and we know how their minds oper-
ate. And that's why this agency, and not Thompson or BBDO or
any other, has this extraordinary challenge and opportunity of

40

really getting something into Stalin's head and the Politburo's head, and making it *stick*. You fellows know that Peace Through Advertising is one of my most fundamental beliefs, but I never thought we'd have such a God-sent opportunity to carry it forward."

Mr. Dascomb removed his nose glasses for polishing. It was Lorbet Neen who broke the silence. "It's tremendous," he said. "Just thinking off the top of my head, I only have a detail. I'm not going back on what I said a minute ago about two million dollars being a lot of money, but the trouble is that you can't *do* much with it these days."

"You can't do everything with it, Lorbet," said Mr. Dascomb gently, "but you can do something. You can make a start. Rome wasn't—*you* know."

Mr. Blandings cleared his throat. He did not enjoy round-table conversations but a question was bothering him. "Just to take an example," he asked, "how would a page in *Collier's* get to Mr. Stalin's attention?"

"We'd send him tear-sheets," said Lorbet Neen. "The whole campaign would call for a huge tear-sheet and reprint operation beamed directly at the focus of resistance."

"Would you take space in the *Daily Worker*?" asked Mr. Blandings. "I'm no media expert, but maybe the Kremlin sees more of it than it does of the *Times* or even the *News*."

"I certainly would not," said Lorbet Neen, raising his voice to a boom and directing an angry glare at Mr. Blandings. "Help those subversive bastards by putting money into their till? You must be crazy."

"Jim was just wondering what was the clearest channel to the Politburo," said George Stout. "It's a perfectly good question."

"They wouldn't take the copy even if it was offered," said Mr. Pflug who, as Assistant Secretary of the Banton & Dascomb corporation, sat in on all meetings.

"The hell they wouldn't," said Lorbet Neen.

A full debate seemed about to open when Mr. Dascomb coughed again.

"I think we're getting to the detail level a little too fast," he said. "That's just one of hundreds of questions we've got to think through before we're ready to present our full-scale recommendations to International. I hope none of us have luncheon dates or meetings tomorrow that we can't break, for I'd like us all to have lunch on the Bridge and spend all the time necessary in assembling the hardest-hitting Task Force this agency has ever brought to bear on an Objective."

Mr. Dascomb was an amateur yachtsman, and so far as possible he adapted naval phraseology to the functions of his land-borne work. The Bridge was the snug private dining room that adjoined his office on the topmost floor of the Posthumous Guarantees and Trust Building.

Mr. Dascomb went on talking in his quiet, rustling voice. You had to hand it to him: when he had an idea, he did something about it, right away. It occurred to Mr. Blandings that Horace Dascomb and Dward Wayburn had something profound in common: they both believed in themselves to the innermost core; both were solidly rooted in their dignity as individuals. Mr. Wayburn loathed Mr. Dascomb, and Mr. Dascomb returned this emotion by stating periodically that although he had never conversed with Mr. Blandings' assistant there was something about his demeanor that suggested he was the thinker of wrong thoughts—but just the same they were blood brothers. I wish I were like them, thought Mr. Blandings; no I don't—what the hell's the matter with me?

". . . and so I think we'll adjourn now," he heard Mr. Dascomb saying. "I have to be at the Cloud Club in ten minutes; I'm lunching with Royal and I'll be learning something about the reaction of his Directors, so I'd like all of us to reassemble here after lunch as soon as I sound Battle Stations."

Silently Mr. Blandings trudged up the hall toward his own office. He didn't know how to characterize Mr. Dascomb's plan for Peace Through Advertising; he just knew it made him uneasy. Whatever there was to say about it, it couldn't be called trivial. It couldn't be called by any of the ugly names that Dward Wayburn softly applied to every known principle of Mr. Dascomb's art. "Not trivial; only silly" came into Mr. Blandings' mind. Well then, think up something better, Blandings, he said to himself

42

savagely; a fat lot you're doing to help the world out of its agony. Smirking inwardly at Horace Dascomb doesn't for one split second let you off the hook. If Horace Dascomb is persuading two million dollars out of an allegedly hard-boiled bunch of American businessmen for the sake of something a kindergarten teacher would know wouldn't work, can't you think up a really brilliant four-million-dollar idea? Or better yet a forty-billion-dollar idea? It's certainly needed, and where are you?

Mr. Blandings came to his office door and a ray of cheer brightened a corner of his mind. He had a luncheon date with Bill Cole. He could usually tell his doubts and troubles to Bill Cole and feel a lot better for it. He perked up and began sliding into his overcoat.

"Mr. Schoonladle is still waiting in reception," said Miss Willersley.

· 6 ·

Mr. BLANDINGS and Bill Cole were nearing the dessert phase of their lunch in the Chestnut Room of the Hotel Marbury. With smart attentiveness a bus boy came to the table and poured luke-warm water into Bill Cole's glass until it overflowed on the table-cloth. From Mr. Blandings' place he removed a plate with two unused pats of butter, emptied the contents of an ash tray upon them, and efficiently disappeared.

The lunch was not being wholly a success; Bill Cole was in one of his unfeeling moods.

"I don't understand all the complaint," he said. "Maybe this morning *was* typical. It doesn't sound so galling."

"Don't you see?" said Mr. Blandings. "I'm the eternal middle-man. I'm perpetually trying to explain and justify Horace Dascomb to Dward Wayburn and vice versa. And that's merely one example. I can see both sides of *everything*."

"Maybe that accounts for your economic value," said Bill Cole. "Something must."

Mr. Blandings speared a piece of lettuce and nibbled at it miser-ably. "No," he said, "I'm just overpaid, that's all."

"By Horace Dascomb?" said Bill Cole, as if he had trapped a hostile witness.

"By society," said Mr. Blandings.

"Oh my God," said Bill Cole.

Two waiters arrived and began clearing off the table as if trying out for the Olympic Games. A maître d'hôtel flopped enormous menus onto the table and poised himself for the dessert order.

44

Both lunchers studied the carte du jour with deep attention and ordered chocolate ice cream.

"Last Christmas," said Mr. Blandings, when the ill-timed flurry died away, "I got a bonus of seventy per cent of salary."

"Dear me," said Bill Cole.

"It's too early to predict," said Mr. Blandings, "but next Christmas there's a strong likelihood the bonus might be eighty-five per cent."

"Does this unwelcome generosity apply to everyone?" asked Bill Cole.

"No," said Mr. Blandings, "just to what's known as Top Creative." He laughed a short, ghastly laugh.

"Bill," said Mr. Blandings, when his companion made no response, "try to be a little understanding about this. When I get back to the office this afternoon I'll have to begin devising a singing commercial for Queeze. What kind of life work is that for a grown man while the world's tearing itself to pieces?"

"What about Horace Dascomb's open letter to Joseph Stalin?" asked Bill Cole.

Mr. Blandings' shoulders slumped. "Yes," he said, "I forgot that. No question I'll be roped in on that. Queeze will have to wait." He pushed his dark globe of ice cream away from him and sat up suddenly.

"There you have it," he said, making a threatening gesture with his spoon. "*That's* what I'm trying to get over to you. It's this perpetual shuttling back and forth between the grandiose and the preposterous and taking it all with total seriousness that destroys minds in this business. Did you hear what happened to Hank Rivvuld?"

Bill Cole shook his head.

"In our radio department," said Mr. Blandings. "Damn gifted young musician. He told me about it himself. He woke up one morning realizing that the theme of the Bach Passacaglia was perfectly adapted to the purposes of the American Tobacco Company; the only flaw was the omission, by Bach, of one dotted halfnote."

Bill Cole made an inquiry with his eyebrows.

45

"You don't believe me," said Mr. Blandings; "I'll show you."
He began to sing, not so softly as he had intended:

So round, so firm, so ful - ly pack't· so free and ea - sy on the draw.

Several people looked up and a waiter captain came hurrying
over. "Please, gentleman," he said.

"Get it?" said Mr. Blandings. "Hank didn't know what the hell
to do. He couldn't get it out of his head. He couldn't make up his
mind whether he ought to explain it to Mr. Dascomb so the agency
could make a bid for part of the account, or go out and shoot himself. He didn't even know whether Mr. Dascomb would understand it if he *did* explain it. Poor Hank."

"What happened to him?" said Bill Cole.

Mr. Blandings looked troubled. "Everybody still hopes he'll be
able to come back to work," he said. "I must say that sort of thing
always brings out the generous side in Mr. Dascomb. He's paying
Hank's sanitarium bills out of his own pocket."

Bill Cole had finished his dessert and coffee, and was drawing
stars, pinwheels, and Roman candles on the tablecloth.

"What you need," he said, "is a harder shell."

"You're very helpful," said Mr. Blandings. "I don't want a shell.
I want a haven. Horace Dascomb can stand anything in this busi-
ness because he believes in everything about it body and soul.
That protects him perfectly. I can only pretend to."

"A lawyer believes in his case," said Bill Cole.

"I don't believe in my case," said Mr. Blandings. "Just consider
me, an advertising man, in relation to the farmer. I take milk and
eggs from the farmer and give him whisky and hair oil in exchange."

"That is exactly what the farmer wants for his milk and eggs,"
said Bill Cole. "Can't you let it go at that?"

"No," said Mr. Blandings. "It isn't just that my daily life gives
me the willies; I wake up in the night and wonder if I'm not fighting with the wrong army on the wrong side of the whole argument.
The whole country's going to pieces. Nobody's honest any more.

The local community's losing its significance. The home's disintegrating. Who the hell's more responsible than an advertising copywriter? He's the guy with the tricky arguments. He's the guy who levels tastes. Is *that* the side I ought to be on?"

Bill Cole picked up a few pennies and nickels from the silver tray and thrust the rest of the change at the hovering waiter, who palmed seventy-five cents with a hiss of contempt and disappeared.

"I think," he said, "the time has come when you should stop seeing both sides of every question. Particularly the major questions. I think you should decide here and now to live and die an advertising man and accept your bonuses with good grace. You happen to be very good at your profession. You happen to be one of its stars. Follow your destiny."

"What is a man to do when he doesn't like what people tell him he's good at?" said Mr. Blandings.

"Continue doing it," said Bill Cole. "Continue implacably."

"There's another alternative," said Mr. Blandings.

"There certainly is," said Bill Cole; "join your friend Hank Rivvuld in his sanitarium."

"Now wait," said Mr. Blandings.

"Or perhaps you're thinking of some gentlemanly good life in the country," said Bill Cole.

Mr. Blandings jumped sharply.

"As a matter of fact I am," he said, bringing defiance up to the challenge. "You've put your finger right on it. I want to find something to do in my personal life that's going to help me compensate for what I have to do in my professional life. That's the clue to the whole business. You can sit there and ask me in that detached and superior way of yours what it is and I won't be able to tell you—but I know there's something. The greatest unmet obligation in American life is the obligation of the superior individual toward something greater than his particular way of making money. In my case that something greater is the community that Muriel and I and our children have gone to live in. One man can't do very much to redress the balances that are out of whack in America, but at least a man can try. Thats what I'd like to do. In

47

Lansdale. Whatever I might get identified with, it might lead to a hell of a lot more satisfaction, and more good, than beating my brains out hunting for a new theme for a dog food."

Bill Cole was making motions preliminary to getting up.

"They're thinking of adding a line of cat food next year," said Mr. Blandings. "That I will have nothing to do with. Nothing. It has a rotten sound to it right from the start."

Bill Cole sighed. "I was never much in favor of your going up to Lansdale in the first place," he said. "You're not my idea of the rural type. If you're going to play at that, for heaven's sake take it slow and easy."

"Obviously," said Mr. Blandings.

"Don't sponsor a zoning ordinance," said Bill Cole. "Have nothing to do with dairying in thought or in deed. Don't decide to buy the local newspaper and be its country-gentleman publisher."

"You needn't speak to me as if I were a child," said Mr. Blandings.

Bill Cole found a waiting taxi a block down Madison Avenue. He settled back in it, his glossy-worn briefcase beside him. "The Criminal Courts Building," he said with a sigh of relief. He lighted a cigarette and took a lung-bursting drag. I made a mistake, he said to himself. I didn't like that gleam that came into his eye when I mentioned the local newspaper.

After all, Mr. Blandings reflected, the office of the Lansdale *Blade* was only a block from the railroad station. He had been conscious of passing it several times even before his lunch with Bill Cole. Tonight, his homebound train was on schedule for the first time in several days, so he could afford to spend a few minutes in the *Blade*'s office before he started up Bald Mountain. He had legitimate business there, too; it wasn't like sneaking into a saloon. Of course, though, the office might not be open.

It was open. Although it was deep winter, the *Blade* office was still protected against insects by a screen door. Mr. Blandings made his way inside and instantly fell into a dreamy stupor. The office smelled of hot type-metal, stacked paper, and a badly adjusted gas burner. From behind a partition came a silvery clinking that Mr.

48

Blandings recognized as linotype matrixes tumbling into the assembler or finding their separate ways back to the proper slots in the big pie-shaped brass-faced magazine that stored them. A heavy rumble, spaced off into bars by a periodic snap, indicated a running press. The smells and sounds together made up an atmosphere in which he would fain live out the rest of his days.

Confronting him in the gloom was an old man wearing very small, very black, dark glasses, and a hearing aid. Mr. Blandings reached into his wallet and brought out a slip of paper. "I would like to insert a classified ad," he said.

It was apparent that the old gentleman's B-battery had reached extinction. There seemed no clear channel to his ocular senses either; he studied Mr. Blandings' slip of paper with fruitless care, turning it over and upside down. Then he pushed it back toward Mr. Blandings with an air of dismissal.

"I want to put an *ad* in the *paper*," Mr. Blandings shouted.

From the back room there emerged in shirtsleeves a heavy, gray-faced man, with gray hair, in gray clothes. "Do something for you?" he inquired.

"Classified ad," said Mr. Blandings. Somewhat shyly he added, "Are you the editor?"

"Yes sir," said the gray man. He counted out the words in Mr. Blandings' copy. "Trying to hire a couple, hey?" he remarked. "That'll be seventy-five cents for one insertion."

Mr. Blandings put a bill on the counter.

"Money down the rathole," said the gray man. "Anybody answer this, you wouldn't want to have them within five miles of you. What's the name?"

Mr. Blandings spelled it out.

"You bought Eph Hackett's place," the gray man announced. "I live up your way but not so far out. You could do me a favor, running me home tonight. My car's got a busted radiator."

"I'd be delighted," said Mr. Blandings. "Could I just look around the plant for a minute?"

"Nothing to see," said the gray man, "but go ahead while I wash up."

All the rest of the evening, seated in his own armchair, Mr. Blandings heard in his mind's ear the exquisite silvery clink of the

49

linotype machine, the snap and rumble of the small press. He had
rather hoped that Mr. Urmot Nellus, the *Blade*'s editor, was going
to invite him in for a drink in return for the favor of being driven
home; it would have been pleasant to have a chat about the ins
and outs of editing a country newspaper. But Mr. Nellus had not
done so. There would, however, soon be a time. It was going to
take at least a week to get Mr. Nellus' car in running order again
and in the meanwhile he had accepted Mr. Blandings' invitation
to be picked up in the mornings and carried home at nights. Nothing about that that Bill Cole could object to, certainly.

You COULD TAKE the Grand Central Zone as your hub; marking off concentric circles you could pretty well figure out who lived within them. It was to the twenty-five-mile circle that the advertising man seemed to cling the hardest. Summit, N. J., Cedarhurst, L. I., New Dorp, Staten Island, Scarsdale, N. Y., Greenwich, Conn. —these he huddled in. If you went much beyond that circle he began to give way to the book publisher, the radio Personality, the public-relations counselor. If you lengthened your radius still more the advertising man would all but vanish and the population at last become rural except for scattered playwrights, artists and the critics of artists, translators from the French, editors of *New Azimuths* and *The Globalist*. By this time, more likely than not, you were in Lansdale County, somewhere in the valley of the great Wintinock River, for when the days of the expatriated aesthetes ended in the 1930's, along with the previous veneration for the Gold Standard, Lansdale County had somehow been the catch-basin for their return. No one knew just why, except that there had always been some sort of tradition of the intellect along the banks of the river. So it was a strange place for an advertising man to live—but Mr. Blandings had not considered that when he and his wife had first seen Lansdale and said to one another, This is the place. The river lay flat and gleaming among the heavily draped folds of high blue-green which here were called the Lansdale Hills, and the Blandings had merely been smitten helpless by the beauty all about them.

Until the twentieth century was well along on its fearful path the natives of the valley had not had to share the beauty—they lived to themselves and were complete. The railroad soared up the valley with the engine whistles haunting the hills, but a trip from

Lansdale to New York was attempted lightly by no one. Individuals had small need and no impulse to leave the fair dream of elms and lawns and slender spires that was Lansdale Town, or to venture more than a few miles from the houses that stood far back from the dust-carpeted streets, robed in their soft, glowing whites. The railroad brought merchandise to stock the stores on Commerce Street, or carried small surpluses of farm produce away to commission merchants in the city. It accepted passengers mostly by courtesy; those it carried were usually in local traffic between Lansdale and the string of towns along its right-of-way to the south or north. If a citizen went to New York there was speculation why he did it; if a stranger came to Lansdale there was speculation who he was, and on what train he would leave.

"When I went to work for the paper," said Mr. Nellus, "it had a paid-up circulation of 2,600 copies. That was back in 1910."

"And what is it now?" Mr. Blandings inquired.

"Not much under 2,400," said Mr. Nellus. He was a big, knobby, gray-haired man, with big, knobby arthritic hands. He usually wore an air of dense discouragement, but unlike most discouraged people he seemed to be always at work; toilsomely, doggedly, without complaint. Tonight he smelled faintly and pleasantly of whisky and was somewhat relaxed. Mr. Blandings was driving him home, for nobody in the garage had yet got around to the radiator job that Mr. Nellus' car must have before it could run again. Secretly, Mr. Blandings hoped the repairs would take a generous time; he was enjoying these twice-daily trips and chats with the editor of the Lansdale *Blade*.

"That's not so damn bad, either," said Mr. Nellus. "I know you're a city man and an advertising man, but look at it this way: all the automobiles and movies and magazines and radios in this county haven't cost me much over 200 subscribers in forty years."

"I wish I could stop being a city man and an advertising man," said Mr. Blandings, "but I would have figured that your circulation would grow more as the town grew."

"What would give you that idea?" said Mr. Nellus. "There's fewer natives in the town than there were in 1910. Thing's made this town grow is this big influx of foreigners."

"Foreigners?" said Mr. Blandings. "I've never noticed many foreigners around here."

Mr. Nellus emitted a *Ha* in which there was no mirth. "Why you're a foreigner yourself," he said; "a typical example of a foreigner."

"Now wait," said Mr. Blandings. "I was born and brought up in Ohio in a town just about this size. If that doesn't—"

"No offense," said Mr. Nellus. "I'm part foreigner myself. I was born here and my mother was born here but my father came from North Carolina. That's always been a part of my trouble. You and your folks coming from Ohio might give you a sort of advantage here. A lot of the old-timers in this state figure Connecticut still owns Ohio, the way it did in the Revolutionary days. It's better than having a Tarheel for a father, anyway."

"I don't get this," said Mr. Blandings. "I thought the United States was all one country."

"I'm just talking about the local situation," said Mr. Nellus. "No question Lansdale belongs to the Union; the question is, who belongs to Lansdale? If your folks were born here and *their* folks were born here, there's no doubt about it. Otherwise you're not a native, you're a foreigner—unless they sort of privately elect you."

"Who's they?" asked Mr. Blandings.

"Why, Anse Dolliver, and Flem Alders and Nobe Eldridge, and that crowd," said Mr. Nellus. "Every one of them has some ancestor helped found this town, and they're never going to let you forget it."

"I should think the local editor would belong to the inner circle," said Mr. Blandings.

"Well I partly do but I mostly don't," said Mr. Nellus. "Like I told you, my father came from North Carolina. He was a tobacco grower down there and he lived in the same town as Josephus Daniels. He called him Josephus and Josephus called him Tom and they were on a very friendly basis."

"My father knew Newton D. Baker," said Mr. Blandings. "He was a Clevelander, and the place in Ohio we lived was practically a suburb."

"Is that so?" said Mr. Nellus. The news that Mr. Blandings could match him in having belonged to a family who also knew a member of Woodrow Wilson's war cabinet seemed to have quite an effect on him. "Is *that* so?" he repeated, and was silent for a moment.

"How did you happen to fetch up a New Englander?" Mr. Blandings asked.

"My father came North to take a crack at the broadleaf tobacco raising that was really something in this part of Connecticut in those days," said Mr. Nellus, "and here's where he met my mother, and here's where I was born. By 1910 my father'd made enough money out of raising shade-grown wrapper so that when the chance came along he up and bought the paper here before anybody else knew it was for sale. He thought of himself as something of a small-town liberal, I guess, and he wanted to be a county-seat newspaper editor like his friend Josephus Daniels. I was the paper's reporter and bookkeeper, sort of. From 1910 to 1920 we had it pretty good here. The state went Democratic in 1912, and my father was so excited you might have thought he did it himself. Then of course he died a couple of years after the war ended and all of a sudden there I was with the whole paper on my hands. Hard to believe that's all so long ago."

"How come the paper is Republican now?" Mr. Blandings asked.

"Who says it is?" Mr. Nellus countered.

"I got that impression," said Mr. Blandings.

Mr. Nellus sighed. "You may doubt this," he said, "and you're too young to remember firsthand, but it was a lot easier to be what you'd call a liberal in 1910 to 1920 than it is now. Course lots of people thought you were crazy, but they joshed you, was all. It wasn't a matter of life and death the way it is today. Why, even the Republican party had a liberal wing. There wasn't anything about people calling other people Communists if they didn't approve of their thoughts—nor Fascists either, for that matter. I've thought about it a lot and I still don't know why everybody's so bitter these days. I don't know when the change came, either. I guess I didn't inherit my father's fighting spirit. Oh, I give the old guard the needle every now and again when I can't seem to resist it, but in general I go along."

"Are there limits to what you'd go along with?" said Mr. Blandings.

"There must be," said Mr. Nellus, "but I don't seem to know just where they are. I guess I'm awful tolerant. When my wife was alive she used to keep some spine in me, but nowadays to tell you the truth I'm so damn mixed up I don't know *what* I believe. So one week I push the paper a little bit this way and the next week I push it a little bit that way, and that's how I get along. But I *am* tolerant, which is what everybody is going around yelling that everybody else has got to be. And yet deep down I feel a man's got to fight for what he believes."

He took a deep breath. "You just tell me how I can combine being tolerant and militant and you can have anything I've got."

After Mr. Blandings had said good night to Mr. Nellus and watched him trudge up the walk that led to a house where all the windows were dark, he drove slowly over the next four miles that brought him to his own well-lighted establishment. He was thinking about the similarity between this aging country editor and himself. Mr. Blandings, the man who could see both sides of a question, or, if necessary, all sides, had been listening to the confessions of a man who was also unsure, and hence at the mercy of all the loud opinionated paranoid cocksure glib undoubting monologists of the earth. He felt a kinship with Mr. Nellus.

· 8 ·

MR. ANSON DOLLIVER swung about in his chair and from the president's glass-partitioned office surveyed his bank. All was of the proper hush. The continuous soft clack of an adding machine had the quality of a grandfather's clock on the turn of a carpeted stair: it deepened the quiet. At a teller's window a dairy farmer from up Bald Mountain way, Libe Watriss, was depositing the milk check he'd got that morning from the Co-operative; at one of the wall desks an old man in overalls was having an unbelievably complex time endorsing a crumpled-looking money order. They were the only two customers in sight. The last-minute Saturday noon check-cashing rush of the city people would not begin for another quarter hour.

Mr. Dolliver picked up the weekly news-letter of the National City Bank and gave it a show of attention. When a bank president had nothing to do he could not put his feet on the desk. But the day's work had really ended for Mr. Dolliver when he had declined a small loan to a young veteran from over Second Valley way. He was a nice-looking boy who'd gone into the Marine Corps right out of high school during the war years. But there was one thing the Marine Corps couldn't give you and that was business experience. "If it was *our* money it would be different," Mr. Dolliver had said. "But it isn't our money, it's the depositors' money, and if anything should happen to it, the depositors and stockholders would have every right, in fact it would be their duty——"

Mr. Dolliver knew from experience there was no way a novice petitioner for funds could get around this one. The kid would be better off working in a filling station anyway; there were six restaurants, tea shops to dog wagons, in Lansdale Town as it was;

56

one more and there'd be too many. "All of a sudden you'd find that nobody could make any money in the restaurant business any more," Mr. Dolliver had explained. "What you'd be distributing then would be *poverty*. Over-expansion leads to cutthroat competition: too many people fighting for the same amount of dollars. You couldn't open a new restaurant here and keep the dynamic American free-competitive economy running the way it should."

There had been a cloud of confusion on the young man's brow at that point, Mr. Dolliver had noticed. Nice boy but hazy thinker.

That's what you had to be on your guard against these days: hazy thinkers. Hazy thinkers and crackpots. They're everywhere. By golly, there's a crackpot right now, just come in to cash a check: Auster Millowy. Tall and noble looking, but a crackpot just the same. Wrote stuff. Signed petitions. Name turned up in the New York papers every month or so. Probably wasn't capable of doing very much harm, but you had to be on the lookout. Coming right up the steps in a boiling hurry was *another* crackpot: Dr. Thellinger Brassells, he called himself—one of these babies who's always talking about an expanding economy, and how infinitely high you could raise the national income. If he knew so damn much about it, how come his average monthly balance never got above $300?

In carefully concealed distaste Mr. Dolliver swung his chair about again and through his glittering plate-glass window resumed a contemplation of the village green. For the ten thousandth time he glanced with pride at the ornamental sign that said *Lansdale: Founded 1719*. The grass plots were still frozen brown and the great trees stood leafless and wiry in front of him, but soon the spring would come, and soon he could move from his house farther up the green to his cottage at the lake. It would not be so hard to take the city people then. He winced, for still another crackpot was mounting the bank's steps: none other than James H. Blandings, a New York advertising man. The last-minute check-cashing rush of the city people had begun.

Why the hell did they wait until ten minutes to twelve on a Saturday morning before they began pushing their checks through the wickets?—their twenty-five to fifty-dollar checks to give them money for their weekend groceries and liquor. Mr. Dolliver knew all these people by sight and most of them by name. He could put

57

any one of them into the right pigeonhole in an instant, and the cordiality with which he greeted them would give no clue to what he thought about them. There were the all-year-round weekend people, who regularly came to Lansdale Town on a Friday evening and left it again for the city early on Monday morning, whatever the season. They were a cut above the summer weekenders, or the vacationers, but not by much. There were the irregulars: the people who managed to make a living out of some New York activity without going to the city more than once a month or so, for two or three days at a time. There were the commuters. Mr. Dolliver might have felt some respect for their desire to sleep every night under the Lansdale skies were it not that the commuters fancied themselves as full-time residents, a preening not to be countenanced. And then there were a few city people who had come to live in Lansdale Town in true permanence. For these Mr. Dolliver had the nearest thing to respect: they had made enough money to need the city no longer. Even so, he could not really like them; they, too, were pretenders to true nativity.

Mr. Dolliver turned back to watch his tellers doling out the cash. By ten o'clock that night, he knew, nine-tenths of it would be back in his bank; stuffed in the big brass-faced night depository by every merchant in Lansdale Town who took in enough of it not to want to trust his own cashbox until Monday morning. Was not this a beneficent process, this money circulation for which his bank was the heart? Most certainly it was; up to a point it was to be welcomed and encouraged, but beyond that point it needed a steely control. Otherwise the city people could well swamp the whole community. Sometimes he thought it was close to swamped already. These damn people, without seeming to know it, were engaged in an attempt to divide and conquer. They had the townsfolk divided already– split right down the middle. If a man was a merchant most likely he *encouraged* these people; their city-earned money raised the turnover, made the cash registers ring oftener at the groceries, the drygoods counters, the drugstores, and the filling stations. On the other hand, if a man was a farmer he hated these people—hated their guts. Except . . . there was never any telling when a farmer might make the clear equivalent of five years' milk checks by selling one of them twenty acres—so

58

you couldn't even tell for sure about that. There was only one thing certain: in the confused and bitter times it was up to him, up to Anson Dolliver, to see that things were kept in balance; that the bank prospered but at the same time the city people gained no further ground in Lansdale at the expense of the ordained order of things.

Anson Dolliver tried not to be proud, but it was difficult. His five-times-great grandfather had been one of the founders of this town. So had Flem Alders'; so had Nobe Eldridge's. Mr. Dolliver wondered how many other towns in New England could boast three of the founding families still standing side by side more than two and a quarter centuries later: not only not gone to seed but still leaders in the community the way their ancestors had been back through all the generations. They might not be friends, ex-actly; the situation was a little more formal than that. The Dol-liver family had always supplied the leaders, and the Alders and the Eldridges had competed among themselves for second place as far back as the records went, and further. Mr. Dolliver like the Dollivers before him was not just the proprietor of the town's bank; he was the proprietor of the town. Some years he might not even bother to hold any actual political post, but that didn't mat-ter. There wasn't anybody who was going to contest matters with him, or anybody that would even think of trying.

That didn't mean things were easy for a Dolliver, or ever had been. The original colony had to be hacked out of the wilderness and defended against the Indians. No sooner than they'd been disposed of, Mr. Dolliver mused, than we had to fight the British, and what was more, fight the American Tories who sympathized with them in our own community, for there were hazy thinkers and crackpots in those times just as there are today.

Somehow, though, they must have been easier to cope with. Because the people who look at things the wrong way today you can't so easily identify. They don't look like Indians, and they don't wear red coats, and there's nothing to distinguish friend from foe unless you have a sharp eye that's trained to look hard and make small distinctions; small but mighty important. What I have against these city people, said Mr. Dolliver, casting another glance at the

59

now swarming floor of his bank, is that they're corrupt; their minds are corrupt. They're soft and they're silly. They're the people who believe in "democracy and more democracy"—and something crazy has gone wrong with this country, because almost every living man in it has been backed into a corner and feels as if he had to say that in public whether he really believes it or not. Now I'm going to be utterly frank with you, Mr. Dolliver said silently to Mr. Joseph Chasuble-Horn, another crackpot about to cash a thirty-five-dollar check, or maybe fifty dollars—he had more money than most of them. I don't believe in that at all, not for a minute, and neither do an awful lot of people who pretend they do. The principal difference between me and those other people is that I'm willing to come right out and say it—well, not in so many words because, damn it, I'm part way backed into a corner myself. But if I can't go as far as I like in saying it you can certainly see my beliefs in my actions. What the right-thinking people here-abouts believe in is the *aristocratic* principle; that is, pick the best men to do the toughest jobs. That's the way every successful business in America is run today, and always was run, and it wasn't until a very little while ago that anybody dared challenge it, be-cause it was evident and right and produced the results everybody wanted; everybody but a few crackpots. And all I'm saying to you is that we run this community of Lansdale, small though it is, in just the same way.

"The greatest unmet obligation in American life is the obliga-tion of the superior individual toward something higher than his own individual way of making money." Do you know who I heard saying that on Commerce Street the other day? That crackpot Blandings. The trouble with these damn fool liberals is that they're always thinking they've discovered something new. This particular discovery we've happened to know about here since before the Revolution and we still act on it every day of our lives. Why the hell else should I be the Chairman of the Town Finance Committee? Or Flem Alders be First Selectman? Or Nobe Eldridge run the Board of Assessors?

With relief, Mr. Dolliver watched Walter Hoag pull down the curtains on the front doors, marking the end of another banking week. As soon as the dozen customers still inside finished their check cashing he would go home. Why the hell was this Thellinger Brassells, the expanding economist, back in the bank for the second time in twenty minutes? Probably didn't know enough arithmetic to draw the right-sized draft the first time. The trouble with you, Brassells, said Mr. Dolliver, in silent contempt, and with all your city friends acting like you owned it up here is that you think *you're* the superior individuals who have all these obligations to fulfill. Every way you can think of, you let on to how much more you know than anybody else knows. And at the same time you're always talking about the masses of the people, and the rights they have coming to them. So you're in an absolute contradiction—talking about individualism, superior individualism, and a democracy in which every man is just as good as every other man.

We want to keep that kind of hazy, crackpot thinking out of this community, said Mr. Dolliver. You know damn well, or you ought to, that the framers of the Constitution of the United States didn't ever trust the masses of the people worth one lead cent. Connecticut has always stood foursquare for the Constitution *as originally written*. It never ratified the Bill of Rights until 1939, that's right, 1939, go look it up in case you doubt what I'm telling you. That was what I call caving in under pressure. It was caving in to the idea of unbridled democracy, which attacked this nation precisely as the Founding Fathers determined it should *not*. This idea was born in the cities, and it got loose in the cities, and now it's spread to the whole country. Once this idea got loose, and enough people fell for it, you could predict everything else that's troubling us today: the steps from this to Socialism and Communism are simple *and they are logical*. All right; we admit we've been undermined by this idea even right here in Lansdale, but we don't admit it has to go one step further. That's why we're determined to see that the city doesn't get one more tentacle around this community here. This is *our* community, see? It belongs to the people who were born and raised here. We can't keep you other people out. We're perfectly glad to have you as visitors, and we'll even take you as residents if you'll submit to the established way of doing things. Why do we insist on this? For the absolutely simple reason that it's our home. We don't aim

61

to be crowded out. We're glad to grow; we're glad to have new trade, but we have one simple rule: you can *be* here, but you can't *belong* here. And you can't belong here *because you've got no right*.

Mr. Dolliver slipped on his Chesterfield with the slightly curled velvet collar, and put his old gray hat inexactly on his head. He waved a wordless goodbye to his staff and slipped out the back door of the bank that gave directly on its parking lot. He was still fuming with unspoken thoughts as he swung his car toward the crosswalk, and it irked him to have to jam on his brakes to avoid a pedestrian who was obviously moving in a trance. Mr. Blandings, his head down, a collection of groceries under his arm, was so busy thinking of the logic with which to convince Joseph Stalin that the American way of life was preferable to the concepts up to now held by the Kremlin that he was not conscious of being almost run down until he heard the bite of Mr. Dolliver's well-shod wheels on the gravel. Then he made an exaggerated leap aside. "Sorry," he said.

"That's all right," said Mr. Dolliver cordially. "Quite all right." He swung his front wheels for the curve at the foot of the green, and was on his way. "Crackpot!" he muttered. "God knows what goes on in a head like yours."

MR. BLANDINGS looked dispiritedly at his typewriter. It was long after office hours and the last train for Lansdale had left two hours ago. He was far behindhand with his work, and this was the third night in a row that he had been stuck in the city. When he had called Mrs. Blandings the news had not been welcome. He put a number of thoughts behind him and tried to concentrate on the matter in hand. With his three-fingered approach to his twenty-year-old typewriter he depressed the shift lock and wrote:

IT'S HERE!

He stared at this for some moments and found it lacking. He put a row of X's through it and tried again:

AT LAST! NO MORE WAITING!

This would not do. He pulled the whole sheet out of the machine and inserted a new one on which he wrote:

NOW, MORE THAN EVER BEFORE—

What the hell was the idea of beginning a sentence before you had any idea how you were going to end it? He must really hike himself out of this slump. He straightened up, went to the drinking fountain and twitched its metal lever. A heavy stream of luke-warm water struck him in the nose. He came back to his chair and lighted a fresh cigarette. There should be an approach from a completely different angle:

TO MEN AND WOMEN WHO HAVE WONDERED WHEN—

That was a hot new angle. He crushed out the cigarette, buried his head in his hands, and stayed immobile for several moments. Then he sat up and attacked the machine angrily:

STRAIGHT AND SWIFT AS AN ARROW
COMES TO YOU NOW—

Once again the steady tap of the X-key obliterated all. He would not give in. He would stick with this until he had the problem licked. Let the mind go now. Let it roam freely over the whole vast spectral range of the English language, the Roman alphabet. Let the fingers respond to the pressure from an overwhelming reservoir of racial memory and personal experience. Unbind the fettering dress of fear and inhibition and let the thoughts flow free and wild. That was the way great things were written: sonnets or advertisements. Mr. Blandings' fingers moved and the keys clacked and a new line stood stark on the paper:

AN ANNOUNCEMENT

Dear Almighty God. This was it. The end, which he had spent twenty years in dreading, had come at last. He was played out. Not one more thought would ever occur to him of enough originality to serve as a headline for an advertisement. Mr. Blandings slumped forward in his chair, his hands pressed against his eyes. Inside him, two glossy, shell-less hard-boiled eggs were playing a gleeful game of billiards; they would strike together, deform, slip off, rebound from the walls of his stomach and collide again. No pain was quite so unendurable as this painless torment; it was bad when the eggs struck their sides together, but when at unpredictable intervals they met tops-on there was no scream hideous enough to relieve the torture.

Just then the eggs did strike their tops. Mr. Blandings slammed his chair back from the desk and strode to the window. Thirty-one stories below him the night's traffic made a curious sound of whish and rattle as squadrons of taxicabs with skid chains plowed up and down streets four inches deep in a melted brown sherbet of snow, rain, and filth. To the west, he could see the enormous electric-spectacular sign of Knapp's Laxative casting fifty thousand watts over Broadway; the three words of its slogan repeated themselves in a red-green-white cycle, over and over, so strongly that they changed the whole color of the drizzling sky. Hell, Mr. Blandings thought; if he could get no comfort from the words he should at least find in them a little courage. Before he had thought of them he had been just another copywriter—one of those well-dressed, pleasantly literate journeymen in words who earned generous salaries when times were good and were fired, a hundred of them in an afternoon, perhaps, when times turned bad or a major advertiser canceled a campaign. But with those three words he had become something else—"a man with an account in his pocket." He could leave Banton & Dascomb tomorrow, if he cared to, and take with him one of the solidest and most profitable accounts in advertising, wherever he should go.

Wherever he should go. . . . Why then could he not relax and take it easier? Just yesterday he had met Thorn Aldable at noontime in the Yale Club; Thorn was his age, and a skilled copy hand by anybody's standards, but he had paraded in and out of a dozen agencies in a dozen years; nobody had anything but good to say for him, but the big accounts he had worked on were always blowing up in his face. Like as not, when he was fired by the agency that had lost the account, the agency that got the account hired him because of his "experience." (The old agency had lost the account because it had gone stale; i.e., it had too much "experience.") But it was a hell of a disconcerting life even so; the everlasting business of fitting in with a new group every year or two, and remembering that your office wasn't at 230 Park Avenue any more but 420 Lexington or 383 Madison instead. "God damn it," Thorn had said, "if I had anything half as soft as Knapp to count on for billings year in and year out, you wouldn't catch me doing anything but just nursing it along and to hell with all the rest of the crap." Talk like this discomfited Mr. Blandings; he found in it the implication that luck, not worth or industry, kept him near the top of the heap. Well, in a sense it *was* luck, because the words that had transformed the Knapp Laxative from a miserable little cat-and-dog account into a weighty and dominant enterprise *might* have occurred to anyone. So there was enough truth in the talk to make it unendurable to him, and to force him every day into new methods of disproving it.

Nothing could be sillier, he said to himself. Nothing could be sillier than the way he tried to force himself to be things he could not be, or the way he thrust himself into situations from which he

65

could not escape whole. The present damnable mess with Dward Wayburn was a beautiful example of the Blandings' incapacity for administration, and Mr. Blandings thought about it bitterly. He had told Dward Wayburn that he did not want him to quit, and Dward Wayburn had at his suggestion gone away for two days to think it over. Then he had come back to announce that he would stay. He had talked it over with his Essie Lou and they had decided he would stay—for a while. He had made it clear to Mr. Blandings in a muffled and ultra-gentlemanly way that he was doing this as a favor and that someday he would have to exact a price for the sufferings of a conscience suppressed out of consideration for another. During the conversation young Mr. Wayburn's pipe had been unusually demanding: a whole pocketful of flaring wooden matches had been insufficient to support its combustion; it had also needed, as tamps, probes, or swabs, a succession of twisted paper clips, pinpoints, rulers, line gauges, pieces of blotter, and other small objects on Mr. Blandings' desk. At the end of it all the pipe's ashes had set fire to the contents of Mr. Blandings' wastebasket, and filled several adjoining offices, including Lorbet Neen's, with smoke, but the pipe and the dark gentlemanliness of its possessor had such an unnerving effect upon Mr. Blandings that he had apologized for his wastebasket's being full.

But when Mr. Blandings, as he had promised, brought up to the Merit and Morale Board the question of a raise for Dward Wayburn, still another snag had, with some violence, been struck. Mr. Dascomb had put his back up and said he did not think this young man had any future in advertising. This was true, and Mr. Blandings knew it was true; indeed it was Mr. Wayburn's own contention. Mr. Blandings had sought to deny it, so now he had a position to defend. And then, as so often, Mr. Dascomb showed how deep ran his capacities as the top executive of a complex business. "You know the procedure, Jim," he had said. "Any chief of section can overrule me without prejudice when it comes to a raise for one of his own men; if he doesn't know his man better than I do, it's too bad. He need only state that he *is* overruling me." Mr. Blandings, caught in a trap, had exercised his privilege of overruling Mr. Dascomb, Mr. Dascomb had smiled his genial, imperturbable smile, and Mr. Pflug, as minute-keeper of all official proceedings, had made the proper note on all the personnel records involved.

But Mr. Blandings had not had the courage to overrule Mr. Dascomb for the full amount of the raise he had in mind, so it was smaller than Mr. Wayburn had somehow been led to expect. The net of the situation thus became that Mr. Blandings had persuaded to stay with the company an employee who had wanted to resign, and who Mr. Dascomb thought should resign, and had persuaded him by the promise of a raise, perilously gained but now delivered half broken—and when thus delivered, accepted with an accusation made terrible by its wordlessness. Since that time Mr. Wayburn had become even darker, more silent, and more gentlemanly than ever, and Mr. Blandings now so shrank from contact with him that, as his salary rose, his value as an assistant declined to zero. But Mr. Wayburn had given the word of a Southern gentleman that he would stay, so the knot was knotted beyond all unknotting.

Damn the whole business to an eternal and everlasting hell, said Mr. Blandings to himself. Why was he in the city and in his office on this foul, witch-ridden winter's night? Because he was supposed to be catching up with his work. And why was he behindhand with his work? Because he had been so upset for the last three days that he hadn't been able to get anything done in its appointed time, that was why. But instead of catching up now he was busy roweling himself with unpleasant memories. But why was he so upset? His mind gave him the answer in terms of homicide: if he could murder Lorbet Neen with a cleaver and go reeling and slipping in his blood he was sure he would no longer be upset at all.

It had been the middle of last week when Mr. Blandings had finished the first part of his task for Mr. Dascomb's series of Open Letters to Joseph Stalin, and had come up with five pieces of trial copy. By the time he had written and rewritten them, polished them and honed them with hours of concentrated work, he had come to think of them as pretty good. George Stout had thought so, too. Mr. Blandings felt a great reliance on George Stout's opinion because, although he was a newcomer of a mere five years' experience in the advertising agency world, he had previously been an associate professor of English in a beautiful, decaying New England college, and was hence a man of cultivation. Then

Mr. Dascomb had assembled the Russian Task Force for an examination of what everyone had written, a determination of what was to be shown the client. Lorbet Neen had been there, and Mr. Dascomb had asked him to express his opinion of Mr. Blandings' copy.

"Stalin," Lorbet Neen had said, "would take it as a sign of weakness."

The unmodified assurance of this had been too much for Mr. Blandings. "How the hell do you know how Stalin would take it?" he had demanded.

"How the hell do *you* know?" Lorbet Neen had countered. "Or have you some kind of pipeline to him?"

Was this a deadly insult? Or only the sort of brutal jibe that businessmen flung at one another? In his ensuing rage Mr. Blandings was not sure—and in his rage he lost sight of his basic belief that the idea of writing open letters to Joseph Stalin was a monumental absurdity, out of which John Milton himself could have produced nothing sensible. Instead he defended his copy on secondary and technical grounds. Lorbet Neen calmly and correctly disclaimed any knowledge of how to write copy and came up, as if it was newly minted, with the word "appeasement" to describe his impressions of Mr. Blandings' approach to the master of the Kremlin. That had been bad enough; it all became very much worse when Mr. Dascomb made it evident that he saw virtue in Lorbet Neen's view. "Appeasement may not be just the right word, Lorbet," he had said, with a cuff-shooting display of judicial temperament; "but Jim, I think there's a good deal in Lorbet's feeling that Stalin might interpret this approach as too soft, too reasonable. I think this is what Lorbet really means, and I think he has a point here."

Mr. Dascomb was always explaining what Lorbet Neen really meant, and thinking he had a point here or a point there. Mr. Blandings didn't know whether it was Lorbet Neen's total, blithering asininity that enraged him so frequently, or whether it was that somehow Lorbet Neen always had Mr. Dascomb's ear, always seemed to say something of the most appalling vapidness in which Mr. Dascomb found whispers of profundity. Occasionally Mr. Dascomb seemed to find it necessary to explain his dependence on Lorbet Neen's beliefs. "Lorbet is *client*-minded," he had said. "He

68

seems to have an instinct for anticipating what the client's reaction is going to be to almost everything, whether it makes sense or not."

It was not like Mr. Dascomb to make so wide an admission; his careful tongue must for once have slipped. But as Mr. Blandings gazed out into the miserable night he could find no comfort in this momentary lapse. For Lorbet Neen's animal instinct had been vindicated that afternoon; it was George Stout who had told Mr. Blandings what had happened. "I was sitting in Mr. Dascomb's office talking about the speech I have to write for him to give before the Association of Car-Float Underwriters next month," George had said, "and all of a sudden Royal Heffingwell came barging in the door, right past the whole secretariat. So I started to get out, but both of them said no, no, stick around, and one thing led to another and the next thing I knew Mr. Dascomb was showing him a piece of your Russian copy—the last thing he was supposed to do under his own rules. You know how he is: you can never figure out whether he's just simple-minded or whether he's working some deep-laid plot. But if he had a plot it was too deep for me because all he said was 'Heff, here's an example of the technically best copy we have, but we're frankly in a division over the basic approach.' That was fair enough as far as it went, and old Heff read it and—well Jim, I'm sorry to be the bearer of the news but he reacted exactly like Lorbet Neen. Of course he doesn't plump out with things the way Lorbet does, but he started to turn blotchy and Mr. Dascomb must have recognized that was a bad sign because he started to backtrack fast, and the next thing he knew he was in a corner, and the only way he could get out of it was by agreeing that everybody knew the approach was wrong as he'd said in the first place. So then they went out to lunch at the Cloud Club and I don't know what happened after that except that obviously Mr. Dascomb knows he got everything screwed up, staff-relations, client-relations, everything, and I'll be fascinated to see how he gets out of it. Because of course he will get out of it. You know, I can't help admiring—"

So tomorrow, Mr. Blandings thought to himself, tomorrow he would be facing a vindicated Lorbet Neen, and a Horace Dascomb who would be full of ultrapolite, extra-ingenious evasions. Lorbet Neen would not gloat; he was obviously too secure to feel any need of gloating. He would see nothing out of the ordinary in the instinctive agreement between himself and Royal Heffingwell, the august Chairman of the redoubtable International Screw, whereas he, Blandings, loathing Royal Heffingwell for a stuffed dummy, would have been as pleased to have had the dummy's approval of what he had written as he was now distressed not to have it. And on top of all this, he himself, the author of the copy, had not one grain of belief in the efficacy of what the copy was attempting to do.

Mr. Blandings' rage against Lorbet Neen suddenly evaporated. Lorbet might be a fool, or maybe he wasn't a fool at all. But even if he was a fool he was a monolithic, conjunctive fool; all of him was idiotic in the same way; his idiocies were consistent, integrated; they all flowed with the same tide. It was a better and even honester kind of fool to be than the Blandings kind of fool, Mr. Blandings reflected; the Blandings kind of fool was inconsistent, fractured, disjunctive, pulverized; lost in the labyrinths of its own four-dimensional mendacity.

Very well. Was this the verdict? Let it be acted upon.

Out of the night that covered him, black as the pit except as modified on an eighteen-second cycle by the Knapp Electric Spectacular, a path of light opened for Mr. Blandings; a group of liberating words formed in his mind. Dear Mr. Dascomb: Throughout the many years of our happy association I have held steadfastly by one conviction—the conviction that should the day come when I felt myself no longer of a usefulness requisite to the position I hold with the firm I would without further ado tender my—

Why not? Indeed why not? He had paltered with his life ever since he could remember, assuring himself that when the time came, when things were *just* right, he would make just such a move as this. But things would never be *just* right; a brave step forward into the dark was the real and only means to freedom. He had enough financial reserve to live and support his family for a year. He had a brave wife; say what you would about Muriel's

70

crotchets she would join her hand in his for any such new adventure. A year was a long time; plenty long enough for carving out a new destiny, whatever it might be. He would abjure the city, live in the peace and quiet of the countryside, and work unassumingly toward a modest appointed end. If success should crown his efforts—but we are no longer talking about success, Blandings, he reminded himself; we are talking about satisfaction, about accomplishment.

The letter of resignation turned out close to perfect on the third draft. It was simple, manly, and direct; no hint of pique or grudge was in it, no innuendo against a colleague, however slight. Would he be urged to reconsider when Mr. Dascomb read it tomorrow morning? More than possibly; in fact, almost certainly. Against such persuasions he was already steeled.

On a little blue square of paper he wrote the words "JW: Please retype," and clipped it to his final draft. Poor Judith Willersley; it would be quite a shock to her. "I'll explain when I see you," he added as a postscript to soften the blow. Then he thrust the draft in an envelope, sealed it, and placed it squarely in the center of Miss Willersley's desk, weighting it down with a thick little glass bowl full of paper clips. The sigh he sighed was of deepest relief: why had he not brought himself to this decisive step long ago? No matter; he was at it now.

He glanced out the window. The skies were still drizzling but he would take a long walk through the winter streets, the clean cold rain stinging his face, and let his mind become serene in contemplation of a new, unfolding future before he turned in at the University Club for the night. He tore up the copy he had been struggling with earlier in the evening; he had accomplished more tonight than he had accomplished in the last dozen years. The hell with that new preparation the makers of Arf were now, after exhaustive scientific laboratory tests, after quintuple-checked kennel trials, about to place on the market for cats. The hell with all of it. He snapped out his office lights with a decisive gesture and went swiftly down the hall toward the night elevators, struggling into his overcoat as he went.

The night elevator arrived after an interval and silently con-

71

veyed him downward. In the lobby of the Posthumous Guarantees and Trust Company one unshaded thousand-watt bulb pierced the darkness with a shriek of light at the watchman's desk. Mr. Blandings signed out on the night register with a flourish, pushed his way through the one unlocked revolving door, and strode briskly to the curb. Like a speedboat on its homestretch a taxicab whooshed by, throwing up a heavy bow wave of slush. The crest of it caught Mr. Blandings just below the waist and dealt him a set of wet, thumping blows. He looked down at himself from his top overcoat button to his shoes, and stood stock-still where he was. Not until another taxicab, slower moving than the first, clipped him with a line of slush around his ankles did he slowly turn and make his way back into the lobby of the Posthumous Guarantees and Trust Company.

"Forget something?" said the night watchman.

Mr. Blandings made a noise in his throat.

"Say which?" the watchman inquired.

"I said *I forgot my rubbers,*" said Mr. Blandings savagely.

The same night-elevator man who had just brought Mr. Blandings down from the thirty-first floor stared at him in smoldering silence as he carried him up again. In his office his rubbers confronted Mr. Blandings, large and black and ugly, under the clothes tree. He sat down and began wearily dragging them over the shoes that were already soaked by their twenty-foot round trip between building and curb. It had been hardly the long, flushed-with-courage walk he was to have taken in the cold, stinging rain to plan his life anew; it had ended before it had begun.

Outside to the west the Knapp Electric Spectacular went on with its ceaseless work, and when his eye caught it, the last ounce of resolution drained from him. Not only was there no courage to be found in it: it fairly shone with despair. It possessed him. He could leave Banton & Dascomb, but he could not leave the world of advertising. Within the world of advertising he was a prosperous man; without it, he was a pauper. He was a captive of his success. Change in his life there must be, but this was not it. One could not escape from the clutches of a wealthy and domineering old aunt by shooting her—a change of jailers was not freedom.

He picked up his sealed envelope from Miss Willersley's desk, and without opening it, slowly tore it and its contents into pieces an inch square. From the palm of his hand he dribbled them into the wastebasket, watching them with care. When the night elevator called for him the second time he not only had his rubbers on; he had found an old umbrella somewhere and was using it like a cane.

· 10 ·

WHEN Mr. Blandings arrived again at Bald Mountain late on a Friday evening he kept the whole complex of his troubles with Lorbet Neen and Joseph Stalin strictly to himself. The emotional crisis that had made him burst out with a letter of resignation to Horace Dascomb, only to tear it up in hopelessness an hour later, was not to be shared with anyone. A man might suffer, but a man's primary duty to wife and family was the stoic preservation of his equanimity. From the male, strength and courage.

"What is the matter?" asked Mrs. Blandings almost immediately.

"Nothing," said Mr. Blandings.

"You're very depressed," said Mrs. Blandings.

Mr. Blandings told her the whole story.

"Darling," said Mrs. Blandings, "it's all a crazy world. Just try not to mind it so much. Do you know what happened here today?"

With a supreme effort, Mr. Blandings lifted his eyebrows.

"A man came along and tried to buy the house. He sat right in your chair and he practically took out his fountain pen and tried to write out a check for $85,000."

"For *what*?" said Mr. Blandings. "He was crazy."

"No he wasn't," said Mrs. Blandings. "He was a completely sane broker who came all the way from New York. He had a French refugee client who wanted security, and he said he had instructions—instructions, mind you—to buy this house."

"That doesn't sound like the French," said Mr. Blandings.

"The security part of it does," said Mrs. Blandings. "Imagine trying to buy security." She stopped short and gave a little secret glance at her husband.

"It still doesn't sound like the French," said Mr. Blandings.

74

"I'm not so sure," said Mrs. Blandings. "When I was in France right after Bryn Mawr I saw a man from Akron try to buy the Château at Blois for cash. I think that's the sort of thing that's given the French their idea of American business methods."

"I don't like strangers barging in here and thinking they can do anything they want because they have a vulgar amount of money," said Mr. Blandings.

"That's not a very nice attitude to take toward strangers," said Mrs. Blandings, "or a very logical one."

"My logic breaks down," said Mr. Blandings, "when day after day in front of my own office jabbering women in minks and emeralds push me away from taxicabs. I have some rights in New York myself."

"You're sounding just a teeny mite like Anson Dolliver," said Mrs. Blandings. "Maybe strangers' ways are a little hard to put up with. Didn't you once tell me about having a row with a Paris taxi driver because you and a lot of Yale boys pasted thousand-franc notes on your luggage like hotel stickers?"

Mr. Blandings looked annoyed. "What did this Frenchman of yours want with *our* house?" he demanded.

"He wasn't *my* Frenchman," said Mrs. Blandings. "He saw a picture of the house in the papers when the Institute of Architects awarded Henry Simms the design prize."

"So what did you say to his broker?"

"I just said that naturally the house wasn't for sale at any price. I should think it ought to make you feel better to think that somebody would buy the house for three times its cost."

"Inflation," said Mr. Blandings. Just the same, it did make him feel better. He kissed his wife by way of apology.

After dinner, Mr. and Mrs. Blandings bundled up in their warmest clothes and went for a walk. The countryside was covered a foot deep with snow. Unlike the city's it was pure and white and crystalline; it carpeted the earth and draped the trees and was an ermine mantle everywhere. Hand in hand, the Blandings walked through the limitless whiteness. A round moon flared in the sky and lighted up the outline of the hills. "You could read a newspaper," said Mrs. Blandings.

The next morning, the iron grip of the winter suddenly relaxed. When Mr. Blandings emerged into the out-of-doors it was to discover that little rivulets of water were gouging the packed white of the roadways. The brook, sheathed over for weeks with ice that had had as many layers and planes as isinglass, was all of a sudden free and roaring. His feet encased in skiboots that had never known a ski, his hands thrust deep into the pockets of his country jacket, Mr. Blandings strolled about his barns and felt hope stirring again in his bosom.

He was interrupted by a cry from his wife, who had been poking about in a lower field.

"Come here!" she cried, her voice tense with excitement.

Down and around the curving roadway Mr. Blandings came; came and joined his wife at the brook's edge.

"Look!" she cried.

Mr. Blandings looked.

Mrs. Blandings made a noise of impatience. "Can't you *see*?"

Mr. Blandings redirected his gaze and saw, furled tight along a rock's edge, a cylinder of live, glossy brown, half buried in the snow.

"A skunk cabbage!" said Mrs. Blandings, in the manner of Linnaeus. "In a day or so it'll unfurl and turn into a bunch of big green leaves. It's the very first thing that comes to life toward the end of winter. It means that before another month we'll see our first crocus, and soon after that the daffodils and the next thing you know spring is going to be everywhere." She jumped up, flung her arms around her husband and gave him a sudden, impulsive kiss.

That noon, the mailman, clanking up Bald Mountain in a car so utterly dilapidated it was impossible to determine its make, left a collection of bulky manila envelopes in the Blandings' mailbox, a hundred yards down the road. News of the death of a wealthy relative could scarcely have brought a healthier, more all-pervading happiness: the envelopes were jammed to bursting with seed catalogs.

By early afternoon the sun disappeared behind heavy banks of clouds, and a drizzle of cold rain began. Mr. Blandings did not

76

notice. He was reading with an intensity he had given to no piece of prose since the day when years ago, as a college freshman, he had first come on Havelock Ellis' *Psychology of Sex*. Now he was discovering something just as new, and just as exciting, if in a different way. When he stopped to think of it he felt a little rueful at what the years had done to him: supplanted nubile young women with radish and tomato seed as a source of inward excitement and desire. Now that was just a cockeyed half-truth, he said to himself impatiently; just because he had newly discovered there were joys in the vegetable kingdom too didn't mean that he was all through as a—

"We could have an asparagus bed," said Mrs. Blandings, deep in the study of pages thick with enormous stalks of something more beautiful than had ever crossed the imagination of Oscar of the Waldorf.

"We certainly could," said Mr. Blandings. In a sort of wondrous waking dream he gave himself completely into the hands of an advertising copywriter operating in realms of which he had no knowledge. No subtlety of understatement, no fear of a Federal Trade Commission or a Better Business Bureau made timid the man who had arranged the fugues for a set of pages reserved to *Lycopersicon esculentum*, or the tomato. "These Wallrath Triple Tested Pritchards," he read, "are of a particularly succulent, early ripening variety. The fruit is fully rounded and of unusual depth. The skin is amazingly thin but of a waxy quality that resists black-pock stemrot or damage from birds or insects. The blossom scar is unusually small, and this variety has been known to bear as many as one hundred perfect fruit from one plant. Resists mosaic. The flavor is regarded by connoisseurs as the most perfect that——"

Mr. Blandings, emotionally unable to read further, glanced at the opposite page. Something the size of a junior basketball confronted him in brilliant crimson—but what really took his breath away was the discovery that enough seeds to raise two tons of these treasures would cost him fifteen cents, postage paid. Mr. Blandings thought of the price of half-a-dozen puny tomatoes, falsely packaged in cellophane at a corner grocery in the city, and his lip curled; he thought of the price of a tomato salad at a restaurant of the *première classe*, and a flush of anger kindled his cheek. Obviously,

77

he had wasted some of the best years of his life in ignorantly paying extortionate profits to commission merchants, gouging freight rates to railroads, burglarious markups to the retailer, when to all intents and purposes these goods were free: free as air. He could raise so many tomatoes that he and his family could wade among them; so many that he could donate them to neighbors for miles around; so many that mischievous and lovable small boys could filch from his vines and he not know or care. The cost would be only a few healthful afternoons in the gorgeous summer sun; afternoons that would brown his torso and make the hard muscles ripple under the flawless skin.

He felt so much better that he went to the bar and made himself a small drink.

Mr. Blandings experienced only a slight trouble: no sooner was he utterly committed to the Wallrath Triple Tested Pritchard as the Finest Tomato ever developed than, turning the page, he would encounter the Wallrath Dowance Pluperfection Ultraglobe, 99 per cent germination guaranteed. "This fruit not infrequently reaches a diameter of four inches without flaw or blemish of any kind" and in numerous other ways, it was apparent, made a simple and obvious bum out of the Triple Tested Pritchard. "Unlike numerous other varieties positively does not crack around the stem end," said the catalog, casting a heavy shadow of doubt over every other tomato cultivated since the poisonous quality of the whole family had been disproved.

Emotionally spent by his bout with only two of some twenty varieties of tomato to be found in one catalog alone, Mr. Blandings rested for a moment and softly sipped his drink. He cast a glance at his wife.

Something was up with Mrs. Blandings. Her hair was in dainty disarray; her curving lips were parted, and in her eyes there lay deep the silent pleading look of love that asks to be requited, never count the cost.

"How much would three yards of manure cost?" she asked her husband gently.

As the afternoon wore on a few things took definite shape. "We'll put the corn in the southeast corner," said Mr. Blandings.

There would be eight succulent rows of it, twenty feet long.

A blast of icy rain struck the Blandings windows; Mr. Blandings craned his neck to where his vegetable garden was to be, popping and sprouting with exquisite green in a mere matter of weeks; he could perceive a skim of new ice forming over a terrain of mud, hummocks, and boulders. He underwent a moment of hesitation and then rededicated himself to the task.

"In that case," said Mrs. Blandings, "as soon as the corn gets high it will cut the sun off from everything else."

After a token resistance the corn was rescheduled in the northwest corner. As the afternoon wore on Mrs. Blandings came to look over her husband's shoulder at the vegetable chart he was laboriously making.

"You cannot," she said, "get one hundred tomato plants into a space five feet square. You've got them planted six inches apart with no space at the edges, and they have to be between three and four feet at least. Also, you don't seem to have any idea how many tomatoes a hundred plants would produce. We'd have all we could possibly handle from sixteen plants—eating, canning, giving away—everything."

"I have to plant six varieties," said Mr. Blandings, "and each variety has to have a fair representation. Sixteen plants is just laughable."

There were so many kinds of everything; that was the trouble. Mr. Blandings had always thought that beans were beans; now he was discovering not only that there were bush beans and pole beans but that each was subdivided into dazzling, glittering, meet-yourself-coming-back subdivisions that were green, or wax, or speckled purple-red; some were smooth, some were wrinkled, some were short and fat, some were long and slender; in their endlessly proliferating descriptions Mr. Blandings could not even tell where botany left off and trademarks began; the Plentifuls, the Streamliners, the Stringless Black Valentines, the Champions, the Last Refugees, the Kentucky Wonders, the Keystonians, the Puregold Waxes, and the Yellow Eye Improveds left him merely wondering and dazed. When it came time to pick and choose between one ecstasy-producing variety and another neither Mr. Blandings nor his wife could do more than point a finger at random and say "*That.*" Yet Mr. Blandings continued to read, with a blessedly hypnotized eye, every line of copy the catalogs afforded him. Whom were they really written for, he wondered? Their advertising prose was as old-fashioned as a circus poster; you could tell that it lied in its teeth and knew that it lied and that its lies were known lies; yet somehow the whole thing was full of charm and gaiety and easygoing loveliness; compared to the crap—yes, crap was the word—that Mr. Blandings himself turned out, it was as drawlingly and charmingly honest as the kitchen-door talk of a nineteenth-century peddler. Obviously the catalogs were partially rewritten in a vague sort of way from year to year but something about them told Mr. Blandings that the basic framework of what they had to say had been composed in the 1890's and not changed much since. Whom were they written for? Him and the likes of him? Not altogether, he felt sure. These catalogs had been written in the days when studying type-on-paper had been one of the world's few pleasures; when compositors with infinite labor had set in nonpareil the characters a writer had scrawled on rag bond with a quill pen and there was nothing, nothing in the rural homes of America to do with leisure but drag hard chairs up to the tiny circle of warm, yellow light from the oil lamp and *read;* read the Bible for comfort, guidance, and the Word; works like *Quo Vadis* or *The Crucifixion of Philip Strong* for culture and uplift—and the seed catalogs for the promise that a new spring was coming, and a new summer when vines and shrubs and bushes would flower and prosper; the corn grow long and fat and flawless; the potatoes swell under the brown earth, and no beetle, worm, insect, blight, or drought corrupt or challenge or dismay. The seed catalogs were a literature of promise and of hope; no heart hearing their litanies could fail to gird for one more struggle, this time at last to be crowned with an unflawed success.

· 11 ·

"HEAVENS," said Mrs. Blandings, "what a be*wil*dering change in the weather."

Mr. Blandings glanced at a window as it shuddered against an elemental assault. With easy grace he slung about him a cloak of detachment from the present. A blast of wind and rain struck the house so hard that the toilet in the downstairs lavatory gulped to maintain its water-balance.

"I think it's changing to hail," said Mrs. Blandings.

"No, no," said Mr. Blandings indulgently. Mrs. Blandings could tell he was far away. She sought to bring him gently back.

"At least if it keeps up we won't be overrun with country salesmen again tomorrow," she said. "Sunday is their big day. A man came around last week and wanted to stock the brook with trout."

"Good idea," said Mr. Blandings.

"They don't charge anything for the trout," said Mrs. Blandings. "Only for the actual excavating of the pond, and building the dam."

"Fair enough," said Mr. Blandings.

"And I scarcely got rid of him before another man came along and wanted to sell us a hundred yards of electric heating cable for the garden," said Mrs. Blandings. "You've no idea how heavy the traffic is, up here."

"What for the what?" said Mr. Blandings, swimming slowly toward reality.

"The same principle as the electric blanket," said Mrs. Blandings, "only you bury it in the ground and it makes everything so warm you can plant your seeds a month ahead of time."

"Say," said Mr. Blandings, "that's an ingenious—"

"No," said Mrs. Blandings. "I sent him away. All we need is a cold frame. A cold frame for the seedlings."

"I'll build one," said Mr. Blandings.

"You?" said Mrs. Blandings. Her inflection may have contained love, but not solely love.

"Certainly," said Mr. Blandings. "Talk about your coincidences, listen to what I just came on two minutes ago under the F's."

He put on a voice of creamy-smooth persuasiveness, like a radio announcer proclaiming the Apocalypse, and from a thick, well-bound red-covered volume intoned: "For the practical home carpenter the construction of a sturdy cold frame need afford few difficulties. Thirty running feet of clear, inch-and-a-half lumber, a generous supply of eightpenny nails, plus hinges, strips of molding section, glass, putty, and glazier's triangles complete the simple supplies necessary. Referring to diagram 127, mark off line A-A, making sure that a perfect right angle—"

"I think it would be cheaper and easier to get Mr. Trer to come up and build a cold frame," said Mrs. Blandings.

Mr. Blandings put down his book. "*Just* why?" he asked.

"Mr. Trer is an experienced carpenter," said Mrs. Blandings.

"Knocking a couple of pieces of wood together doesn't call for an experienced carpenter," said Mr. Blandings.

"And I think even an experienced carpenter like Mr. Trer would buy the sash from a mill instead of making it himself," said Mrs. Blandings.

Did all women, Mr. Blandings wondered, have his wife's ability to puncture a man's soft, rosy moods? Here he had offered the household a favor of work with his own hands, and the answer was an immediate and routine rejection.

"Muriel," he said, "I don't pretend I'm an experienced carpenter, any more than I'm an experienced farmer or gardener or anything else, but it makes me just a little vexed to be told off as an incompetent bungler every time I suggest doing something myself. How am I ever going to get the feel of things in the country if I don't pick someplace to begin?"

"I'm merely thinking," said Mrs. Blandings without rancor, "of the time you crated the phonograph records. It was just knocking a couple of pieces of wood together, but the nails went through all the Brahms and part of the Sibelius."

So. A wave of irritation swept Mr. Blandings. He had been about

82

to seize on the business of Mr. Trer, the experienced carpenter, buying sash from a mill instead of himself assuming the delicate joining of woods with love and glue, and from that proceed to a few comments on the decline of craftsmanship in America. This topic was now limp and slain at his feet, thanks to his wife's ill-timed reference. The nails had *not* gone through all the Brahms; they had gone through *all but one* of the Brahms, but you couldn't expect women to play fair when they were out to make a point. Besides, it had been dark, he had been in a hurry, and the nails were admittedly the wrong size. None of this was to say he was incapable of doing a precision job if that was the thing called for.

"Must you sulk?" said Mrs. Blandings. "If you want to build a cold frame and it will make you happy, please do. Only I've been making a list of things that have to be done this spring, and it's so long I don't know where anybody's going to begin."

"For instance?" said Mr. Blandings.

"For instance the orchard," said Mrs. Blandings. "Every single tree has to be pruned."

"I suppose you think I can't saw a dead branch off an apple tree without knocking it over," said Mr. Blandings.

"Well, can you spray them?" asked Mrs. Blandings. "Three times? That's what they need. Can you mix fifty gallons of arsenate of lead, blue vitriol, and lime in the cellar and spray it at a nozzle pressure of two hundred pounds to the square inch?"

"Well," said Mr. Blandings.

"It's not just the apple trees," Mrs. Blandings went on. "How about those three gorgeous maples by the road? Did you know the biggest one has a girdle root that'll kill it in a year if something isn't done about it? Do you know what to do? Did you know that we have eleven elm trees on this property and that they're all threatened with Dutch Elm Blight? Can you prevent Dutch Elm Blight? Do you know what to do with an oak that has a Strumella canker?"

"Now just a minute," said Mr. Blandings. "Where did you get all this?"

"From The Man," said Mrs. Blandings. "The Man from the College of Arboreal Surgeons."

"What was anybody from any such outfit doing snooping around up here?" Mr. Blandings demanded.

"He wasn't snooping," said Mrs. Blandings. "He came here most politely and asked if he could be of any service. He was just overcome by the beauty of everything up here. He said he'd often looked up at this mountain from down in the valley across Gay Head Bridge, and this time he just impulsively came up to take a look for himself. He didn't expect to *find* anybody."

"I'll just bet he didn't," said Mr. Blandings.

"He wasn't a salesman," said Mrs. Blandings. "He was a *technician*. He gave me his card and he turned out to be Assistant Chief of the Deciduous Service. He asked if he could just look around without even bothering me, and when he came back he was just literally breathless. He said our oak grove was absolutely unlike anything he'd ever seen in the whole state. Absolutely first-growth timber, and the biggest trees must be five hundred years old. His eyes were just popping. He said our trees should be the envy of everybody for a hundred miles around."

In spite of himself Mr. Blandings felt mollified that a staff member of the College of Arboreal Surgeons should find so much to admire so deeply about the Blandings oak grove. It covered two acres to the south of the brook and its stately beauty had been a matter of remark even before this professional opinion. Pretty smart, Mr. Blandings thought; pretty smart to have acquired a piece of property of which one aspect alone was a cynosure for practiced professional eyes. He reflected for a moment in the same mood that came over him whenever he thought of the incredible richness of the flora and fauna of Lansdale County, and particularly of that rich, mountaintop speck of it that he had purchased from Mr. Ephemus Hackett—at the time, with so much pain.

"But he was deeply concerned," said Mrs. Blandings; "really *deeply*."

"About what?" said Mr. Blandings.

"About the condition of our trees," said Mrs. Blandings. "All of them."

"I thought you just told me he said they should be the envy of everyone for hundreds of miles," said Mr. Blandings.

"I did," said Mrs. Blandings. "But the man said it was obvious

84

they were suffering from *years* of neglect. He said it made him sick to think what might happen if we had a really bad storm. He said we might lose half of them if we didn't take steps."

A hideous blast of wind struck the house; for an instant even the oil burner faltered. "Oh dear," said Mrs. Blandings; "I think I heard one groan right then."

"What kind of steps?" Mr. Blandings demanded.

"All sorts of steps," said Mrs. Blandings. "Trimming, genetical pruning, filling decay cavities, bracing—things like that. He asked if he could leave an estimate with absolutely no obligation, and he seemed so thoroughly *interested* that I thought the least I could say was yes."

"And?" said Mr. Blandings.

"Well," said Mrs. Blandings, "absolutely everything considered, and to put every tree on the property in apple-pie order, between twelve hundred and fifteen hundred dollars."

Mr. Blandings sat bolt upright.

"That doesn't count the spray mixture," said Mrs. Blandings, "but that would be only a dollar a gallon, and we'd only be charged for what they actually used."

"That's damned sporting of them," said Mr. Blandings. Suddenly he exploded. "Good God," he said; "do I have to spend fifteen hundred dollars just to keep the trees standing up on this place? Not to build, not to beautify, not to get ahead? Just to keep these bloody trees from not lying down like sick horses the next time there's a mild breeze from the northwest?"

"Don't *bellow*," said Mrs. Blandings. "Really, sometimes you seem to delight in being unreasonable. If something is complicated and silly enough, like putting electric cable under the garden, why right away you're interested, but a simple and straightforward proposition like trying to preserve some priceless trees makes you fly off the handle."

"I don't see what good pouring yourself another drink is going to do, either," she added.

Mr. Blandings halted himself on the way to the bar and set down an empty highball glass with excessive dignity.

"Very well," he said. "But you might ask your medicine man from the College of Arboreal Surgeons one simple question: if these trees are five hundred years old what's been keeping them upright all this time without his help? Why is it that just as I come along, a soft, virginal pushover from the city, all of a sudden it's going to cost fifteen hundred dollars to keep these trees standing up?"

Mr. Blandings fixed his wife with a glare of unassailable logic. As he lifted his chin to improve his posture, a gorgeous flash of pure actinic blue-white lit up every ice-shrouded window-light in the living room. Simultaneously there was the sound, rising and riding above the storm, as of ten thousand heavy-starched linen collars ripped asunder, and the lights went out.

"There!" said Mrs. Blandings. Into her monosyllable she comressed the tone of a prophet vindicated. A whole series of thick, searing flashes lighted the living room as if an asteroid had burst just outside, and there were further sounds of *sarkasmos*, literally a ripping and tearing. They came from somewhere to the south of the oak grove.

A heavy clank indicated Mr. Blandings was in motion and had come into contact with the firetongs and poker. "You'd better call up the electric light company," said Mrs. Blandings.

"What else did you think I was going to do?" said Mr. Blandings. Another moment of groping, with several smaller collisions, brought him to the phone. He did not recognize the sound the receiver gave forth as he pressed it to his head, but a communications engineer would have immediately identified it, in the language of his trade, as an open-circuit hum.

The world, the next morning, was too beautiful to be true. The lashing rain of the storm had frozen on every object it touched, and the planet lay ensheathed in ice. Now, under a cloudless blue sky, the hills glittered like flexed steel, and a thousand unfamiliar objects struck back at the eye with tiny, explosive, golden flares. In the fields near him, Mr. Blandings could see clumps and bushes and shrubs and evergreens in some supranormal state; it was as if he were looking at them with a vision given a false, fascinating sharpness by a drug. They looked of unearthly beauty, but edible. Everything had the glitter of hard candy; the polished, immobile glow of objects encased in crystal. But it was the trees that held the

86

most incredible enchantment, for they were sculptures out of transparent rock.

Mr. Blandings called his wife to see, and in the vision before them the two forgot the asperities of the evening before. It was a full quarter hour before they could take their eyes away from the burst and dazzle of the countryside and assign themselves the tasks of a new day.

Mr. Blandings padded to the bathroom. The water that issued from the hot faucet was a thin and lukewarm stream. Mr. Blandings' electric shaver would not work—but not until Mrs. Blandings remarked that the bedroom clock was stopped did he integrate these facts in his mind. Whatever had gone wrong with the electric current the night before had not been put right.

In its absence, the Blandings house was a sepulcher. The hot water died away; soon, in the inaction of the pump, there would be no water at all. The electric stove was a chilly lump of porcelain; there was nothing on which to fry an egg or make coffee; no means of scarring a piece of bread into toast. The refrigerator was mute, and dripped. Probably it would not drip for long, for the oil burner, whose flawless performance depended on fuel injected by an electric motor, was more silent than any tomb, and the whole house would soon reach a temperature at which a refrigerator would not be missed. It occurred to Mr. Blandings that he would like for the first time in an uncountable number of months to turn on the radio and get news of the outside world, and how much of it lay in the same glittering paralysis; only when he clicked the *on* switch did he realize that this, too, was dead. He bundled himself up in as many layers of textiles as he could find and went outdoors. Instantly, he fell down; the ground was everywhere covered with half an inch of glass-smooth ice. He picked himself up and crawled back into the house; the beauty of the ice storm's aftermath no longer held for him its earlier appeal.

In the afternoon, soon after Mrs. Blandings had succeeded in producing a few cups of coffee stewed in a sauce pan held over the living-room fireplace, three unbelievably hardy men knocked for admission on the Blandings' back door. They clumped into the kitchen, faintly scarring its battleship linoleum with their hobnailed boots and the heavy climbing irons that identified them as linesmen for the electric company. "We got to saw out a couple of your trees," said their spokesman. "They come down last night in your grove, and took a transformer and a quarter of a mile of our three-phase wire with 'em." Seeing on Mr. Blandings' face an expression he mistook for truculence, he added: "Property owners can be held liable for that, you know, if the home office wants to enforce its contract."

Mrs. Blandings looked at Mr. Blandings, who looked out the window. It was not possible to see anything, but the sound of saws was in the distance.

"I hope," said Mrs. Blandings, "that when the children come home from Barleydew next week you'll make some effort to curb your language."

"Furthermore," said Mrs. Blandings, "there are few things a woman finds so irritating as a ceaseless flow of profanity. It isn't the actual words she objects to so much as the numbing, unimaginative monotony of it."

"Are you listening?" Mrs. Blandings inquired. The two candles in the living room gave an uncertain light in which she could see her husband only indistinctly; he had on a fleece-lined country greatcoat and a hunting cap with the ear muffs turned down.

"And while we're on the subject," Mrs. Blandings continued, "it might not be a bad idea for you to stop talking about being psychoanalyzed and actually do something about it."

"It frankly disturbs me to hear you make those constant references to some kind of *plot*," Mrs. Blandings continued. "That's not normal thinking. Surely it must be evident to you that when the tree man called on me, neither he nor I had any knowledge that there was going to be a freak ice storm at this time of the year. As a matter of fact, it was over two weeks ago he was up here, and if I made any mistake at all it was the mistake of waiting to bring the whole subject up until I thought you might be in a receptive mood."

"In one of your increasingly rare receptive moods," said Mrs. Blandings. "Psychotherapy might help you a great deal."

With painful brightness the lights came on. From the cellar came a sound that ranged upward three octaves in the fraction of a second, indicating the resumption of the oil burner. Mr. Blandings blinked in the sudden glare. Suddenly the voice of a stranger boomed through the Blandings' living room. "Friends," it said, "do *you* suffer at times from sour eructations, gassy distentions, furred tongue and oppressive breath? Tell you what you do. Take—"

One leap brought Mr. Blandings to the radio. As he wrenched at the switch he had not turned off that morning he was made no happier by recognizing himself as the author of the solicitous words he could not bear to hear.

· 12 ·

ON A SUNNY DAY in springtime the air on Bald Mountain was like champagne: everybody said so. As Mr. Blandings moved up the road toward the house he took deep drafts of it, and felt cheered. A man might have his troubles, but it was wonderful how fresh air and warm sunshine in the country could shrink them to a more fitting proportion.

The men in the neat blue dungarees with blue caps to match nodded a cheerful greeting as he passed. In a tasteful embroidery of red cord the initials C.A.S. gave their work uniforms a natty look, and it was evident in the agility with which they went about their tasks that there was little they did not know about trees Already the Blandings acres and the oak grove had taken on a look of discipline they had never had before.

Inside the house, there was a warm, nourishing smell of lunch about to be. Mr. Blandings cast an indulgent look at his two daughters in the living room, and poured himself what he considered a modest drink of sherry, using an old-fashioned glass as a container. It was wonderful to have the kids at home again for a while; their vacation from Barleydew would last three full weeks. Betsy was so unbelievably beautiful; Joan was so solemnly charming. It was a poignant thing to be the father of daughters. He felt the suspicion of moisture in his eyes as he looked at the two of them, curled up on opposite ends of the long divan. "Take your feet off that upholstery," he snapped.

Joan continued to read a heavy work on atomic physics; Betsy maintained a show of interest in the latest copy of the Lansdale *Blade.* Neither child moved, except that Betsy turned the paper inside out, untidily. Mr. Blandings sipped his drink and waited for his wife to emerge from the kitchen. Several couples had come and

90

gone from the Blandings' employ in the last two months: this was a period in which Mrs. Blandings was again the family cook.

"Well for heaven's sake," said Betsy, "look who's dead now." She did not seem to be addressing anyone. "Mr. Preebles."

"He was quite old," said Joan, not looking up or apparently breaking the stride of her own reading.

"The only Preebles I know around here is the feed-store man," said Mr. Blandings.

"That's the one," said Betsy. "He was very nice to me when we were buying the grass seed; I'm sorry he's gone."

"There's some mixup," said Mr. Blandings. "He wasn't old."

"The paper probably has everything wrong as usual," said Betsy, "but it says here '—proprietor of Preebles' Seed and Feed store, Mr. Preebles, age 44, was a member of the Lansdale Board of Education, a past Ruler of the Lansdale Lodge of the Benevolent and Protective Order of——' "

"Well?" said Mr. Blandings.

"Well?" said Betsy. "He was forty-four."

"How old do you think I am?" Mr. Blandings asked.

"Let's not get personal," said Betsy.

American schooling, thought Mr. Blandings, must be the worst in the world; you sent your children to expensive boarding schools and they acquired nothing outwardly visible except a set of these harsh, vulgar, pseudo-witticisms, designed to be conversational "stoppers."

"Plenty of people are perfectly hale and hearty in their fifties," said Joan. "The life span is increasing." She appeared to be offering him comfort.

"Mr. Preebles was a grandfather," said Betsy, letting the paper slide to the floor where it assumed a tent-like shape at which she began softly kicking.

"That's ridiculous," said Mr. Blandings. "A man of my age wouldn't be a grandfather." He had not intended to remind his children that his last birthday had marked his entrance into the same year of decay that had just finished off Mr. Preebles, but now the fact was out. He reached for the newspaper, to restore it to its intended two-dimensional form; as he stooped he felt a heavy twinge in his back.

91

"It isn't ridiculous, Father," said Joan. "If a man married at twenty-one and had a daughter who married at eighteen he might be a grandfather at forty-one, allowing ten months for gestation in each case."

"Nine months, silly," said Betsy.

"I was giving them a month's courtesy," said Joan. She turned a sweet smile on her sister. "But you know best," she added.

Betsy narrowed her eyes. "Listen, you little toad," she said.

"*I* didn't say anything," said Joan; "*I* wasn't in a parked car for an hour with Vincent Spelly at Spring Dance, and *I* didn't get called into Miss Lanphry's office the next day—"

"Keep on chattering and I'll beat the pie out of you," said Betsy.

"Father," said Joan, "Betsy—"

Betsy leaned across the divan and delivered a smart slap to her sister's cheek. Without altering her scholarly expression in the slightest Joan leaned back and flung her book into her sister's stomach.

"Stop this," Mr. Blandings shouted. "Shame on both of you. Let's have a little peace and gentility in this home. God damn it—"

Mrs. Blandings entered the living room. "Lunch is ready," she said. She glared at her husband. "Apparently my comments about profanity have had little or no effect."

Lunch was a divided feast. Since the sisters refused to sit down together Betsy was banished to the pantry, Joan to her room. Mrs. Blandings made an attempt to discover the cause of the outbreak, but Mr. Blandings, even if he had felt talkative, would have found it hard to reconstruct the exact sequence whereby an obituary notice in the Lansdale *Blade* had led in half-a-dozen sentences to an outbreak of violence between his daughters. He could not appraise the quality of Joan's remark to Betsy, and so he could not possibly convey it. It was no news to him, or to his wife, that Betsy loved boys and that boys loved Betsy; what Mr. and Mrs. Blandings shied from discussing with one another was the precise shading of the verb, someplace between transitive and intransitive, that would express the true state of affairs.

"You're becoming very secretive," said Mrs. Blandings as she walked from the dining room. "You didn't tell me about your letter to the paper, either."

Mr. Blandings, who had just stuffed the Lansdale *Blade* into the wastebasket, straightened up in surprise.

"It was certainly very well expressed," said Mrs. Blandings, "but if those were your sentiments you might at least have warned me you were going to spread them on the record. It creates a rather peculiar position."

"Muriel," said Mr. Blandings, "I haven't written any letter to the paper recently. I guess I'd know if I had."

Mrs. Blandings retrieved the *Blade,* opened it to page four, and pointed. Mr. Blandings read:

Editor *Blade,* Dear Sir: In the midst of today's crisis, we too often overlook the source of the greater part of our confusion as to the place and meaning of Democracy. This is our American Educational System. Few of us realize the enormity of the gift won for us—

Mr. Blandings glanced downward. There was his name, without a doubt. But in the phrase he had just read he was pretty sure he had discerned the true author. He went on:

—the enormity of the gift won for us three hundred years ago—the gift of universal free education. Granted that the working out of a perfect public school system leaves much to be desired, what is to be said of that large, powerful, and prosperous segment of our population that has, in effect, seceded from this entire system and instead placed its children in private schools? What becomes of the ideal of Democracy when it can be practiced or not in terms of what parents do with their children? If we are really serious about Democracy these people must answer a huge question—the question of whether or not—

Mr. Blandings went to the foot of the stairs and raised his voice.

"Joan," he called, "I'd like you to come here for a moment, please."

Joan came slowly down the stairs, achieving various complex dragging sounds with her hands and feet. She looked very solemn.

"I didn't mean anything by what I said to Betsy," she said; "it's just that—"

"Never mind about Betsy," said Mr. Blandings. "I just thought that maybe you could enlighten me about this." He handed her the paper. She gave it a swift, incredulous look and passionately flung it on the floor.

"Oh!" she wailed; "that stupid old man; he signed your name to it."

"You wrote it?" Mr. Blandings asked.

"Certainly I wrote it," said Joan, "and now he's gone and spoiled everything. I wish I could die."

"When did you write it, Joan?" said Mrs. Blandings.

"When I had the mumps," said Joan. "You mailed it for me yourself. I couldn't go out. I kept looking and looking for it to come out after I sent it in and it never did, so I thought they'd thrown it away."

"It places me in a rather peculiar position," said Mr. Blandings.

"Well don't blame *me*," said Joan. "I signed it Joan H. Blandings and somebody who can't even read made Joan into James."

Mr. Blandings crushed out a half-smoked cigarette and immediately lighted another. He did not know how to deal with the situation.

"Have you written any other communications?" he asked.

"Several," said Joan.

"Are they likely to appear over my signature?" said Mr. Blandings.

"Joanie dear," said Mrs. Blandings, interrupting; "you're an unusually gifted and intellectually mature child for your age, and your father and I take joy in your abilities, but if you're going to express yourself on public matters I really think you ought to consult the family before you go and—"

She paused; the right words would not offer themselves.

"Furthermore," said Mrs. Blandings, "if you're going to reconstruct everything you've got to start being more careful with your handwriting. I've watched you signing your name and you begin by making a big J with squiggles after it, and I'm not at all surprised that someone who didn't know thought it looked as much like James as Joan."

"Go and what?" Joan repeated. "I'll print my name in big block letters if that makes anybody feel better, but you dodged the point."

"Look, Joan," said Mr. Blandings. "It happens that you and

Betsy are both in a private school, and to have a letter appearing with my name on it calling parents who send their children to private schools snobs makes me out to be a fool or a hypocrite, or both. If you and Betsy—"

Out of the dining room Betsy appeared.

"If anybody is discussing me," she said with icy hauteur, "I'd like to be present."

"Nobody's discussing you," said Mr. Blandings. "Go upstairs."

"It happens that I'm being called for in a few minutes," said Betsy. "I may or may not be back for dinner, so you needn't bother about *me*."

"Who is calling for you, may I ask?" said Mr. Blandings.

"Vincent Spelly," said Betsy, "since you wish to know."

"Ah ha," said Joan.

"Be quiet," said Mr. Blandings. "Who is this Spelly kid, anyway?"

"Mr. Spelly," said Betsy, "is not a kid. He is a freshman at Princeton, or is almost entirely certain to be next autumn."

"Where are you going?" said Mrs. Blandings.

"Do I have to account for every minute?" said Betsy. "His father has loaned him the convertible and there is the possibility of a cocktail party and perhaps dinner afterward."

"Has he a license to drive?" Mr. Blandings asked.

"I haven't inquired," said Betsy scornfully. "I consider that *his* affair."

"I consider it *my* affair," said Mr. Blandings, "if some sub-freshman full of cocktail-party gin is going to hurtle over the public highways with my daughter and crash into—"

"If you wish to make charges against Vincent Spelly," said Betsy, "you might wait until he gets here."

As if on cue, the door opened without announcement, letting in a glory of afternoon sun. Framed in the opening stood an enormous figure, his features momentarily invisible in the flooding light behind him. He stepped inside and briskly closed the door. "Hello honey," he said to Betsy. "Family row?"

"Why Vince," said Betsy, "we were just speaking about you." With the utmost grace she made the introductions; with the utmost aplomb Mr. Vincent Spelly shook hands all around. He appeared to be much taller than six feet and much heavier than two

95

hundred pounds, but he had the carriage and posture of a fencing master at top form.

"I was just on the verge of telling the family about how it was your plane that dropped the bomb right down the smokestack of the Krupp plant at Essen," said Betsy.

"Just a coincidence," said Mr. Spelly.

"He was the third-youngest bomber pilot in the Eighth Air Force," said Betsy.

"We never reckoned things that way," said Mr. Spelly.

"He lied about his age," said Betsy, "and they never found out. Well, goodbye, everybody. Expect me when you see me."

She paused at the door.

"By the way, Vince," she said, "have you a driver's license?"

Mr. Spelly looked nonplussed.

"Golly," he said, thumping himself lightly, "I think I left my wallet home. It's a good thing you spoke."

"Never mind," said Betsy; "we can stop there and pick it up on our way."

The door closed behind them, but it was some moments before Mr. Blandings raised his eyes from the floor.

"Now I suppose you're going to start browbeating me again," said Joan.

Mr. Blandings sighed deeply. "No, Joanie," he said, "I'm sorry if I browbeat you. I seem to be confused about everything. I thought your sister said that this young man was going to be a freshman at Princeton next fall, but he seemed to me more like a major."

"A lieutenant-colonel," said Joan, "that's what he was. But you're right about his going to be a freshman. He's starting a new career. He's going to study botany."

"Botany?" said Mr. Blandings. "He doesn't look much like the botanist type to me."

"He's doing it on army orders," said Joan. "The Joint Chiefs of Staff have put botanists on the AAA priority list of scientists for the next war. We haven't one-tenth the number we need, we haven't even a hundredth. There's an absolute connection between botany, aerodynamics, and atomic warfare in the future."

"What kind of connection?" said Mr. Blandings.

Joan shrugged her shoulders. "Top secret," she said.

· 13 ·

HAVING LIVED for some weeks on the depressive slopes of his psychic curve, Mr. Blandings was now on the upgrade again. He drove his station wagon with relaxed, easy care down the twists and turns of Bald Mountain Road toward Lansdale Town, and marveled at the sky. Daylight Saving Time had been in effect a week; it was extraordinary what that did for a man's spirits. Bill Cole was due on the late afternoon train to spend the weekend, and Bill would be bound to notice the improvement in his feeling-tone since the time they'd had lunch in the Hotel Marbury, back in January. It would be a pleasure to have a quiet home dinner, just the three grownups and Joan, and then after dinner Mr. Blandings would take Bill into his study, and show him how well his affairs seemed to be going these days. He must be careful not to put any particular emphasis on his growing acquaintance with Mr. Nellus of the *Blade*; the old boy had formed the habit of dropping in a couple of times a week. He was so obviously a lonely widower that the Blandings felt gratified when he occasionally stayed and took potluck at the dinner table. But Mr. Blandings felt that Bill Cole might take this to be a disregard of his injunction not to get interested in a country newspaper. It was nothing of the sort. How could you get in trouble by writing Letters to the Editor every little while? If an increasing variety of country matters was catching his interest it was certainly healthy and harmless that he should express himself. Mr. Nellus was delighted to publish these simple offerings: they reduced by just so much the amount of text he had to write himself. Profit to all, harm to none. Lawyers were rather obtuse in catching connections in a profession so far removed from their own.

97

"Been doing anything foolish?" said Bill Cole, as he and Mr. Blandings drove together back up Bald Mountain Road. His train had been half an hour late; he was full of cinders and a little irascible.

"Not a thing," said Mr. Blandings. "How's everything at Laird, Leeds, Firkin, Drizdall and Emphy?"

"Rocking along," said Bill Cole.

"I hope you don't mind that we haven't anything planned for the weekend," said Mr. Blandings. "We just thought we'd sit around and everybody relax."

"Suits me to a T," said Bill Cole. "I'm sort of tired."

Mr. Blandings drove the station wagon smartly into the driveway. "We'll all just do as we please," he said. "Muriel's in her overalls somewhere in back."

Mrs. Blandings was no longer in overalls but in a skirt of vivid green corduroy, topped by a sweater gleaming with metallic threads. She was freshly showered, coiffed, and perfumed. "I said we'd go over for cocktails," she said.

"I don't want to go to a cocktail party," said Mr. Blandings, "particularly on a last-minute invitation, and with Bill up here for a rest. I've just got through promising him."

"It's just for one drink at the Joseph Chasuble-Horns'," said Mrs. Blandings. "She sounded as nice as could be over the telephone. It's just a few people at their cottage and she explained it was one of those mixups—*she* thought her husband had called *you* up, and *he* thought—"

"I know," said Mr. Blandings. He put up a sulky resistance for a few more moments. Then he found himself in doeskin trousers and a tweed jacket, driving his wife and Bill Cole in the station wagon over the five-mile hill-and-dale back road that would bring them to the cottage of Mr. and Mrs. Joseph Chasuble-Horn. "They're the parents of Amy Horn," said Mrs. Blandings to Bill Cole. "Joan and Amy have got to be lifelong friends just in the time since Joan's been going to the Lansdale School."

"When was that?" said Bill Cole. "I thought both the kids were in Barleydew."

"Joan begged and begged," said Mrs. Blandings, "and finally

98

her father gave in. She can twist her father around her little finger."

Mr. Blandings gave all his attention to driving the car.

"If you ask me," said Mrs. Blandings, "it was all a pretty silly business. But Joan didn't like Barleydew, and she called her father and me snobs for not letting her go to public school right here at home, and when she won her father over there was very little left that I could do. So now we're experimenting with democracy."

Mr. Blandings put the brakes on suddenly, having come upon a driveway sign that said *The Joseph Chasuble-Horns* in bright, nobby buttons. "This must be the cottage," he said heavily. Abreast was an enormous house and a long driveway lined solidly with cars. "Yes, this is the cottage and I can hear the intimacy from where I sit." He found an awkward place to park the car and switched off the motor. A roar of sound from the house engulfed everything; it was the sort of organ note that came over the radio from Times Square at ten seconds before midnight at New Year's.

"Oh dear," said Mrs. Blandings.

Mr. Blandings was in tow of Mrs. Chasuble-Horn. He had lost his wife, who had been shooed upstairs to the ladies' disrobing room by a Scandinavian maid. Bill Cole was already at ease with a drink in his hand, chatting happily. Mr. Blandings, looking about the room in a faint panic of distaste and strangeness, could recognize not one familiar face. Then his condition worsened. He saw a familiar face with neither name nor background to attach to it. ". . . Dr. Stoss, Mr. Blandings, and Dr. Opart . . . Dr. Füchtler, and behind him Dr. Boomper and *Mrs.* Opart, Mr. Blandings . . . Dr. Mardable, Dr. Shallot, and Dr. Brassells, Mr. Blandings . . . Dr. Proscu and Mrs. Brassells, here, Mr. Blandings, and now . . . Professor Mieullont and Colonel Blieiux, Dr. Worplin, Dr. Lillinger. . . ."

Apparently he was the only mister in the whole company; every other male and even an occasional female seemed to have an honorific of some sort. He had met only a small fraction of the throbbing roomful and he was in a state of total confusion. At parties like this in the past nobody ever seemed to mind asking him who the hell *he* was, but somehow he always felt the obligation to know

99

instantly, or be previously aware of, the fame of anyone to whom he was introduced, no matter how dim it might be. As a result, he never got anything straight.

". . . and I want you to meet our guest of honor," he heard Mrs. Chasuble-Horn saying. She maneuvered him by the elbow as if she were docking a small boat. "Sir Zooanian Dree, may I present Mr. James Blandings. Sir Zooanian is here from Bombay for a visit, isn't that nice," said Mrs. Chasuble-Horn.

Standing with his hands behind his back, Sir Zooanian Dree made a remarkable appearance. He was dressed in a gray claw-hammer coat of heavy wool, unskillfully cut; its tails reached close to his ankles, so that his striped trousers were almost concealed except in front. On the left thumb of his coffee-colored hands he wore a ring in which a glassy red stone was embedded. His head was surmounted by a magnificently involuted lemon-yellow turban and on his feet were a pair of blue sneakers. He wore an Ascot tie, but did not appear to have any socks.

"How do you do," said Mr. Blandings.

Sir Zooanian focused on Mr. Blandings and then while continuing to face him relaxed his ocular muscles for distant vision. He seemed to make a tiny, sidewise inclination of the head, but he said nothing.

"Do please find yourself a drink," said Mrs. Chasuble-Horn, guiding Mr. Blandings in the direction of a built-in bar with a white-coated servitor behind it. "And do make yourself at home."

Mr. Blandings had no trouble finding a Martini. It was deathly pale, and he downed it at a gulp. The admiring bartender instantly presented him with another. This one he took at a more leisurely rate; then with a third in his hand he began a slow aimless wander, setting his countenance into lines he hoped would be taken for abstraction. Immediately he saw bearing down on him the face he knew without the name. It was a face of healthy pink extraversion, surmounted by a crew haircut and decked with spectacles made of chased white gold and octagonal lenses, lightly tinted.

"Well, Mr. Blandings," said the face, in a voice that added another haunt of familiarity. "How have you been? I am Dr. Boomper, Elgin Boomper. I have not seen you since we worked on

100

the Grassroots Intercultural Program together. Interesting party, is it not?"

The full memory of Dr. Boomper flooded back to Mr. Blandings. He was one of those newer things on earth, the radio Ph.D. Mr. Blandings had once been impelled to look him up in *Who's Who* to see if he was real—and there he was, "author, educator, publicist." He had written three or four works of such miscellaneous categories and unlikely titles as to be unrememberable by a professional mentalist, but one smash hit stood out. Dr. Boomper was the author of *The Conquest of Intercostal Serenity*. It had been a runaway success for its original publisher and was now a fixture rooted apparently forever in the dark devious business of mail-order bookselling. Dr. Boomper's qualities as an educator were much more vague, except that Mr. Blandings was this moment gathering the intelligence that Dr. Boomper was now Deputy-Director of the Educational Division of ORPS. He did not know what ORPS was.

"Tell me who some of these people are," said Mr. Blandings. He had always regarded Dr. Boomper as an overeducated ass, whose talk was so abstract and full of jargon as to be unintelligible in a real world. Now, however, in the midst of this sea of strangers, Mr. Blandings was glad to have someone to talk to. And Dr. Boomper, Mr. Blandings remembered, always knew who everybody was, even if not exactly. He spoke like a trained radio orator, using no contractions and avoiding any change in voice dynamics that would send the needle too far over on the control-room dial.

"Well," said Dr. Boomper, "the gentleman in the brown coat who is just lighting that lady's cigarette is Dr. Adrian Stoss, who heads up the School of Mundane Relations down on 24th Street. Part of the I.A.O. that operates under a grant from the Sykes Foundation, you know; Adrian is doing a perfectly marvelous job for them; I understand their load factor is up to 87 per cent. Next to him, let me see, is Dr. Heinz Füchtler—"

Dr. Boomper pointed out a pale, ascetic man talking to a companion with a deep, humorless intensity. "He is the ex-Chancellor of—oh you know the country I mean, I know its name as well as I know my own. First Hitler took it over and then the Russians took it over, and nobody knows just how Dr. Füchtler got out, but

101

he is giving a course in Political Theory at Lovegrove Southern and doing a marvelous job."

"Who is that he's talking to?" asked Mr. Blandings.

"That is Dr. Opart," said Dr. Boomper; "Dr. Bezling Opart, the Executive Secretary of the League to Combat Opinion. It is quasi-governmental and the State Department uses it a good deal. Dr. Opart is doing a magnificent—"

"Who is the guest of honor?" Mr. Blandings inquired. His cocktails were at work and he was beginning to enjoy the loud, egotistical din of the Chasuble-Horns' enormous living and dining rooms. He could see his wife in gay conversation on the other side of the room, and thought she looked pretty.

"There I am afraid you have me," said Dr. Boomper. "I have asked Dr. Shallot and Dr. Brassells and several other people here this evening, but I did not find any clue. I believe that he was at one time a Premier of some Indian state, but other than that I am afraid I have no information."

"He doesn't seem to be very outgiving," said Mr. Blandings. Sir Zooanian was no longer standing; he now rested with utmost composure in a heavily upholstered armchair, his hands clasped in front of him, his legs thrust out so that his ankles crossed. He was looking at nothing in the physical world.

"No, he does not," said Dr. Boomper. "I think perhaps he does not speak English. I endeavored to engage him in conversation when I first arrived, but I had no success."

"He certainly didn't say anything to me," said Mr. Blandings.

"Nor to anyone," said Dr. Boomper genially; "I have rather trained myself in observation, and I think I can say with assurance that our distinguished guest has not said anything to anybody since he arrived."

Mr. Blandings studied Sir Zooanian without being able to arrive at a conclusion.

"It was unfortunate that someone offered him a cocktail sausage and a rum collins the moment he came in," said Dr. Boomper. "I rather assume that pork products and alcoholic beverages must be equally anathema to him. In fact, I am rather afraid that perhaps even the *offer* of such things, no matter how well intentioned, might be negatively construed."

"How did he get here?" asked Mr. Blandings. "Who did he come with?"

"So far as I know—" said Dr. Boomper, but that was all: he was suddenly seized by Mrs. Chasuble-Horn and borne rapidly away. "Excuse me," he said over his shoulder in his conscientiously polite way, just before he vanished.

Left to himself, Mr. Blandings twirled his empty cocktail glass thoughtfully for a second and then in the counterfeit of a casual saunter made again for the bar. "How about a double?" said the bartender. Without waiting for an answer he pushed toward Mr. Blandings a wide-brimmed champagne glass, filled with liquid of the most barely perceptible amber cast.

"You can't tell me you can do it with that few people," said Dr. Lispetha Suellity Worplin.

"You certainly can," said Dr. Orpen Shallot, "it's mathematically exact."

"In a pig's eye," said Dr. Worplin. She was a loud, large woman of determined bearing.

"You don't know what you're talking about is the trouble with you," said Dr. Shallot, courteously. "You don't know any mathematics."

"I'll bet I know as much mathematics as you ever will," said Dr. Worplin, "and maybe a hell of a lot more."

"You take four hundred beans—" said Dr. Shallot.

"*You* take four hundred beans," said Dr. Worplin. "Take four hundred *million* beans and see what it gets you." She unloosed a wild bellow of laughter and brought her heavy palm down with a smack on the knee of the man next to her. It was Mr. Blandings' knee. "How about it?" she inquired of him, and entwined her arm with his. "My boy friend," she announced.

"You take four hundred beans," said Dr. Shallot, with angry persistence; "two hundred white ones and two hundred black ones, and shake them all up in a jar—"

"Serves a family of eight," said Dr. Worplin.

"—and after you've withdrawn fifty beans the distributions of white and black according to probability—"

103

"But there's such a difference between beans and *people*," said Mrs. Brassells.

"Not *some* people," said Dr. Worplin. She gave Mr. Blandings a ferocious nudge. "How about it, dream boy?"

Mr. Blandings was trying to determine how drunk the eminent child psychologist and author of *Toward the Emergent Sibling* might be, and how much his own perceptions were off their normal key due to five extra-dry Martinis.

"—and it is on that Law of Probability that we base the entire system of Scientific Sampling," said Dr. Shallot, glaring at Dr. Worplin. Mr. Blandings suddenly remembered about Dr. Shallot; he was a public-opinion analyst from whom dozens of advertising agencies drew for research support on their marketing and merchandising problems.

"Come back in five hundred years," said Dr. Worplin, "and I'll tell you whether your beans have the power of predicting human behavior." She cuddled close to Mr. Blandings. "Don't disturb us," she said at large, leaning her head on his shoulder.

"It's already worked for over a quarter of a century in the profession of advertising," said Dr. Shallot, taking a large swallow of his drink. "Market research was founded on it."

"The *profession* of advertising," said Dr. Worplin. "What kind of talk is that?"

"Ask your friend," said Dr. Shallot. "How about it, Blandings?"

The rest of the talk had been dying down as the shouting between Dr. Worplin and Dr. Shallot had become louder. By comparison with fifteen minutes ago the room was semi-quiet.

"That's right," said Mr. Blandings. "It certainly was."

Dr. Worplin disentangled herself from Mr. Blandings and sat up with a lurch. "What the hell do *you* know about it?" she snarled.

"I'm in the advertising business," said Mr. Blandings. "Not that that—"

"Oh *ho*," said Dr. Worplin. She could be seen cranking her guns to a new deflection, and Mr. Blandings could feel the attack coming—headed by Dr. Worplin, but backed up by the whole multitude here assembled.

"Oddvertising? You are in oddvertising?"

The room quieted as if a tube in a sound truck had burned out.

Sir Zooanian Dree had spoken, had asked a question, and had asked it of Mr. Blandings.

Mr. Blandings hesitated. "Yes, I am," he said.

"American oddvertising," said Sir Zooanian, so quietly that the room strained to hear him, "is thee hope of thee world."

There was a light buzz of surprise. Nothing came from Dr. Lispetha Worplin.

Mr. Blandings laughed as he would not have laughed had it not been for the Martinis. "You sound like Horace Dascomb," he said.

"Horace Dascomb," said Sir Zooanian; "do you *know* him?"

"Well yes," said Mr. Blandings. "Yes, I know him. I work for him."

"Ah," said Sir Zooanian, "I am very proud I should meet someone who is disciple of Horace Dascomb."

The little noises in the hitherto deafening room were now all indicative of a general change in the axis of thinking.

"In my countree," said Sir Zooanian, in his soft, slurring voice, "thee greatest need is thee cultivation of wants. If my people could be made to want more they would at last bestir themselves to have more. American oddvertising and oddvertising methods are making now a small beginning, very small but a beginning, in thee cities. Ah yes."

"Fascinating," said Mrs. Chasuble-Horn. "Isn't that fascinating, Auster?"

Auster Millowy, author of the poetical works collected under the title of *Animus-a-um*, was noted in his prose essays for the contempt he poured out on people who held the points of view he had himself espoused two years before. Having written "Advertising: Moloch of Modern Man" in *The Globalist* just after the war, he agreed that what Sir Zooanian had just said was fascinating indeed. The endorsement rapidly became general.

"In India," said Sir Zooanian, "there is *too* much contemplation. As a nation, as a continent, we are in great need of laxatives."

He picked up a card of matches from a little polished table beside his chair. "For example," he said.

The company leaned forward earnestly for a closer view of Sir Zooanian's demonstration. Mr. Blandings did not need to. Even from a distance he could see the red, green, and white logotype he had conceived for the Knapp account; below it were the three words that constituted an admittedly major contribution to American advertising.

"Genius," said Sir Zooanian.

It was nice to be admired, but not for all the precious stones in India would Mr. Blandings reveal to this roomful the authorship of what Sir Zooanian Dree was now so extravagantly praising.

"I have sought in every way to find an adequate translation for these words into Hindustani," said Sir Zooanian, "but thee difficulties are too great. It is most unfortunate."

"It is amazing, Sir Zooanian," said Auster Millowy, "that a statesman so wrapped up in world affairs as yourself should also find time to become such a student of the peculiarly American art, for art it must be called, of advertising."

"Ah yes," said Sir Zooanian; "you are mistaken. Or perhaps I should more kindly say merely out of date." He inclined his head with a tiny smile toward the most advanced prosodist of his times.

"It is five years," he said, "since my political enemies misrepresented my position to my constitu-*ency* in such a way as to make necessary my retirement to private life."

There was a little pause, which no one filled.

"Since that time," said Sir Zooanian, "I have been working in thee Bombay office of thee J. Walter Thompson Company. I am in this country for what is known as a refresher course. I find it every day more full of fascination."

What must have been a giant sneeze shattered the air of the room, and Mr. Blandings looked behind him to discover Bill Cole mopping his face with an immense handkerchief which a moment later he used on his legs. It was evident that in his spasm he had spilled most of his highball.

· 14 ·

IN THE MORNING, the Blandings and Bill Cole sat about the table at a late breakfast, and discussed last night's affair. It was Mr. Blandings' huffy position that Mrs. Blandings had had no business revealing to the company at Mrs. Chasuble-Horn's cottage the facts of authorship of the Knapp Laxative Account. It was true Sir Zooanian had become almost lyrical on discovering that he was face to face with the man who had composed the Three Words, but Mr. Blandings' strong feeling was that no matter how well the news had been received at the time, fumed in alcohol and sycophancy, it would in the long run degrade him. If there was anything in God's name he wanted to do it was keep his city profession and his country life two things separate and apart.

Besides, he hadn't liked those people very much last night. He knew their kind. All through that cocktail party he had been the object of fishy eyes, the recipient of limp handshakes, the auditor of "Oh reallys." And he knew why, Mr. Blandings asserted: it was obvious that he did *not* write poetry, he did *not* have the lowdown on what U.S. policy toward the Viet Nam should infallibly be, he did not contribute articles to *The Globalist* or *New Azimuths;* that he could translate nothing from the French if it were less evident than a steamship poster, that he could *not* scan a five-beat accentual line. And so he had been condescended to in a nice, well-bred way, because all these intellectual folk had gained the idea, and gained it correctly, that he was "in trade." And then all of a sudden that mysterious Hindu to whom everybody was kowtowing had up and claimed him as a fraternity brother, after which everybody fell all over themselves to listen to his ideas, and to find out more about him, and elect him to their damn snooty lodge.

"I don't want any of them, thank you," said Mr. Blandings.

107

"They think all the right things—but when I hear the way they talk about them, it just makes me want to think the opposite. Liberalism in America has been taken up by snobs, and I want no part in that."

"I can't think of anything more snobbish," said Mrs. Blandings, "than not wanting to let people know how you make your money. So the last thing I can understand is how you can be vexed with me because when your Hindu was going on about Knapp I up and told him that he was talking face to face with the man he was calling a genius."

Mr. Blandings was not able to answer this, so instead he proposed to Bill Cole a walk over the hills that were drenched in the sunshine of a perfect spring day.

"Very smart of you to have invested in the upkeep of your trees this way," said Bill Cole.

"I rather thought so," said Mr. Blandings.

"Tell me," said Bill Cole, "are you able to be up here enough to make this place really work out for you?"

"Well," said Mr. Blandings, "in recent weeks I've had to stay in town a good deal, and Muriel has been a little peevish, but things have slackened off quite a bit now."

"What was the big push?" asked Bill Cole.

"That open letter to Joe Stalin," said Mr. Blandings. "Golly, how we worked on that one. I did about thirty pieces of copy myself, none alike."

"When will it start coming out?" asked Bill Cole.

"Never," said Mr. Blandings. "The whole idea blew up."

"I suppose that means that now you'll have to hunt for another one," said Bill Cole.

"No," said Mr. Blandings. "We lost the account."

"You seem very calm about it," said Bill Cole. "I guess I don't understand the advertising business."

"Who does?" said Mr. Blandings. "I just happened to come out of this particular smashup with flying colors."

Bill Cole waited.

"The client started off by thinking my copy was terrible," said Mr. Blandings. "But by the next morning the client said it was

108

growing on him, and by the *next* morning he said that with a few simple changes, as attached, there was no question it would make a very strong campaign. Of course the changes ruined the whole point, but who was I to kick? I made the inference that the client had taken the copy home and showed it to his wife."

"Who is the client, remind me," said Bill Cole.

"International Screw," said Mr. Blandings. "Royal Heffingwell's outfit."

"Ah," said Bill Cole. "I was once on a committee with Eloise Heffingwell."

"Then the rest of the story won't surprise you," said Mr. Blandings. "We got OKs, we sent out the plates, the stage was all set for the first ad—and forty-eight hours before deadline we got orders to cancel the whole works. The client had decided the printed word was obsolete. Couldn't budge 'em."

"So?" said Bill Cole.

"So they bought a radio show from another agency instead," said Mr. Blandings.

"For Joe Stalin?" said Bill Cole. "I didn't think—"

"No, no, no," said Mr. Blandings impatiently. "The whole Joe Stalin idea is dead. Just cross it off."

"But you told me you came out of it all with flying colors," said Bill Cole.

"I did," said Mr. Blandings. "There's a newspaper in North Carolina that either didn't get our cancellation notice or wouldn't honor it, so they ran the ad." He threw his head backward and laughed a hearty, generous laugh. "And within forty-eight hours we had a new account out of it. Gilbertson Extrusion."

Bill Cole looked blank.

"See?" said Mr. Blandings, pleased. "You've never heard of them. They make practically the entire world output of Botular Closures, but you've never heard of them. Why? Because they've never done a line of advertising in their lives. Old man Gilbertson came all the way from North Carolina to New York to tell Horace Dascomb that when he read that Joe Stalin ad he decided that if any agency could produce copy like that it was time he started advertising. So now the whole account is ours. It could run to three times International Screw. Why every agency in the country has been trying to crack Gilbertson for fifteen years. So you can see I'm quite a fair-haired boy with Horace."

"The copy ran by accident?" asked Bill Cole.

"Yes," said Mr. Blandings, "I told you."

"But it was your copy?"

"My copy," said Mr. Blandings.

"It must have been the copy that'd had its whole point ruined by Eloise Heffingwell, wasn't it?" said Bill Cole.

"Are you practicing for district attorney?" said Mr. Blandings. "All you do is ask questions. Certainly it was if you want to put it that way, but it brought in the business, didn't it?"

Bill Cole and Mr. Blandings walked along in silence for a moment. They were nearly back to the house. "The man who really got his ass in a sling in the whole business was Lorbet Neen," said Mr. Blandings, his voice glowing from some inner warmth. "He was having a knock-down-drag-out fight with the newspaper that ran the ad because of course he'd sent out cancellations and he told them he wouldn't pay for the space. That almost lost us the Gilbertson account the day after we got it; it turned out old man Gilbertson owned the newspaper."

"Well, well," said Bill Cole. He sounded bemused.

"Mr. Dascomb never loses his temper," said Mr. Blandings, "but it's very unnerving when he has a trembling fit at you. He had a beaut at Lorbet. And who do you suppose had to go down South and straighten things out?"

"You?" said Bill Cole.

Mr. Blandings nodded; a slow, sage, smiling nod.

"Well," said Mrs. Blandings, coming downstairs in a hostess gown as her husband and Bill Cole sat down with four o'clock drinks in their hands, "*you'll* be surprised. Who do you suppose called up while you were out for your walk?"

Mr. Blandings waited.

"Sally Chasuble-Horn," said Mrs. Blandings, "and wait till you hear."

Mr. Blandings waited.

"It's all practically decided," said Mrs. Blandings. "She and I decided it between us."

110

Mrs. Blandings turned to Bill Cole. "Do you know what Jim's going to do?" she asked. "He's going to run for the school board."

"I never heard anything so—" said Mr. Blandings.

"Sally was just full of the idea," said Mrs. Blandings. "After we left last night Auster Millowy and Dr. Boomper and the Shallots stayed on and talked and talked, and they decided that Jim was the man they'd been looking for."

"That might be quite true," said Bill Cole.

"Sally said what we all know perfectly well," said Mrs. Blandings. "She said it was an absolute shame that a lot of brilliant people had moved to this part of the country with their children, to bring them up here and give them the advantages of country life, and then have to put their education into the hands of a lot of antediluvian know-nothings."

"Interesting," said Bill Cole. He glanced at Mr. Blandings who was looking elaborately at the fireplace. "Why do they think Jim is their man?"

"For several reasons," said Mrs. Blandings. "In the first place there was a letter signed by Jim in the *Blade* a few weeks or whatever ago on the subject of education and democracy that got Sally quite stirred up."

"So," said Bill Cole, looking sharply at Mr. Blandings. "Writing letters to the papers?"

"Oh no," said Mrs. Blandings; "Joanie wrote it, bless her soul; Jim's name got signed to it by mistake."

"Ah," said Bill Cole. "I often wonder what Jim would do without the loving help that womankind seems to pour out at his feet."

"Typographical error," said Mr. Blandings. He felt huffy and defensive.

"I didn't bother to correct Sally," said Mrs. Blandings, "though naturally I will. Because that wasn't the main reason why they were thinking of Jim. Sally said Auster Millowy in particular believes that advertising has within it the seeds of a great moral and spiritual force, and he thinks—"

"My God," said Mr. Blandings; "Auster Millowy has caught up with Horace Dascomb. After all these years he's actually—"

"—and he thinks," said Mrs. Blandings, overriding the interruption, "that just because it may have been used to unworthy ends

111

in the past that's no reason why it may not become the mechanism through which some great future movement is brought to fruition. Isn't that exciting?"

"Is getting Jim on the school board the first step toward that end?" asked Bill Cole.

"Sally said," said Mrs. Blandings, "and she said that Auster agreed with her completely, that the greatest unmet obligation in American life is the obligation of the superior individual toward something higher than merely his own way of making money. I must confess I was a little amused at that, because the first person I heard say that was Joanie right in this living room when she was getting over the mumps, and she was quoting Miss Stellwagon."

Bill Cole shot another look at Mr. Blandings, who finished his drink abruptly, and walked to the bar to make another.

"Now where Jim *really* comes in," said Mrs. Blandings, "is that Sally and Auster and all the rest think that anyone with Jim's advertising background would have all the means at his fingertips to make a practical, effective, realistic campaign, based on the best modern principles of attention-getting. I must say it's logical."

"Who's the opposition?" asked Bill Cole. "Isn't it all cut-and-dried bipartisan up here?"

Mrs. Blandings hugged herself and gave a little squeal.

"That's what makes it so perfect," she said radiantly. "The man Jim would be running against would be Ephemus W. Hackett."

Mr. Blandings put his new drink down with a whack on the tabletop. His eyes were sparkling. "No!" he said.

"Yes!" said Mrs. Blandings. "Bill, there was a Mr. Preebles who died last month, in the second year of a three-year term. They've appointed Hackett to his place on the board, but by the laws of this township, Sally says, there's got to be an election this fall to see if he stays or goes. Wouldn't it be wonderful if—"

Mr. and Mrs. Blandings were suddenly seeing the same vision: the vision of discomfiting and humiliating the man who had sold them their country property for too much money and never spoken to them since.

"Now look," said Bill Cole. "This is all very well but has Jim the faintest idea of what's involved here?"

"Well—" said Mr. Blandings. It came to him that he knew noth-

112

ing about how to go about getting what he suddenly knew he wanted. But that did not matter. He could find out. Something had dropped into place. Whatever it was he had been searching for so vainly in his talk with Bill Cole at the Hotel Marbury in January, he knew he had it now. Something had taken the place of nothing. The details could be filled in in due course.

"Take my advice," said Bill Cole, "and don't get mixed up with that bunch of do-gooders. You said yourself this morning you didn't like them."

Mr. Blandings cleared his throat. A new light had been cast on things rather abruptly. He now needed to explain that although he did not take back anything he had said that morning this was not inconsistent with an altered viewpoint; that although things were precisely the same there was also a difference to them.

"Quite true," said Mr. Blandings. "But I also said that they stood for the right things. For the common man and against privilege. For minority rights and against discrimination. For positive social policies and against the resurrection of William McKinley. If a few of the people who think these things happen to be horses' asses that's unfortunate but it can't be helped."

"All right," said Bill Cole, "but just don't expect any of these people ever to *do* anything helpful for you. That's not their specialty. And I know that you could get into quite a lot of trouble by stringing along with them."

"I take it," said Mr. Blandings, "that as always your advice is to do nothing, let the opportunity pass, look the other way, and just keep on stewing in my own juice. Well maybe I will and maybe I won't. Look Bill: this is the sort of thing I had in the back of my mind the day we talked at lunch at the Marbury, only then I didn't have anything tangible I could put my finger on."

"You haven't got anything tangible to put your finger on now either," said Bill Cole. "Somebody's wife has just had a talk with a poet and called up Muriel about it. Don't confuse that with the voice of the people."

"I'm not," said Mr. Blandings irritably. "But somebody's got to do something about things like education in this community. Muriel says Joanie talked me into sending her to school here, and maybe she did. Anyway now I'm stuck with being the parent of a

113

Lansdale schoolchild, and I admit it's terrible. Fortunately, Joanie seems to pick up her own education out of the air wherever she is, but this Mrs. Horn has it dead right about the state of the schools around here. There isn't anything this community needs worse than some adequate, up-to-date ideas about what a child's education ought to consist of."

"I don't doubt it," said Bill Cole. "And maybe that's the last thing this community wants."

"That's just cheap cynicism," said Mrs. Blandings.

"No it isn't," said Bill Cole. "You inveigh against advertising and all its works, but your thoughts are colored by it just the same. You think progress is a good thing. You think a competition of ideas is a good thing. You ought to be aware that there are millions of people in America who don't agree with you on either point. You ought to be aware that it's not competition but privilege that a community like this believes in. You and Muriel moved to the country, according to your story, because you wanted to re-capture some of the ancient virtues for yourselves and your kids, and get out of the expensive, noisy, dishonest squalor of New York. Have it that way if you want to; it's a perfectly good way. But don't forget that one of the ancient virtues of rural America is the virtue of sticking in the mud. Don't make speeches about progress around here; it's dangerous talk."

"You're putting on an attitude," said Mrs. Blandings. "I know *you*."

"No I'm not," said Bill Cole. "I'm giving you a genuine warning. You and Jim think that because the city is complex the country is simple. That's a false contrast. The city is complex, all right, but the country is super-complex. Don't monkey with it. For heaven's sake don't think that because Jim can persuade the people of the United States to buy seven hundred tons of one brand of laxative per year that gives him any insight into how to become a working part of rural America. It simply doesn't."

"All the same," said Mrs. Blandings.

"I should think you'd remember," said Bill Cole, "how Ephemus Hackett made idiots of both of you in the simple process of buying a few acres of land. You took him for a hick but he took you for thirteen thousand dollars. That was just a money transaction. Now

114

here you are thinking that you can walk right into Mr. Hackett's own private lair and take away from him, without the lure of cash, or without the thought of any effort, or even a scrap of knowledge about where any effort should be applied, what is probably his proudest possession—his membership on the Board of Education. I never heard anything so silly."

"All the same," said Mrs. Blandings.

After Bill Cole had taken the Sunday evening train back to town and the Blandings were re-established by themselves in their living room, each one of them tried to put the whole business out of his mind. For Mr. Blandings this was a little hard. He could somehow see himself, all difficulties surmounted, a power for education first in Lansdale Town, eventually in the state. Something called the Blandings Plan would find notice, through no self-seeking of his own, in the press, and after a while educators would come from far and near to watch it in daily operation. That the Blandings Plan was at the moment a Euclidean cube with boundaries but no content was not a matter for concern. When the time came for definite ideas, they would infallibly appear.

And Mrs. Blandings, too, kept the idea vivid, although she spoke no more about it that evening. The notion that her husband might best Mr. Ephemus W. Hackett in some contest was too bright to be ignored; wherever she turned her inward eye, there it glittered at her. True, this was only May; it would not be until the autumn that any such luscious fruit could be savored. But planting time was close, if ever there was to be such a harvest.

15

ALL IN ALL, it was the perfect summer, and it had stemmed from the perfect spring. April had been such an idyll of lovely warmth by day and gentle showers by night that when its end came the cherry and apple trees from foot to tip of Bald Mountain burst into bloom like exploding popcorn. This was unprecedented; almost a month ahead of time. In general, however, the onset of May was greeted with foreboding by the dozen or more farmers on Bald Mountain with whom Mr. Blandings had some small acquaintance; it would be a bad month for sure. There had been fog in February; everybody knowed "Fog in February, frost in May."

Mr. Blandings waited with towering impatience. The garden plot was ready and newly fenced; the weather was perfect, the earth warm and moist, and Mr. Blandings wanted to plant everything—at once and immediately. But his wife forbade him. He could plant some root crops if he liked; some radishes and beets and carrots, but he could not touch a seed of corn, or transplant as much as one tomato seedling from the cold frame Mr. Trer had built. All the garden books frowned on over-early eagerness and there was not one farmer on Bald Mountain who bothered to plant anything until after Decoration Day. But there was no frost; the month of May ended without one night that could be described as even chilly; Libe Watriss, down the road, the local weather oracle, said he would be damned; this was the first year in history he could remember—

By mid-June it was evident the Blandings had green thumbs, both of them. Mr. Blandings felt pretty impatient and a little condescending toward the farmers on the mountain. Doubtless complex operations like dairying and tobacco-growing took a man's full patience and skill, but to be a successful truck gardener was obviously the easiest and simplest and most gratifying occupation a man could find: these funny books about a man's misadventures with the soil were just so much silliness. The Blandings garden, rectilinear as a battalion of West Point cadets, was a study in greens from glossiest black to palest olive. Mrs. Blandings weeded every hour, on the hour, so that not one alien blade of crab grass, plantain, or purslane, no swift-springing Jerusalem artichoke, should mar a square inch of the softly crumbling brown-sugar earth. The earth had not been that way in the beginning; at first boulders the size of cobblestones had to be cast out of it; by slow degrees Mr. Blandings had reduced, with rake and spade, the size of the intruding stones to eggplants, to potatoes, to walnuts, to almonds, and at last to diamonds. But all it took was a system and devotion. Nature did not exact struggle; Nature merely asked for love. And love the Blandings gave her. In accord with some deep law of harmony the whole of Lansdale County, that spring, was scarcely touched by insects. Mosaic and black rot were unknown. By July 4 the early corn was up a foot in the Blandings garden, the tomatoes were putting forth new stems and axils by the hour, and what had been bare squash hills three weeks before were covered now with green leaves the size of elephants' ears. If there was any flaw in Mrs. Blandings' pleasure it was that the squash vines were a little assertive; their springy tendrils were showing a tendency to reach out and grab. Mrs. Blandings did not like it one evening when she saw that a coiled green tendril of the squash had seized a carrot top. She pinched it off and threw it away. Next morning, two squash tendrils had seized two carrot tops.

Flawlessly, the weather continued. As it was with the garden, so it was with the meadows. The rhomboid fields below the Blandings house lay warped on the hills, and each was a bedazzling flung scarf of wildflowers. The spears of timothy and redtop came to stand so high that from one oblique angle the fields looked dense white-green and from another, a rippling, half-transparent red. It occurred to Mr. Blandings that he was going to have a bumper crop of hay; in fact, that he had it already.

117

This was surprising and delightful; Mr. Blandings had never thought of hay; not actively, anyway. Was hay not worth $20 a ton? The *Countryman's Hand Book* said that under certain circumstances it certainly was. Mr. Cornish, an aged and arthritic farmer down the road, happened by one day and was moved to reminiscence. He squinted at the Blandings fields and allowed himself to remember there was once a time when Pop Hackett, the old drover, not the present son, used to get a hundred ton off'n the property Mr. Blandings now owned.

"Why at $20 a ton that's $2,000," said Mr. Blandings to his wife. "I don't mean it would be $2,000 *clear;* whoever's going to buy it would deduct the cost of his labor for mowing, and raking and loading and hauling. But still—"

The question was now: to whom would Mr. Blandings sell his hay? Libe Watriss seemed the most likely possibility; he was the most successful or at any rate the most industrious dairy farmer whose property lay along Bald Mountain Road; everything about him, from his long red neck to his torn and thickened fingernails, made him almost a parody of what in reality he was—but Libe Watriss was a friendly man, and not standoffish like the most of them. Often on the way to his own farm two miles farther down the road, he would stop and chat with Mr. Blandings in the long, light evenings. It was difficult to understand him because he never finished a sentence: "Let me tell you something about, why there's people that'll take and, I've seen a man who'll, not that I've anything against it, some do it that way, still you can't tell me it don't make any difference, why up here one time we had a fella, come from over in York State, he thought he knew all about it, well sir first thing you know there was a crowd around yellin'—" But Mr. Blandings thought he would be a good one with whom to start proceedings.

Mr. Blandings began by offering his hay, in his slightly over-hearty country manner, to Libe Watriss, at "whatever price you think is fair." In the ensuing conversation it was impossible for Mr. Blandings to discover whether Mr. Watriss had accepted or rejected this offer, although as the days wore along and Mr. Blandings' fields began to appear slightly rank it seemed as though he must have rejected it; for some time he did not come near the

118

Blandings place at all. Somewhat in doubt about the next step, Mr. Blandings brought up the subject of his hay to Mr. Dud Palters. "Thought you'd already promised it to Libe Watriss," said Mr. Palters, snappishly. "I did," said Mr. Blandings, "but—" "Can't sell the same hay twicet," said Mr. Palters, glaring at Mr. Blandings and seeming to find him guilty of sharp practice on a closely regulated commodity exchange. When next Mr. Blandings saw Libe Watriss, Mr. Watriss was cordial but on the subject of hay said only, "I hear you want to give it to Dud Palters." There seemed to be two misunderstandings here, one inside the other; at last, when a sharp rainstorm one evening bashed down a lot of the timothy, Mr. Blandings realized he had a problem on his hands.

Mr. Blandings was bound to confess, after a little, that he was baffled, pure and simple, by farmers as he saw them. They seemed to be against everything and for nothing. It was not hard to discover that the Bald Mountain farmers like the Messrs. Watriss, Palters, and Cornish heartily disliked Mr. Anson Dolliver and his bank. Their reaction to him would have gratified the most rudimentary Marxist: he was a practitioner of usury, battening on the misfortunes of the worthy poor, a money monopolist supported in his existence by a sinister conspiracy among unnamable Interests. God knows, thought Mr. Blandings, the Bald Mountain dairy farmers were poor; poor and industrious. They worked like serfs under the lash and one of them had once defined a "good" year as any one in which he ended up with $300 in Mr. Dolliver's bank. Yet it quickly became evident that there was a force for Evil greater than Mr. Dolliver, the Capitalist. This was Socialism-and-Worse, which had been brought to a once proud and self-reliant nation by the Democratic party under Franklin Delano Roosevelt. There was something wrong with the size of the Bald Mountion farmer's milk check; to discover the reason it was needless to cast one glance further than the White House. Wall Street and the White House, there they were: the final ultimate conspiracy.

It surprised Mr. Blandings to discover how farmers could hate farmers. To the New England dairyman, the Wisconsin dairyman was a man of wicked practices; a tariff should be imposed by other states on low-cost Wisconsin butters and cheeses to keep them from ruining the markets for honest toil in the East. The farmers of the Great Plains were conspirators in evil, helped and encouraged by the Federal Government. How was a man to keep his herd alive against the extortionate prices those bastards were permitted to exact for the grains and the baled hay the New England farmer had to buy? As for the Southern farmer, his very existence was intolerable to a believer in Natural Law; his tons of cottonseed oil, made into oleomargarine, were bringing ruin to honest creamery butter. He was also a callous exploiter of the Negro; yet the Negro's perverse unwillingness to work for starvation wages also received heavy and unfavorable scrutiny.

Mr. Blandings who, as an advertising man, thought he knew something about the problems of Distribution, soon came to realize that this city-acquired education would not fit any place into the wide assortment of injuries and injustices his farming neighbors so passionately felt. Their demand seemed to be for unfettered individual initiative, generously subsidized. He tried to think of whom they reminded him and suddenly he knew: they reminded him of his clients; of businessmen everywhere as he had met them; in one breath yelling for freedom eternal, in the next for protection everlasting. As a city man, Mr. Blandings had thought of farmers as a "class"; now he saw that there were as many classes of farmers as there were castes in India. This might be wisdom, but it did not help him sell his hay.

As July wore on, the sun shone brilliantly and the rains ceased. Mr. Blandings gave up person-to-person contact in the matter of his hay and inserted a classified advertisement in the Lansdale *Blade*, once more against Mr. Nellus' advice. The reaction was immediate. The Blandings telephone began ringing briskly, and over the weekend seven people appeared at the top of Bald Mountain. All this attention, however, came from agricultural-equipment salesmen; there were no offers to buy the hay.

The following Wednesday a prospect appeared. He was a farmer alien to Bald Mountain and came, in fact, from "over to York State," as Mr. Blandings himself had now learned to call the neighboring commonwealth to the west. Whatever might have been his need of hay was never discussed; he took one look at Mr. Blandings' fields, spat in disgust and began berating himself, almost as if Mr. Blandings had not been there, for having used the gas for a twelve-mile round trip so ill conceived. He was younger than the average of Bald Mountain farmers, and somewhat more articulate.

"Maybe this is hay in Connecticut," he said, "but over where I come from we'd say it was mostly overgrown weeds and wildflowers. And see this here? This is wild onion: I guess you got enough to stink up the milk of every cow in the state." Having plucked a pretty purple-flowering plant and rolled it between his fingers he let it fall contemptuously in the dust of the road.

Mr. Blandings looked so mortally damaged that the York State farmer modified his tone.

"I ain't saying a man couldn't use this stuff for hay if he was des'prit," he said. He seemed about to sympathize; then his eye caught something and he squatted suddenly, running the palm of his hand down close to the grassroots. "How long you been on this place?" he asked, shooting a quizzical glance at the profferer of forage to the needy.

"Oh, maybe a year, more or less," said Mr. Blandings, overcoming a tendency to gulp.

The York State farmer straightened up, a clenched fist full of something. "Must be four-five years since these fields been cut over," he said. He opened his fist and displayed a big handful of curling shreds, wispy brown and far gone in desiccation. "Last year's, year before's, year before that's . . ." he said, talking to himself, as he picked strands out of his palm. "Yep; four-five years."

"What is it?" asked Mr. Blandings.

"Mat," said the farmer. "Look close down between this year's green; see that brown stuff?"

Now that his attention was called to it, Mr. Blandings saw it crystal clear.

"Your fields is covered with it," said the farmer; "inch, inch-and-half, two inches deep, maybe. I was figuring how many years back the fields had died uncut. Anybody go in there with a machine now, he'd have one sweet time climbing down every two minutes to unfoul his cutter bar."

The last threadlike notion of hay as a cash crop disappeared from Mr. Blandings' mind. He could see that a classic pattern in his country experience was about to be repeated. The pattern always began with his bright hope of selling something. When circumstances bludgeoned this hope to death he would have the task of reconciling himself to the necessity for giving it away. In the city there was nothing ever that could not be given away; the idea of being unable to rid oneself of anything unwanted was ridiculous. But in the country there were hundreds of things that could not be given away, and now his hay was one of them. The classic pattern would complete itself when Mr. Blandings would finally have to pay for the removal, as refuse, of something that he had begun by thinking was a source of income. But he would not give in yet. He apologized somberly to the York State farmer for having caused him a fruitless trip, and bade him farewell. "Burn it off, my advice," yelled the farmer as his truck began to jounce away. "But take it careful."

Eventually Mr. Blandings humbled himself to offer cash to Libe Watriss or anyone else who would clear his nine acres of hayfields and cart away the trash. For once, no one in the countryside came forth to take his money. At last, when Mr. Blandings' fields were in such a state of disarray as to spoil the appearance of the whole mountainside, Libe Watriss explained; Mr. Blandings might just as well stop trying to get his fields mowed this year by *any* consideration; he, Libe Watriss, would have been glad all along to take the hay, such as it was, in return for the labor of mowing if he'd had the time. But the summer was too busy; nobody else had any time either. Libe Watriss invited Mr. Blandings to consider a point that city people frequently overlooked: what the hell good was money if you had to let your own place go to pieces while you made it off someone else, and then never could get caught up with your own work again? Leave the fields go another year, and if he spoke up early enough maybe somebody could help him out. Meanwhile he might as well relax.

It was a hard blow. In all of country living there was no more

rudimentary crop than hay, yet here he was, powerless to do anything about it. He could, as Libe Watriss pointed out, put a herd
of cows in his fields, but that would mean, as Mr. Watriss also
pointed out, a considerable amount of repair to the Blandings
fences so as you wouldn't find the cows all fetching up on the
railroad tracks a mile and a half away, and nine hundred feet below, in the valley of the Wintinock. Or Mr. Blandings could get
himself a hired man, God knew just where, though, and pick up a
mowing machine and a rake and a wagon secondhand somewheres.
Sure, then he'd either have to get a couple horses or a tractor, and
either way, Mr. Watriss conceded, Mr. Blandings would be in the
farming business. Thing city people don't ordinarily realize, Mr.
Watriss went on, was that thirty acres of land was a lot of land.
If they was nobody on it, why then it just went its own way, but
if they *was* somebody on it, why they had to make plans to take
care of it, one way or another. If city people didn't want to take
care of their land, and didn't plan all the way through to take care
of it, what he, Mr. Watriss, couldn't understand was why
they come to the country in the first place. Mr. Watriss then
launched on some cow-and-fence talk that Mr. Blandings found
unintelligible, the upshot of which seemed to be that maybe they
could go shares on something next summer. Mr. Blandings could
not have been more confused. For a moment, his office life seemed
less galling. On his desk were two push buttons: one summoned
his secretary; the other summoned office boys. When he pushed
one or the other, somebody else immediately did what Mr. Blandings wanted. But in the country there were no push buttons.

16

EXCEPT OF COURSE for the radishes, the peas had been the first
thing the Blandings had savored from their own garden. They
were magnificent, and Mrs. Blandings was damned if she would
ever bother with them again. The rows sprang up, green and fresh,
and instantly needed the support of brush cut to their measure and
stuck in the garden like little dead trees. Then they yielded a few
cupfuls of matchless product, enough for one meal for a statistical
family of 2.3 persons, and shriveled brown and died.

Funny that none of the books made really sensible differentia-
tions between what one should plant and should not plant, Mrs.
Blandings mused during several solitary days in the country while
her husband found himself bound to the city. There were the
beans, for example. Whereas a twenty-foot row of peas had let
her down completely, an equal length of beans threatened to engulf her. Every sunny morning as she strolled through the garden
she would examine the plants; she might have picked them clean
the evening before, but there was a brand-new crop; a little larger
and a little coarser than its predecessor of twenty-four hours. It
had been Mr. Blandings who had finally determined the quantity
of planting in the garden; Mrs. Blandings, out of the female instinct having to do with bearing and rearing, knew that it was all
vastly too much, but Mr. Blandings, by instinct the blind scatterer
of seed, could characteristically not be stopped at the time. And
nothing was intervening to set a balance. Where were the rabbits
and the woodchucks who ate the green tops and the lettuces?
Where were the fieldmice and moles who gnawed the root crops?
Where were the crows that pecked the corn? Where were the
squash bugs, the potato beetles? Everything this summer seemed

to be Malthus in reverse: the Blandings family consumption was stationary, but the means of subsistence was increasing in geometric ratio, or better. If the summer came to an end without some sort of Malthusian check, Mrs. Blandings reflected, it was going to be hard on her; she had already canned thirty quarts of beans in an effort to avoid serving them on the table three times a day, but still they marched at her every day, rank on rank, like Meredith's army of unalterable law. Mrs. Blandings asked Libe Watriss one morning why everything was going so alarmingly well; Mr. Watriss had said he'd be danged if he knew; it was the greatest, most flawless growing season they'd ever seen in the county. The dry spell was getting very long, but everything had got off to such a perfect start in spring and early summer that it'd hardly made any difference yet. The great central fact about farming, Mr. Watriss emphasized, was that you never could tell; you couldn't tell nothing about nothing from one day to the next and don't let any of the boys from the State College tell you different.

Not even Mrs. Blandings had realized the reproductive capacity of that great genus gathered together under the name of *cucurbitaceae;* the squashes, cucumbers, pumpkins, and melons. Here the copywriters of seed catalogs had seriously, and no doubt deliberately, understated their case: three cucurbit seeds of any one variety were more than enough to sustain a township. Mr. Blandings had heavily overdone things and had thus cast himself and his wife in the role of sorcerer's apprentices: the process had been started, but there were no instructions for shutting it off. Conditions were now becoming serious.

In the beginning, the lovely, long dark striped-green tubes known in the catalogs as zucchini, or Italian squash, had introduced Mrs. Blandings to a new and temporarily intense joy: barter. The agreeable manager of the vegetable department of the big chain-store supermarket had said sure, he'd take some of it and give her canned goods in exchange. Day after day, Mrs. Blandings trundled the station wagon, loaded with zucchini, down Bald Mountain Road to Lansdale Town, the squashes growing slightly larger and darker with every load; day after day she came home triumphant with canned exotics. But after a while the cordiality of the vegetable department manager began to fade. There came a
125

visit when he solemnly enjoined Mrs. Blandings from bringing any more of "that stuff" into his store; the squashes were growing too huge and coarse, and people were sick of seeing them. The morning after this depressing passage Mrs. Blandings went out to the vegetable garden; picking her way through a jungle of leaves she hacked with a rusty little hatchet at what she hoped were the very roots of all the squash vines; next day in the broad waving carpet of green three shriveled brown threads of vines and leaves, each perhaps twenty feet long, made inconspicuous radii to mark what she had succeeded in disconnecting from the earth. This seemed merely to offer more scope for the survivors. Mrs. Blandings looked at her garden and realized that all of a sudden part of it had become trash; burgeoning, proliferating, exponentially expanding trash; trash that could overnight engulf the mountaintop that was her home. The vines kept on bearing; sucking nitrogen from the soil and converting it into Hubbard, crookneck, pattypan, and acorn squashes. As for the zucchini, there seemed to be uncountable grosses of them, a foot and a half long, six inches in diameter; the size of a newborn babe, but three times as heavy.

Suddenly, everything went out of control at once and Mrs. Blandings at last perceived what was happening. They were in the midst of a glut. The corn was twelve feet high and bursting with tasseled ears. The eggplant vines were collapsing with the weight of their glossy purple fruit. The okra, which had started as half-a-dozen droopy little seedlings, had grown pods six inches long that were beginning to burst and spill their seed upon the ground. The broccoli went to flower before it could be cut; what had been plump round heads of lettuce suddenly shot up tall spiky stalks that budded and bloomed. When Mrs. Blandings gazed at Mr. Blandings' sixty-four tomato plants, of eight different varieties, she all but sank to the ground, for although the fruit was still green, most of it was "whitening"; the vines dragged at the raffia nooses that struggled to hold them to their heavy wooden stakes, and it was apparent that every tomato in the garden—a hundred thousand, Mrs. Blandings felt sure—would ripen with one accord: next Saturday afternoon, she said to herself, at exactly three forty-five.

And probably they did. But something else happened at three forty-five that next Saturday afternoon, and it subsumed the tomatoes.

Mr. Blandings too had become dimly aware that the *oikonomia* of his country home was not quite right. In the kitchen there was the magnificent electrically operated Kitch-N-Glutt-N, which instantly chewed up the garbage and sluiced it into the septic tank in such a way that it would never again enter the nitrogen cycle of the life process. On the other hand, the house was innocent of any machine for disposing of the vast array of paper products that accumulated in a country home: the wrappings, the cartons, the old cracker boxes, the busted bags, the old newspapers, the tissues, the consumed paper towels and napkins, all made a wild miscellany that had to be carted and burned out of doors; neither the oil burner nor any other device in the house could deal with them, and so it was one of Mr. Blandings' lesser pleasures every weekend to drag a barrel of the stuff out to a wire-mesh paper burner near the barns and there supervise its consumption. This Saturday, he did it just the way he did it every Saturday, wondering sulkily why neither he nor anyone else had thought of the need of a country house for a built-in incinerator. The phrase that always formed in his head was "If I were ever to build another house——" but it never went any further.

The afternoon sky was flecked with clouds, but the thunderheads in the west probably meant nothing; they were too far away and the wind seemed to be in the wrong direction to bring the storm they carried anywhere near Bald Mountain. Mr. Blandings touched a match to the bottom of the paper burner and the flames shot up. As he lighted a cigarette and turned his gaze on a hundred-foot row of starlings who were holding a convention on one wire of a high-voltage transmission line, there was a small explosion inside the paper burner, as there often was when an old light bulb had found its way into the refuse, and a large sheet of tissue paper, half alight, took wing from the top of the burner and floated placidly away. It came to rest, burning gently, about thirty feet distant, in the middle of the field nearest the Blandings house. Dutifully, Mr. Blandings followed it. By the time he reached

127

it, an area of the dried, matted, dead grasses of the last few years was burning with a bright, homey crackle; just a small area, a disk of a diameter no more than five feet.

Mr. Blandings stamped it out. That is, he stamped out about half of the circumference of bright little flames, hampered slightly by the country sandals he was wearing instead of shoes. But by the time he turned to the other half of the flames they had doubled their circumference and were not so easy to handle. He went at them methodically but when he looked up he saw that the fire had eaten around the small spot he had previously stamped out and was as merry and as busy as if no one had interfered with it at all. He paused, paralyzed to realize that he was standing in the burned-out smoking center of an area larger than a skating rink, and terror suddenly seized him by the throat. Toward every one of the three hundred and sixty degrees of the compass the flames, still small, still intimate and friendly looking, were making their inexorable way. They headed for the house. They headed for the barns. They headed for the oak grove. They headed everywhere at once.

"*Pi r* square," Mr. Blandings thought idiotically; "the area of a circle is the constant *pi* times the *square* of the radius."

He commanded his motor centers back into being and raced for the house, shouting "Hey!" at the top of his lungs. Mrs. Blandings seemed to be nowhere around. In the house, Mr. Blandings seized the first weapon against disaster that came to his hand, and a moment later found himself outside again, dementedly squirting a seltzer bottle from the bar at a perimeter of flame that must now enclose half an acre. The crackling had grown loud, and smoke was billowing into the blue sky.

"Brooms! Git brooms!"

Libe Watriss swung down off his truck and seeing that Mr. Blandings was a rooted statue, loped into the kitchen. A moment later he loped out again with a cleaning bucket and mop, two brooms, a couple of burlap bags, and Mrs. Blandings. All of these he systematically put to work. From close to Mr. Blandings' feet he turned on a hose bib, and a stream of water gushed forth. Disdaining a coiled length of garden hose Mr. Blandings had also failed to notice, Libe Watriss filled the bucket, and in it soused the brooms, mop, and burlap bags. Into the hands of Mr. Blandings and his wife he thrust the brooms. "Now whack at it," he said. He himself took the sopping bags and with them began flailing the earth; his slow, unhurried, matter-of-fact motions brought into the Blandings' minds the first dim notion of how to fight a grass fire in the country: hoses, extinguishers, and volumes of water were all beside the point: you beat out the flames by smacking them with something damp.

This went on for several minutes, Mr. Blandings and his wife working with desperate inefficiency; Libe Watriss proceeding at half the pace but making all his strokes count. "Better go call up the fire department," he said after a little while, in a casual tone; "we're goin' t' need a little help."

Mr. Blandings made his telephone call, saying he knew not what to he knew not whom, and again rushed outside. The scene struck primordial horror into his marrow. With every instant of time the fire expanded; the dense dry-dead grasses of yesteryear were a burning mattress spread over the globe. The earth was ablaze as far west as Nebraska. Gray, pungent smoke polluted an ocean of air. Mr. Blandings gazed wildly about him; in his ears the crackling of flames had reached a roar, yet over the roar he could hear, and be appalled by, the inner voice that told him it was his own carelessness and incapacity that had brought this ruin upon the United States of America.

Whack, pause, *whack,* pause, *whack.* Libe Watriss was not bothering to look up. A man can 'tend to just so much by hisself, his back muscles said; beyond that he'd got to leave things go. Some two hundred yards of the line of fire were now dead and smoldering in front of the Blandings house thanks to Libe Watriss, but on all other fronts it was still advancing: north toward the barns, south toward the oak grove, west toward a forest of evergreens on the land still owned by Mr. Ephemus Hackett. Mr. Blandings resumed his spasmodic beatings and then, at last, at last, after the passage of two-and-a-half eternities, the wail of a siren was heard far to the east. "Here come the boys," said Libe Watriss.

In another five minutes the volunteers of Aquaskat Hose & Engine Company No. 2 arrived. Following the huge red ultramodern pumper up Bald Mountain Road came a stream of cars that stretched behind it like a tail to a comet. The cavalcade came to a brake-shrieking halt, and the Blandings acres were instantly overrun. Men in overalls, men in grocers' aprons, men in business suits, men in white doctors' coats, men in lumberjacks' checked shirts, men in every costume, and some women, deployed into the fields. As if with the benefit of a dozen rehearsals, the big red pumper maneuvered to the brook and dropped a six-inch rubber-and-canvas intake line into a shallow pool. Mr. Blandings could see hose lines running suddenly toward his house, toward the barns, toward the oak grove. Pails and soaking flails appeared everywhere, and there were shouts and runnings, and orders given and countermanded, and although the burning shores of grass widened and widened still, it was apparent within ten minutes that the Aquaskat Volunteer Hose & Engine Company No. 2 had the situation well in hand. "Best thing for you to do is go inside now," Libe Watriss bellowed to the Blandings; "the boys usually appreciate a little refreshment after one of these things is over."

That was the day, as the Blandings looked back on it, when they really met the natives of Lansdale Town. As the fire diminished they had the wits to lug up from the cellar every bottle of Old Supine to be found, to lay out on the dining table every glass that Mrs. Blandings could commandeer from her best crystal to ex-containers of jelly and cheese, to haul out cases of Coca-Cola and ginger ale, and denude the refrigerator of its ice cubes. By the time Aquaskat Hose & Engine Company No. 2 had finished its work and the Blandings fields were a dark smoking black, its members fell on these supplies with relish. They used very little ice, no more than two dozen bottles of Coca-Cola, and practically no ginger ale, but all the Old Supine and three dozen cans of beer, most of them warm, vanished swiftly. There must have been several hundred people at the Blandings place during the height of the excitement; it was impossible to separate onlookers from official members of the brigade. It was obvious that the Blandings house had for some time been an object of curiosity now being thoroughly sated. The crowd tramped wet ashes into the carpet and

130

up the stairs; they left streaks of sweat and soot on the slip covers of the furniture; several glasses and fragile ameublements and objects of art came apart in some spontaneous way. But everybody was in a roaring good humor, everybody recounted to everybody else his own and therefore officially correct version of the sequence events had taken, and for the better part of an hour the fire was refought in the Blandings house, its rooms and porches. Mr. Blandings must have given himself several huge jolts of Old Supine somewhere along the line, Mrs. Blandings reflected; he was innocent of any tensions or symptoms of shock, and seemed to take as much pleasure as anyone in Libe Watriss' endlessly repeated account of how he had been driving back from town and had come on Mr. Blandings trying to quench his blazing fields with a bottle of seltzer water from the bar. It seemed obvious that a piece of Bald Mountain folklore was in the making.

Gradually the crowd thinned. At length, Fire Chief Luden Posker rose to go and became momentarily embarrassed, but not so much so as not to be able to set forth what he had to say. "There's supposed to be a charge for answering calls outside the District," he said to Mr. Blandings. "Now if it was some Polish farmer that'd just lost his barn and half his stock that'd be one thing."

He ended the sentence there.

"Much obliged," he said to Mr. Blandings a few moments later, a still wet check for $50 between a gigantic thumb and forefinger. It was for double the official amount, but Mr. Blandings felt in an expansive mood.

"Well," said Luden Posker, "got to be going. Don't let Eph Hackett get in your hair. Guess he wasn't up here today cause I heard him say he was going over into York State. But when he serves you with a warrant just pay your fine quiet like and forget it, my advice."

"*Fine?*" said Mr. Blandings.

"Yep," said the Fire Chief. "I know all you were aiming to do was get rid of a little trash, but still and all some nine acres got burned over this afternoon and a grass fire that size is usually took as prima fayshee evidence of negligence when the party concerned don't turn out to have a fire permit. There was quite a little breeze

131

from the northwest this afternoon, too. Eph Hackett's fire warden, you know; he'd be kind of likely to stand up sort of straight on this one, it having been his father's property one time, and all."

He took his departure. Libe Watriss rose from the depths of an upholstered chair, leaving it dark and damp. "Well," he said, "I guess I got t' get back to m' caows."

· 17 ·

THE FIRE had been one of those blessings in disguise, Mr. and Mrs. Blandings had come to agree. For one thing, as Libe Watriss pointed out, the burned fields were now in better shape than they had been for half a decade. The Aquaskat volunteers with a skill masked under their seemingly random approach had kept the flames away from the oak grove, the orchard, the barns, and the house, yet the empty fields were burned clean, right to the stone walls that marked the boundaries of the Blandings property. The deep-tangled mat in the fields was gone and a fluffy carpet of ash replaced it. The fields looked as forlorn as a shaved cat, and a smell of deep scorch enveloped Bald Mountain, but both these immediate evidences of mischance would soon disappear. The fields would fuzz and feather over before the autumn, even, and next spring they would sprout clean and green and virgin.

The fire had also proved to be the long overdue Malthusian check to the vegetable garden. The flames had burned one side of the fence and someone had backed a truck into the other side, and and thereafter the garden had been used as a thoroughfare. The cornstalks were still standing but they were confusedly awry and when inspected were discovered no longer to have any ears. Looking back on yesterday afternoon Mrs. Blandings realized that during the height of the flames and confusion she had seen a large, swaybacked piebald horse standing in the garden; at the time his presence had seemed no stranger than anything else, but now that she thought of it she realized it had not been normal. Where the horse had come from, whom he belonged to, she had no idea, but she would continue to feel his presence for the rest of the season. Having made a substantial meal of the corn he must then, the evidence seemed to show, have suffered a severe fall among Mr.

133

Blandings' tomatoes, most of which were now a muddy pulp. Indeed, the whole garden was a wreck in various other mysterious ways; Mrs. Blandings noted with bitterness that only the squash vines seemed untouched, still waving the triumphant green banners of their leaves, still bearing their enormous twenty-pound off-spring under these leaves with the skulking secrecy of cats.

But the principal accomplishment of the fire seemed to be the betterment of relations between the Blandings and their neighbors. Bald Mountain Road on Sundays was a sort of late afternoon local scenic tour; on this particular Sunday a car went by every five minutes or so, and slowed or stopped to view the blackened fields. The occupants were mostly the folks of the town who as members of the fire department had yesterday come roaring up the hills in answer to an emergency; now with the emergency past they were bringing their wives and children to look at the scene of their latest prowess. They were all highly amiable—although it was clear that the episode of the seltzer bottle would be permanent in the annals of Aquaskat Hose & Engine Company No. 2. Nor were the townsfolk the only displayers of the new cordiality; half-a-dozen farmers of Bald Mountain were among the visitors, and in these too there was manifest a change in attitude. Mr. Blandings had plunged himself into catastrophe; they had plunged in and dragged him out; he was unmistakably indebted to them and his sense of obligation would be permanent; suddenly, therefore, they were willing to display a certain careful measure of friendship. It was a somewhat obscure and involute emotion but Mr. Blandings felt that in part at least he understood it. He expressed considerable gratitude, and the expressions were passed unheeded; it was part of the act.

During the afternoon also a variety of salesmen from neighboring counties as well as Lansdale drove up Bald Mountain to discuss the merits of various products for the prevention, detection, or extinguishment of fires, and Mr. Blandings was in a poor position to resist them.

It was late on Sunday afternoon, and a fiery sun was approaching the rim of Westland Mountain, fifteen miles away, when Mr.

Ed O'Neill arrived. Mr. O'Neill was the head man of the Wintinock Realty and Insurance Company. It had been a long time since Mr. Blandings had seen him; scarcely at all since the time, over a year ago, when Mr. O'Neill had sold him a series of elaborate and expensive policies to protect his country establishment from almost every imaginable disaster. Mr. O'Neill was not at all in the regular cut of the Lansdale County native; he was a large, freckled, enormously genial and hypereuphoric red Irishman. He hopped nimbly out of an enormous sedan, followed by his small dark-haired wife, and then, one by one, by five children. His wife's figure made it evident that a sixth could scarcely be more than a month removed from a separate existence. "What have you been doing up here?" Mr. O'Neill bellowed to Mr. Blandings.

The circumstances of yesterday were discussed for the twelfth time. Grass fires, forest fires, holocausts, conflagrations, were deplored for some fifteen minutes. Mr. O'Neill seemed to have every detail of every disaster in the New England states at his fingertips. It developed that he came from Boston and was, as he described it, a newcomer in Lansdale County; it had been a bare quarter-century since he had settled here.

"Well," said Mr. O'Neill at length, "I guess you got a claim."

"Claim?" said Mr. Blandings.

"That's the trouble with you fellows from the city," said Mr. O'Neill. "Too busy and important to read your policies. You lost a privy, didn't you?"

Mr. Blandings said why yes, he had lost a privy; a mysterious, dilapidated old outhouse had stood askew in a lower field in the rough right angle of two stone walls. Mr. Blandings had never known how or why it had ever been hauled there, and he had always had in mind to have it torn down and carted away. Now that it was consumed almost without trace it suddenly had value.

"And I see where the fence around that garden got busted down in the excitement," said Mr. O'Neill. "And your hay was worth something; not very much, but something."

This was a reversal of all the country tactics Mr. Blandings had ever known.

"Why say," said Mr. O'Neill, "when I sell a man insurance I don't just collect the premiums and go way and forget him until next year. That's not the way I do business, and it wouldn't be the way the Farriers' and Steam Boiler Casualty would want me to do business, either. I sold you a Complete Coverage Comprehensive; when we wrote the policy on your house we put in a clause that everything else on your property is automatically covered up to 10 per cent of the face value of the policy. Would well say fifty dollars satisfy your claim?"

"Well," said Mr. Blandings. He was thinking that fifty dollars would precisely cancel out the check he had given Luden Posker yesterday. That would leave him out the amount of the fine he was going to have to pay for having accidentally set fire to his own property without having had a permit to do so. The fine would probably be ten dollars, but that was a lot less than he'd have had to pay to get his hay out and carted away—and the mat would still have been there, a fire hazard for the future. Everything was obviously going to come out all right; maybe this was the way you did business in the country; maybe he was getting the hang of it at last.

"Up to fifty dollars," said Mr. O'Neill, "they usually take my sayso; above fifty dollars they're likely to send somebody around from the Home Office."

"Fifty dollars," said Mr. Blandings, abandoning the idea of sixty dollars, "would be entirely satisfactory."

"I'll write it up," said Mr. O'Neill, "and we'll get it in the mail tomorrow."

He pulled a notebook from his back pocket, made an entry in a careful hand, and stowed it away in a manner that announced the end of business. "It's a wonderful place you have up here," he said admiringly. "Mighty lucky thing you didn't lose it."

"Yes," said Mr. Blandings; "believe me I'm grateful."

"And *that* reminds me," said Mr. O'Neill. "I *knew* there was something else on my mind. I was talking to some of the folks over in Art Hollow about you just the other day. Dr. Boomper, Mrs. Horn, and that crowd. They gave me to understand you have some ideas about education around here. They thought real well of that letter you had in the *Blade* a while back."

"Well," said Mr. Blandings, "it's just that I think every child's entitled to a—"

"So do I," said Mr. O'Neill. "And around here they don't get it."

"I understand there's a good deal of—"

"You said something," said Mr. O'Neill. "There's altogether too much. What they need is new blood, but they're never going to get it unless somebody like you is willing to pitch in and help. These old boys around here, some of them's been in office a hundred years, and it's time they moved over. It used to be the Democratic party around here didn't have a chance, but these are changing times, yes sir, changing times. We're ripe for—"

"We certainly are," said Mr. Blandings. "We're ripe for—"

"Correct," said Mr. O'Neill. "I like your views; like the way you express them. Now you take this fire you had; you're probably still a little shook up by it, but twicet-three-times as many people know who you are today as knew yesterday, just on account of it. Take what I heard about you and that seltzer bottle—probably not a word of truth in it, but if one person's told me that story since last night, I'll bet a hundred have. That's the way a man gets famous."

"As a matter of fact—" said Mr. Blandings.

"What did I tell you," said Mr. O'Neill, admiringly. "Well, if you want to find yourself on the school board ticket, just say the word to me. Just because this is an off year don't say it isn't an important year."

The conversation went on and on in looping ellipses that made Mrs. Blandings grind her teeth. Men were the most extraordinary, vague creatures; they had a demented fear of coming to the point. No wonder the world's affairs, consigned to their fumbling hands, were on the verge of final collapse. When the O'Neills at last departed without any conclusion to the conversation of the males, Mrs. Blandings turned on her husband in well-bred anger.

But before she could say what was on her mind Mr. O'Neill returned.

"Say," he said, "I'm certainly a hot salesman. First thing I should have done was sell you some more insurance on your house, but I got so interested talking about other things I plain forgot."

Mrs. Blandings watched in silent female scorn while this transparent deception enmeshed her husband. When Mr. O'Neill was ready to leave a second time Mr. Blandings had approximately

137

doubled his insurance and had thanked Mr. O'Neill for his thoughtful kindness in bringing the subject forward. Somehow, Mr. O'Neill had heard all about the anonymous Frenchman's offer for the Blandings house; you couldn't beat the French for shrewdness in values, could you, Mr. O'Neill inquired. That had done it.

But at any rate, the school board matter had advanced a few dim steps.

"What would I have to do if I were to . . . run?" Mr. Blandings had asked, halting and feeling foolish over the verb.

"The less the better," Mr. O'Neill had bellowed. "I mean," he said, having himself heard an overtone in his remark that was not in tune with what he had intended, "don't do anything; just leave it to me. Busy man like you, there's no reason you should bother your head more than you have to."

It had all left Mr. Blandings with a fine sense of growth, accomplishment, and internal ease. At last, a goal was ahead of him, a definite tangible goal. Somebody wanted him to do what he himself wanted to do. It even looked as if somebody was going to do it for him.

"Friends," said Mr. Blandings quietly, "a relative newcomer in this community must show a fitting modesty in bringing forward new proposals, particularly when they affect the lives of the generation that will someday succeed us, and render their judgment on us, good or ill."

There was an intense silence.

"Education," Mr. Blandings continued, "is the keystone of our social arch. Every ill in our community, our country, indeed in our present-day world finds its root-cause inevitably in a failure of education. Such failures are *our* failures."

If this was a daring way to open the topic, there was no indication that the audience was made hostile by it.

"My plan," Mr. Blandings went on, "is neither complex nor expensive. It is, however, far reaching, and the one absolute requisite for its success is the boldness of vision with which it be applied. Halfway measures will not do. The time for faltering and indecision has passed. We are at last brought face to face with inescapable alternatives. The hour has struck."

There was a rap, and Mr. Blandings turned in its direction.

"Is that you in the bathroom?" said Mrs. Blandings.

Mr. Blandings opened the door sulkily. The full-length mirror on its back swung his image out of sight; with it into oblivion went the sea of faces upturned to hear the Blandings Plan from the lips of the man whose revolutionary proposal it was.

There was a moment during which wife and husband debated whether to pretend that the one had not caught the other in the midst of an unusually full-blown fantasy with sound. Mrs. Blandings found a middle course.

"If you really want this school board job as much as you seem to," she said, "I think it would be a fine idea to give that speech to a live audience. I'm sure with all your practice it must be really good by now."

The trouble was, Mr. Blandings said to himself later, that the Blandings Plan wasn't yet entirely clear; something always threw a distraction into the works just as he placed the two fingers of one hand in the palm of the other and said "Firstly."

It was Mr. Urmot Nellus, editor of the Lansdale *Blade*, who eventually spilled the beans. Mr. Blandings met him on the threshold of Lansdale Liquors one sunny Saturday morning when both of them were stocking up for the weekend.

"I'll have to hand it to Ed O'Neill," said Mr. Nellus.

Mr. Blandings issued a smile. He knew perfectly well what Mr. Nellus was talking about, or thought he did, but modesty forbade any forthright rejoinder.

"Yes sir," said Mr. Nellus, "and I admire you too."

"Why," said Mr. Blandings, "nonsense; there's nothing to admire about merely—"

"Sure there is," said Mr. Nellus. "Takes nerve. Too few people would do it."

"Well," said Mr. Blandings, "I suppose I ought to go out and do a little campaigning. My wife thinks so. After all, I've got an uphill fight on my hands."

"Fight?" said Mr. Nellus. "You haven't got any fight on your hands. That's why I said I admired you. It's what I mean by having nerve."

139

It was apparent there was a misunderstanding somewhere.

"Take my advice," said Mr. Nellus, "and don't complicate things by doing any fighting. Last thing Ed O'Neill would want or expect. Like he was saying to me when I covered the caucus last night: 'Blandings is ideal—just new enough to fill the bill exactly.' Ed has just one job when something special like this comes up, and that's to find somebody's willing to stand up and get walked on. He just wanted somebody to lend his name to a show of opposition, sort of—a name to go on the ballot. I thought he explained that to you."

"But—" said Mr. Blandings. A high-speed transvaluation of values was taking place in his mind. He was the fall guy, the patsy, the easy mark—it was instantly and painfully apparent to him, and he wondered why he had not known it all along.

"But there are Democrats on the school board," he said, in a vacant-sounding voice.

"Sure," said Mr. Nellus. "The board's bipartisan; three Republicans, two Democrats. Regular times, soon as a person gets named in the party caucus he's as good as elected. But this is something different; you're a candidate to fill a vacancy, so there's only one to be elected but there's two candidates; in a deal like that there's never been a Democrat elected in this town since anyone can remember."

"I'll be frank with you," said Mr. O'Neill. "If you were to be elected to the school board in this town I for one would be surprised. Pleasantly surprised, that is, but surprised." His large Irish face beamed with what appeared to be candor of the first order.

Mr. Blandings looked glumly about him in Mr. O'Neill's bare, echoing office. He had come for a showdown, but Mr. O'Neill displayed no consciousness of guilt.

"I don't see where I didn't put the proposition to you just the way I'd put it again if I had it to do all over," he said. "We're the minority party up here when it comes to town elections, but we're making progress. The reason we're making progress is that we're trying to get good candidates to run for office."

This was mildly mollifying.

"I don't mind not being elected," said Mr. Blandings; "what I mind is being licked as an absolutely surefire proposition. No

140

chance; no whisper of a chance, and nothing I can do about it."

"Why worry?" said Mr. O'Neill. "Just relax and take it easy. Look. This crowd of New Yorkers that's come to live more or less in Lansdale is always talking about improving the standards of this and that, but they don't never *do* anything at all. Anse Dolliver spends his life being afraid they will, but he's safe as a church. But *you* can really do something by just standing up on election day and getting mowed down. I didn't tell you you were going to be elected. We agreed there ought to be some new blood in the situation, that we did. I just happen to think that on account of your fire—and not forgetting that letter of yours in the paper a couple of months back, of course—you might get as many as one vote for every two for your opponent, and that would be far from bad, believe you me. The question none of this New York crowd, or most people that are always yelling about politics, can answer is, how are good people ever going to get elected unless you *start* somewheres? The way you start in politics is by getting licked. It's as simple as that. If you want to help this community, one way you can help it is letting Eph Hackett tromp on you. 'Twon't hurt you none, and it might do some good."

"Besides," said Mr. O'Neill, "there might be a miracle happen. How do *you* know?"

· 18 ·

MR. BLANDINGS would always remember the hour of the telephone call, for he had just looked at his watch and risen to go upstairs to bed when the bell rang. It was 10:32 P.M. New York was calling. What would New York want at this hour of the night?

"Mr. Blandings," said a sepulchral voice in the receiver, "this is the Associated Press."

Every impropriety in Mr. Blandings' life since pubescence passed instantly before him.

"Yes?" he said.

"Sorry to break in on you at this hour of the night," said the AP man. "I just wanted to ask a few questions in regards to Joan H. Blandings, age fourteen. She's your daughter, is that right?"

For a moment, Mr. Blandings' voice was muted altogether by an elemental fear. But Joan H. Blandings, age fourteen, his beloved, serious, little blond-and-brown-eyed daughter was indubitably at this moment asleep in her bedroom, just above him. Only an hour ago she had gone to bed, the picture of serenity and self-composure. Why should the great Associated Press want to know anything about her? Mr. Blandings took a deep breath to quiet his beating heart.

"That's right," he said; "what's—"

"Just give me a brief line on her personality," said the AP man. "Would you describe her as a healthy, normal, out-of-doors type girl, still too young to have much interest in boys?"

"Certainly I would," said Mr. Blandings, trying to still the shaking hand that held the receiver.

"Likes to help her mother in the kitchen, and all that sort of thing?" said the AP man. "Does she have any unusual pets or anything like that?"

142

"No," said Mr. Blandings. "I'd like to be told—"

"Just one more question," said the AP man. "Has she ever done anything like this before?"

"Like *what* before?" said Mr. Blandings. "I'm trying to find out what this is all about."

There was a moment of silence at the other end of the line. When the AP man spoke again, it was in a different tone of voice. "You really don't know anything about this?" he asked.

"I don't know a thing about anything," said Mr. Blandings. "I'm trying to find out from you."

"That certainly adds a colorful angle," said the AP man. "What about your wife? She didn't know anything either?"

"When I don't know what a thing's about I can't very well determine whether my wife knows about it or not," said Mr. Blandings; "but nothing has come up between my wife and myself about our daughter except routine parental matters."

"Just a moment till I get that down," said the AP man. "That'll do for a quote." Mr. Blandings contained himself while a typewriter at the other end of the line clacked out a long sentence.

"I'm sorry," said the AP man, coming back on the line, "I assumed you'd have known already, but I guess we're a little ahead of you. By the way, my name's Robard Splinters—R-o-b—"

"Let me have it, Mr. Splinters," said Mr. Blandings.

"I have a fourteen-year-old girl myself," said Mr. Splinters, "so I know how you're going to feel."

Mr. Blandings waited.

"Well," said Mr. Splinters, "here it is."

Fifteen minutes later, dazed, Mr. Blandings put out the lights in his study, put out the lights in the empty living room, and slowly mounted the stairs. The eleventh tread emitted a desperate groan. He faced the door of his younger daughter's room, and slowly opened it, waiting for it, too, to groan, as all otherwise silent things did in a country house after ten o'clock at night. It gave out no sound.

Before him lay his younger daughter, locked fast in sleep. The picture that confronted Mr. Blandings was the sort of picture he had seldom seen except in the four-color double spreads of bed

143

and mattress companies. Joan's face was relaxed and beautiful as a seraph's. She lay on her side, one hand between her cheek and pillow, the other trailing just outside the covers. Her pretty hair was divided into two clusters behind her neck, each tied, for the night's safekeeping, with a small blue bow. To complete the whole candybox composition, bright moonlight struck a shaft across her pillow.

I can't wake her, Mr. Blandings said to himself. I thought I could, but I can't. I even feel like an intruder, opening her door and looking at her this way. Good God, I begat her, and I watched her mother suffer giving her birth, and I used to change her damn little didies twenty times a day. Now she's not my baby any more, and I'm intruding on her.

Joan stirred faintly in her sleep, and Mr. Blandings made haste to close himself out of his daughter's room.

In the master bedroom, Mrs. Blandings was poised to snap out the reading light between the beds.

"Muriel," said Mr. Blandings, "Joanie has just won first prize in an international contest on what to do about the Atomic Bomb."

"Wait a minute," said Mrs. Blandings. She sat up and removed from her ears two pledgets of soft rubber which she inserted every night, not to be awakened by the thunderous morning symphony of the birds on Bald Mountain. "Now."

"Joanie," said Mr. Blandings, a vast impatience roiling within him, "has just won the first prize of a medal and a $500 bond from *Nubile Girlhood Magazine.*"

"Good heavens," said Mrs. Blandings, "*what* for?"

"For the best essay on 'What the Atomic Age Means to a Girl on the Threshold of Life,'" said Mr. Blandings. "She gets a free trip to Washington and the magazine is trying to get Vannevar Bush of the Carnegie Institution to present the medal, and she's to be the guest of honor at the Bureau of Standards, and maybe she'll be given her bond by the President on the White House steps."

"She hasn't a thing to wear," said Mrs. Blandings.

Downstairs, the telephone rang again.

"Hello," said Mr. Blandings. "Yes, I'll be glad to talk to the United Press. That's right. Fourteen now, fifteen next February. Just a normal, healthy, out-of-doors type. Little too young to be

144

interested in boys yet. Yes, a great help to her mother in the kitchen. She hasn't any dogs or cats for pets, but she's raising hamsters in the cellar. Hamsters. Oh yes, she confides everything in her mother and me; naturally we're very pleased and proud."

"Muriel," said Mr. Blandings, upstairs again, "that was the UP." Mrs. Blandings once more removed the stopples from her ears. The telephone resumed its ringing.

It was the New York *Times.* A gentlemanly voice apologized for the lateness of the hour. "That's a very attractive human interest story we've just picked up from the AP," the voice said, "particularly the angle about neither you nor her mother knowing anything about Joanie's being in the contest."

Mr. Blandings lost himself for a moment in the recollection of what he had just told the UP to the contrary. "Pardon me?" he asked the voice from the *Times.*

The voice cleared its throat for a more succinct repetition: "We'd like to send our own man up to Lansdale first thing in the morning for a follow-up. We want to make certain that Joanie will be around for a little talk and a few pictures and so on."

"She'll be here," said Mr. Blandings, "as far as I know."

He answered the telephone four more times before he got to bed

During the course of the Saturday morning it was inevitable that Mr. Blandings should bump into Mr. Dolliver. Mr. Blandings had a deep-seated loathing for Mr. Dolliver as a skinflint country banker, but this morning he wore a different aspect.

"I think it's up to me to congratulate the father of this splendid little girl," said Mr. Dolliver. He smiled and held out his hand. Mr. Blandings shook it gravely, wishing that Joan had not winced so noticeably when Mr. Dolliver patted her on the head. "That's very generous of you," he said, setting the muscles of his face in a smile.

"Mighty proud," said Mr. Dolliver. "Mighty proud." His radio had broadcast the news last night, and he had seen the morning papers. The wire stories, at various lengths, were to be found in the *News,* the *Times,* the *Mirror,* the *Herald Tribune.* Despite various excisions the phrase "typical American community of Lansdale" occurred in each. In each paper also young Joanie

145

Blandings was listed as a student in "the Anson Dolliver High School"; the ultra-conscientious *Times* had even pointed out that the school was named after Mr. Dolliver's great-grandfather, and had been built in the 1920's when the present Mr. Dolliver had been the school board chairman.

It was wonderful the way the press of America served America. Mr. Dolliver was untrained in journalism, but his eye for special situations was very keen. If four New York newspapers carried a story about a young girl's brilliant accomplishment in the typical American community of Lansdale with which the name of Dolliver was prominently associated, then, over the nation, four hundred newspapers would doubtless carry the same story. The clipping service to which, for years, he had subscribed for anything with the name of Lansdale in it would cost him quite a sum this time at a nickel a clipping but he would not begrudge it. Mr. Dolliver decried "publicity," but an occurrence like this was another matter.

Dr. Wambly, the high-school superintendent, came flying down the schoolhouse steps in front of which a score of people were already gathered, Saturday though it was.

"Mr. Dolliver," he said, "there is a man here who says he is from *Life*, and he and his young woman assistant are rearranging the science laboratory rather drastically."

"Well," said Mr. Dolliver, who had lighted a cigar and was flicking at it gently, "I think whatever breakage is incurred can properly be charged off to, ah, call it a good cause."

"That was rather my own thought also," said Dr. Wambly, who up to that moment had been empty of any mentation whatsoever.

"Why don't we all go up and see if we can give him a helping hand," said Mr. Dolliver, selflessly.

"Precisely what I was about to have suggested," said Dr. Wambly.

Shoulder to shoulder, Mr. Blandings and Mr. Dolliver, strange companions, walked up the long shallow steps of the high-school building, a crowd slowly thickening behind them. As they approached the science laboratory at the rear of a long gloomy hall, there came a sound as if a heavily ornamented Christmas tree had been run into by a blimp. A voice spoke, with heavy emotion.

"I don't care if you are from the New York *Times*," it said; "the

146

next time you decide to sit down just kindly look where you are going to put it, that's all."

"Good morning, gentlemen," said Mr. Dolliver, striding in with an air of modest self-confidence. "A small mishap?"

The *Life* photographer, obviously the aggrieved party in the crash, withdrew a malevolent stare from a tall man who was fumbling unhappily with the seat of his trousers, and turned something less baleful on Mr. Dolliver. A blazing ten thousand watts of light flooded the little laboratory, and showed a brilliant multicolored carpet of powdered glass on the worn linoleum floor.

"Are you in this act?" he demanded of Mr. Dolliver.

Dr. Wambly stepped forward, trembling violently, and effected a set of introductions that mislabeled everyone. "All right, Mr. Dolliver," said the *Life* photographer, addressing Mr. Blandings, "if you're the head of this show maybe you can help us get a little co-operation. We're paying demurrage on a DC-6 that's waiting for me at the airport. I've got to be in Trans-Jordan come hell or high water tomorrow afternoon and I've got to get this out of the way first. Meanwhile I'm getting no place fast."

"I've made an inventory, Mr. Eiskerat," said a brisk young lady in gray, addressing the *Life* photographer.

"Thanks, Snooty," said Mr. Eiskerat; "this is Miss Snoodarian, my researcher, ladies and gentlemen. Three Erlenmeyer flasks, one half-dozen Petri dishes, two burettes and stand, two 500 cc. retorts, three pipettes, six 500 cc. beakers, and one set of Geissler tubes on mahogany base."

He looked at Mr. Blandings. "Frankly, Mr. Dolliver," he said, "I don't know how Steichen himself would go about creating the Atomic Age out of this stuff—particularly since All the News That's Fit to Print has sat on the Geissler tubes, which were my only hope. I think our best bet is to pack up this whole crowd and fly it up to M.I.T. in Cambridge, where we could really have something to work with. This the young lady?"

"Mr. Hicks particularly said he wanted the rural schoolhouse element stressed in the pictures," said Miss Snoodarian.

"It's just dandy for Hicks to sit in his office and sound off," said Mr. Eiskerat, "but how does he expect me to get the twenty-first century in the background with a couple of pieces of china and

147

a burette? That's what he said to me: 'Get a sort of atmospheric suggestion of the twenty-first century by background laboratory glassware.' The most modern piece of equipment in this place dates back to 1882, it was made in Germany, and into the bargain it's busted."

"In recent years," said Mr. Dolliver, "there has been a dearth of funds expendable for equipment, and then of course the war—"

"Look, Mr. Blandings," said Mr. Eiskerat, "your gratifying position as the father of this little girl—"

"I want to correct an unfortunate misapprehension of which I am the guilty one," said Dr. Wambly. "Inadvertently, I—"

He attempted to re-identify Mr. Blandings and Mr. Dolliver in Mr. Eiskerat's mind, but in his anguish got it wrong again. "That's the way I understood it the first time," said Mr. Eiskerat. Before Mr. Dolliver could fix Dr. Wambly with an outthrust jaw all the ten thousand watts of lighting went out.

"*Now* what the hell," said Mr. Eiskerat.

"Fuse must of blowed with all that load on it," said the school janitor, speaking for the first time. "Coulda told anybody."

"Look," said Mr. Eiskerat; "if I'm not in Trans-Jordan by six o'clock tomorrow afternoon—"

"Merv," said Mr. Dolliver, speaking to the janitor and using his authoritative voice for the first time that morning, "get the fuses fixed up and let us try to offer every co-operation to the press."

"Time out," said Mr. Eiskerat. "Snooty, I have an idea. Go to the dime store. Buy one of everything in the place that's made of glass, and be back here in as close to half an hour as you can. And I'll go to that hardware store we saw down by the station, and come back with as much aluminumware as I can carry. We may not be able to give Hicks the twenty-first century, but maybe we can give him an itty-bitty taste of the twenty-second."

"Dr. Wambly," said Mr. Dolliver, "in the interval might I see you in your office for just a moment?"

A large, unidentified lady, radiating the principles of creative living, circled and landed in front of the heroine and her father. "This must be darling Joanie," said the lady. "Joanie, sweetest, aren't you just too thrilled to be alive?"

Joanie looked at the lady with displeasure.

"I'm Mrs. Hinchcliff," said the lady, "Dillys Hinchcliff. I'm Director of Special Events for *Nubile Girlhood*. I declare I don't know when I've been so excited myself."

She turned a look of inquiry on Mr. Blandings.

"This is my father," said Joan.

"Oh," said Mrs. Hinchcliff. "I thought that other gentleman—"

A siren sounded in the street below; not the shrieking siren of a fire truck but the urgent-moaning type associated with ambulances. Everybody moved toward the windows just in time to see two enormous trucks, painted a sleek purple and entirely closed in, draw up to the curb. On their sides was lettered in shaded gold "Sight & Sound Division: Intersensory Corporation."

"I declare I don't know when I've been so embarrassed," said Mrs. Hinchcliff. "Joanie was supposed to get her letter of notification before any of this happened, but somehow it just didn't get sent out. I guess we'll just sort of have to make things up as we go along, won't we, Joanie?"

"I guess we will," said Joanie. She said it with a sort of relish that was lost on Mrs. Hinchcliff but that caused her father, during the rest of the morning, to study her inscrutable young face with anxiety.

The miracle of what Lorbet Neen called Mass Communication Media, Mr. Blandings decided during the next few days, as his daughter's publicity bandwagon kept roaring on and on, was that out of the vast, shallow confusion of their inquiries anything remotely resembling actuality could emerge at all. There certainly was freedom of inquiry in America, he reflected. Let a piece of news break, or even a piece of pseudo-news like this, and an army of men and women with repeater pencils, headphones, miracle shutters, ultra-lenses, throat mikes, parabolic reflectors, and amphibious darkrooms were on the scene in a flash. The men who so deftly handled this complex equipment were a little on the tough side, a little inclined to order everybody around in the name of their freedom, but certainly good-natured and well disposed. But they provided, as Mr. Blandings saw it, one more example of what was happening in twentieth-century America: the substitution of activity for thought; of technique for understanding. At the center

149

of their labors, as at the center of a hurricane, there was a vacuum.

Why, Mr. Blandings asked himself, were press, radio, and newsreels spending so much time and money on the whole business anyway? His daughter, who was bearing herself with a mature dignity through everything and was turning out to be remarkably photogenic, had written a young and nobly serious theme on the atom, radioactivity, and the female sex, and somebody had decided it was better than all the other pieces so written—some of them by older girls or young women. For that matter, thought Mr. Blandings, it's better than I could do myself, but still what of it, what's the vast excitement? He could only wonder. He was slightly galled by the role assigned him in the saga: the father of the Genius, so dull a clod as not to know what he harbored under his own roof. He had been interviewed and photographed extensively, but everything about him seemed to have landed in the wastebasket except for a sentence from a three-column story in the *Times'* best monotone, which read:

> Joan's father, a New York advertising executive, is active in local politics.

MR. DOLLIVER had reached a conclusion, radical but sound. Over his radio he had listened to Joanie Blandings' reception of her medal of honor, pressed upon her by the head of the Bureau of Standards, acting in place of Dr. Vannevar Bush, who had suddenly pleaded a confusion on his calendar. And every news commentator that day had had two minutes' worth to say about the simple, touching ceremony in which the President of the United States had taken time off from the world crises that engulfed him, left Ambassadors and Foreign Ministers and Special Missions waiting while he stepped to the microphone and newsreel cameras to hand to Miss Joan Blandings a $500 bond of the United States of America and make a little speech about Our Children, the Heritage of the Future, Enduring Peace, and our excellent rate of progress in stockpiling atomic bomb matériel. Mr. Dolliver's own name had dropped by the wayside in this secondary wave of publicity, but he did not care too deeply: "the typical American community of Lansdale" was still in copper-riveted apposition to every mention of his homeland in every broadcast. And there had also come over the air an announcement that the gifted young girl scientist, Miss Joanie Blandings, would be a guest star on the Hot Tots Program next Thursday night. That had pretty much settled things in his mind.

Now, as he sat on his wide screened porch, overlooking Shamalaug Lake, Mr. Dolliver glanced among his visitors, and quietly flung his bombshell.

"But Anse," said Mr. Ephemus Hackett when he got his breath, "you can't do this to me. You just can't. Particularly not with *him*." He gestured in a northwest direction with a dark brown bourbon highball.

Mr. Dolliver took a small sip of White Rock, lightly iced.

"Martha," he called into the living room, "get Urm Nellus on the telephone at the *Blade* office, tell him who's calling, and hand me the phone out here on the porch."

He looked at Mr. Hackett mildly. "Let's not get sentimental," he said.

"But Anse," said Mr. Hackett, "why do you want to do such a thing to me?"

"Just take it easy, Eph," said Mr. Dolliver; "I'm not forgetting you're a cousin of mine. This election is just to fill an unexpired term, remember; next year, when all this business is forgotten, you'll be just as well off as you ever were. Meanwhile, it wouldn't hurt you to pay some attention to that lumber business of yours."

Martha silently presented the phone to Mr. Dolliver.

"Urm?" said Mr. Dolliver; "where you been keeping yourself?"

An answer crackled in the receiver.

"It's mighty funny," said Mr. Doliver. "*Life*'s had a couple of people up here, the newsreels have all sent crews, the wire services have come and gone, the New York *Times* sent its own man up, the Sunday supplements are digging in, but I don't see any evidence the Lansdale *Blade* knows anything's going on at all."

The receiver crackled again.

"Certainly I'm in favor of it," said Mr. Dolliver, "and what difference do my opinions make anyway?" He glanced irritably at Mr. Hackett, who had fumbled his drink onto the floor.

"Okay, Urm," he said. "Now, I have a suggestion to make about an editorial, which I think would make a very good one, if it was worded right, but you can take it or leave it, just as you please." There was a pause.

"Maybe you'd better get out a pencil," said Mr. Dolliver. He waited a minute, and then on some unheard cue from the other end, he resumed.

"It would be about this school-board election coming up next week. If I was writing it I'd call attention to the fact that the Anson Dolliver High School has just enjoyed a signal honor in having one of its pupils get national attention in the most important situation confronting the whole world, see? I'd name the girl, and then I'd walk right up to the fact that her father is a candidate for the board in the elections, see? I'd say that Eph Hackett, his Republican opponent, has been a faithful and efficient servant of the town in various capacities for twenty years—and here's where how you word it would be important—not come right out and say new blood is needed, but somehow get it across without saying it. You'd know how to do that better than I would. And then you could quote me as having shaken hands with this Blandings and saying, 'We will abide by the decision of the voters and may the best man win.' Just that, Urm, nothing more. I think it would make an attractive item."

Mr. Dolliver said an elaborate goodbye, and replaced the phone carefully on its cradle. Nobody said anything at all.

"No questions?" said Mr. Dolliver.

"Yes," said Mr. Hackett, in a strange, underwater voice. "For the third and last time I'm asking you why you're pulling the plug on me and letting this guy from York State and the City get my seat on the school board. I got a right to know."

Mr. Dolliver turned on him suddenly.

"Because it'll look good, that's why," he said, between his teeth. 'Suppose we go down the line and let Blandings be counted out next Monday, right after all this talk about his genius daughter as the product of Lansdale, the typical American community, and before *Life* comes out with its pictures, even. How'll that look? This election right here in Lansdale next Monday is going to be the only school-board election in the country that ever made news across the whole United States. If he loses it's going to be messy reading. It ain't going to seem very democratic."

"How long since you been interested in being democratic?" said Mr. Hackett.

"There's such a thing as knowing a good time to lose an election," said Mr. Dolliver. "When Blandings' year's up you can come back, stronger than ever, because he'll have made a fool of himself in the meantime. It's a smart idea to give a little ground when it's in the cards that you're going to get it all back later, *with* interest. You learn a few things running a bank, you know."

153

"Anse," said Mr. Hackett, "you and I had the same maternal grandmother, and so help me, if she was alive today—"

"Don't fret, Eph," said Mr. Dolliver. "Why my goodness, I don't even know for sure that Blandings is going to make the school board. It's just a surmise on my part, that's all."

Of course it was unfortunate that when *Life* appeared with six of the two hundred pictures that Mr. Eiskerat had taken before the flight to Trans-Jordan on which he had crashed and died, the captions on the pictures of Mr. Blandings and Mr. Dolliver were reversed. Mr. Dolliver, a realist, wasted no time composing a letter to the editors. He merely summoned Dr. Wambly and gave the unfortunate originator of the misunderstanding a hideous repetition of the upbraiding that had almost destroyed him the day the pictures were taken.

The election was over, anyway. Mr. Blandings was in. Precisely as Mr. Dolliver had predicted, it had been the most publicized election to a school board in all America. The follow-up stories on Joan Blandings' father were beginning to cost Mr. Dolliver a new mountain of nickels paid out to the clipping bureau, but it would all die down fast, now. Mr. Dolliver was so pleased with his stratagem of losing an election for the greater good of the Grand Old Party that when he met Mr. Blandings on the village green he tried out the effects of a synthetic chagrin. It worked beautifully. Mr. Blandings wrung Mr. Dolliver's hand, acknowledged the good fight, and became vaunted and puffed up in a concealed way. The finest traditions of Anglo-Saxon good fellowship were regnant.

The first suggestion that events were to take an unfortunate turn occurred far from Lansdale, in Studio Five of the Interworld Broadcasting System. It was not that Joanie did not distinguish herself as the guest star of the Hot Tots program, but rather that she distinguished herself too well.

"I never dreamed our little baby would be so completely placid about something like this," said Mrs. Blandings, as she and her husband listened fondly to the radio. Joan's calm, precise voice had just finished discussing the equivalence of mass and energy.

"Excellent," said the Master of Ceremonies—the emcee, in the

154

language of Mr. Blandings' trade. "And now here's our next question: the Ancients used to think that there were four elements: earth, air, fire, and water. How many elements do we know about today?"

It was obvious from the scrabble that came over the Blandings' radio that every little hand in the studio had shot up in answer to this primary-school question. The emcee picked the youngest.

"All right Jimmy. Plutonium was the ninety-fourth? Well, that is . . . yes, that is correct. Joanie, you want to add something?"

"It won't stop there," said Joanie. The studio audience roared appreciation of some learned jest. "There are going to be a hundred or so before it's all over."

"Gosh," said the emcee in his most eloquently human vein, "that's a lot of elements. What makes us so sure?"

"The Periodic Table," said Joanie.

"Now what's that?" said the emcee. "I've heard of kitchen tables and railroad timetables but—"

"The Periodic Table," said Joan, crisply, after the roars of laughter had died down, "was invented or discovered or whatever you want to call it, by a Russian—"

A deadly echoing silence came over the studio audience. In the control room, an agonized engineer raised a trembling hand toward a switch that could cut the program off the air and flood the ether with organ music from the mighty Wurlitzer. Perhaps in a second the sharp stab of a telephone bell would give him vice-presidential aid in the name of Policy.

"—a Russian scientist by the name of Dmitri Mendelyeev," Joanie went on. "He died in 1907. In the past quite a number of Russian scientists have made notable contributions to progress. This was one of the greatest ever made by anyone."

The control-room engineer sat like an ice statue in the sun: frozen but dripping.

"Speaking of great contributions to progress," said the emcee, "here's Earl Hibbic, to say a word to us about the new, *improved* Zafties that everyone's talking about: the only atomized breakfast food that—"

It was cuing the end commercial thirty-five seconds too soon, and unless Earl Hibbic could slow himself down a little, or try

155

the dangerous expedient of ad-libbing, there would be a spot of
organ music at the end of the program after all. But the situation
was saved.

In the living room of his home on Bald Mountain, the adoring
father of Miss Joan Blandings, age fourteen, rose to snap off the
radio. "What lucky parents we are to have such a brilliant, en-
chanting little daughter," he said.

"Oh but aren't we," said Mrs. Blandings, fondly. "If the child
has a single fault it's that she has just the slightest, teeniest inher-
ited tendency to volunteer more information on a subject than
she's been asked for." She offered her husband a slow, sweet smile
and picked up her sewing basket.

Mr. Blandings considered four possible retorts but dismissed
them all. He rediscovered the place in the volume he had set aside
as the radio time approached, and bent himself again diligently
over a page.

"It should not be thought," said Dr. Abraham Udderweld on
page 384, "that the *id* is necessarily the reservoir out of which
abreaction is always spontaneously generated in those cases where
a psychic lesion has previously been determined. On the contrary,
the *id* . . ."

As things turned out, it was unfortunate also that no one, up
to now, except presumably the judges for *Nubile Girlhood,* had
ever read the essay with which Joanie had won her gratifying
prize. The instantaneous swarm of mass communicators to the
scene of an Occurrence had ferreted out practically everything
except the Occurrence itself.

This natural oversight now came into process of correction.

Perhaps Joanie could have avoided all the trouble by a few simple eliminations in her essay if she had just had a little friendly
advice from a competent adult. Months later, testifying before a
Congressional Committee, she solemnly stated that it was her belief that she could not have. By that time, however, the whole
question of whether she could or couldn't was an academic matter,
and it brought no mitigation of the corroding bitterness that was
eating out the soul of Mr. Anson Dolliver.

The hideous defect in Joanie's essay, a great columnist began

156

by pointing out, was its attitude of drooling veneration of Madame Curie. Through the exercise of unusual enterprise, nature not stated, the columnist had come on a copy of this essay and could state that not once but half-a-dozen times the juvenile author had cited the co-discoverer of radium as *the* woman of the modern world who should be the model for conduct among women who would live in the age of the sundered atom. Now the first time Joe Glunk, American, got a whiff of this, the columnist went on, it probably smelled all right. Radium cost $25,000 per gram and its discoverers were French. Joe knows the Frogs came to the aid of the American colonies during the war for independence from England, and twice within the present blighted century Uncle Sam paid off with everything he had to get the Frogs turned belly down again.

So far so good, the columnist continued. The smell began to get a little high when you looked more closely at the Curie dame—who was not French by birth at all, but a Pole from Poland, of the original name of Sklodowska. La Curie's Frog husband had died in 1906, so you couldn't put the tag on him, but the lady of his choice had lived until 1934, which as the faithful well remember was a year after Franklin Delano Roosevelt and his crew took over the White House. In the twenty-eight years between her mate's death and her own, this Mrs. Curie, or Sklodowska, had made no bones about her own political views. La Curie was a Socialist, which in 1906 talk meant what we mean today when we say a man is a Commie.

Nor is that anything like near all. Let us now take up the thread of some of this lady's direct and collateral relatives. It is interesting to note that more than one of them had been personally befriended by the Great Eleanor in the days when she made the White House a hot-dog stand for every stray political cur who happened to be within sniffing distance . . .

Certainly nothing much will come of that farrago, thought Mr. Blandings.

It was to the credit of Mr. Anson Dolliver that when it turned up among his clippings he did not understand it at all. He was an un-paranoid man, who had never had any luck in following involutional thought.

The day of Mr. Dolliver's great betrayal was in mid-November. He had been sitting in his office reading a document from his clearinghouse district when Mr. Ephemus Hackett clopped wordlessly in and handed him a city newspaper with a great deal of heavy type for the headlines. Smack in the middle of page one was a two-column heading with the simple words, An Editorial. Mr. Dolliver began to read. His face became a mottled purple.

"Me!" he said.

"Yep," said Mr. Hackett. He had little experience of how to feel or express exultation but for a late beginner he was not doing badly.

It was too much to be believed. It was fantastic and a delirium. Mr. Dolliver gathered all his strength and wrenched at himself like a man in the last stages of a nightmare. But the horror did not abate.

"Like it says here," said Mr. Hackett, reading aloud, "'A fourteen-year-old girl who pens a clever justification of subversive characters in the guise of writing about our own American Atom Bomb cannot herself be blamed.'"

"Don't read another line of it," said Mr. Dolliver.

"'However,'" Mr. Hackett continued in flat disobedience, "'the true culprits must be ferreted out and publicly exposed. What kind of TEACHERS set this girl on the path of PERFIDY AND BETRAYAL? What is the Anson Dolliver High School? What sort of SCHOOL BOARD governs it? That such an outrage could happen in a typically American community like Lansdale, an outwardly tranquil New England town that boasts of its proud AMERICAN heritage, is just one more example of the terrifying ability of our ENEMIES to spread a poison at the very roots of AMERICAN life. The little red schoolhouse, that was pure & white inside, is no more. Instead we have WHITED SEPULCHERS—million dollar edifices like the ANSON DOLLIVER HIGH SCHOOL—and inside they're dyed RED.'"

It was impossible to tell whether Mr. Dolliver was conscious.

"The next sentence is *all* in capitals," said Mr. Hackett. "That's where it begins to talk about you personally."

158

Mr. Dolliver's telephone chose that moment to ring. Mr. Dolliver got the receiver to his ear by a series of coarse twitches. Republican State Headquarters was at the other end of the line.

"For Christ's sake," said Headquarters, with no preliminaries, "what sort of a mess have you got everybody into down there?"

Mr. Dolliver said something that was not only not convincing but not coherent.

"Speak up," said Headquarters. "What is this Blandings father-and-daughter act that you've swallowed hook, line, and sinker?"

Mr. Dolliver made an attempt to explain.

"Don't tell me any more," said the Headquarters' voice. "I know the type. Class traitors. I've seen 'em by the hundred. Plenty of money in the bank thanks to the Capitalistic System, but want to get out and destroy what's put them where they are. Roosevelt type. He doesn't surprise me half as much as you do. He must be a damn smart guy to pull the wool over your eyes so that he can actually use the head of the Lansdale G.O.P. organization as a Front for Moscow."

There was more. There was the suggestion that Mr. Dolliver might not be a delegate to the next Republican National Convention. There was the further suggestion that Headquarters might want to see a successor to Mr. Dolliver installed as the boss of Lansdale immediately. There was a great deal more, and Mr. Ephemus Hackett heard it all, for although nothing could be gained from Mr. Dolliver's answers, the vibrant voice on the phone could be heard five feet away.

When it was all over, Mr. Hackett was no longer exultant. If his own betrayal by Mr. Dolliver had now resulted in Mr. Dolliver's scalding discomfiture that was one thing; but as the facts seemed to be looming, a great and more terrible crisis might engulf every right-thinking member of the community—and all as the result of one moment's relaxation of the vigilance that was the everlasting price of—well, if not Liberty then certainly that higher discipline, Conformity.

Mr. Dolliver faced Mr. Hackett, and a slight measure of strength returned to him. "You're the guy who let this Blandings family into the community in the first place," he said. "You and those

159

thirty-one and one-half acres, more or less, you sold him out of your top land back when you did."

"Now look," said Mr. Hackett.

"Look nothing," said Mr. Dolliver. "I'm in a jam because I let myself be misled by a kind instinct. It's not the first time, but it's the last. If I have some cleaning up to do around here, by God it's going to be thorough, and it won't necessarily stop with Blandings." He glared at Mr. Hackett; he was not sure what crime he wished to pin on him, but he needed a temporary scapegoat. "So watch your step," he snarled. "If anything leaks out about this telephone conversation I'll know where it came from, and whose head to break. Go out and sell somebody some lumber; you've got an overdue payment on your note with us right now, and maybe one of those bank examiners is going to walk right in here this morning."

That evening, on Bald Mountain's top, Mr. Blandings finished Chapter XIV of Dr. Udderweld's *Ego, Id and Anxiety*. He felt delightfully at ease. He was now not merely a dweller in the community of Lansdale Town, but part and parcel of its being. He had arrived. He had yet to attend his first meeting of the school board but he felt more pleasure in his membership in it than in any reward of money, medals, or prestige that his profession of advertising had ever brought him. He glanced at his little daughter and observed with pleasure the gleam on her slender wrist of the silver watch he had given her to show his pride in her accomplishment. In a way, he thought to himself, in a way Joanie has had something to do with my own success. It was drawing a rather fine bow to put it that way, but he felt so relaxed and mellow that he was happy to share a little extra credit here and there. It was not a bad old world. Momentarily, he could think of no flaw in his relationships with Lansdale, the United States of America, or the spinning globe.

"You take this Dolliver chap," he said suddenly aloud to Mrs. Blandings. "He's not a bad fellow at all. I shouldn't be surprised if he and I got along pretty well together, the way things are turning out."

160

BOOK TWO

· 20 ·

MRS. BLANDINGS, in an India-print dress that swirled about her ankles, looked tall and graceful. She was also manifestly eager for the occasion, whereas Mr. Blandings, although he followed his wife up the graveled walk, had faintly the look of being pushed.

Against the dark sky the barn looked huge and soaring as a cathedral; at one angle a wintry crescent moon rode on a corner of it like a weathervane. Inside, the rafters stretched away into darkness. The floor was of oaken boards as solid as the earth itself. With loving care someone had relaid them, and joined and fitted and chinked and planed them so that now they seemed to make one vast glossy surface, faintly scored with parallel lines. They must have given footing to cows and horses one day in the long ago, but they could do duty for a ballroom now.

"Look at the harnesses," said Mrs. Blandings in a whisper. From a peg in a girder of the barn's frame there hung coiled a luscious tangle of leather; smooth, oily-black, and limp as a sleeping snake, but caught up at junctions here and there with cleats and diamonds and lozenges of heavy polished brass. Mr. Blandings nodded and peered around the barn for other evidences of antiquity lovingly preserved.

There were not many of them. Mr. Henry Simms' barn was not a restored showplace; it was where Henry Simms worked. Pushed out of the way into a far corner were desks and drafting tables: the T-squares, triangles, boxes of draftsman's instruments, rolls of translucent tracing-cloth and blueprints, and all the other apparatus of a practicing architect were compacted into a temporary

161

neatness and, for this evening, set aside. From chestnut wall to chestnut wall the barn was an arena.

So far as Mr. Blandings could see, no smallest nail had been used to fasten it together. The enormous foot-square girts and beams joined one another in heavy square mortices and the ends of the beams had been drilled for delicately pointed dowels that were an inch in diameter at their butt ends. Whatever had once been the partitioning for stalls and cubicles, it had all been swept away.

Mr. Blandings made a comparison between his smaller barns and Henry Simms' vast one, and wondered what was the degradation that had overtaken American life. What had been the slow but accelerating sloppiness that had started to overwhelm it as the twentieth century began? Why had owners and workmen once taken pride in their work, and why had they ceased to? Why had it been that, as tools grew more remorselessly precise, more icily sharp, the people of rural New England had been more and more content to bang things together without caring for the looks or strengths or morals of construction? If an oak board on a bin had come loose and had been lost it had been replaced, if at all, by a couple of pieces of cheap tongue-and-groove pine, neither sawn straight nor hammered home; where the knots had fallen out of this in a still later generation, the holes had been covered over by the rusty tops of tin cans; when these had torn loose they had merely been left to hang there, dangling from a few bent nails of the wrong size. It was this sort of patchwork, successively compounding in stupidity and cheapness, that Henry Simms had ripped out of his barn; now he was back to the layer where the wood was oak and chestnut, and the workmanship was honest.

The big barn was aglow with shaded electric lights, and on a confusion of benches, chairs, and stools some fifty men and women, boys and girls, were sitting. They made up a stratum of Lansdale society new to Mr. and Mrs. Blandings; the only familiar face they saw belonged to Mr. Urmot Nellus, who waved them a greeting with a hand clutching a large glass.

A rush of sound suddenly woke the barn alive; a harmonica, banjo, and accordion went soaring off into the measures of a

162

country dance and all about, from chairs and benches, a swirl of women rose up in response. With instinctive knowledge they began to balance and arrange the social order. The men were constrained in clumsy poses or postures of pseudo-gallantry, but the painful counterfeit did not seem to matter to the women; if they had been squired by bronzed young wing-commanders they could not have appeared more radiant. It's a damn good thing, I guess, thought Mr. Blandings, but a damn curious thing. Here was his wife, as much a stranger to this gathering as he, yet suddenly she was ready to gambol as lightheartedly as a kitten. One hand clasped her husband's; the other was outheld, graceful, white, and patrician, to offer itself to the clumsy paw of any male within distance. Having spied one, she said "Come *here*," in a voice suffused with gaiety, and stamped her foot in a tiny mockery of impatience. Then she reached out and grabbed the hand of a miserable-looking man. He had innumerable bumps: his Adam's apple, his eyebrows, and the structure behind his ears all made planes and solids that should have been more interesting to a sculptor than to a female. But having grabbed him, Mrs. Blandings proceeded to engulf him. "Yes ma'am," Mr. Blandings heard him say in answer to some question his wife had asked in a caressing voice.

As he observed this, not without wonder, Mr. Blandings found his own hand seized by something small and soft and warm; looking about, he discovered that a dark girl with creamy skin and lustrous eyes had secured him firmly and was now turning on him the full voltage of her womanly charm. "That your wife?" she inquired in a gleaming contralto, inclining her head toward Mrs. Blandings. Mr. Blandings nodded.

"We'll have to break it up," she said. There ensued a complex maneuver; in a moment Mr. Blandings found himself far away from his wife, each hand grasped by a woman completely in tune with the spirit of things.

"I'm your partner," said the contralto girl, "and this"—indicating an attachment to Mr. Blandings' other hand—"is your corner lady."

"I don't—" said Mr. Blandings.

The two head ladies cross over
And by that gentleman stand;
Side ladies cross over
And all join hands.
Honor your corner lady
Honor your partners all
Swing your corner lady
And promenade the hall . .

The unbelievable sonority of the harmonica, banjo, and accordion made the whole barn seem to swell and tremble. Clem Sprickles sat on the platform, a foot-long harmonica clasped to his mouth in a ravishing kiss. The shudderous vulgarities of glissando, tremolo, vibrato, *vox humana,* and echo-organ effects were unknown to him; he merely inhaled and exhaled through the forest of brass reeds in his mouth organ, his cupped hands at either end acting as resonators. As in every parody of a country band, Clem Sprickles' right foot, encased in a long shoe with a loose sole, beat out the time by slapping the floor like a seal's flipper. But so sharp was Clem Sprickles' sense of rhythm, and so richly did the three instruments reinforce each other that Mr. Blandings felt a delightful stirring in his limbs. "Just listen to the caller and go where I push you," said his contralto girl. "This is Mrs. Hacker, and my name is Esther Deeming."

Mr. Blandings introduced himself.

"Oh," said both ladies in unison, "you're the father of the little girl."

"Sets in order," bellowed the caller, and new groups of eight formed squares all across the barn. Clem Sprickles delivered a prodigious slap with his foot and the music engulfed everything.

Head couple lead up to the right
And balance there so kindly
And pass right through
And balance too
And swing that girl behind you.

Mr. Blandings got the hang of it in a tentative sort of way. "You'd better take your coat and tie off," said his contralto girl, after the number had ended. "This is hot work even in February." She looked deliciously cool in a white blouse and a full-cut skirt that swirled when she swung her hips.

> *For it's lady 'round the lady*
> *And the gent around the gent*
> *And the gent around the lady*
> *And the lady 'round the gent . . .*

After a while, when Mr. Blandings was so thoroughly enjoying himself that he no longer cared about the cascades of sweat that poured from him, there was a sort of intermission. "Come and say hello to Mr. Sprickles," said his contralto girl. They walked over to the band platform. "Mr. Sprickles, this is Mr. Blandings," she said.

"The father—" said Mr. Sprickles.

"—of the little girl. Yes," said Mr. Blandings. Clem Sprickles' thin red face, his corded, roosterish neck, his wrinkled, cloudy eyeballs behind a pair of gold-rimmed glasses askew on his long nose, all spelled out some archetype of aged bumpkin. He had a cackle to go with it all, and his knees were so thin they made spiky points through his worn blue trousers. He was given to slapping his thigh, just as he should. Mr. Blandings thought that his one gallus was probably an affectation, but the rest of him could not be questioned. "Your music is wonderful," said Mr. Blandings.

"Don't know how to play this thing now never will," said Mr. Sprickles.

At his feet Mr. Blandings saw a large, luxurious box. Its padded leather lid was open; inside it were twelve glittering mouth organs, cuddled niche by niche in beds of purple plush. "Why do you have so many?" asked Mr. Blandings. "Are they in different keys?"

"Th' git *wet*," said Mr. Sprickles. " 'Fi didn't change 'em every number they'd play mushy. Your little girl here tonight?"

No, Mr. Blandings explained, his little girl was at home tonight. He went no further in elaboration. She was spending too much time at home. The vast to-do, first of praise and then of censure she did not understand, had now mostly died away, but it had left Joan a conspicuous character; a circumstance she liked no better than Greta Garbo.

As Mr. Blandings walked away Clem Sprickles nudged his accordion player. "That's the man teaches his little girl the multiplication table in Rooshan," he said. "They're after him, but they ain't caught him yet."

Mr. Blandings sat on the sidelines and watched. He had lost his contralto girl somewhere, and his wife, blissfully happy by the look on her face, was now at the head of a set in a far distant corner. She seemed to know everything about square dancing and with complete assurance moved through the most intricate steps and countersteps, imparting some of her own lithe grace to the men who sludged about her.

. . . ladies twirl and the gents plow under . . .

Under the soft light, the couples dipped and swung. The women were tall flowers swaying in a gentle wind; the men had achieved a sort of clodhopper dignity; whatever had been artificial as the evening began was now transmuted into genuine. A mood struck Mr. Blandings so suddenly that he caught his breath; this was all familiar; he had been here many, many times before. As he sat on his rough stool the clock and the calendar went whirling back, and he was in the midst of an America of lanterns and churns and shallow milkpans and cool root cellars and homespuns and candle molds. There were no wires in this world, and no noises louder than the shout of a man's voice; nothing ran by cycles except the ceaseless, unhurried seasons. Mr. Blandings watched the women, their long hair bound with ribbons, their dresses billowing, their feet shod in daintiness. He watched the men, oafs and clods and gallants alike, now clad in wools and buckskins, their hair gathered roughly at their napes. He was seeing America in its proud young might, strong and rude, strong and unkempt, strong and honest. The girls vied to be feminine and alluring, for who should capture the saturnine young males was a matter of life and death. Those who failed would soon put on spinsters' caps and live out the rest of their lives in unspoken agony; those who succeeded would run a different risk. "Let them bear children until they die of it, for that is what they are for," the Reverend Jonathan Edwards had recently said: there was general assent, no less among the women, to the soundness of his view. There was nothing, in this rough world, of faintheartedness or hanging back; if a thought could not be set

166

down with a gnawed pencil on the breadth of a shingle it was no honest thought. A man was grim if he felt grim, courtly if he felt courtly: there was no pretense, and all were intent, and all concerned. . . . Mr. Blandings drew out a great round watch from his elaborate weskit and studied the hands through the thick bull's-eye glass; he must leave here soon, for it would take a horse full two hours to bear him home over the dark rocky road to the top of Bald Mountain. And tomorrow was Sunday, which meant that he must be up early to listen to three hours of the word of God thundered at him while he sat on a hard bench and thought on his chances of salvation. . . .

"Hello, Jim."

Mr. Blandings refocused his vision with a start, and beheld Henry Simms beside him in modern dress. *Déjà vu*—that's what it was! The psychiatrists had a name for this weird, engrossing feeling of experience revisited, even if they could not explain it; perhaps it was the memory of a dream, perhaps it was a true vision of the past through a rent in the veils that enshrouded the past. Whatever it was, it was uncanny.

"Hello, Henry," said Mr. Blandings, hurriedly tucking these thoughts out of sight. "It's a wonderful party you're giving."

It was something, Mr. Simms explained, that he liked to do two or three times a winter. "You'd like most of these people," said, Mr. Simms. "Take old Doc Outcleff over there; he doesn't look like much, and nobody round here thinks of him as anything but a pretty good veterinary, but all of a sudden the Swedes up and gave him a whopping medal a couple of years ago. I don't mean a Nobel, but something not too far from it. He'd isolated some virus that was killing all their cows, or something. Very unassuming man."

"Yes," said Mr. Blandings, "I'm on the school board with him."

"Why of course," said Henry Simms. "I keep forgetting."

"But I didn't know anything about him," said Mr. Blandings. Upon my soul, he thought, so *that* was this quiet man whom everybody called Doc and who never offered an opinion except in the most tentative, hesitant way. You certainly couldn't tell the players without a score card in the country. Mr. Blandings had mentally put Doc Outcleff down as a third-rate country physician; instead,

167

he turned out to be a man of international fame. Let that be a lesson to you, Blandings, said Mr. Blandings. . . .

"When you get a chance," said Henry Simms, "say a word to Urm Nellus over there. I'm always glad when he shows up at one of these things; he leads a sort of lonely life. He thinks a lot of you, you know."

Presently Mr. Blandings found himself sitting side-by-side with Mr. Nellus and experimenting with an occasional sip of hard cider from a stone jug to which Mr. Nellus seemed to have free access. He was too tired to dance any more, but Mrs. Blandings had fallen in with a little group of diehards who seemed to be contesting whether they or Clem Sprickles and his men would give out first. Mr. Nellus had danced no sets during the evening, but neither did he appear to be present as a member of the working press. "Lovely group of people here," said Mr. Blandings.

Mr. Nellus seemed a little sullen from his cider. "You think so?" he said. He waved an arm at large. "You can have 'em," he said.

"Now didn't you have a good time?" asked Mrs. Blandings. "I practically had to drag you there, but in spite of all your fuss I'm quite sure you enjoyed yourself."

"Yes," said Mr. Blandings, "I had a good time." He pulled off his undershirt in a meditative sort of way, and dropped it in his laundry hamper. It was still drenched.

"You know," said Mrs. Blandings, "I kept thinking and thinking what it was that made those people so much nicer and more interesting than the cocktail-party bunch of the Joseph Chasuble-Horns', and it's just finally come to me: they never sounded off. They never blathered. It was even hard to find out just who they were, or just what they did. They're QPs—they're quiet professionals."

"Why Muriel," said Mr. Blandings; "why sweetie."

Now that his wife had said it for him, it was perfectly clear. All the way home in the station wagon he'd been thinking about his vision of the past, and why that scene and those people had evoked it. He hadn't known.

"Golly," he said. "What an improvement over that bunch of Poets and Peasants." He was thinking of how right Bill Cole had been to warn him off the chattering glib of the Chasuble-Horns, who talked of steelworkers but stalked celebrities. He had thought they were the only alternatives to Mr. Anson Dolliver and his crew of right-thinking Republicans, but now it seemed to him that here was a third force, if that's what you'd call it, and it was to this that his sympathies of temperament truly went. He thought of the mild and apologetic Dr. Outcleff and his international medalist's fame, all but unknown in his home town. It suddenly occurrred to Mr. Blandings that he, too, had once won a gold medal: a gold medal from his world of advertising for having written the best laxative campaign of a particular year.

"Why are you blushing?" Mrs. Blandings asked.

21

Mr. BLANDINGS glanced out his office window into the dusk that settled so early over the city. The weather was freakishly warm, and in the winter's midst a gentle, springlike breeze was curling through the partly opened sash; loaded with its tons of colloidal bituminous soot, he could still somehow get from it a notion of green shoots in moist earth, buds swelling red, and wands of willow turning yellow. Yet at four o'clock the day was already dark enough that the Knapp Laxative sign was on and spraying its glaring colors over half the Manhattan skies. During the war the accursed thing had been blacked out—not without some protest from Lorbet Neen at regimentation and some gentlemanly complaints from Mr. Dascomb about the U.S. Navy's inability to cope with the Nazi submarine menace except by this encroachment on the free-enterprise system. God, thought Mr. Blandings, it had been wonderful not to have that sign thrusting its dazzle into his face for almost four years. But now . . .

He turned back to the sheet in his typewriter. It was a memorandum, a formal memorandum, typed on white paper instead of interoffice blue, to Mr. Dascomb, and it called for some neat wording. Mr. Blandings looked at his typing. "I was very gratified," he read, "at your recent kind words about my association with the Lansdale school board, and by your stated belief that members of the B. & D. Organization who become identified with situations in their home localities increase their understanding of what you so aptly call Motives that Move. I have no personal desire—"

What a liar I am, said Mr. Blandings softly to the water cooler in the hall outside his office. Of course I have a personal desire. The personal desire I was about to deny was the desire to be an effec-

170

tive, respected member of the Lansdale school board. On the contrary: I want to sit around a table and plan things for other people's good. That's what I'm supposed to be doing in Plans Board meetings on this very floor, except that it isn't the same. I don't want to plan things so that a lot of fat boys can get a lot fatter; I want to plan things for a community that needs help, and that I believe in, and where I can see the results of the plan grow into a reality that will make my soul expand. Don't give me any of that no-personal-desire stuff.

"I have no personal desire," Mr. Blandings resumed, "to become immersed in local politics, but perhaps this is one time when I should not consult my purely personal wishes. You may remember that when Lorbet Neen conducted his Area Study of Thought Molders last year, Lansdale County turned out to have more Thought Molders than the Dakotas and Alaska combined. Even more surprising was that Lansdale showed a higher proportion of Thought Molders per thousand Inert Population than any other non-metropolitan county in America. I think this makes it an extremely interesting locality, and one I might well profit by getting to know in considerably greater intimacy. This is all the more so because we were all concerned that Lorbet's study indicated that, as the number of Thought Molders in an area went up, the per capita use of most of the products on our account list tended to go down, with the single exception of Distilled Beverages. I do not for a moment pretend—"

Mr. Blandings took his hands from the typewriter, folded them behind his head, and observed himself on the threshold of another lie. It was a little frightening the way the lies kept cropping up. Was he lying more, or just catching himself oftener? He wondered if Mrs. Blandings had known about this for years, and kept a wifely silence; whether everybody knew about it, and discounted him accordingly. . . .

"I do not for a moment pretend," Mr. Blandings' typewriter continued, "that my own studies could fully explain the curious situation presented by Lorbet's figures. But I do think I might be able to gain some personal insights which might be valuable. There is also another reason why I should like to consider a closer associa-

171

tion with Lansdale activities at the expense of some time spent in the office during the next six months. It is that—"

Mr. Blandings paused again. He was reminding himself of a small child. You gave reasons to your parents why you wanted something. If they did not suffice you said, "And *besides* . . . ," and only then the true reason emerged. He was at last coming to the point of his memorandum.

Horace Dascomb had been in his profession long enough to have seen everything. Being himself as uncreative as a newt, he could not understand at first hand the sufferings of the creative but he was always prepared for them; if he was no physician he was at least an actuary. And with his actuary's eye he had long ago observed the terrible restlessness that was likely to strike a writer of advertising copy in his late thirties or early forties; a restlessness that made him yearn to snap the golden cords of salaries and bonuses and profit-sharings and stock dividends and find, by some means, in some obscure place or bizarre fashion, something he thought would be simpler and more rewarding.

Mr. Dascomb's onetime senior partner, Suggerd Banton, was himself a case. Banton & Dascomb as a business entity had been formed out of several of the ribs and part of the spinal column of an old established agency from which the Messrs. Banton & Dascomb, two bright young men, had walked one weekend after the end of World War I. The new agency had found recognition and prosperity from the start—but after twelve years of moil and toil Sugg Banton had suddenly thrown in the sponge. Except that he had not quit; he had merely divested himself of all offices except the chairmanship of the board, and gone far, far away. What the arrangement now was between the Messrs. Banton & Dascomb only the two principals knew. A leased wire of the American Telephone & Telegraph Company directly connected the thirty-first floor offices in the Posthumous Guarantees and Trust Company with the remote New Mexico ranch where Mr. Banton had gone to live and search for New Values; on this wire the two partners talked every morning for half an hour or more. With the rest of his time Mr. Banton seemed to have founded a new religion based equally on the ageless wisdom of the East and the more immediate effects of

172

colonic irrigation; he had also bought an old factory and was having a very prosperous time selling Aztec pottery facsimiles by mail. He came to New York only once a year, to preside at the annual stockholders' meeting—and as the years went by it must be that Mr. Banton's long series of daily telephoned suggestions to Mr. Dascomb grew to be of less and less practical value. But if Mr. Dascomb ever had any complaints about the relationship he was never heard to voice them.

The world of advertising was full of such arrangements. And so, whatever emotions Mr. Dascomb may have encountered on feeling Mr. Blandings begin to tug at the rope, surprise was not among them.

"He wants to go on a two-day week for the rest of the year," said Mr. Dascomb, snapping into place the black tie that made him in uniform for the Waldorf dinner to which he and Mrs. Dascomb had been bidden to meet a South American Minister of State who was going to explain, informally, the significance of the revolution that had recently swept his country from the Left or Right; the dispatches were not clear.

"Are you going to let him?" said Mrs. Dascomb.

Mr. Dascomb shrugged. "If he keeps the Knapp account happy I guess that's the main thing," he said. "We'll find some compromise. He's mixed up in some sort of small-town politics; it'll wear off."

"It seems to me," said Mrs. Dascomb, "that no sooner do you get everything at the office all neatly rearranged than it all starts coming apart again. I'm sure other agency heads don't for a minute put up with so much temperamental nonsense. I'm sure Stanley Resor—"

"We're going to be late again," said Mr. Dascomb.

"If that's all," said Mr. Rocklett, "somebody could make a motion to adjourn."

Mr. Blandings made the motion; a mumble and scrape indicated that another meeting of the Lansdale school board had come to an end. He liked to move adjournment; it gave him some feeling of certitude to propose something he knew would be agreed and acted upon. He needed this, for otherwise he was more mixed up than he had ever been before.

173

As time wore on it was more and more apparent to him that he had misconceived what a school board was for. Whatever it was for, it had nothing to do with education. "The curriculum is not the concern of the board," Mr. Rocklett had said at Mr. Blandings' first meeting, not in rebuke but in simple explanation. Mr. Rocklett was the chairman of the board, the proprietor of the largest hardware store in town, and the possessor of a most agreeable personality. Mr. Blandings, who had hitherto known him only across the counter, was amazed at his skill in rustic debate. He reduced everything to the smallest and simplest terms imaginable and then applied his solution to problems that would have given pause to Oliver Wendell Holmes. "You wouldn't want *political* control of education, now would you?" he asked Mr. Blandings genially. "You and I are just political hacks, when you come right down to it. It's our business to see that the schools in our district are going concerns—but education? That's for the superintendent and the teachers. Once the board started sticking its nose into the curriculum you'd have a bad situation." As Mr. Blandings studied the board he began to think that this might indeed be true.

Mr. Rocklett's method in debate was to assume that he and his opponent really agreed, and that the opponent was taking the opposite view for the dialectical fun of it; he used a broad grin and a heavy wink as auxiliaries to this method and on Mr. Blandings in particular it was disconcertingly successful; it nurtured his inborn abilities to disagree with himself at a crucial moment. Moreover, to his bewilderment, he liked Mr. Rocklett. Republican, skinflint, wily infighter, taker of the small view: on all counts Mr. Blandings wished to dislike him. The trouble was that Mr. Rocklett was a very pleasant fellow.

On the other hand, when Mr. Blandings contemplated his fellow Democrat on the board he was filled with dismay. She was Mrs. Editha Ormerary, a square, massive lady of brick-red color who wore middy blouses the year round, and had apparently done so since adolescence, from time to time making the necessary concessions to size but standing pat on style. How she had ever made herself acceptable to the Lansdale Democratic organization Mr. Blandings never expected to discover, certainly not from Ed O'Neill. Presumably she represented Woman and, to some lesser degree, Culture. She had been to college, she ran an herb garden, she wove textiles. Her own skirts were made of these, usually in a nubbly gray. They were free of the taint of professionalism, but no hand-operated loom could weave tightly enough to resist the stresses that developed when she sat down; although there was no record of an actual tensile failure her hem lines were always wavy and drooped at the rear. She had been taken up by the Poet and Peasant party that centered about the home of Mr. and Mrs. Joseph Chasuble-Horn; one baleful result of this association was her voluble infatuation with the works of Dr. Lispetha Worplin.

Who or what Mr. Ormerary was or had been Mr. Blandings did not know and did not want to be told. The most charitable view he could take of Mrs. Ormerary was that she was crazy. Where Mr. Rocklett's views were small, hers were so large as to be indiscernible. If there was method in her thought it was a method Mr. Blandings could not follow. When she occasionally said something that was undoubtedly true but had always been known, Mr. Blandings found himself wishing that he could be dissociated not only from the speaker but the truth as she had uttered it. Unfortunately, the converse was not true: Mrs. Ormerary had a marked tendency to take Mr. Blandings' side in matters of controversy, embracing him as a fellow exponent of progress and enlightenment. It was the indescribable horror of being agreed with by Mrs. Ormerary that began to crush the breath and heart out of Mr. Blandings, and was slowly to render him a silent, brooding, impotent member of the educational system of Lansdale Town.

It was all the worse that Mrs. Ormerary was on Mr. Blandings' side, for it was evident that her fellow feeling for him sprang from something deeper than political partisanship. Mr. Blandings soon came to realize that party labels meant next to nothing in the board room. If he could not abide Mrs. Ormerary it was apparent that the Republican ranks were also split. Mr. Rocklett was having his troubles with a blood brother in the G.O.P., a tall, pink, delicious-smelling gentleman by the name of Coswin Causeway. Unlike Dr. Outcleff, whose pioneering spirit did not extend into political realms and who could always be counted upon to vote with the chairman, Mr. Causeway would not stay on the reservation, but for reasons of his own was all too likely to go cavorting in the pastures where Mrs. Ormerary pawed and stamped.

Mr. Causeway had lived in Lansdale for a long time but he was a commuter, not a native. Mr. Blandings used elaborate stratagems avoiding him on the morning and evening trains, unaware that at least half his success was due to Mr. Causeway's similar maneuvers. Mr. Causeway was an insurance executive, much too high in his hierarchy to bother any longer about "contacts." He must have come on the Lansdale board at a time when Mr. Dolliver had thought it wise to throw a small sop to the commuter element and had singled out Mr. Causeway as the most rock-ribbed defender of the faith that could be found in that area. The flaw in Mr. Causeway was only that in the nature of his daily life billions were a commonplace; he could shove a decimal point two places farther over to the right in a way that made Mr. Rocklett and Dr. Outcleff shudder. This taking of the large view of everything was what created, between him and Mrs. Ormerary, a sort of solidarity that collided with the solidarity of Mr. Rocklett and Dr. Outcleff. The former solidarity dealt in terms of the large and loose; the latter in terms of the small and pernickety. Mr. Blandings found it increasingly impossible to choose between them. Why, he asked himself, was his life always a series of dilemmas? He was a liberal, was he not? Then why did a labeled liberal make him sick? And did he not believe in progress, and were not Mr. Causeway's concepts those of progress? Then why could he not abide Mr. Causeway? What are you doing, Blandings, that you should have a sneaking affection for two political reactionaries, just because they're pleasant people personally? Where are your convictions, your dedicated ideals? To your baffling ability to see both sides of a question you now seem to be adding the psychological feeling of necessity to reject them both. Should you have your head examined?

"Why doesn't the *Blade* print the school board meetings?" Mr. Blandings asked Mr. Nellus. "Why don't you come to them as a reporter?"

"Norb Rocklett would make it mighty uncomfortable," said Mr. Nellus.

"The meetings are supposed to be open," said Mr. Blandings. "I
176

read that in a state pamphlet. It might help the deliberations quite a lot if there was a reporter listening."

"There's a tradition in this part of the country that the best way to conduct public business is in private," said Mr. Nellus.

Mr. Blandings made a noise of impatience.

"Look," said Mr. Nellus. "There used to be a time when I thought I could be William Allen White. But that's past. Either there's some difference between this part of the country and Emporia, Kansas, or else there's some difference between me and William Allen White. Probably both."

"But the public doesn't get a look-in at the way anything's done here," said Mr. Blandings. "Maybe you could put the shoe on the other foot. Maybe you could conduct some public-opinion polls and shed some light on what the people are thinking."

"The people are thinking of rape and pillage," said Mr. Nellus. "I don't need to go to any expense to find that out."

"I only meant," said Mr. Blandings, "that maybe some feature of that general sort might brighten up the paper."

"Who'd want that?" Mr. Nellus demanded. "Anybody start brightening things up around here likely to get himself into a peck of trouble."

"Maybe," said Mr. Blandings, "the paper would *look* more interesting if you changed the typography."

Mr. Nellus dropped part of his defensive attitude. "I wouldn't object to some new type," he said, "except it costs money."

A wild irrational idea, the kind he liked, formed in Mr. Blandings' mind. He must not blurt it out. But he could be shrewd and wary with it, and stalk it through the underbrush. He assumed what he believed to be a soft-focus look, blank and bland.

"Much money?" he inquired.

"Depends," said Mr. Nellus. "Not worth doing anything unless I had a thousand dollars to put into some new linotype mats and a couple of shirttailfuls of new foundry type."

"It might make a lot of difference," said Mr. Blandings.

"It wouldn't make any difference at all," said Mr. Nellus. "Besides, it would be more like fifteen hundred before you got through. The *Blade* makes a living for one man right the way it's running now, after I get through paying my help, and if I was to start putting any money back into it I'd have just that much less to eat, that's all. No sense to it."

"Look," said Mr. Blandings, no longer able to contain himself; "if somebody were to offer you fifteen hundred with the understanding it was all yours if you'd spend it on new type and such, would you accept it?"

Mr. Nellus looked puzzled. "Well I don't know, I guess so," he said.

"Well that's just what I'm going to offer," said Mr. Blandings.

Mr. Nellus looked at him; first at his face, then down to his toes, and slowly back to his face again. He knocked the ash off his cigar.

"You're crazy," he said with finality.

"No, I'm not," said Mr. Blandings. "Maybe you don't understand how people like me feel. All my life I've been hipped on publishing. I don't mean big city stuff. I mean publishing right down at the grassroots, where you know the people you're writing about and you can *feel* their reaction to what you're printing."

"There hasn't anybody given me any reaction to anything I been printing for the last five years," said Mr. Nellus. "Good *or* bad."

"They would," said Mr. Blandings; "I just know they would if you went after them. The last thing I want to do is sound conceited, but after all my business is influencing people by the written word, and I've had some success at it. The trouble is there isn't much satisfaction in influencing people to buy laxatives and hair-restorers when the world is in such a state, and most of the people I know in my business wish just what I wish—that they had something to do with publishing something more important."

For what seemed to Mr. Blandings a long time Mr. Nellus sat silent. When he did speak it was not to the point as Mr. Blandings saw it. "What beats me," said Mr. Nellus, "is where you city people get the money you have to throw around."

"I haven't any money to throw around," said Mr. Blandings. "In the advertising business you get fired very fast if things turn bad, but when times are good they pay you a lot of bonuses and things because there isn't anything else to do with the money. Right now I have a little cash left over from a Christmas bonus, and I suppose I could buy bonds with it but it just came over me I'd rather invest in something close to home; something I could watch."

"Invest, hey?" said Mr. Nellus.

"Yes," said Mr. Blandings. "It would be a perfectly businesslike deal. What I'd offer you is a small amount of new capital to make an improvement in the *Blade,* and in return you could give me a small fractional interest—a sixteenth, or an eighth, or whatever was fair."

Some perplexity was continuing to gnaw at Mr. Nellus; obviously he could not bring it to the level of speech.

"You wouldn't need to be afraid of my trying to interfere," said Mr. Blandings. "If I could be of any help I'd be glad to, but otherwise—"

"I wouldn't be afraid of your interfering," said Mr. Nellus. "For all anybody knows I might welcome a little interference."

"Will you think it over?" asked Mr. Blandings, trying to keep the pleading note out of his voice.

Mr. Nellus snubbed out the remains of his cigar. "I guess so," he said. "I guess I don't commit myself to very much if I say I'll think it over."

"I think maybe Mr. Nellus is going to give me a small interest in the paper," said Mr. Blandings.

"Oh?" said Mrs. Blandings. Her female extrasensory-perception apparatus told her instantly that she was confronting a falsely presented proposition, and that when the proposition emerged in its true light, as she would force it in a moment to do, she would not approve of it. "And what would you do with it if he did give it to you?" She stressed the word *give* in such a way that her husband would not know whether she had stressed it or not.

"What do you mean what would I do with it?" said Mr. Blandings.

"What purpose would be accomplished in your mind if you were to acquire an interest in the Lansdale *Blade?*" Mrs. Blandings asked, smoothly. Was there any stress on the word *mind,* Mr. Blandings wondered. Was his wife being mean to him?

"The purpose," said Mr. Blandings, a trifle grandly, "would be. . . ." He paused. There was a purpose, not only a good but a compelling purpose, in his wish to be a minority partner in the fundamental human activity of publishing a country newspaper; of being a member, however small and inconspicuous, of the Fourth Estate. It was there, shining clear, in his mind; he was sure he could clothe it in lustrous words if he were just asked about it sympathetically. This cross-questioning was something else again; it served to inhibit.

"The purpose," he began again, "would be to help the *Blade* render a better service to the community."

This was trite and bombastic and not at all what he had meant to say. His wife paid no heed to these defects.

"Did Mr. Nellus come to you and ask for help?" she inquired.

"N-o-o," said Mr. Blandings. "Not directly, at least."

"Then how is it he's going to give you a part interest in the paper?"

The time for subterfuge was past.

"Because I offered to buy it," said Mr. Blandings.

Mrs. Blandings whacked a bracelet down hard on her dressing table.

"Damn it," she said.

22

NOTHING under the pavements of New York was as complex as
what was under the earth of his countryside, Mr. Blandings reflected. The roots, the rocks, the worms, the burrows of rats and
moles and woodchucks—it would take Consolidated Edison and
New York Steam Corp. a frenzy of work in the next hundred years
to achieve one per cent of such labyrinthine complexity. The simple city, the complex country. In the city, all was indifference. In
what election district of Manhattan Mr. Blandings had once lived
he had never been able to remember. Under the same roof with
what felons, traitors, or wife-poisoners he and Mrs. Blandings had
been domiciled they had never known. The arrival of a police riot-
and-disaster truck at one end of a block was unnoticed at the
other. But in the country the most delicate shifts of poise-counter-
poise could be instantly felt and wantonly misinterpreted. In
country loam, hate could grow like a weed.

"Anse Dolliver," said Mr. Nellus, "has something against you out
of all proportion."

Mr. Blandings shifted his weight on the one visitor's chair in
Mr. Nellus' tropically disordered office. He had stopped by partially in the hope of getting an answer to his proposal of a fortnight
ago, but Mr. Nellus seemed to be steering the conversation into
other channels.

"I wouldn't borrow money from Anson Dolliver once," said Mr.
Blandings. "I went to a bigger bank in a bigger place. Maybe that's
it."

"That sort of thing certainly riles Anse," said Mr. Nellus, "but it's
not that. I happen to know."

"How?" said Mr. Blandings.

181

"You'd have to promise not to tell," said Mr. Nellus.

Mr. Blandings made his most solemn vow.

"A week before the election the *Blade* ran an editorial about new blood on the school board," said Mr. Nellus.

"I know," said Mr. Blandings. "I've never thanked you enough."

"No thanks to me," said Mr. Nellus. "It was Anse Dolliver suggested it. Course I was glad enough to do it."

Mr. Blandings was thunderstruck.

"Don't ask me why," said Mr. Nellus. "When he called me up I just assumed he'd had another of his bone-cracking rows with Eph Hackett, but the fact is, he was willing to have you on the school board."

Any remaining sense of triumph at being on the school board drained away from Mr. Blandings. He was there not out of merit after all, but because some small-town political deal had put him there.

"If I'd known you'd take it so hard I wouldn't of told you," said Mr. Nellus. "Anyway, point I was making was, whatever's got Anse Dolliver so down on you must have happened *after* the election."

"Of course there was all that rumpus about Joanie's piece," said Mr. Blandings.

"Yes," said Mr. Nellus, "but it died down mighty fast after Conant and Compton and Bush and Oppenheimer and all those high muckymuck scientists testified for her."

"That's right," said Mr. Blandings. "They all certainly came through handsomely for my little girl. It was mighty nice of Mrs. Roosevelt to invite her to Hyde Park, too." He sighed. "Poor Joanie," he said. "She can't figure out why there was such an outburst because she said something nice about a Frenchwoman who died in 1934 and a Russian who died in 1907. For that matter, neither can I. Just what is your friend Dolliver saying about me?"

"Don't call him any friend of mine," said Mr. Nellus. He lowered his voice to a hoarse whisper. "Obviously," he said, "I wouldn't be telling you this if I believed it myself." He cleared his throat elaborately, while Mr. Blandings waited.

"Well," said Mr. Nellus, "you know about the Needlework Society, I guess."

Mr. Blandings did. The Needlework Society was a group of

182

hard-riding Saturday-night poker players to which any man could belong if he played good enough poker; it had to be very good.

"Last Saturday night at the Needlework Society," said Mr. Nellus, "Anse Dolliver said he had it straight from a man who knows somebody high up in your office that you'd been acting as a transmission belt to the Kremlin, and that it was common knowledge."

Mr. Blandings' brows contracted until his memory, caught unaware, filled the gap. Then he deliberately took his time in framing an answer. "There's a certain amount of truth in that," he said.

Mr. Nellus' eyes grew enormous.

"I wrote over thirty letters to Joseph Stalin," said Mr. Blandings, "but I did it as part of my job and on the orders of a client who is a member of the National Association of Manufacturers."

Mr. Nellus' eyes grew more enormous still. "Have the Russians got spies in *there?*" he asked in a trembling voice. "By golly, I've often thought—"

"No, no," said Mr. Blandings. "Or how do I know? Maybe they have. But let me tell you the straight story."

Mr. Blandings told Mr. Nellus the straight story, complete with Mr. Dascomb, Royal Heffingwell, and Lorbet Neen.

"Well," said Mr. Nellus, "it just goes to show."

It certainly does, Mr. Blandings thought to himself afterward as he walked down Commerce Street. But what? All over America, Americans were busy impugning the Americanism of other Americans. Mr. Dolliver was now, for some reason unknown to Mr. Blandings, impugning his. What used to be calumny confined to the last week of a nasty election campaign was now stock and stencil of everyday utterance. Without realizing what he was doing, Mr. Blandings began to vilify Mr. Dolliver. God damn him, he thought; the stinking little black reactionary. Five times in a row *I* have voted for the man whom popular preference has put in the White House. That is more than Anson Dolliver can say: infinitely more. By that simple yardstick I am infinitely more an American than he is. But he still arrogates to himself the right to say who is a "regular" American and who is not. I'd like to meet him face to face and tell him just what I think of him.

Just then he did meet him.

"Good afternoon," said Mr. Dolliver.

"Good afternoon," said Mr. Blandings.

Mr. Dolliver's eyes were narrow as he continued his walk up Commerce Street, but he prided himself that his greeting to Mr. Blandings could not have been more controlled, that not one vestige of his hatred had been visible. This man was the author of a humiliation unique in Mr. Dolliver's experience. Presumably he did not know it, but this altered nothing in Mr. Dolliver's emotions. The threat of discipline and demotion in his party's ranks still hung over him. So far as Mr. Dolliver was aware, no one in Lansdale Town with the single exception of Ephemus Hackett was aware of Mr. Dolliver's possible fall from grace. There was small danger of a leak from that source. Mr. Hackett was still angry at the stratagem that had tweedled him off the school board, and had exhibited more than a measure of bitter glee at how that stratagem had backfired in Mr. Dolliver's face. But he would not spread the story around town, Mr. Dolliver knew: the penalties he could exact of Mr. Hackett were too severe and too well known. Mr. Blandings, however, was another matter; he ought to go back where he came from.

Mr. Dolliver had no immediate plans, and felt the need for none. He was not only the best poker player in the Needlework Society; he was also good at chess, and in sitting cross-board from someone whose game he did not know he merely deployed his pieces, made no aggressive move, and waited for his adversary to entangle himself. Nine times out of ten, the strategy worked. Mr. Dolliver did not know what Mr. Blandings was going to do; from all reports he had not done anything on the school board except rake up, as if they were brand new, all the old chestnuts that wide-eyed new members always had raked up, time immemorial. So the main thing to do about him now was just to watch him: watch him and wait for his overt act, whatever it might be. This man, playing the country gentleman, was a queer and obviously treacherous type: engaged in a profession, advertising, which was the handmaiden of free competitive capitalistic enterprise, and of some stature in that profession; yet at the same time mixed up, in Lansdale County, with that bunch of crackpots to whom he himself had given the contemptuous name of Poet and Peasant party, this cancerous yeast of intellects which were fermenting in the political party that used only to be the refuge of the down and out, the Polacks, the bums, the malcontents. On top of all this had come the revelation, from a friend who knew a man by the name of Neen, or Leen, or something like that in Blandings' office, that Mr. Blandings was one of a group that was trying to sell something—scrap iron? uranium?—to Russia. Every now and again you came up against some college professor with a twist in him like that, even some famous ones, and although it was monstrous wherever found, it was not wholly unexpected among the crackpots of college campuses. But an advertising man—that was more than a healthy mind could comprehend. Well, Mr. Dolliver thought, the sooner we can get him swept clean out of here the better, but I guess I can afford to take my time.

"You never talk about the school board any more," said Mrs. Blandings, one evening.

Her husband shrugged.

"Not very interesting," he said. "Not very interesting, talking about push brooms and locker paint. I don't want to bore you."

"But surely the Board of Education discusses more important things," said Mrs. Blandings.

"Yes," said Mr. Blandings. "We talk about the furnace."

"You're in one of your moods," said Mrs. Blandings.

"No I'm not," said Mr. Blandings. "Last time we talked about the furnace and about the Integrated Child. The talk about the furnace made a lot more sense. Besides, there's something we can *do* about the furnace. We can replace it. After we talk about it for another six months I think maybe we will. I don't know, though; maybe we won't."

"But what about *education?*" said Mrs. Blandings.

"I've told you," said Mr. Blandings. "Education is the forbidden topic. Mrs. Ormerary is always bringing it up, and to tell you the God's truth, by now I'm relieved when Norb Rocklett knocks her down."

"But this is ridiculous," said Mrs. Blandings.

"All right, it's ridiculous," said Mr. Blandings. "But it's the way

185

things are. I've learned something. I've learned there's no hope for education in America. The whole damn plan and purpose is lost; it got lost nobody knows where or when. And if it's ever found again it won't be by a rural school board—thank God. Norb Rocklett thinks education should be 'something practical'; Mrs. Ormerary thinks it should be 'self-expression.' You just get whipsawed between the two of them. You turn to the furnace for relief."

"Very well then," said Mrs. Blandings. "Forget education for the moment. How about an increase in teachers' pay?"

"Un-American agitation," said Mr. Blandings. "That's the board's majority view."

"Surely it's not yours," said Mrs. Blandings.

"No," said her husband; "no, I was in a minority of two, on that. Mrs. Ormerary was on my side there." He shuddered.

"Well then, what about the welfare of the child?" said Mrs. Blandings. "What about the hot-lunch proposal?"

"Communist-inspired," said Mr. Blandings.

"Now you're joking," said Mrs. Blandings. "Now I know you're joking."

"But I'm not," said her husband. "Schools can get a federal subsidy for hot lunches, if they apply for it. And what's that? That's the entering wedge for Socialism, for undermining the home, for making children the wards of the State. Listen, Muriel: the reason I know these arguments is that I got them all thrown at me when I muttered something about your damned PTA hot-lunch proposal, meeting before last. Norb Rocklett pulled a clipping out of his pocket from a paper over in York State where some defender of democracy traced the hot lunch spang back to the French Revolution. Let me tell you—this is a more dangerous issue than sex education. The hot lunch is part of the cold war."

Mrs. Blandings was silent.

"What I didn't know," said Mr. Blandings, "is that everything a school board could concern itself with has been fought over, in Lansdale and every place else in the country, since before I was a schoolboy myself, and every cause is lost. The truth itself is lost. It's all too discouraging to talk about. The school board works for no pay and no thanks and one way or another they all mean well —I suppose—but the only thing that comes out of it is chaos. The

186

strong, clear, unhampered man in the whole system is the janitor. He tends the furnace."

Mrs. Blandings shifted in her chair. "Is this the sort of thing you plan to tell your constituents?" she asked.

"Screw my constituents," said Mr. Blandings.

Mrs. Blandings sighed.

"And that's another thing," said Mr. Blandings. "I get sorrier and sorrier we ever got mixed up with that Chasuble-Horn crowd —all those poets and Ph.D.'s and stuff. I think they're a bunch of fakes."

"I think you should stop calling them the Poet and Peasant party," said Mrs. Blandings. "I've heard you do it several times recently and it won't make you popular."

"Maybe I don't want to be popular any more," said Mr. Blandings. "I'm getting mighty tired of listening to guff. Maybe what I'd like to do is just get cracking rude in somebody's living room and tell him he's full of—"

"Don't get yourself worked up just before bedtime," said Mrs. Blandings.

"What I need is a forum," said Mr. Blandings. "I'm tired of doing the listening: I'd like to do a little of the talking."

"About how the strong man in the whole system is the janitor?" said Mrs. Blandings. "Anybody who wanted to could give that a sort of Made-in-Moscow ring without half trying."

"No, no," said Mr. Blandings. "Just the reverse. Take this Auster Millowy. He's the boy whose heart is always bleeding for the steel-mill hunky. What the hell have a poet and a steel-mill hunky really got in common?"

"They're both men," said Mrs. Blandings.

"Maybe," said Mr. Blandings. "But I'll bet you the steel-mill hunky, if he could understand what Auster Millowy was talking about, would say 'I don't want your gracious consideration, I don't want your good will, I don't want your Christ-bitten compassion.'"

"Before you get yourself a forum," said Mrs. Blandings, "shouldn't you figure out a little more exactly just what you want to say on it? Your position isn't always clear even to me."

"All right," said Mr. Blandings. "Take Auster Millowy again.

187

He thinks business profits should be confiscated: I heard him say so. How the hell does he think the whole show got started? Take this town. Fifty years ago you'd be damn lucky to be able to buy a turnip and a chamber pot in a place this size. Now the stores and the windows and showcases are full to bursting with frozen foods, and fancy cheeses and good meats, and radios and washing machines, and pretty dresses for $11.95. How the hell does the Poet and Peasant party think they got there?"

"You sound like Horace Dascomb," said Mrs. Blandings.

Mr. Blandings slapped the arm of his chair. "That's *just* what I don't like about Auster Millowy," he said.

"What is, for goodness sake?" said Mrs. Blandings.

"He makes me sound like Horace Dascomb," said Mr. Blandings.

It was too late at night for the telephone to ring, but it rang. "I suppose that's him now," said Mr. Blandings petulantly, "with some cockeyed idea that he wants me to rush right into town about."

But it was not. The conversation, which Mr. Blandings began in a burst of cordiality, became full of jolty monosyllables. These in turn gave way to a series of explanations. In all of it Mrs. Blandings could find no clue to the person at the other end.

Mr. Blandings resumed his chair. "That's a very awkward place for the telephone instrument," he said, looking harshly at his wife.

He took out a handkerchief and blew his nose.

"I think my cold is getting worse," he said.

"I didn't know you had a cold," said Mrs. Blandings.

Her husband replied that he had not wished to worry her. "It's getting into my joints," he said. "They ache."

"I'll get you a couple of aspirins and a hot lemonade," said Mrs. Blandings, rising. "Who was on the phone?"

"Bill Cole," said Mr. Blandings.

"It didn't sound like that," said Mrs. Blandings. "What did he want this time on a Sunday night?"

"He wanted me to have lunch with him tomorrow," said Mr. Blandings. "But he didn't put it that way. He said 'I think we'd better have lunch tomorrow.' He can be very unmannerly."

When Mrs. Blandings came back with the hot lemonade and

188

a few thin cookies she sat down on her husband's ottoman and put her arms around his knees as she had been wont to do in the days when their marriage was young.

"Jim," she said, looking up at him, "have you done anything you haven't told Mummy about?"

"No," said Mr. Blandings. "At least . . ."

"Oh dear," said Mrs. Blandings. She knew her husband was telling her the truth, but that it was not the whole truth, and that she could get the whole truth more quickly from someone other than him. She snuggled her head against his knees and made her plan.

23

"HE SAID he felt just miserable this morning," said Mrs. Blandings, "so I said all right he could jolly well stay in bed. I said I'd been planning this trip to town for the last ten days and I wasn't going to change it. I didn't tell him I invited myself to have lunch with you in his place. I thought it might make him pettish."

Bill Cole smiled. "It's a break for me," he said. "You know how much I love you."

"I'm dying for a shrimp cocktail," said Mrs. Blandings. "I haven't had a shrimp cocktail since I don't know when."

"A shrimp cocktail and a cup of consommé," said Bill Cole to the waiter captain in the Chestnut Room of the Hotel Marbury. "How do you like it in the country with another spring on the way?"

"Oh, *wonderful,*" said Mrs. Blandings. Her face fell. "Sometimes I get so lonely I think I'll die."

"The next time you feel that way—" said Bill Cole.

"And then I'd like the sweetbreads *glacé,*" said Mrs. Blandings. "I don't want anything I could possibly have in my own home."

"Does Jim have to stay in town a lot?" asked Bill Cole.

"Altogether too much," said Mrs. Blandings. "He's supposed to be on part-time at the office but I can't see that it makes much difference. First there's one crisis, then there's another."

Bill Cole made an involuntary half-gesture toward the briefcase on the chair beside him.

"What is it, Bill?" said Mrs. Blandings quietly. "I'm sure Jim's in some sort of a jam again, but what's it about?"

"It isn't necessarily a jam," said Bill Cole. "Jim can punch his

190

way out of it. It has to do with the Lansdale *Blade* and your friend Mr. Nellus."

"I *knew* it," said Mrs. Blandings. "I've known it ever since last night. Oh dear, I'm afraid I can't finish my shrimps."

"Just be easy," said Bill Cole.

"Bill," said Mrs. Blandings, "if Jim's been flimflammed again, that's one thing. He's been flimflammed by everything in the country—land, house, neighbors, school board, I don't know what. I could stand his being flimflammed again, I suppose, but if he's been flimflammed by Mr. Nellus I think it would break his heart, and I think it would break mine too, because we've both gotten so fond of the old gentleman, and he's the one person who seemed so thoroughly . . ."

She dropped her hands in her lap, and the waiter slid the sweetbreads before her like a conjurer.

"Maybe it would be helpful if you told me what you know," said Bill Cole.

"All I know," said Mrs. Blandings, "is that one night Jim told me that he thought Mr. Nellus was going to give him an interest in the paper, and I wormed it out of him that he'd offered Mr. Nellus fifteen hundred dollars to buy some new type and whatever. Wouldn't you know, Jim left it open to Mr. Nellus to decide what Jim should get in return. I was vexed, and I made a scene."

"Rather deliberately," she added.

"Did Jim tell you he'd actually given this Nellus a check for fifteen hundred dollars?" asked Bill.

"No he didn't," said Mrs. Blandings.

"Well he did," said Bill Cole.

Mrs. Blandings set down her fork, and her eyes began to glitter with tears.

"And now I suppose Mr. Nellus has absconded," she said.

Bill Cole unsnapped his briefcase and began pulling out some papers. "In the literal sense of the Latin *abscondere*," he said gently, "he has."

Mrs. Blandings looked in misery at the plate from which she had eaten one forkful. The waiter captain came hurrying up. "Sweetbreads satisfactory to your liking, Madame?" he inquired.

"*Very* nice, thank you," said Mrs. Blandings.

"However," said Bill, "there isn't any question of fraud involved. Fraud isn't the point. It's rather more complex."

"Jim said," said Mrs. Blandings, "that he'd suggested to Mr. Nellus a sixteenth or an eighth interest in the paper in return for the fifteen hundred, but I suppose that's all spilt milk."

"Yes it is," said Bill Cole. "The check has gone through the banks. Look, Muriel, I think it's a splendid break that you came in today instead of Jim, because we've got to move fast, and you and I can decide the best course and put a united front up to Jim. The fact is that in return for the fifteen hundred dollars Nellus did not convey any fractional interest to Jim at all."

"No fractional interest," said Mrs. Blandings, tonelessly.

"No," said Bill Cole. "He conveyed the total property."

"I beg your pardon?" said Mrs. Blandings.

"I have here," said Bill Cole, "a bill of sale made out to Jim, 'in return for one dollar and other considerations,' a sworn statement from Nellus to whom it may concern that he is the sole owner of the property known as the Lansdale Blade Printing and Publishing Company, that it is free of any mortgages, liens, or other encumbrances, plus an audited balance sheet and income statement. Also—"

The dam burst, and the tears that Mrs. Blandings had been holding back came welling over her lower eyelids. She put her handkerchief up to her face, and her shoulders began to shake with laughter. "I'm having hysterics," she said. "Hold my hand."

"Something for dessert?" said the waiter captain. "Glass vanee, shokolaa, strawberee . . ."

"Not for years," said Mrs. Blandings, "have I had a glass of brandy after lunch. Will you take me to a matinee?"

"There aren't any matinees on Mondays," said Bill Cole.

"A movie, then."

"Let me call my office," said Bill Cole.

When he came back, Mrs. Blandings was pulling on her gloves. "Before we go on our tear," said Bill Cole, "you should read the letter Nellus sent me with all this."

Mrs. Blandings shook her head. "Just give me the gist."

"By now," said Bill, "I guess Mr. Nellus is in Santa Barbara,

192

California, where he said he was going to join his married sister. He gave me a post-office box number and he said that if he had done anything actually illegal to write him there. He said that when he got Jim's check it was just too much for him: that Jim obviously wanted to be a country publisher as much as *he* wanted to stop being one, and that giving Jim the paper in return for the fifteen hundred dollars seemed the perfect way to make everybody happy. He said he'd left things so that the paper would run itself for three weeks, and that Jim could depend on Verm Booler. Who is Verm Booler?"

"The *Blade*'s reporter," said Mrs. Blandings. "He's rather old and he wears a hearing aid and he can't see very well, but apparently he's a wonderful reporter, as they go."

"Anyway," said Bill Cole heavily, "Nellus explained that he was writing to me instead of dealing direct because he felt that this was the last chance in his lifetime he'd have to get away from New England and he was afraid that if he stayed to talk it over the thing would strike a snag somewhere. He's right there. The snag would have been me. As things stand now, there's a sort of default, but in another sense there isn't. I don't know just where we'd find a statute that would apply. And if the old man wouldn't waive extradition from California—" he shrugged.

"At the beginning," said Mrs. Blandings, "you said Jim could punch his way out of it."

"Certainly," said Bill Cole, "he can resell the thing just as fast as we can find a buyer."

The Hotel Marbury doorman swept them into a taxi. Mrs. Blandings, although the mother of two teen-age children, had never lost her awareness of what the smell of cool fur did to an adult male. She adjusted herself so that her companion would be unable to breathe without savoring it. "You're wonderful," she said. "You always know what to do. Where are we going now?"

Nutmeg Day came on a Thursday that year; on such bank holidays Mr. Dolliver liked nothing better than to spend some time with his stamp collection, and that was what was now occupying him on an exceptionally raw afternoon. There had been some years during which he had given it up completely; in the 1930's it had irked him beyond endurance to realize he shared a hobby pursued also by the man in the White House. Gradually he had overcome this repugnance; the man in the White House also liked old-fashioneds, and Mr. Dolliver, come to think of it, had never switched to Martinis on that account. It was getting close to time for an old-fashioned right now, too; the small thump on the front door fifteen minutes ago meant that the delivery boy had flung on Mr. Dolliver's stoop the weekly copy of the Lansdale *Blade,* and that meant it must be rising five o'clock. He would put away his stamps, get out the bottle of Old Supine, the cherry, the slice of orange, the lump of sugar, the bitters, and the ice, and then with slow, pleasurable ceremony make himself the one drink per day that was at once his custom and his limit. More and more men of *calibre* were switching to Old Supine: Mr. Dolliver seemed to encounter their faces from every printed page.

When, after one sip, Mr. Dolliver opened the Lansdale *Blade,* his casual glance turned into a stare of blank incomprehension. There was a two-column box under the banner; in Old English type, Mr. Nellus' immemorial signal for an announcement, it was headed To Our Readers. It said very little except that the old editor and publisher, with so many years of toil behind him, felt that the best interests of the paper and of the community would now be served by a change of direction and that for his successor he bespoke from the *Blade*'s patrons, editorial and advertising alike, those same qualities of loyalty, forbearance, and understanding which it had been his pleasure and reward over a period of et cetera, et cetera, et cetera. If there were to be any alterations of policy their announcement would come in due course from the new proprietor, Mr. ——.

It was this that Mr. Dolliver could not get through his head. Some things were too big for indignation, too big for a show of expostulation. Mr. Dolliver laid the paper aside, and gave himself over to thought. That Nellus; that old fool. He's been half off his rocker, one way or another, all his life, and more particularly so since his wife had died three years ago, but to do a thing like this, so utterly grotesque, so perverse, so unfair to the community, to himself—why even unfair to this Blandings man: even if Nellus had up and *given* it to him he wouldn't know how to work it, or have the time for it, or anything. Mr. Dolliver wasn't sure that Lansdale needed a paper; he wasn't sure there need be newspapers at all; in fact, the more he thought about it the more he winced and winced again to think of the personal agony he had endured because a columnist back last November . . .

"Martha," he called into the next room, "get me the *Blade* office on the phone."

But of course, with the paper having just come out today, there was no one there. No one except old Verm Booler, obviously sitting there in the gloom with his dark glasses on. By the scrabbling noises in the receiver Mr. Dolliver could tell that the old man was trying to bring the receiver into some sort of contact with his hearing aid, but nothing came of it. "God damn it," said Mr. Dolliver, "I'm going down to the hardware store and buy you some batteries for that thing with my own money."

Mr. Dolliver resumed his solitary brooding. He had a pretty good idea of where the Lansdale Blade Printing and Publishing Company stood financially, even though Urm Nellus had always managed to avoid being a loan customer. The paper itself, Mr. Dolliver reckoned, couldn't net more than five hundred dollars a year, the cockeyed way it was run; the job-printing business— drug and grocery store handbills, political posters, stationery, raffle tickets, town reports, tax lists, church programs—might run to a good deal more, provided Urm Nellus kept after his collections, which was doubtful. Make everything conservative and say that after the supplies were bought and the help was paid, Urm Nellus had had for himself something like a hundred and fifty dollars a month. That just about fitted in with his scale of living; yes, that was about it. Make everything efficient and shipshape and you might be able to double that. Of course, if you could ever make the paper into a real county-wide carrier of classified advertising for real estate, livestock, and what-have-you, you'd really have something. Take that paper over in Winbury; it was a gold mine, just on that account. But one smart, industrious family had worked, father, son, and grandson, to build that property up over fifty years, with that one everlasting end in view, and that was the only formula.

What would this Blandings do with the *Blade* now that he had

195

it? He'd either have to run it or hire somebody to run it; there was nobody there now who could. Was he going to take to slanting the news some New-Dealing, Russia-loving way? If so, it wouldn't be long before—

"By golly," said Mr. Dolliver, aloud to himself in the dusk-filled room. "Right under my nose. Right under my nose."

With relish restored, he ate the maraschino cherry he had previously impaled on a green toothpick. "Martha," he called, "look up his number and get me that Blandings fellow on Bald Mountain."

"Now who was soft-soaping you?" said Bill Cole. "Isn't there some way of shutting off that telephone?"

"That was Mr. Dolliver," said Mr. Blandings. "I can't make him out. First he spreads stories I'm a Communist and next he calls me up to congratulate me. He was really very hearty."

"About what?" said Bill Cole.

"About the *Blade,*" said Mr. Blandings. "He'd just got his copy. Butter wouldn't have melted in his mouth. I guess he thinks he'd like to lend me some money again."

"He won't need to," said Bill Cole. "Muriel and I have a plan worked out for you."

"I see," said Mr. Blandings. "Do I just make my mark where you tell me?"

"Jim, dear," said Mrs. Blandings, "during the last few days while you've been sick in bed Bill and I have been working together rather constructively."

"You've certainly been spending plenty of time in town," said Mr. Blandings. "From the time all this broke until today I've scarcely seen you."

Mrs. Blandings rumpled her husband's hair. "Erna's looked after you better than I could," she said. "You know perfectly well you've loved lying in bed and having her bring you fluffy omelets and wine jelly and boned, glazed squab, and goodness knows what else. So why should you grudge me a little time in town now that we have a wonderful cook for the first time in ten years—particularly since it's all in your best interests?"

196

"All right," said Mr. Blandings. "But if it concerns me I'd like to know what you've been up to."

"It concerns you," said Bill Cole. "You're very fortunate in your wife and you're very fortunate in me. While Erna's been feeding you on the fat of the land Muriel and I have arranged things so that you can turn a pretty little profit of 100 per cent on an accident. Ever hear of the firm of Downt and Downt?"

Mr. Blandings shook his head.

"Brokers," said Bill Cole. "Newspaper brokers. You'd be surprised what a profitable business it is."

Mr. Blandings lighted a new cigarette.

"Thanks to Muriel," said Bill Cole, "whose sharp eyes found something in Mr. Nellus' monumental docket I had overlooked, we discovered that not six months ago Downt and Downt had written to your friend Nellus to ask him if he was interested in selling the *Blade*. They said they had a possible interested party."

Mr. Blandings felt a hardening in his arteries. He could see something coming that he would not like.

"There's no copy of Nellus' answer," said Bill. "But I managed to wangle a little information just the same. Downt and Downt were making the inquiry on behalf of Fassett Newspaper Enterprises. They were willing to offer three thousand dollars for Mr. Nellus' newspaper, *and they still are*."

So that was it.

"You're shot with luck," said Bill Cole. "You get five tons of disordered type metal dumped on your neck on a Monday, and on a Thursday you have a chance to get rid of it at twice what you inadvertently paid for it."

Mr. Blandings went to a window, and with meaningless care adjusted a Venetian blind.

"No," he said.

In the freemasonry of American business, enemies continued cordially to call one another by their first names. "Lorbet," said Mr. Blandings into his office phone next day, "may I call on you for a piece of advice?"

"Any time, Jim," said Lorbet Neen, in his bass voice.

"I'll be right over," said Mr. Blandings. His Miss Willersley was troubled by this; it was her belief that Mr. Neen should come to her employer's office, not vice versa. Whenever she called Lorbet Neen she and Mr. Neen's secretary had a quiet, tense, indrawn female battle as to which of their respective principals should be the first to pick up the telephone receiver. Usually Miss Willersley lost, and it gnawed at her.

"Lorbet," said Mr. Blandings to the head of the B. & D. Media and Research Department, "what can you tell me off the top of your head about Fassett Newspaper Enterprises?"

It was the sort of question Lorbet Neen loved. He need not, as was necessary when a question of intellect was involved, answer off the top of his head. He could reach down to a deeper layer, where the close-packed statistics lay.

"A sound, aggressive, up-and-coming outfit," said Lorbet Neen. "They're on their way toward creating what might become a new media field. They own twenty-two county-seat newspapers within a radius of a hundred and fifty miles of where they head up, with an aggregate of between sixty-five and seventy thousand circulation and a milline rate so cheap it would knock your hat off."

He began reaching for a set of huge, leather-bound looseleaf volumes. "Look at these figures," he said.

"I don't want to get into it too deeply," said Mr. Blandings.

"You ought to know more about it," said Lorbet Neen. "Take one of your own accounts; take Old Supine. Do you know what would happen to the sales of that product if it did as well per capita in places under ten thousand population as it does in the big cities? I thought not, and I'll tell you: their sales would damn near quadruple, that's all."

Of course, Lorbet Neen had gone on, happy to have instructed Mr. Blandings about one of his most important accounts. Fassett was too damn perky about its success so far. They talked about their seventy-thousand circulation as if it were a hundred times as great. But it was obviously something to watch. Centralized buying of paper and all supplies. Six-page papers, everything delivered printed except one side of the loose middle sheet, which was where the local news was set up and run off in the local plant. If the local manager (that was what they called him) needed more space for news or local ads, that could be worked out too; they had a fast-moving teletype interconnection between headquarters and every one of the member papers. It wasn't *chain* publishing, Lorbet Neen emphasized; it was what you might call *branch* publishing—the basic pattern centrally established, local variations as needed. When you let yourself think, said Lorbet Neen, damn if it didn't seem as if this was the basic direction in which all publishing had been going for fifty years, except that maybe the Fassett idea could possibly turn out someday to be just a little smarter than anybody else thought so far. Too early to tell, but it was Lorbet Neen's personal idea that Fassett was a Growth Company.

Mr. Blandings thanked Lorbet Neen with hearty insincerity. If there had been the slightest trace of doubt about Fassett in his mind, Lorbet Neen's endorsement had swept it away.

"So you see," said Mr. Blandings that evening, back again in his own living room, recounting to his wife and Bill Cole the substance of his conversation with the Banton & Dascomb expert on media.

"I certainly do," said Bill Cole. "I see clearer than ever. I think maybe with a little skillful negotiation we could hike up Fassett's price to four thousand or even five. The paper is dull as ditchwater, and old man Nellus was a completely unbusinesslike old rattlepate, but everything considered it's probably worth more than I thought."

"I wouldn't dream of selling the *Blade*," said Mr. Blandings. "I'm going to publish it."

"Jim," said Mrs. Blandings, "I don't think you realize how much work Bill's put in on this problem ever since Monday."

"Yes I do," said Mr. Blandings. "And I'm grateful. But I want to state my position."

Until he said that, his mind had been teeming with ways to explain himself. Now that his wife and Bill Cole sat in silence waiting for him, he found the arrangement of his thoughts going random inside him.

"I don't like standardization," he said. "I don't like things stamped out with hundred-ton cookie cutters, so that you can't tell one from another with a microscope. I like handwork. I like to

199

see where the tool slipped a little and the man had to fix the scratch. I—well, that's it."

Bill Cole waited for him to go on, but he did not. "I suppose," said Bill, "that you carry out these idiosyncrasies in buying your car, and your typewriter and your soup. I never heard a man contradict himself so. You deplore people who don't want progress, but here you are defending a pure nineteenth-century concept. *I* love the thought of blacksmith shops under chestnut trees, but the chestnut trees are gone and so are the blacksmith shops, and the lovable rural editor and the old family physician are on the way, and I cannot afford to mourn for any of them. Time bears them away, that's all."

"Who is contradicting himself now?" said Mr. Blandings, gaining a little momentum. "You're trying to persuade me that nobody should fight against economic determinism. I thought you were a Republican, for God's sake: I thought you were against the collectivist idea wherever you found it. Now here you are talking like Karl Marx."

"Jim," said Mrs. Blandings, "do you think it's any nicer of you to imply that Bill's a Communist just because you disagree with him than it is for Anson Dolliver to imply that you are, for the same reason?"

"I'm sorry," said Mr. Blandings who wasn't sorry. "All I want to be is an individualist in my own way. I can't draw a logical line except to say I'm willing to buy canned soup, but not canned ideas. Old man Nellus was an individualist, at least of sorts. Maybe he was a pretty dull, timid individualist, and maybe that's the kind I am too, but at least I can stand up and be counted as *some* sort of individualist in this rapidly collectivizing world. I'd rather see a dull, individual piece of printed matter than a glossy piece of machine-made standardization."

There was a silence.

"Right here in my own back yard," said Mr. Blandings, "I've been given a chance to fight out this fight in small, simple, local, understandable terms. It doesn't involve fighting with personal enemies; it merely involves fighting for what I think is a good principle against what I think is a bad one."

200

"You had the same sort of religious call when you thought you might get on the school board," said Bill Cole. "And nothing has come of it."

"All right," said Mr. Blandings. "Now I've got a vehicle that I can use for my own ideas. I've been more disappointed about the school board than anybody else. But now, instead of being just a member of a committee that rules ideas off its agenda per se, I can be a—a—"

What could he be? Where was the word?

"An autocrat," said Mrs. Blandings. "An autocrat, fighting for individualism and democracy, two contrary ideas at once, with twenty-four hundred circulation from a busted old paper in a town that doesn't like you. A setup for success."

She was somehow very angry.

"Let us bring the conversation down from this lofty and confusing plane," said Bill Cole. "You can either sell this windfall and pocket some money, or you can refuse to sell it, and have it milk you instead. If the latter, I do not see how you can edit a paper here and run an advertising job in New York."

"I'll find some way," said Mr. Blandings.

"I wish to God," said Bill Cole, "I could find some legal means of extraditing that renegade Nellus from California and bringing him back here to face the music. If I could find some sort of flea-bitten relative who'd sue him for dissipation of assets—"

"Men seem so strong and self-reliant," said Mrs. Blandings, "until one tries to depend on them."

Mr. Hackett sat down in Mr. Dolliver's leather-upholstered chair, the one with the brass studs.

"Originally," he said, "I was just walking around to see that he wasn't setting any more grass fires without a permit, like he done last summer, when my eye caught on this."

He held out a sheet of bright yellow memorandum paper, of which the bottom third was burned away.

"So I clumb over the wall and picked it up," said Mr. Hackett. He handed the paper, headed "From the desk of J. H. Blandings," to Mr. Dolliver.

"Still careless about burning papers," said Mr. Dolliver.

"I'll say," said Mr. Hackett. "Read it."

Mr. Dolliver read:

Dear Mr. Stalin:

This is the third letter we are addressing to you. Its purpose, like its predecessors, and those that will follow, is to impress on you the deep significance of figures relating to the industrial capacity of the United States. Most of these figures are not generally known in the United States itself. For example:

The U.S. can produce 275,000 aircraft motors annually.

The U.S. can produce 195 million barrels of high-octane gasoline annually.

Line after line the figures continued, down to the edge where the paper was burned away.

"Cracky," said Mr. Dolliver. *"Espionage!"*

"More like spying to me," said Mr. Hackett.

"I guess," said Mr. Dolliver, "that J. Edgar Hoover might like to know about this."

202

· 24 ·

"IF YOU WERE to ask my opinion," said Harry Silber, "there is more value in this one at $2.39 than in the fancier one at $2.98, although don't misunderstand me, they're both very good shirts."

"I guess," said Mr. Blandings slowly, "I'll take two of the cheaper ones, but I want them to have different patterns."

Mr. Silber flopped out three different numbers in the cheap plaid $2.39's and waited for Mr. Blandings to make his choice. "And what else?" he said.

"With the sun getting warmer I guess I need a work cap."

"Right over here," said Mr. Silber. He gave Mr. Blandings an appraising glance. "You look like a seven-and-a-quarter, but take a three-eighths; they shrink when you sweat, I don't care what anybody tells you."

He began disarranging a high pile of neatly stacked caps. Silber's Dry Goods was a long, narrow store with an ornamental tin ceiling. The fluorescent lights were new; the painters were yet to arrive to touch up the scars left by the electrical installers. "Eight weeks I've been waiting for them," said Mr. Silber. Mr. Blandings had said nothing, but Mr. Silber had observed him looking at the ceiling.

Mr. Silber was a little under fifty, Mr. Blandings thought. There was no trace of accent in his speech, but his voice was always hoarse, as if he smoked too many cigarettes guaranteed by ten thousand throat specialists to be free of irritating tars and resins. Mr. Blandings could somehow see the picture of Mr. Silber lying as an infant-in-arms at his mother's bosom while the family waited in the filthy cavernous room at Ellis Island in some year like 1902. On the other hand, Mr. Silber might just as well have come from

203

Indiana. Mr. Blandings had once had the impulse to ask him where he was born, and had stopped himself just in time: this simplest, most elementary inquiry might, for all Mr. Blandings knew, bear to Mr. Silber's ears the horrible overtones of an OGPU question. No, you couldn't ask a man where he was born, any more. You couldn't tell him where *you* were born, either: "I was born in Ohio," coming from Mr. Blandings' lips, might sound like a challenge.

Mr. Blandings had long ago discovered that everything in dry-goods was to be found in Mr. Silber's store; everything from a pair of copper-riveted overalls to a dress collar. When Mr. Blandings had once been caught collarless it had amazed him that Mr. Silber could immediately supply a clean non-yellow wing collar of the correct size and style. Mr. Blandings could not imagine how Mr. Silber could profit by carrying such merchandise, for his store was at the inelegant bottom of Commerce Street, with the railroad station just opposite, and not at its black-glass-and-chromium top. "You'd be surprised," was all Mr. Silber would say in answer to Mr. Blandings' question. There was always some restraint underlying Mr. Silber's merchant manner; if you wanted to be seized by the lapels, gathered up at the waist, and thrust into triple mirrors, your store was J. Donald Robinson's, at the top of the street.

"How is everything going with the paper?" Mr. Silber inquired as he handed Mr. Blandings his change.

"Fine," said Mr. Blandings. "If it weren't for this recession we'd really be doing very well."

"Which recession is that?" Mr. Silber inquired.

"Well, you know," said Mr. Blandings, "this—" He did not know which recession himself.

"We are not members of the Merchants' Association, as you know," said Mr. Silber, "because we consider a store's closing hours a matter for the proprietor to decide, not an association. Nevertheless, we have been here quite a long time, and compared to what I know I would not call this any recession. That is from me who my wife says I complain all the time."

"There's been a little falling off in advertising," said Mr. Blandings, trying to sound professional. After all, it was his business.

"When you cut off the five hundred delinquents who hadn't paid

204

their subscriptions for three years or more, and lowered your rates," said Mr. Silber, "I said to my wife, I said I wonder if he's doing the right thing. I don't question your judgment: I'm just wondering."

"I had to make up my mind one way or another," said Mr. Blandings. "I thought I ought to make the circulation as clean and tight as I could."

"Nineteen hundred circulation sounds quite a lot less than twenty-four hundred is the only thing," said Mr. Silber.

"You've kept up your patronage, anyway," said Mr. Blandings. "The *Blade* appreciates it."

"Don't mention it," said Mr. Silber. "With us it's a business proposition."

Mr. Silber was fond of using the plural pronoun to describe his establishment; he seemed to do it as naturally as if he were a vice president of Macy's. The little bell on the clock-spring coil jingled wildly for an instant as Mr. Blandings opened Mr. Silber's front door after saying good night, and to his ears it brought a tiny breath of Europe and poverty and irremediable sadness to mingle with the loud, careless blast of neon-drenched America on Commerce Street, of a vernal evening.

It was all incomprehensible to Mr. Silber. One need only look at Mr. Blandings to perceive him as a Nordic among Nordics. His eyes were blue, his thinnish hair must once, in boyhood, have been blond. Not by manner, address, carriage, posture, gait, expression, voice, gesture, or build did he differ notably from his fellows. But Mr. Silber's eyes, sensitized by several thousand years of peering in the dark, easily perceived something: Mr. Blandings was a man with a pack at his heels.

"Why?" he said to his wife, who had no answer to give him.

Mr. Silber and his wife had many reasons to be grateful to the part of America in which they lived. No chalked door, no smashed window had ever anguished or terrified them. Their two children had made uneventful trips through the school-mill of Lansdale's education and were now in college; no taunt had ever blasted their childhood beyond the usual sufferings of small creatures everywhere. Mr. and Mrs. Silber were lonely, but perhaps they preferred it so; they were used to standing by themselves and had not sought to have it otherwise. The business with the Merchants' Association was typical; a group had once sought out Mr. Silber, and suggested that if he would close his doors at six in the evening and at noontime on Wednesdays in the summer he might receive in return the benefits of some fraternal give and take. To Mr. Silber this had seemed merely foolish, since he did quite a tidy business between six in the evening and eleven at night when he put up his own shutters. He had declined, and that had been the end of it; no other suggestions were made to him, no other proffers of brotherhood. Whatever conspiracies against the consumer were locally arranged Mr. Silber had to ferret out for himself, and then decide how to meet with the virtue of his individuality.

With the advantage of his considerable practice, Mr. Silber had no trouble seeing what was being done to Mr. Blandings as the publisher of the Lansdale *Blade:* he was being boycotted. The reason was darkly hidden from Mr. Silber, but the evidence was shining clear. And it was being done with the utmost delicacy, Mr. Silber was bound to admit. Mr. Silber had a keen eye for areas and observed with what almost imperceptible slowness the size of the local advertisements declined. Any sudden change, any abrupt cancellation, would have been perhaps suspicious; but so long as Lansdale's businessmen cut off only a quarter of an inch of their patronage at a time, continued to express cordiality and plead a decline in the margin of business, there wasn't anything to be done or remarked on. The same contraction must be happening to the printing of handbills and the like. Mr. Blandings had spoken of "recession"; could it be possible that he had no suspicion of what was really going on?

"I wonder if I should say anything to him," said Mr. Silber.

"And get yourself into a fine mess of trouble poking your nose into things that are none of your business?" said Mrs. Silber.

"What Jim needs is a cause or a crusade or something," said Mrs. Blandings. "Henry, don't you know any sort of issue he can lay his hands on, ready-made? The *Blade* gets duller every week, right in front of our eyes. Circulation goes down a little, advertising goes down a little. I don't blame anybody but ourselves."

Henry Simms was a pipe smoker, too. Unlike Dward Wayburn in the Banton & Dascomb office, he needed no auxiliaries at all. He did not even put tobacco in his pipe; he just used it as a sort of perpetual, insoluble lollipop.

"Afraid not," he said.

Henry Simms was a gifted man, but he had the most unjournalistic mind in America. Mrs. Blandings did not know why she had asked him the same question a dozen times during the harried last two months; the answer was always the same.

"Stop worrying Henry," said Mrs. Blandings. "We'll find something after a while."

"There's always the old lake project," said Mr. Simms.

"What old lake project?" said Mrs. Blandings. "Shamalaug Lake?"

Mr. Simms nodded.

Lake Shamalaug was about three miles long and three-quarters of a mile across at its widest point. It lay in a complex fold of hills six miles from the center of Lansdale Town, and its waters were clear and cold. Mr. and Mrs. Blandings were conscious of it mostly at those times when Betsy was home; at one end of it was a sagging and decayed amusement park set in a huge, handsome pine grove that provided unexampled opportunities for adolescent lovemaking. Mrs. Blandings wished it was in hell.

"I never knew it had a project," said Mrs. Blandings, with a well-go-on intonation.

"Oh yes," said Mr. Simms. "I worked on it. As a transitman. In the 1930's every residential architect in the country was starving, and I thought I was pretty lucky to get a $35-a-week job with the State Engineer's Office as a surveyor. I was, too."

It was the end of his narrative.

"Is there any way I can crank you up so you'll go on?" said Mrs. Blandings.

"That's all there is to it," said Mr. Simms. "We finished the survey, and then like hundreds of other things like it at the time it all collapsed, got buried and forgotten."

"What did?" said Mrs. Blandings.

"The project," said Mr. Simms.

"*What was the project?*" said Mrs. Blandings. Her husband was beginning to think she would make a very good reporter.

"Oh," said Mr. Simms. "Well, it was a very sound and attractive idea. The State Engineer's Office was ordered to report on what would happen if a dam were built at the lower end of Shamalaug, where it empties into the Wintinock, and do you know, it would have increased the size of Shamalaug by over ten times. I forget the name of the old state senator who was sponsoring it, but he wanted to build the dam, enlarge the lake, and take a thousand acres around it by eminent domain and make a state park out of the whole business. But as I say it all fell through, and about that time residential construction woke up a little and I went back to the practice of architecture."

"Jim," said Mrs. Blandings. "There's your cause. There's your crusade."

"Of course," said Mr. Simms, "the bigger lake would have drowned out all the cottages that Anson Dolliver and the Alders and the Eldridges and the rest of them own, and taken quite a sizable bit of acreage from Anse Dolliver in particular. It would have drowned out the amusement park, too, and a lot of farms, and made all sorts of changes."

"Jim," said Mrs. Blandings again, "there's your crusade. There's something to make the *Blade* halfway interesting. Revive the state park idea. How simply wonderful."

She was beaming. Her husband made no response. Neither did Henry Simms.

"Jim," said Mrs. Blandings. "I'll tell you what I'll do. I'll go to the capital and I'll see what I can find out about all this. Henry can give me the names of some people to look up in the State Engineer's Office, and I'll find out what happened to the whole project."

Mr. Blandings straightened up in the chair in which he had been slumping deeper and deeper. "Well," he said, "maybe."

After Mr. Simms had gone home, Mrs. Blandings looked with sad love her husband in the eye. "Why is it," she asked, "that you're so wild with enthusiasm at the beginning of something, and that you get so down in the mouth about it later on?"

"I guess you and Bill Cole were right about the *Blade*," said Mr.

208

Blandings. "I guess the shoemaker should have stuck to his last."

"The time for thinking that was when Bill Cole had a buyer," said Mrs. Blandings. "Now we have to *do* something. And I'll help do it."

She leaned over and kissed her husband. "Don't be discouraged, darling," she said. "We can work this out, just you see."

The letter that came back to Mr. Dolliver from the Federal Bureau of Investigation was anything but satisfactory. "The vigilance of the individual citizen," it said, "was never more necessary for the preservation of our democracy than at the present time. However, in the instance of the memorandum forwarded by you, involving the use of figures by one J. H. Blandings in a document purportedly addressed to one Joseph Stalin, the figures used appear to be derived entirely from the Annual Report of the Department of Commerce of the United States, an official document issued from the Government Printing Office and available to all persons for $1. Accordingly it is not thought—"

Very well, thought Mr. Dolliver. It was characteristic that Washington should be drowsy and complaisant. He would not bother Washington further. Things had better be handled on the local level after all. On the local level they were proceeding satisfactorily.

25

WHEN MR. BLANDINGS came home from the *Blade* office one sunny afternoon he found the house much too quiet. He made for the bedroom and discovered his wife lying down; the shades were drawn and a damp cloth lay across her forehead. "Erna and Amby are going to leave," she said.

Since the day when Mr. Blandings had first made the acquaintance of Urmot Nellus by inserting in the *Blade* a classified ad offering employment to a country couple, a lurching procession of male-and-female Serbs, Croats, and Slovenes had wandered in and out of the Blandings home; Finns, Germans, and Italians bound in unwelcome wedlock had also contributed their national peculiarities to the house on Bald Mountain. Between times, Mrs. Blandings had been the family servant, and said, in listless sorrow, that she preferred it so. There had seemed no solution to the problem of getting country work done until the blissful day when Erna and Amby had appeared. Amby was an amiable and persuasive slacker with a weakness for the bottle, but Erna was worth three of anybody. Not only was she the best cook Mrs. Blandings had ever dreamed of; she worked with hard, willing cheer at every household task and in the time of her presence on Bald Mountain had made domestic life a song. Now this heavenly situation was about to be destroyed.

"Why?" said Mr. Blandings.

"I don't know," said Mrs. Blandings. "Erna's as miserable as I am. It's something about Amby, and you've got to find out—I can't."

After a grave dinner, Mr. Blandings paid a call on Erna and Amby in their rooms off the kitchen. If managing people in the office gave him trouble it was nothing to the distress he felt at coping with a crisis under his own roof. He fumbled with the conversation until Amby came to his rescue.

"I'll tell you," said Amby; "it's nice here, but there ain't enough to do."

This rocked Mr. Blandings on his heels; he thought of Erna's prodigious housework and *per contra,* of the untidy barns, the ragged garden, the lawn that was never weeded until the weeds had already won the battle: Amby's domain.

"I don't know what you mean," he said.

"You take a place like this," said Amby, "it ought to be farmed."

"We told you in the beginning we weren't going to farm it," said Mr. Blandings. "All we ask of you is to keep the place neat and good looking, and there's plenty of work just doing that."

"Not a gardener," said Amby. "Never claimed I was."

It was not the first time this country matter had come up. If a man thought of himself as a farmer he was not a groundsman; he resented lawn mowing, or even work in a small truck garden. He considered his domain the fields and the barns; somebody else could pretty things up.

"I'm not going to get drawn into farming," said Mr. Blandings. "It costs too much money."

"You mean to tell me," said Amby, "it costs you less to have me working at something that don't bring in any money than working on something that *does*?"

This was a direct hit; whatever Mr. Blandings had planned to say, it blew up. Amby pursued his crippled foe.

"You take where I was before," he said; "I used to make twenty-nine hundred pounds of milk a month for him. I went shares with him until he had a stroke."

Him *who*? One reason Mr. Blandings had such communication difficulties with country people was that he was always tripping over pronouns left in dark corners.

"You take me," said Amby. "All my life I been with cows. First thing I can remember in all my life is milking. Wasn't four years old yet."

Mr. Blandings cleared his throat.

"Why hell," said Amby, "if they was as much as one cow on this place it would make all the difference."

211

"You mean . . . ?" said Mr. Blandings.

"Why sure," said Amby. "You take you folks, you don't know what a difference even one cow makes to a place in every particular."

Mr. Blandings was at a point of inflexion in his entire life; a point as important as a proposal of marriage, but darkly inconspicuous.

"How much would a cow cost?" he inquired.

"Why now you take a Guernsey or a Holstein," said Amby. "I wouldn't let you have one, and I'll tell you why. Just one cow, she'd sicken without she was with a herd."

Amby was now an alert and interested human being.

"But you take a Jersey, now," he went on, "she don't need a herd. She's just as happy by herself. My, what a beautiful cow a Jersey is—and a good producer, why you can get forty pounds of milk off'n her a day."

The dairyman's measurement of milk in pounds would always sound strange.

"Approximately how much, Amby," said Mr. Blandings, trying not to sound pleading, "would a Jersey—"

"You take ten years ago," said Amby, "I could of picked up a first-class registered Jersey for seventy-five dollars. I'm not saying the price wouldn't be higher today, but look what's happened to the price of the milk and cream and butter you'd be saving."

"Why don't you sort of—" said Mr. Blandings.

"Leave it to me," said Amby.

When Mr. Blandings told Mrs. Blandings that Erna and Amby had withdrawn their notice and would stay, the tortured look went out of her eyes. When he told her the terms, her forehead creased and a long tremulous sigh escaped her. "Still," she said, "I'm not criticizing; I guess it was the only thing to do."

Three days later, a Jersey cow was in the Blandings barn. Indeed, she was beautiful. She seemed not only female but feminine. Her coat was a dreamy faun color, and her eyes were a lustrous brown. Into her right ear was clamped the long, thin piece of metal stamped with her registration number. It was to none of these points that Amby was drawn. "Look at that bag, will you,"

212

he said. "I had to pay a little more for her, but she's one in a thousand."

"How much?" said Mr. Blandings.

"Don't give it a thought," said Amby. "He don't care whether he gets paid now or six months from now."

Dairy products now began to inundate the Blandings. The milk was gorgeous; the yellow cream clotted as in Devonshire; no butter, no cottage cheese could be bought to compare with what Erna made from the Jersey's outpouring. With unlimited supplies of cream and butter to draw on, her cookery leaped another five notches in the scale of perfection. The cow had to be milked three times a day and even so became alarmingly restless after 5 P.M.; her bag, taut to translucence, dragged cruelly at her hindquarters. No question but that Amby knew cows, and had acquired a prize one. "My God, I think she's agonta drowned us," he said one day after she had dispensed enough for twenty well-located soda fountains.

A complete change came over Amby. He gave up drinking. Into the hitherto neglected barns he moved like an avenging angel, and cleared away the debris of twenty years. One afternoon Mr. Blandings came home and discovered a concrete mixer and two conspiritorial Italians at work. "What is this?" he demanded.

"Man getting a concrete floor in his barn free ain't got any kick coming, has he?" Amby answered. To Mr. Blandings, *sotto voce,* he added, "I made a *deal* with 'em."

What it was, Mr. Blandings could not discover. He was on the run again, and this time his pursuer was Amby Sillcox. Bills began arriving. None came for the cow, doubtless owing to curious credit practices among cattle dealers, but Mr. Rocklett's hardware store was more forthright. Invoices turned up for milk pails, milk pans, milk strainers, milk cans, a small cream separator, a small electric churn and ice-cream freezer. None of these had been authorized, but none of them did Mr. Blandings feel he could protest. In the aggregate they did not come to much over a hundred dollars, and Mrs. Blandings reported that they were saving almost ten dollars a week in dairy products unpurchased at retail prices. Therefore, in a little over ten weeks . . .

In far fewer than ten weeks everything was wildly, loopingly, out of control. Amby now saw his function as the manager of an estate whose owner should not be bothered with trifles. A sow and two piglets appeared. "We was wasting garbage and wasting skim," said Amby. He was using as the pigsty a small, elderly building Mrs. Blandings had thought she might someday turn into a guest house. His construction methods were poor, and the run for the pigs was a ragged trapezoid of chicken wire, conspicuous by the side of the road. "You'll feel pretty good about it when you have your own hams and bacon," said Amby.

One afternoon when Mr. Blandings came home he found the Jersey with a companion in the field. "He had to go out West," said Amby. "I said we'd board his cow till he come back. She's going to drop a calf next couple of weeks, and we git it in return for the board. I acted just quick enough. The Jersey was starting to pine."

What was past was prelude. The cows began to multiply as if by fission. Mr. Blandings sought out Amby. "No need to get upsot," said Amby. "He had to go and have an operation, so I rented his herd. Give him enough money to pay his hospital bill, and we get the milk. You and I going shares now, don't forget."

When Mr. Blandings counted, there seemed to be seventeen cows on his land. The last increase had a curious effect on the domestic economy: the flow of milk into the Blandings household absolutely ceased, and there was a reversion to store purchase. Amby said nothing until questioned. "Got t' make all the milk we can," he said. "With the milk checks we get from the co-operative we can buy all the stuff anybody can stomach." Mr. Blandings noticed this total reversal of Amby's economic and emotional approach to milk, but kept silent. He himself had felt rather awash with the product when the Jersey was in full output; his insides seemed so coated with cream that alcohol would not diffuse into his bloodstream in any satisfactory concentration. This he had resented. Amby, he noticed, seemed to use no dairy products except evaporated milk which he dribbled from a boughten can into his coffee.

At the end of the first month Amby presented Mr. Blandings with $5.75 in crumpled paper and worn silver; it was his share of the proceeds from dairying. The accounting was done on the back of an old envelope and needed a great deal of explanation. Mr.

Blandings tried to follow but gave up. More and more bills from more and more stores or dealers were arriving; more and more equipment was finding lodgment in Mr. Blandings' barn. One day Amby came home in triumph with a field mower, a hayrake, and four spools of rusty barbed wire, bought at auction; they were on a one-ton truck which itself was a mystery. "B'longs to Erna," he explained. "Got it out of storage over to Hartford." A large, strange dog, wolf-like but yellow-colored, was trotting at his heels. Amby called him Spot, and he instantly obeyed Amby's lightest command. There was some old-time intimacy here that Amby was not going to explain. "There isn't any place here for him to sleep," said Mr. Blandings, snappishly. "He's a house dog," said Amby.

Mrs. Blandings announced to her husband that night that the dog was the last straw. In this, she was wrong. Almost immediately and out of nowhere two handsome dapple-gray work horses appeared in the barns, so big that their fat rumps were a foot above eye level. "Well I can't pull the field mower by m'self," said Amby. Mrs. Blandings had tackled him this time, and was having wild internal feelings as she saw unheralded chickens pecking about the barn floor. "He died and his widder didn't have any use for a team so I took 'em off her hands. Let me tell you it's a lot better than having one of those tractors; you don't get any manure off a tractor and the price of gasoline, they've got it where it's outrageous."

There were mysteries within mysteries. No bill for the original Jersey cow ever arrived. Amby seemed to have bought many of his new acquisitions with his own money. The general running expenses of the establishment rose considerably, but there was never any more talk about Mr. Blandings' monthly share of the business proceeds. The landed proprietor fell deeper and deeper into unease but in his efforts to bring things clear again he could only thrash like a wounded perch.

The truck was loaded. "I want you," said Mrs. Blandings, "to have a good, thorough, *sensemaking* talk with Amby. You'll be on the road over an hour each way, and that's plenty of time to get a few fundamentals thoroughly understood."

Mr. Blandings nodded gloomily. His wife had maneuvered it

215

so that he and Amby were about to start out for the State Agricultural College. The ostensible reason lay in a dozen glass gallon jars of corn preserved by Erna. She had packed whole ears, a foot long, five to a jar, and for the first three months they had been so beautiful in their glass casements that the Blandings had preferred looking to eating. Then, jar by jar, their liquid had turned cloudy and a contention arose whether the corn was edible or did death by botulism lurk there. Mr. Blandings was sure it was edible; his wife had somehow used this as a lever to force him to make the trip to the college's Analytical Canning Laboratory along with Amby, to find out.

"Why did you put *all* the jars in the truck?" Mr. Blandings asked. "Two would have been enough."

"I figured take one take all," said Amby. "Some of 'em's milkier than others."

The trip began in silence. After a while Mr. Blandings said, "Amby, I want to talk to you about the general situation."

"Go right ahead," said Amby.

There was a loud bang. "God damn it," said Amby, "I been afraid of that left rear tire right along."

Mr. Blandings glanced at the spare-tire bracket. It was empty. "Where is it?" he demanded venomously. "In the barn?"

"Yep," said Amby. He stopped and swung out of the cab; Mr. Blandings tried to marshal his anger into orderly rows of stinging sentences to fling at him when he came back.

"Joke's on you," said Amby, hopping back under the steering wheel. "The tires is okay. It must been Watriss' truck backfired just as it passed us."

The journey was resumed. What with trying to dissipate his unusable anger Mr. Blandings was less than ever inclined to chat. When the second bang occurred, very loud, about five miles after the first, Amby did not stop. "Muffler," he said. " 'Bout ready to fall off anyway."

The third bang was the decisive one.

It occurred as Mr. Blandings and Amby were passing through the only city on their route large enough to have a traffic policeman. It shattered the air just as the truck jounced over the old disused trolley tracks on which his kiosk stood and Mr. Bland-

216

ings, looking in the rearview mirror, saw the officer cringe, recover, blow three piercing blasts on his whistle, and begin reaching for his service revolver. Wordlessly Amby pulled over and stopped in the middle of the block. By the time the officer reached them, livid with rage, a large crowd clogged the sidewalks.

"What are you two sons of bitches doing with that truck?" he bellowed. His uniform was strangely bespattered. With the truck at a dead stop, the fourth bang took place, and sent a shower of substance all about. The crowd retreated. "All right, wise guys, step down," said the officer. He reached for something and pulled up not the revolver Mr. Blandings expected but a large, thick notebook, and fixed his antagonists with a terrible glittering Irish eye.

When the fifth bang occurred some moments later he reversed his tactics and wearily slapped his notebook shut. "Just get out of town," he said. He glared at the floor of the truck body, awash with blasted corncobs and shards of glass. "What do you mean, you're going to have it *tested*? What the hell do you want to know about it you don't know already?" His attitude softened a little as he pocketed $10 from Mr. Blandings to have his uniform cleaned. "Don't take it to the Agricultural College," he offered in parting. "Save it for the Rooshans."

It was unfortunate that the next mile of route was over cobblestones, and with two poorly graded railroad tracks to cross, for three more of Erna's handsome gallon jars of corn exploded here. There was something about jostling they could not seem to stand. Once the truck was again on the open highway Mr. Blandings spoke to Amby, but very gently. "Slower, Amby," he said; "not more than fifteen miles an hour. There's still four left." As he spoke, there became three.

The rest of the trip was as a hone rubbed on the long vagus nerve. Two of the jars held out until almost within sight of the goal, but suffered the fate of Moses. As the truck swung slowly into the college driveway and parked by its beautifully kept grounds, the one remaining jar stood like a cathedral that had by the grace of God come through an air raid. With infinite caution Amby and

Mr. Blandings descended from their opposite sides of the truck's cab, and for a few moments their actions, under the warm morning sun, seemed aimless. What was evolving was the psychological distinction that separated the officer class from enlisted men.

"I wouldn't touch that thing," said Amby, "for a hundred of thousands of dollars. No power on earth going to make me go near it."

"Very well," said Mr. Blandings. "I'll take it in." A fine tremor was shaking him, but into his voice he was able to inject a small note of gentlemanly condescension. "If it's stood this much of the journey, I think it can go the last hundred feet. At least you can open the doors for me."

The finality took place in a broad corridor, opposite a desk with a brass standard saying MISS QUIMBAT—ENQUIRIES. Mr. Blandings was never to know whether Amby saw what really happened and slyly pretended not, or whether his solicitude for Mr. Blandings was as real as it seemed. In either event, Mr. Blandings could not conceal the truth from himself: although Miss Quimbat screamed, and a colored porter eventually came and sprinkled sawdust over the corn and glass and sticky liquid on the travertine floor, the twelfth stout jar of Erna's corn had never exploded. It had fizzed slightly at the neck, and Mr. Blandings, of the officer class, had dropped it.

26

MR. BLANDINGS was sprawled on his living-room couch, and Henry
Simms sat with his coat off in a chair.

"That wasn't the end of the story, of course," said Mr. Blandings.
Mr. Simms looked inquiring.

"When I got home I had a row with Muriel because the first
thing she asked me was if I'd had a thorough *sensemaking* conversation with Amby about the whole snarl this place was in. Of
course I hadn't. Going over, the corn was blowing up every couple
of miles, and coming back I simply wasn't in the mood to talk
about anything."

He found himself recounting again, always with the same veil of
dishonesty drawn over the degrading part of it, the episode in the
hall of the State Agricultural College.

"Anyway," he said, in a heavy effort to dismiss it, "after that
Muriel rather took things into her own hands. She called up the
County Agent and asked him to stop around and inspect things. He
showed up one afternoon and Muriel took him all through the
barns. When they came back to the house Muriel called Amby in
and got the County Agent to repeat what he'd said. He'd said that
it was a sanitary offense to quarter the horses and cows in the same
barn, and that anyway the state would stop letting any more milk
come out of those barns by summer unless we installed an electric
cooler and so many other things I don't even remember. He said,
'Lady, you've got a losing proposition here; either you've got to
spend four thousand dollars on your barns or get rid of that herd,
and there's only one way I'd look at it if I were you.' So Muriel
turned to Amby and said, 'You heard that,' and Amby said, 'Well,
I guess we get rid of the herd,' and the County Agent left.

"I thought it was all being a little too easy. That evening about nine o'clock Amby came into the living room, and he was very drunk. I thought maybe if I could get a few more drinks into him he'd pass out, so I had a few with him, but it didn't work out very well."

Mr. Simms made a sympathetic noise.

"The more he drank the meaner he got," Mr. Blandings resumed with a sigh. "He began accusing me of leading him into a trap; said we'd made a solemn vow to go shares together and now I was walking out on him. And finally he hit a sort of keynote, and over and over again he said, 'We're building a new America, and there isn't going to be any room in it for millionaires like you.'"

Mr. Blandings twitched on the couch. "What I want to know," he said, "is why these things happen to me. So help me, I never intended to do any farming here, as you damn well know. I consented to that one cow only to please Muriel; to set things up so she could be happy keeping the best cook she ever had. But of course that's all lost anyway—obviously Amby and Erna couldn't stay after that terrible outburst of Amby's, and Muriel and Erna went around weeping together and cursing men for the three final days while we got all the livestock and stuff cleared out. So here I am, poorer by I don't know what, and Muriel doing all the housework again, and a lot of mysterious bills drifting in, and people calling up asking when I'm going to pay something I didn't even know they thought I owed them . . .

"*But more than that*," said Mr. Blandings. "More than that, I want to know how it can be that Amby Sillcox can denounce me as a millionaire who's going to be liquidated in the new social order at the same time that man Dolliver in the Lansdale bank is going around saying I'm a Communist. I have never done anything to anybody, and I want to know why I am in this situation. *And I want to know what is going to happen next.*"

He stopped, out of breath, and glared at his companion.

"I don't know," said Henry Simms. "Maybe nothing at all. Maybe now things will really begin to settle down. What do you hear from Muriel?"

Mrs. Blandings' visit to the state capital was being a great deal more fun than she had ever allowed herself to imagine. Not since her college days had she tried to cope with the mechanics of library research, but she was beginning to get the hang of it again, and felt a sense of pride and excitement in what she was discovering.

It was amazing, too, what a good time she was having with Daisy Fay. Daisy and she had been roommates at Bryn Mawr. Parting at a June commencement in a year between the wars, they had sworn a lifelong friendship and then vanished from one another utterly. But there must really have been something worth preserving in their undergraduate intimacy, for now, after so many years, they had come together again without so much as half an hour of awkwardness. Mrs. Blandings had merely written to say that she was coming to Hartford for a week or so; Daisy Fay had telephoned in answer the next morning that her husband was away, and Mrs. Blandings must stay with her. "Eldo's in Washington, and I don't know *when* he's going to be back," said Daisy Fay. "The Department of Justice is calling him a monopoly, the poor darling."

Very little seemed to worry Daisy Fay. From a slim red-haired undergraduate she had painlessly progressed to the point where now her three sons were in college and she was fifteen pounds overweight, in a loose, uncaring, comfortable way. The well-polished house in the Hartford suburbs said plenty of money; the distorted springs in the upholstered chairs even spoke that there was enough money to make ostentation unnecessary. Eldo Fay would telephone to Daisy every evening about half past nine; from Daisy's murmurs of sympathy or outbursts of indignation Mrs. Blandings could infer the daily going-over that Daisy's husband's firm of machinery manufacturers must be receiving from the Anti-Trust Division. In Daisy Fay's comfortable cosmos only one thing was awry: the National Administration. But even when she discoursed on this it was evident her indignation did not corrode her: with whatever was wrong, all would come right in the end. "I wish Jim and I could be more like you and Eldo," said Mrs. Blandings.

221

"Isn't it dreadful we've never met one another's husbands," said Daisy. "Tell me more about Jim."

"There isn't much more to tell," said Mrs. Blandings. "He just happens to be superbly competent at work he happens to hate. That's putting it rather more clearly than I think Jim's able to put it to himself. So far, we haven't been able to find out just what to do about it."

"And I don't think we're on the right track," she added.

"You mean with the *Blade?*" said Daisy.

"The *Blade* and everything," said Mrs. Blandings. "Nothing seems to work out properly. We're engaged in a pretense that we belong in Lansdale but it's grotesque, because the other side isn't playing. We're outlanders, and everybody knows it, including Jim, but that's another thing Jim won't admit to himself."

Daisy Fay sat in sympathetic silence.

"In some ways Jim is the most naïve man I've ever known in all my life," said Mrs. Blandings. "Advertising men are supposed to be so cynical and calculating. I just wish there was a little of those qualities in Jim. He *thinks* he has them, of course, but that oleomargarine editorial was all the proof anybody'd need to the contrary."

"I don't think you told me," said Daisy.

"That's what just about wrecked the *Blade,*" said Mrs. Blandings. "It did prove one thing. It proved that the *Blade* got read by an awful lot of people who never admitted it before."

"What happened?" said Daisy.

"Well," said Mrs. Blandings, "Jim read an article that was just bursting with facts and figures about oleomargarine versus butter, so he sat down and wrote an editorial and headed it 'Let's Give Oleomargarine a Break' and I never even saw it until it came out."

"Don't think," said Mrs. Blandings, her voice rising, "that editors are only threatened with shotguns down South or in the nineteenth century, because that's just what happened to Jim. It made him feel terribly brave at the time, but then a couple of days later when everybody stopped speaking to him the bravado element went out of it. Imagine, Daisy; right in the middle of the Connecticut dairy-farming country, Jim writes and publishes a hymn to oleomargarine. Really, if he'd've gotten up in Town Meeting and said 'Let's all buy Turkish tobacco' it wouldn't have been a tenth as bad."

"Why did he do it?" asked Daisy.

"Because he *believed* it," said Mrs. Blandings in an exhausted voice. "It's his economic creed—'the Consumer, first, last, and always: what's best for him is best for all.' It sounds so true and so innocuous, doesn't it? I know Jim thought it would make a very popular editorial. Of course he was having a bad reaction from cows when he wrote it—but so was I, the filthy, horrible, treacherous beasts. Yet I could have told him not to publish such an absolutely incendiary thing."

"But here you are," said Daisy, "busy working up material for him that maybe he'll use to blow off his other foot."

"No," said Mrs. Blandings; "I'm going to be of help to him in spite of himself. I've dug out a wonderful story about how this old Lake Shamalaug project got suppressed back in the thirties, and I'm sure I could hang all the town fathers with it—but I'm just not going to give it to Jim."

"Deceiving your husband?" said Daisy.

"Yes," said Mrs. Blandings. "And don't think I don't feel very uncomfortable about it, too. In one sense," she added; "in the broader sense I'm doing it to protect him. And it isn't as if I hadn't done something nice and constructive for him, because I have. I have a fine story about how the lake project was conceived, why it was a good idea then, and why it's an even better idea today. All I'm leaving out is the messy part; Jim can have a nice *pro bono publico* crusade that ought to make him popular with everybody —everybody except the Dollivers and the Eldridges and the Alders."

"Heavens," said Daisy Fay, "those are all Founders' Names."

"How did you know?" said Mrs. Blandings.

"Why bless you, they all came from Hartford," said Daisy with a merry laugh. "There was another one, too; what was *his* name?"

"I don't know," said Mrs. Blandings. "Those three are the only ones you keep bumping into all the time, because the families are still right there in charge of Lansdale more than two hundred years later."

"Well," said Daisy, "their originals were riffraff, or so their contemporaries here used to think. What was the name of that fourth one? He was a minister or something; it'll come to me in a minute."

"I love to think Anson Dolliver is descended from riffraff," said Mrs. Blandings. "He's the whole show in Lansdale, you know. He's the one who incited the farmers to make such an issue with Jim over the oleomargarine editorial—not that they needed much inciting. Oh dear, isn't there anything a free press in America can talk about without making *some*body angry?"

"If you ask me," said Daisy, "there's altogether too much free press in this country right now. Look at what some of these newspapers have been calling Eldo. Why? Just because he and his father and family before him were a little extra hard working and ingenious, and used their heads and put some patents together and built a substantial business, and were honest, upright, God-fearing people."

"Now Daisy," said Mrs. Blandings. "It isn't consistent—"

"*Lendicks*," said Daisy, "that was his name. The Reverend Jonathan Benjamin Lendicks. The minute I said God-fearing I thought of it. You've never run across his name in Lansdale?"

Mrs. Blandings shook her head, "Never," she said. "What's he to you?"

"Nothing," said Daisy Fay, "except that with Eldo being so wrapped up in old Connecticut names I hate to lose a thread, and there's something about this old Reverend Jonathan I can't bring out. It's funny the one man of property should vanish and the riffraff still be there. Or maybe it isn't at all. Maybe it's always been that way. Maybe conditions today are nothing new."

Mrs. Blandings could see a political speech rising in Daisy Fay's bosom, and sought to avoid it. "Let's talk about our children," she said brightly.

"Let's," said Daisy Fay. "Didn't your younger daughter—"

224

27

"WHEN is Mother coming home from Hartford?" said Betsy.

"You can read it, all but the postscript," said Mr. Blandings. He withheld one private page, and tossed the rest of his wife's letter across the breakfast table. "All she says is that maybe she'll be away another four or five days."

Betsy and Joan read the letter over one another's shoulders. "What does she mean by 'on the track of something that might change the whole situation'?" said Joan.

"You know as much as I do," said Mr. Blandings. He hoped his fourth cup of coffee would have some helpful effect on him. "I haven't the remotest idea."

"Why don't you call her up?" said Betsy. "Hartford isn't so far away we can't afford to, is it?"

"I've told you," said Mr. Blandings, "that until we can get a single-party line installed up here your mother and I don't think it's advisable to talk over the phone any more. We don't know who's listening in."

"Do you mean to say we're *tapped*?" said Joan.

"No," said Mr. Blandings. "Not as far as I know. It's just all the busybodies on a party line in the country. We were stupid not to think about it before."

"Do you think that's how the rumor got around that Mother was pregnant again?" said Betsy.

"It's possible," said Mr. Blandings. "Anything's possible."

He brushed himself free of toast fragments with a paper napkin and rose from the table. "Time I got down to the *Blade*," he said.

"How are you going to get along if we have to go to camp before

Mother gets back from Hartford?" said Betsy. "You can't possibly take care of yourself alone in this house."

"I'll manage," said Mr. Blandings. He wasn't being much of a father these days, he realized. He wasn't being much of anything.

Betsy curled an arm through his and rested a glowing cheek and strands of golden hair on his shoulder. "I'll stay here and take care of you, and not go to camp, and Mother can stay away as long as she likes."

Joan surveyed her sister. "*Freudian*," she said. "That's what it is."

"Do the dishes, scullery maid," said Betsy, "and don't let Father's plate slip out of your baby hands."

"God help the man who marries you," said Joan with a glare of fury at her sister. "You're a bitch."

"Children," said Mr. Blandings, "I absolutely forbid—"

"The man who marries me," said Betsy, unruffled, "will get a mighty fine cook." She cast her eyes for an instant heavenward. "And that ain't all," she added in a Mae West voice.

"The first thing an intelligent man would want would be loyalty," said Joan.

"Come back in two years and I'll tell you the first thing a man would want, intelligent or not," said Betsy.

"Listen to me," said Mr. Blandings. "I absolutely forbid—"

"Maybe at first," said Joan, "but then he'd begin to wonder. Look at you, just this year. First it was Vincent Spelly, then it was Alan Hepsworth, now it's Nadwell Neen. Same thing with all of them."

"That's enough, Joan," said Mr. Blandings.

"It *ought* to be enough," said Joan.

Mr. Blandings was seeing diplobic visions of Dr. Udderweld, his mind shocklessly packed with all knowledge of infantile sexuality, rejection images, incestuous drives, and guilt-fear constellations. They did not add to his peace of mind.

"Listen, children," he said, "you've been taking care of me very beautifully while Mother's been away, what with Betsy's wonderful cooking and Joanie doing the housework on scientific principles, but this squabbling is enough to drive a man out of his head, particularly with this constant vulgar reference to—"

"You can't dodge biological facts," said Joan.

226

"Who is this Nadwell Neen?" asked Mr. Blandings, his anxieties taking an abrupt new turn.

"A boy," said Betsy.

"We're lucky, Father," said Joan. "He could just as well be an orangutan."

"I mean what does his father do?" Mr. Blandings asked. "I'm not prying—I have a reason for asking."

"I really don't know," said Betsy. "He told me, but it's slipped my mind."

Mr. Blandings gave up trying to fathom the minds of human beings in the larval stage, and in the warm June morning drove the station wagon down Bald Mountain Road and through the mild traffic of Lansdale Town to the parking space behind the office of the Lansdale *Blade*. The badly adjusted gas burner under the linotype's melting pot still bore its fumes through the building. He had been trying to get it fixed ever since Mr. Nellus had left him the paper.

On his desk the day's mail usually deposited only the most inconsequential third-class matter. Today was different: there were two envelopes sealed and bearing three-cent postage. Both bore the corner card of Banton & Dascomb. Without opening the envelopes he knew from whom they came: the monarch-sized one, hand-addressed, could only be from George Stout; the long, fattish one, faultlessly typed by an electric machine, was out of Horace Dascomb's office. Mr. Blandings turned them over and wondered which to open first; both bore identical postmarks; there was no clue to which should have precedence. He weighed the two in his palms, and decided that George Stout's should have the first attention.

George Stout's cultivated handwriting always impressed Mr. Blandings: it had the appearance of flawless calligraphy in a language he did not understand. He had to read it twice before he felt he had mastered it, although it was no more than the sort of friend-to-friend document that was growing rarer and rarer in the United States as mass communication slowly strangled every other variety:

227

. . . miss you sorely for reasons professional as well as personal. They have dumped a lot of your work on me, without easing up a whit on my own. The whole thing was vastly complicated last week by the sudden rupture of relations with Dward Wayburn, who . . .

But Mr. Blandings knew nothing of this. It must be the subject of Mr. Dascomb's letter; he should have opened it first, after all.

. . . who will be with us no more after this week. I wish I could give you the cold dope on this, but I haven't got it. In the old days the employee always insisted he'd resigned and the management said he'd been fired. Now, with all this severance pay business, it is just the other way around . . .

When are you coming back? I hear all sorts of things about you, and I don't know what's truth or what's rumor. That oleomargarine editorial of yours was a dilly, but wasn't it a little rash? I showed it to Mr. D. and it made him pensive enough to say there was 'a serious gap in Top Creative' so long as you're away. Things always happen in bunches, you know: just a few days before your editorial came out we landed a handsome piece of new business from Soap-oleo Producers, and Mr. D. made some noises about wishing you were here so we could have the benefit of your touch with the theme copy. Without you, I seem to be elected. The sort of reason that makes me not sorry your Mr. Wayburn is gone is the way he reacted when I told him all this. He said it was 'one of those amazing coincidences.' Of course it was a coincidence, but he said it in such a nasty way that I got mad and forgot for a moment that I used to be a professor of English. My only other news . . .

George Stout's only other news was that the Open Letter to Joseph Stalin idea had blown up again, this time into so many fragments that all seemed irrecoverable; the State Department would have to go it alone after all. Mr. Blandings scarcely bothered to read the details; he was thinking about "a serious gap in Top Creative" so long as he was away. It was nice to be missed. Sometimes a man got so lost and lonely that it was nice to be missed even in the foundlings' nursery from which he had run away. For the first time Mr. Blandings wondered who was sitting in his office. He wondered why his once-devoted Miss Willersley had not written to him, and who was using the special office chair he had once bought with his own money. As to the Dward Wayburn business, that was disturbing. Dward Wayburn's specialty had always been insinuations made with such careful modulations of his gentlemanly voice that a reply was difficult. Well, Dward Wayburn was now leaving, after all Mr. Blandings had done to keep him; when Mr. Blandings examined his thoughts he seemed to find he was disturbed less at this than that the sands were drifting over the footprints that once he resharpened every day as he trod the corridors of Banton & Dascomb, Advertising. Yes, he was missed, but even while he was missed, little pieces of him were being mislaid in what had been his daily haunts.

He thought of George Stout, the one man among all the Banton & Dascomb personnel whose friendship he really valued. In George's career he saw the precise reverse of his own; George, having forsaken his beautiful New England college, had found on Madison Avenue a serenity he had never known before. "I wouldn't go back to that campus for anything," he had told Mr. Blandings in the days when their friendship was first growing. "The freedom here, my God, the freedom. No Trustees, no Provosts, no Chancellors! No faculty teas, no campus politics, no miserable, pimply students! Bring on every bastard client in the world of advertising —it'd still be heaven here compared to Oliensis!" At this very time Mr. Blandings had been hell-bent to escape from everything that to George Stout was heaven. As a result, he was today caught in a trap door that separated one world from another. He had neither made good his escape from the city nor found any haven in the country. He was just stuck.

The telephone on Mr. Blandings' desk offered a weak tinkle, altogether unlike the authoritative one-two one-two with which city telephones announced their demands. He put the receiver to his ear and heard Harry Silber's hoarse voice:

"I got something I need to talk to you about but I can't leave the store."

"If it's important I'll come right over," said Mr. Blandings. After all, Harry Silber was an advertiser; by now, with all the shrinkages elsewhere, his largest.

"The sooner the better is all," said Harry Silber.

"I need another cup of coffee anyway," said Mr. Blandings. "I'll meet you at the Greek's."

"I said I couldn't leave the store."

"Be right over, Harry," said Mr. Blandings. He had been first-naming Harry Silber for some time, in the hope that Harry Silber would do the same by him, but Harry Silber did not seem to get the point, and Mr. Blandings was not the sort of person who could say "call me Jim" to anyone. So now he was wondering if Harry Silber thought him patronizing. But there was no way he could go back to "Mr. Silber." As he rose from his desk he knocked to the floor the still unopened letter from Horace Dascomb; he rescued it and put it squarely in the midst of the disorder so that he could not fail to see it first thing when he got back.

When Mr. Blandings entered Silber's Dry Goods he wondered why Mr. Silber could not leave the store, for there was Mrs. Silber, waiting on the only customer. She caught Mr. Blandings' eye and gestured with her head: "In back."

Mr. Blandings, his heels making a loud noise on the bare floor, walked the depth of the store and found a little curtained hallway he had never seen before. It gave onto a small office in which Mr. Silber, a rolltop desk, an adding machine, and a set of ledgers produced an almost intolerable congestion.

Harry Silber swept the ledgers to the floor, motioned Mr. Blandings to the swivel chair, rose and closed the door. Then he said, almost inaudibly, "If you were to say I ever told you this I would have to call you a liar to your face."

"You can trust me," said Mr. Blandings. It was nice to be made a confidant, no matter of what.

"Listen," said Harry Silber, "I been waiting and waiting for you to catch on to what's happening to your paper, but you don't seem to, and now yesterday something happened I have to tell you against my wife's advice, even."

"There's no reason why we shouldn't be frank with one another," said Mr. Blandings. "Business is rotten."

"It'll get rottener," said Mr. Silber. He lighted a cigar, and one exhalation turned the air in the tiny cubicle blue.

"Yesterday," he said, "this fellow from the Merchants' Association, I can't use any real names, came to see me, and to make a long story short he wanted me to quit advertising in the *Blade*. First he put it like that, crude, and then he began to pretty it up. Part of what he says is true: the Winbury paper trucks copies over here

230

now from thirty miles away and sells almost as many right here in Lansdale as you do. It always was a good paper for advertising; that, anyone has to admit. What it comes down to is the Merchants' Association boys are aiming to take a page or maybe a double spread every week in the Winbury paper and, you know, divide the space and the cost among themselves—drugs, sundries, dry-goods, hardware, car dealers, all the rest, and they're telling me I can come in if I'll go pro rata with them. You know—not exactly take my space out of the *Blade,* but fix it so I run out of money before I get to it."

"Well," said Mr. Blandings, "all I can do is urge you not to—as a salesman, that is."

"I know," said Harry Silber. "I don't want to, but I got another thing to consider. If you lose enough more advertising it wouldn't be good for either of us that the *Blade* should start looking like a throwaway printed by Silber's Dry Goods, would it?"

"No," said Mr. Blandings; "it certainly wouldn't."

"Of course," said Harry Silber, "I could always buy a page throwaway from you without any of the editorial stuff, but what I gather is you're interested in being a newspaper publisher, not a job printer, is that right?"

"That's right," said Mr. Blandings. "Even so, right now the job-printing business can scarcely keep the paper alive."

"You didn't go at things right if you'll pardon me for saying so," said Mr. Silber. "Take that oleomargarine editorial."

"No, Harry," said Mr. Blandings, "let's not take it. It was a mistake—it was about the biggest mistake I could have made. I wrote it out of honest conviction, and the facts were right, but that didn't keep it from being pretty dumb."

Harry Silber shrugged. "It was a good piece of writing," he said; "I was for it. But live and let live is the only way."

"I've been pretty stupid with the *Blade,*" said Mr. Blandings, "and it's cost me a lot of money. But now I think I have something that's really going to put the paper on its feet—something to make it really popular with all but the very smallest, snootiest group around here; the ones I can't possibly have on my side and wouldn't want to if I could."

Harry Silber assumed an air of interested attention.

231

"The credit for this really belongs to my wife," said Mr. Blandings. "She got hold of the idea, and she's done all the work on it. I'm going to run it in big space with a lot of pictures and maps for four or five weeks."

Then Mr. Blandings, in full detail, told Harry Silber the idea for making a journalistic crusade out of the revival of the Shamalaug Lake State Park. It took him fifteen steady minutes; Harry Silber never uttered a word, and listened as though entranced. When Mr. Blandings finished there was a silence.

"You like it, then?" said Mr. Blandings in a modest way.

"Yes I like it," said Harry Silber. "If your idea is to cut your own throat from ear to ear and pour iodine on it, I like it fine."

"But what—why?" cried Mr. Blandings.

"I guess we got to have a fundamental conversation," said Harry Silber. "You are making a proposal for the common good. In this part of the country that is called Communism. I don't know why the insurance companies in this state are not called Communistic, but they are the only exceptions I know of."

"I told you in the beginning," said Mr. Blandings, "that Anson Dolliver and his bunch would be against this but for everybody else it should be wonderful."

"For nobody else," said Harry Silber. "Nobody would look at it that way."

"Look what they'd get," said Mr. Blandings. "A beautiful—"

"Don't tell me again," said Harry Silber. "It is very pleasant in this part of the country and I have no personal complaints, but it is a political jungle, and you keep thinking it is a lawn party. I do not come from a long line of old New England families as we both know, but I know something about this part of the country that you don't know."

"Let me tell you," said Harry Silber, before Mr. Blandings could draw his breath. "There is this big bunch of phony liberals living near you, is that right? In Art Hollow. You call them the Poet and Peasant party, which they do not like, but you are identified with them just the same. That is unfortunate. They are no more Communists than Mr. Dolliver, but they used to say nice soft pretty words about Russia, not out of any conviction one way or another, but because it used to be the high-style thing to do, get what I mean? Now it isn't, so they ve given it up, but the rest of the people are very slow to recognize this, so they keep on thinking this is a bunch of Communists. And this Poet and Peasant bunch are the only people who will say they are for your idea, and this will hang a millstone around your neck with everybody else, right away."

"That is not the worst of it," Harry Silber went on. "These people will only *say* they like your idea. If the state captures land by eminent domain to make the Tennessee Valley Authority that s fine by them, because they don't live in Tennessee, see? Hundreds of farms inundated to build Grand Coulee? Good. That's on the Columbia River, not the Wintinock. Were you at that Town Meeting the time Mr. Auster Millowy got up and yelled because the highway department was going to take five feet off one side of his twelve acres for that new blacktop road?"

Mr. Blandings had indeed been at that Town Meeting. He could recall, in a flash of unwelcome memory, the poet's peroration, parsed and punctuated to the last perfect point: "If the Police State is to cast its shadow over this hitherto gleaming land, let us at least have the courage, as our last gesture, so to recognize it, and so to label it."

Out of nowhere, a hiccough racked Mr. Blandings.

Harry Silber did not seem to have any more to say.

"I can only hope you're wrong about this," said Mr. Blandings.

"I'll hope so too," said Harry Silber.

"Just tell me one thing," said Mr. Blandings. "A bunch of merchants getting together to buy group space in the Winbury paper with the incidental idea of putting me out of business—why isn't that a collectivist, Communistic idea and a conspiracy into the bargain?"

Mr. Silber shrugged. "An idea depends on who has it," he said. He stood up. "I'm not going in with it," he said; "but maybe you should figure out what is the lowest price you could give me on three thousand throwaways, same general style as the ads I've been using in the paper."

"Much obliged, Harry," said Mr. Blandings. "I'll get the figure around to you."

233

· 28 ·

IN THE TWILIGHT, Horace Dascomb's unopened letter gleamed faintly at its addressee. Why was it so bulky? Mr. Dascomb, who could be endless in conversation, could not sustain the writing process for more than half a page, so there was some enclosure. Mr. Blandings looked at the envelope with foreboding; although he held in his hand a plastic paper knife which said Compliments of the Lansdale First National Bank, Anson Dolliver, President, he could not quite bring himself to use it. Things certainly came in bunches, as George Stout's letter had said; he didn't think he wanted anything more from off this present bunch. After his long discouraging talk with Harry Silber he had gone home for lunch, lain down for a while, and then spent the afternoon looking over his checkbooks and bank statements, and the neat but depressing records his wife kept of the condition of the *Blade*. It was becoming apparent to him that he was approaching the end of something or other; just what, he did not know because he kept a veil over it.

Cocktails had helped. His daughters had collaborated in serving him a tasteful dinner; they had neither quarreled nor involved themselves in innuendoes about sex. It was amazing what a good cook Betsy was; apparently she loved it. So all in all he had been a little cheered up, and after dinner he had driven back to Lansdale Town. It was close to the summer solstice; in the *Blade*'s little office he would not need to turn on the lights for another twenty minutes.

Open that letter, Blandings.

Now just a minute, said Mr. Blandings. It's either good news or bad news or neutral, so I have only one chance in three of enjoy-

234

ing myself. Is it worth taking? He opened his desk drawer, poured a swig of Old Supine into his dusty desk glass, and downed it. Then he slit the envelope.

"Well for God's sake," said Mr. Blandings.

As he suspected, the letter from Mr. Dascomb was very brief:

Dear Jim: It never occurred to me that we as an agency might be sending you as a publisher a space order on behalf of a client we both know so well, but a lot of strange things are happening these days, and so I hope you will accept the enclosed in the knowledge that my very best personal good wishes go with it. Cordially.

Methodically, Mr. Blandings unfolded the enclosures. The space purchase forms of the American Association of Advertising Agencies, blue and white and tastefully typographized, had been familiar to him all his business life, but always he had been the sender, never the recipient. He made out the bold, stolid signature of Lorbet Neen, Chief, Media Department at the bottom of the first sheet, then swiftly snapped on the light and stared. It was an order for fifty-two pages in the Lansdale *Blade* on behalf of Old Supine Blenders, Inc., "full back page to be guaranteed at rates prevailing." Clipped to the general order was a specific order for the first insertion, and stapled to that was a large, handsome proof of the ad to be run.

From far away Mr. Blandings heard the heavy mountain locomotive of the night freight sound the blasts, two long, two short, that are the grade crossing signals on all the railroads of America. The freight would sound four more such warnings before, like a horse with its hooves set against all motion, it would be dragged shrieking into the Lansdale station by an invisible force which would suddenly give up and let it stop as if it had struck a claybank. There would then ensue half an hour of clashing shifts of cars in the Lansdale Yard before the freight would be on its way again, its lone, mysterious way.

Mr. Blandings got up, and with a filthy towel that was hanging beside a filthy sink, began cleaning the glass in a filthy window. It was important to see the freight come in, tonight. All railroad trains, freight or passenger, were called "he," Mr. Blandings knew. "He ought to be on the crossing bell any minute now," or "He's running half, three-quarters hour behind" was sound railroad

235

talk; "she'll be comin' 'round the mountain" was just unknowing balladry. "Interfere" was a good railroad word, too. "He interfered with No. 73" meant he had knocked the hell out of No. 73, either denting a gondola car or killing twenty people: the verb did not specify. Life is certainly a string of euphemisms, Mr. Blandings thought, polishing his windowpane with full industry; we cannot any of us say what we mean because it is always too terrible or too obscure or too hopelessly entangled with something else. That space order from his own agency to his own paper and for his own account—what could he say about it? It was, of course, a lifesaver, but it was also a host of other things. It was seductive, frightening, repellent, and irresistible. That one order for Old Supine would bring the *Blade* over five thousand dollars if the account really ran a full year. And Horace Dascomb would hardly have sent it to him with that personal note if there had not been a good deal of assurance that the schedule was solid. Moreover, if anybody knew the account backward and forward it was Mr. Blandings himself, and very seldom did it ever cancel a schedule. Not all publications would accept liquor advertising, and radio networks not at all, so Old Supine was sometimes hard put to it to find the space on which to spend its heavy appropriation.

Wait a minute, though; Horace Dascomb might be offering him a little charity. He sometimes did strange sentimental things; George Stout's letter indicated that Horace Dascomb was concerned about him. Quite possibly Mr. Dascomb felt a little guilty toward him because of something about the Dward Wayburn business, not even mentioned in his letter. So maybe it was charity, maybe it was hush money, maybe it was—

The fact remained it would be a lifesaver. The Methodist Ladies' Evening Guild would certainly hit the roof if such a torrent of whisky advertising ever started appearing in the local paper; they used to be mad enough about the local liquor stores' price-list ads back when there were any. Well, that would be fun; he would publish their stupidest letters, along with an editorial rejoinder that would make them madder than ever; at that sort of thing he was good, he was deft, he could work with a twist of the wrist. But above all, with this advertising windfall, he could stay in busi-

236

ness. He had made his mistakes; he had paid for them dearly; he had done everything the hard way. But he knew better, now, and with a fresh start . . .

Just a minute, Blandings. Do you *really* know better now? Have you *really* made your last mistake, your last major miscalculation about the way you live in this community—indeed, about the whole way you live your life? Just today you felt ready to give up; now there comes to you a windfall right out of the purse of the domineering old aunt of advertising from whose strings you have been trying for so long to disentangle yourself. If you're going to do *that*—take money for the *Blade* from your own dishonest capacity for writing advertising copy for a rotgut whisky—you might as well go the whole hog and go back to New York, and not walk the same streets with Methodist ladies whom you will dispose of by some simian trick with words that they don't have. . . .

When he awoke from his reveries, the freight was gone. Through the window he had so carefully polished, the semaphore lamp high above the station showed a clear, luminous green, and the night was quiet.

Mr. Blandings knew what he must do. Into the crazed typewriter that had belonged to Urmot Nellus he carefully inserted two pieces of copy paper, and after a stretch of five minutes devoted to getting the paper absolutely level and even between the guides, he began to type. The machine made a sort of batting noise that fluttered his ears uncomfortably.

Dear Mr. Dascomb: It was typical of your generosity that you should find so pleasant and courteous a means of throwing a lifeline to this sinking raft. In fairness, however, I must tell you that the *Blade*'s days are numbered—at least under my management. I have made a good many mistakes up here and one result is that I shall soon have to get rid of this little publishing property for whatever I can get. I am sorry to have to acknowledge this, and I must obviously ask you to keep my news in complete confidence. I burden you with it only because the paper is beyond the aids of charity and under the circumstances it wouldn't be fair to take the client's ill-gotten funds. That is why I must turn down the order. I must tell you more about this when I next have the opportunity of seeing you.
P.S. The copy absolutely stinks. I ought to know—I wrote it myself six months ago.

237

Mr. Blandings signed the letter with a blunt copy pencil and addressed the envelope. There was a down train, mail and milk, that made Lansdale a few minutes after six in the morning, and anything put into the green box stenciled "Train Mail" on the station platform would be picked up and delivered in New York by afternoon. He looked at the letter for a long time, and in a sudden flash of honesty with himself he saw right through it. It purported to be a quietly resigned acceptance of Fate; actually it said in a coy, veiled voice to Horace Dascomb, "Invite me back and I shall come." With cold premeditation, Mr. Blandings seized the neck of the Old Supine bottle and flung it as a juggler would whip a flashing Indian club to his partner. It made a fair hit right on the door of the potbellied stove in the middle of the room and burst with a ring and a splash, its thick fragments wobbling for a moment on the stove's zinc apron before they came to rest. Mr. Blandings sat quite still for a moment; then he folded his letter, and sealed and stamped the envelope. It took him five minutes to gather up the broken glass and sop up the Old Supine with handfuls of paper towels. When he had done that, he walked to the dark station and plunked his letter into the green box on the platform. Then he found his car and drove it slowly to the top of Bald Mountain, seven miles from town.

The house was ablaze with lights, but empty. As always, the children had gone to bed without snapping off a single downstairs switch. As soon as Mr. Blandings cut off the station wagon's engine he could hear the telephone ringing in the middle of the house. He dived for the kitchen extension, but when he said hello, blankness greeted him. Then the line awoke and the operator said, "I had a call for you but now I have a disconnect. Wait a minute."

A switch opened somewhere, and Mr. Blandings could hear the voices of women arranging the world's communications in the night.

"Hartford."

"Thank you. . . . N.C., operator. Change over and ring again, please."

"Thank you, operator. . . . Hartford, please."

"Surely."

"Hartford."

"Hartford, your O.T.C. had a call for Lansdale that was D.A., but W.H. now. F.C., please."

"Thank you, one moment please."

Rome, Utah, and Buenos Aires suddenly entered the symphony, and as suddenly faded away.

"L.K. but C.F., operator."

"Keep trying, operator, please. I am holding for A.G."

"Surely, operator."

The switches closed again, and Mr. Blandings was alone in the night with the local operator at Lansdale. "Will you hang up please and I'll ring you as soon as I have your party."

Mr. Blandings hung up and made his way to the living room. As he passed the bar, three bottles of Old Supine stared at him. He turned each bottle so that its label faced the wall. Then he poured an inch of water-clear gin into a glass and hunted for something with which to mix it. Finding nothing, he downed it straight.

The telephone rang again and his wife's voice sounded in his ear. "Darling!" she said, and she sounded enraptured.

"Listen! I know we can't talk over the phone. I'm just calling to say I've made the most miraculous discovery, and everything from now on is going to be gorgeous. I can't wait to tell you, I'm so happy. And you'll be as happy as I am, or even happier. Believe me!"

"That's fine," said Mr. Blandings.

"Are you all right?" said Mrs. Blandings. A tiny bit of joy went out of her voice, but a warm solicitude took its place.

"Never better," said Mr. Blandings.

"You're not reacting very much," said Mrs. Blandings.

"I'm just being cautious," said Mr. Blandings. "You know."

"Of course I know," said Mrs. Blandings. "But darling, you won't have to worry about things like who hears what on the telephone any more. Never at all again, once everybody knows what I know."

"How's Daisy?" said Mr. Blandings.

"Oh, wonderful," said Mrs. Blandings. "Would you like to talk to her?"

"I guess I'd better not," said Mr. Blandings. "Just give her my very best regards."

"I will," said Mrs. Blandings. "Aren't you going to ask me when I'm coming home?"

"Yes," said Mr. Blandings; "that was the main thing on my mind."

"Well, I'm not quite sure," said Mrs. Blandings. "I'd leave to-morrow except it would be foolish to come back until the very last thing's done, so maybe I ought to stay another couple of days. I'll let you know."

After he had hung up, Mr. Blandings sought out a canvas chair on his screened porch, and slumped in it while he wondered what had gone dead in him that he could share so little of his wife's pleasure at some unknown turn of events. He thought of his letter to Horace Dascomb, lying darkly inside the mailbox in the dirty, deserted Lansdale station seven miles away, and wondered if his wife's news should modify anything he had said in it. No, he decided; other times in his life he had tried to outwit circumstances by some last minute retrieve, and it had always made things worse. Do something and then stick by it, Blandings. That letter is very comfortable right where it is, and tomorrow Horace Dascomb will have it and then he will—

Mr. Blandings got up from his porch chair and stepped out onto the lawn that he had cut a week ago and now should cut again. It was a beautiful night, with an acetylene moon far up in the sky. But a bullying little wind had sprung up and was snapping his trousers about his ankles, and several huge cirrus clouds were in the sky, and above them the moon was riding, riding.

MR. DASCOMB was good and peeved; Mr. Blandings could see that by the tremulousness of the signature; so marked that a blob of ink had splashed on the bottom of the otherwise immaculate letter. Mr. Dascomb had been anxious to have it mailed, too; otherwise his secretary would certainly have recopied it. He was not offering charity to the *Blade* or its publisher, Mr. Dascomb explained. His charitable contributions came out of a personal account and were not intermixed with the firm's business affairs. Since explanations seemed to be in order in this correspondence, he himself would burden Mr. Blandings with one. It was perhaps a little egotistic to assume that the *Blade,* which Mr. Dascomb regretted he seldom saw, had been in any way singled out. Let Mr. Blandings remember a conversation he had recently had with Lorbet Neen, who for a long time had been studying the city versus rural sales of Old Supine; studies which had led him to the conclusion that there was a potential quadrupling of the market for Old Supine should its rural sales per capita approach the cities'. As the result of Lorbet's monumental study on Mr. Blandings' old account the client had made a massive incursion into the country weekly field, with a goal no less than eventual Dominance. Some five hundred space orders had thus gone out in the same mail that had borne Mr. Blandings his. The extremely unsatisfactory business methods of these papers (Mr. Dascomb seemed to be saying *ahem*) made the operation a headache for the Media Department, but if Lorbet Neen, always a good soldier, was willing to have his department take the brunt, that was that. Meanwhile, Mr. Dascomb was sorry to hear of the *Blade's* troubles, which of course he would keep entirely to himself; if Mr. Blandings, the author of the Old Supine copy, now wished as a publisher to decline it, Mr. Dascomb was afraid the appropriate persuasions to the contrary escaped him. Cordially as always.

It was a long letter for Mr. Dascomb. When Mr. Blandings finished it his ears were pink and his face felt stiff.

There were always the tomato plants. Mr. Blandings worked hard at them all that day, and most of the next. It was not much of a growing season, this year. Rains had battered the garden when it was young and fresh; there had been day after day of mizzling dampness, and just before summer was officially due there had been one night of sharp, incredible frost that had curled and blackened the edges of the lettuce. Even so, Mr. Blandings thought with a tired satisfaction, I have learned to be a pretty good gardener. I really know how to keep the checkrein on the squashes. I no longer pull up the young carrot tops under the impression they are weeds. I don't plant the corn too soon. I lay out my rows with taut mason's twine before I make a furrow. Above all, I have learned to give the tomato plants four feet of space in every direction. It looks ridiculous until July, but I have learned. He bent and stooped among the tomato plants, making expert knots in the raffia with which he tied the well-pruned plants to the neatly sharpened stakes he had driven into the chocolate earth beside them. He was even learning why most of the farmers around him were so hopelessly bogged in unsuccess: there was such an infinitude of things to do every day that the choice was paralyzing. Now that he was finished with the tomatoes, should he begin flipping squash bugs into kerosene, or would it be a good idea to go on a flame-throwing expedition against some of the twenty tent caterpillars' nests he had counted among his trees? The poison ivy he had killed forever last year was springing up anew around the apple trees, and a huge maple branch had mysteriously split a few days ago and was dragging, dying, on the ground. He looked at his watch and discovered he could undertake none of these things: he must hurry down the hill to meet Betsy and Joan on the train coming back from the city where they had spent a day and a night;

242

the day, shopping for last-minute things before they went off to summer camp; the night——? Well, Mr. Blandings did not know how they had spent the night; he could only be glad that the Hotel Marbury was a Banton & Dascomb account and that he had a long-time acquaintance with the Resident Manager, who had made him feel his daughters would be safe under its roof—if that was where they had been . . .

"Have you seen Vascal?" Betsy asked as soon as she got off the train.

"I never read Vascal," said Mr. Blandings.

"Well you're in him," said Betsy.

Mr. Blandings' stomach gave a lurch, but he drove impassively out of the traffic tangle at the Lansdale station platform.

"Is Mother home?" said Joan.

"Not until tomorrow," said Mr. Blandings. "What have I done to get into Vascal's column?"

"I've got the clipping in my bag," said Betsy. "Nadwell gave it to me at lunch today."

"Betsy didn't get in until three this morning," said Joan. "She thought I was asleep."

"It was mighty sneaky to pretend you were asleep if you weren't," said Betsy.

"It certainly was a late-closing ice show you went to," said Joan.

"Don't start fighting the instant you get back," said Mr. Bland-ings. "What about me in Vascal's column?"

"Father," said Betsy, "I was perfectly chaperoned practically all the time. You know what? I found out the most fascinating thing about Nadwell Neen. His father is the head of the some-thing-or-other department in Banton & Dascomb, so it was old school ties all around."

Oh God, thought Mr. Blandings; oh God, oh God, oh God.

"A bunch of us went to dinner at Nadwell's parents' apartment," said Betsy; "and then we went to the ice show, and then we broke off from the old folks and went to the Persian Room. I just adore Nadwell's manner with waiter captains. And his father is an old sweetie, and his mother's very nice too, and they're both the *greatest* admirers of yours, Father."

243

"I've never met Mrs. Neen," said Mr. Blandings, through feelingless rubber lips.

"Well anyway," said Betsy, "nobody could have said nicer things about you than Mr. Neen. He said you had genius. Then he went on to say all geniuses were crazy but of course he was joking all the way through."

Mr. Blandings tried, but could not recall having seen Lorbet Neen smile in the office; not once, ever.

"He's always a little foolish with me," said Betsy; "he's sort of the ancient gallant type."

Lorbet Neen, Mr. Blandings reflected, was his own age, precisely. Years ago they had discovered they had the same birthday. He looked at himself in the rearview mirror, and got no reassurance.

"Come on, Father," said Joan; "goose it a little. We're just poking along."

There had been a time in his own youth when that had been a washroom vulgarity among the coarser boys of his Midwest school. Now it came tripping in all innocence from the lips of his younger daughter.

Oh God.

"Where is that Vascal clipping?" Mr. Blandings called upstairs as his daughters were unpacking.

"I must have left it in New York," said Betsy as she made a stately descent. "I can't find it anywhere."

The only thing worse than seeing it was not seeing it.

"Could you describe it at all?" He knew it was a fool's question the instant he asked it.

"It had the words 'advertising biggie' in it," said Betsy, thoughtfully, "and something about whisky. That's all I remember."

Mr. Blandings was preparing himself for a night on the rack when Joan came downstairs with a flutter of newsprint between a thumb and finger.

"Here it is," she said; "it was in her underwear." The sisters favored one another with reptilian smiles.

Mr. Blandings took the clipping, and ran head-on into further evidence of his decay. "One of you find me my new reading glasses like dear good girls, will you?" he asked in a senile voice.

Glasses adjusted, he stared at the small, smudgy type:

> What advertising biggie turned down the liquor copy he himself wrote when his own agency offered it to the country newspaper he publishes, not too successfully? Said it stank. Odd.

His life was becoming one long blush, thought Mr. Blandings, feeling himself turning pink again. It was so fascinating to read stuff like this about somebody else, so shocking to encounter it about oneself.

"What makes you think this has anything to do with me?" he demanded.

"I don't know," said Betsy; "something at lunch that Nadwell told me his father'd said, maybe." Obviously her principal interest was not in anything *said* in Homer Vascal's column; only that something had *been* said.

Mr. Blandings threw the clipping in the wastebasket. Then he pulled it out again. It was an embarrassment, a major embarrassment, but at least there was no catastrophe in it. The appalling thing about it was its correctness; it said nothing, but its question could not have been asked without an exact knowledge of the facts. Mr. Blandings, like so many thousands before him, asked between his clenched teeth the choleric question: *where* did he get it? What bastard fed it to him? It could only have been someone in the Banton & Dascomb offices. Mr. Blandings had kept no carbon of his letter, had seen practically no one in the forty-eight hours it had taken his letter to Mr. Dascomb to wing its way straight into Homer Vascal's types. He thought of the enormous surge of anger he must have caused in the bosom of Lorbet Neen by declining the space order he had signed . . . and straightway he was sure he had his man. Lorbet always blurted things out; this time the blurt had been loud and indiscreet enough to do the damage.

Mr. Blandings cast an angry look at Betsy. "I don't know that I'm crazy about having any daughter of mine playing around with somebody like this Neen kid," he said.

245

Betsy gave him an incredulous look and her eyes filled with angry tears. "I'm not 'playing around' with him," she said. "I think that's a pretty nasty expression for a father to use to a daughter." Her anger kept rising faster than she could express it. "I think Nadwell Neen is the nicest boy I've met in a long time anywhere, and even if I didn't I'm at the age when it's my privilege to make my own friends without interference from the older generation, and you can get your own dinner and I hope it *stinks*."

The curtains made a graceful swoop as they tried to follow her boiling wake out of the room, and when the house ceased rocking from her slammed door the muffled sobs came drifting down the stair.

Joan shook her head gravely. "You shouldn't have taken that line, Father," she said, standing up and smoothing her skirt, "but I'll get your dinner."

Considering everything, the rent in the domestic fabric rewove itself with surprising speed. Joanie was no cook by Betsy's standards; she followed formulae with scientific exactness instead of using Betsy's mixture of empiricism and instinct. But she could do well enough so that Mr. Blandings was able to leave her in the kitchen while he toiled back to Lansdale Town in the station wagon and bought the best five-pound box of candy he could find in Scadron's stationery store. It was the *Blade*'s publication day, but there were no copies on the counter; instead lay a high, fresh mound of the Winbury *Times*. While Mr. Blandings waited for his package a customer came in, asked for a *Blade*, and was supplied it from under the counter. Scadron's had never reduced its draw from the *Blade*, but this was why the number of copies they returned for credit every week was mounting higher and higher. This evening, however, Mr. Blandings was concerned with parenthood more than publication.

Back up the hill, Mr. Blandings gained entrance to Betsy's room and presented his gift and his abject apologies. The painful period of forgiveness then began; at dinner the unnatural solicitude of everybody for everybody clogged the air. Mr. Blandings was praying for the return of the moment when his daughters would once again clothe their affection for him in the gossamers of their light, easy, offhand scorn, but that would not be until tomorrow at the earliest; tonight everything was carefully wrapped in cotton wool.

When the telephone rang it was a shock but a relief. Everybody rose to answer it on behalf of everybody else. It was Betsy whose solicitude won.

"Hello," said Betsy; "why he*llo*. Oh I'm so glad you called. I had such a lovely time last night; truly, I did. I'd rather see an ice show than practically anything else I can think of."

Oh God.

After a moment the conversation took a different track.

"Yes, he's right here. Would you like to speak to him? No, it wouldn't disturb him the singlest little bit."

"For you, Father," Betsy called in a beautiful, escalloped voice. "Mr. Neen." As she passed him in the hall she said "*Senior.*"

Mr. Blandings and Mr. Neen inquired for one another's health and discovered flawless conditions. "Say Jim," said Lorbet Neen, "there's a good deal of hell breaking down here and Mr. Dascomb, who went home this afternoon not feeling very well and left word he didn't want to be disturbed; as I say Mr. Dascomb asked me if I wouldn't call you and see if you wouldn't drop whatever you were doing and be in the office tomorrow morning for consultation. It's because of that piece in—"

"We're on a party line up here, Lorbet," said Mr. Blandings loudly. "Let me guess: has the client left the rails?"

"That would be one way of putting it," said Lorbet Neen, his deep voice sinking deeper still.

"All right," said Mr. Blandings, "I'll be there. Wait a minute; my wife's just getting home tomorrow."

"Mr. Dascomb asked particularly," said Lorbet Neen.

"All right," said Mr. Blandings, "I'll be there."

Fortunately, dinner was over, and the dishwashing made too much noise for conversation. Mr. Blandings went to bed very early, to be ready for the early morning train.

· 30 ·

THE ELEVATOR OPERATORS in the Posthumous Guarantees and Trust
Building had on summer uniforms, and seemed to be a different
crew from any Mr. Blandings remembered. When he got out on
the thirty-first floor he thought for a moment he must have mis-
called his stop: He saw nothing familiar at all. Then it became
apparent that Banton & Dascomb had gone through still another
of their space rearrangements "designed to speed up communications and provide for a more orderly flow of traffic." He made for
where his office had been and encountered a maze of new steel
and plaster partitions. He was really shocked, and completely dis-
oriented. Where was Miss Willersley? Where were his desk and
chair, his entire onetime habitation enforced? A stranger in shirt
sleeves came hurrying by. "May I help you?" he said with extra-
mural courtesy. By the time Mr. Blandings had been conducted
to Mr. Dascomb's office, which alone seemed to have survived the
changes, he was already softened up for whatever was going to
occur.

"They're waiting for you, Mr. Blandings," said Mr. Dascomb's
secretary. "Go right in."

Mr. Dascomb was flanked by Lorbet Neen and George Stout.
"Jim," he said in his quiet voice, "it's very good to see you." The
handsome face seemed as imperturbable as ever, but Mr. Blandings noticed Mr. Dascomb's hands were trembling.

"I've asked Lorbet to sit in with us," said Mr. Dascomb, "because at their last meeting our directors did a very good day's work
and chose him for the newly created post of Executive Vice President. There won't be any announcement until the first of the
week."

248

So. Well, after all, it was little more than a recognition of the *de facto* state of things for the last several years, but still it was a hard, grating fact to come on suddenly, and in the morning. With Lorbet Neen officially elevated to the right hand of Mr. Dascomb himself, life in Top Creative would no longer be a simple hell. Mr. Blandings strongly clasped the hand of Lorbet Neen and wished him endless success in the high post to which the directors had so wisely bidden him. He began counting up the directors: Mr. Dascomb and Lorbet Neen were the only two he could think of off-hand.

"And at the same time," said Mr. Dascomb, "the announcement will go on to say that our friend George, here, will be a Vice President, too, in charge of public relations."

This was a shock of a different type. Mr. Blandings was deeply fond of George Stout, but he was scarcely five years in the service of the agency. Good God, thought Mr. Blandings as he shook his friend's hand, how life is catching up with me; for six months I have slackened the pace on this treadmill I have trod for twenty years, and see what is happening.

Mr. Dascomb cleared his throat and thrust two neat folders onto the back of his desk to indicate a clearing of the decks for action. His hands began to tremble more noticeably.

"Jim," he said, "there's some pretty bad trouble afoot because of that Vascal piece yesterday. We're on a nasty spot, a really nasty spot." He sighed, and passed a hand over his forehead.

"It would all have blown over, Jim," said George Stout softly, "if the client himself hadn't put his foot in it. *You* know."

"Yes," said Mr. Dascomb. "I wish something could be done with retired army officers instead of making them board chairmen in American businesses. I forget whether General Slocum headed up Old Supine's board when you were active on the account, but in any event he made the considerable tactical error yesterday of having his office call Vascal direct and, uh, threaten him."

"General Slocum," said Mr. Blandings. "Is he the one the Italians pushed into the Cisterna Puggi in 1943?"

"*That* war is ancient history," said Mr. Dascomb, with a flicker of irritation; "I'm speaking now of what he did to Vascal yesterday, or more precisely what Vascal did to him. Of course nothing

249

could have made Vascal happier; the General's phone call was the complete admission that his story had struck home, and it gave him half-a-dozen more new stories, too. So he let the General understand he'd run a piece a day on the whole business for a year if he felt like it, and he was beginning to feel like it. It was a little after that the General called me."

There was a most uncomfortable pause.

"I suppose he threatened to take the business away from us," said Mr. Blandings.

"Naturally," said Mr. Dascomb, quietly.

"Just the Old Supine Blend or the whole line of whiskies and gins and wines?"

Mr. Dascomb said nothing and the reply fell to George Stout. "The whole line," he said, "right down to the imported prune cordial."

There was another pause.

"I don't suppose, Jim," said Mr. Dascomb, "that you have any more idea than the rest of us here as to how the substance of your letter got to Vascal so quickly and exactly?" The trembling of his hands was now being communicated to his arms and shoulders.

"No," said Mr. Blandings. He raised his eyes and looked hard at Lorbet Neen, who looked hard back.

"I think you ought to lay every card face upward with Jim, Mr. Dascomb," said Lorbet Neen. "Otherwise, we're beating around the bush."

"Perhaps Lorbet has a point there," said Mr. Dascomb. "I think what he is trying to say is that I should report that among several very intemperate things General Slocum said to me yesterday was that if we were to accept your resignation he would consider the matter honorably closed."

That was it. Mr. Blandings had known that was it all along; last night, when he read Vascal's piece; when he talked to Lorbet Neen on the phone; all the while in on the train this morning. Unconsciously, he had set himself to meet it, so that now he did not stumble over a single word.

"Mr. Dascomb, please don't have another minute of embarrassment or anxiety about anything. Consider my resignation is in this moment, and I'll go and find a desk and write the first draft and

George and I can go over it until we get the phraseology just the way you and Lorbet want."

The trembling fit now came full on Mr. Dascomb.

"May I ask," he said, his voice shaking with the rest of him, "if you mean to suggest that I could sink to the point of permitting—"

His epiglottis did him in; he choked and had to swallow.

"—of permitting," he went doggedly on, "a client to dictate the terms of *my* relationships with *my* associates? Upon my soul——"

His breathing made a harsh sound that drowned out the growl of the air-conditioning machine.

"The business Suggerd Banton and I created out of nothing a quarter of a century ago," said Mr. Dascomb, "was not set up without principles and has not grown to greatness without principles. If the day should come when I must violate those principles, I will let the business die."

He stopped, and commanded his head to stand still. For an instant he was able to look full and steady at Mr. Blandings.

"I could wring your neck," he said in a strangled voice.

It was the most terrible thing he had ever said to anyone in his employment.

"Mr. Dascomb——" said Lorbet Neen.

"Excuse me, Lorbet, excuse me, everyone," said Mr. Dascomb. "I'll have to leave you for a moment." He arose and pressed a button; from floor to ceiling a section of bookcases a foot thick swung open on olive hinges, disclosing Mr. Dascomb's retiring room of lavatory, bath, shower, toilet, cot, ultraviolet lamp, and telephone. He entered it with dignity, and a ton of rare books, resuming the plane of the wall, shut him away.

"Now I've heard everything," said Lorbet Neen. "That's the first time in all my experience I ever saw anybody insult Mr. Dascomb, right to his face, right in his own office."

"I wasn't insulting him," said Mr. Blandings, shaken. "I was trying to make it easy for him."

"It was a rotten thing to say," said Lorbet Neen. "People like you have no consideration for the feelings of others, is your trouble."

"It was the only honest and decent thing to say," said Mr.

251

Blandings. "It was what he wanted, it's what you want—well, you've got it."

"Listen," said Lorbet Neen. "Don't act like you were born yesterday. Maybe you think this business is a racket. Maybe I do. Maybe even George here thinks so. But all Horace Dascomb asks of anybody is one very simple thing: that they don't act like it's a racket when *he's* around. *He's* got *Ethics*."

Lorbet Neen's stress on the last word had a peculiar ring; it was neither sympathy nor admiration, but just a blurt.

"I know that," said Mr. Blandings.

"Do you?" said Lorbet Neen with a vulpine snarl. "Then why don't you know that when anybody comes to the old man with as crude a proposition as 'fire Joe Doakes or lose the account' there's only one thing he's going to tell them? If you hadn't butted in with your goddamned martyred resignation talk you'd have learned what the old man *did* say to General Slocum."

The phrase "the old man" had never before occurred in Lorbet Neen's language, or anyone's else, to describe Mr. Dascomb. Hearing it now, Mr. Blandings knew for sure that Lorbet Neen was heir-apparent to Mr. Dascomb's long-held throne.

"I'll tell you what he said," said Lorbet Neen. "After General Slocum had batted his ears back for fifteen minutes he said, 'Neither I nor this agency ever permit ourselves to be intimidated by threats or pressure, so we will now resign from your account.' And you know as well as I do he'd stick to that line even if it meant the agency losing every goddamn penny of its business—unless somebody got him honorably and ethically off the hook."

Mr. Blandings sat silent. "As a matter of fact," said Lorbet Neen in an altered mood, "that *is* the same General Slocum the Eyetalians pushed into the Cisterna Puggi."

Mr. Blandings nodded. "So he might crawl," said Lorbet Neen. "But if he doesn't this agency will have to go out and scramble around for a new four-million-dollar account to make up for Old Supine Blenders." His anger rose up again like a roaring flame. "So not only won't there be any back pages for Old Supine in your Lansdale *Blade*," he said, "but you've queered the account for four hundred and ninety-nine other publishers, too. God damn it, don't you realize the old man could have made a perfectly good

252

explanation to Slocum about how it all happened except he felt he had to protect you and your news about how your lousy newspaper is going to blow up? That's more Ethics! If I ever control an agency there won't be any of this Ethics, let me tell you."

"Everything you say," said Mr. Blandings, "indicates more and more clearly that my usefulness to Banton & Dascomb is at an end."

"Oh no you don't!" said Lorbet Neen. "We're not going to have any more martyrs to the system around here as long as I'm Executive Vice President." He leaned forward and shook a thick, well-groomed forefinger at Mr. Blandings. "You pull any fast stuff about resigning, and you'll have a lot more to answer for than losing this agency a four-million-dollar billing. What couldn't Vascal do to us with *that*?"

George Stout, who seemed to be feeling beyond his depth in his new capacity as Vice President in charge of public relations, let his breath escape through his front teeth in a quiet moaning whistle.

Lorbet Neen flung a paper clip angrily into an empty wastebasket. "In fact," he said, "you'll have to come back to work. You'll have to come back to work, and we'll have to find some way or somebody to take over your newspaper. That's the only way I see to get the whole business straightened out. *Then* Vascal won't have any more story, *then* we can explain the whole situation to Slocum . . ."

"Wait a minute," said Mr. Blandings. "There's such a thing as slave labor. We don't live in the police state *yet*, you know." As he heard himself say it, he winced.

The door of precious volumes opened, and the three juniors rose to their feet as Mr. Dascomb walked carefully back to his chair. The faint odor of aromatic spirits of ammonia wafted itself about.

"My apologies to everyone," said Mr. Dascomb. The smile was once more imperturbable, and only the faintest tremor now disturbed the hands. With solicitude he turned to Mr. Blandings. "Jim," he said, "when I asked you to come in this morning it was merely to confer on some of the knottier aspects of our little problem. During the last few moments I have been wondering if perhaps the very best thing all of us could do would be to lunch together at the Cloud Club. Could you put aside any other plans and let us make it a foursome?"

"Certainly, Mr. Dascomb," said Mr. Blandings.

"Good," said Mr. Dascomb. His secretary entered silently in answer to some radar impulse. "Four at the Cloud Club at twelve forty-five," he murmured. He turned again to Mr. Blandings. "General Slocum and two or three of his headquarters staff almost invariably lunch at the Cloud Club on Fridays. My thinking is that if they should see the four of us lunching amicably together it would show them that we were all standing shoulder to shoulder, impregnable to threats."

"And of course," he added, "if any of us, best of all you, managed to have an amicable little conversation in the lounge where the General usually smokes his after-luncheon cigar we might find a few knots unraveling in an almost magical way. Eh, Jim?"

On the Catatonic Express to Lansdale (Fridays only), Mr. Blandings sat in the swaying club car and tried to relax. He had seen the General. The General, in fact, had been seated in his luncheon chair when Mr. Dascomb and his three associates had entered the Cloud Club's lofty dining room. He had got up, walked menacingly over to Mr. Dascomb, and then heartily clapped him on the back, uttering obscenities with a brigadier's grin. Mr. Blandings, being introduced to him, remembered a lady reporter's estimate of him made prior to his being pushed into the Cisterna Puggi by the Italians: "Just a great big impulsive boy." That lady, Mr. Blandings thought, had a gift for phrase deeper than she knew. The great big impulsive boy had crushed Mr. Blandings' hand, roared a couple of hideous insults at him, and ordered the waiter captain to merge the two luncheon groups. Everyone except Mr. Dascomb had had three old-fashioneds made with Old Supine and everything had straightened itself out completely even before the General's after-lunch cigar. "Have to talk that way sometimes, commanding troops," the General had said. It was his only reference to his yesterday's phone call to Mr. Dascomb. Obviously, the General's staff had worked hard the previous evening to regroove and rechannel his emotions, and find proper means of letting him know that a brigadier general (ret.) was no

254

match in this democracy for Homer Vascal. The mystery of how Vascal had come by his item had been given up as insoluble, but Mr. Blandings had explained everything else. The General had not seemed to comprehend the explanation, but was wholly ready to accept it. "Who says there's *anything* the matter with the copy?" he had thundered when Mr. Blandings was trying to say that his criticisms of Old Supine to Mr. Dascomb had gone no further than that. Led by General Slocum, whose demeanor was of a strong man determined to fuse bickering groups, there had been general agreement at the close of the occasion that nothing was the matter with anything.

"I couldn't be more grateful to you, Jim," said Mr. Dascomb as the two were parting at the end of the afternoon. "You played a major part in the restoration of harmonious relations."

But now, in the club car, Mr. Blandings could find no pleasure in that. Mr. Dascomb, always tactful, had made only the vaguest references to Mr. Blandings' status, whether as an employee on leave of absence or as the publisher of a small-town newspaper soon to collapse under its burdens. Everything he said had been an invitation to Mr. Blandings himself to say something, but Mr. Blandings had said nothing, since he neither knew what to say nor how he felt. Mr. Dascomb, as so often, had crossed him up: having first shown that he would defend Mr. Blandings to the death, he had then maneuvered him into making his own explanations and apologies to General Slocum. Damn the old man!—he was as crooked as a ram's horn, yet there was nothing, nothing that anyone could ever pin on him.

The train flashed past Darien; soon it would leave the main line and set forth on its own. Mr. Blandings examined the horizon of his world, degree by degree over the full circle of the compass, and could nowhere find surcease. He was heartily glad to be leaving the city; his day there had been a perfect miniature of his professional life: the taut nerves, the crisis, the clash of egos, the false good fellowship, the panting sense of triumph at having merely regained a momentary, newly doomed, control over the stone of Sisyphus.

And so was he glad to be returning to the country? Alas, the thought of the country, where he never did anything right, made

255

him think for a bewildered instant with pleasure of the city, where occasionally, as today—occasionally, by accident, at random, out of the blue, and in the category of events for which there is no cause—he did something right.

But at least Muriel would be back in the country. It had been too many days since she had been away, and he wanted her, he hungered for her, he loved her. Also she had something nice to tell him. In the stress of the last two days he had forgotten that.

Mr. Blandings opened the evening paper and found himself through some hypnosis reading Happy Heidsic, whose column offered a mild sort of postmeridian competition to Vascal's morning thunders. Heidsic's style was less like Milton's, more like Addison's:

> Switcheroo of the week: That adman who threw the whole liquor industry into an uproar—

Oh my God, said Mr. Blandings, aloud. The conductor, hurrying through the car, paused to glance at him sharply.

> —liquor industry into an uproar earlier is in a funny light again. His assistant, who wrote a lot of his copy, quit his agency last week to go to work for Consumers Militant, the outfit that believes and works for the abolition of national advertising. Heard on Ad Row: 'An Army back should enroll in Notre Dame?'

Dward Wayburn.

Mr. Blandings wondered for a minute whether this latest intelligence, which would obviously also be news to Mr. Dascomb and Lorbet Neen, would again unhinge General Slocum. It probably would, he thought—and then decided he did not care. In that moment he knew precisely how his letter to Mr. Dascomb had found its way to Vascal. He could not prove anything, and he would never try to prove anything, and he would never confide what he felt to anyone else, not even his wife. But he knew. Dward Wayburn, wandering among the corridors of Banton & Dascomb, still an employee waiting his severance pay, his keys and identification card still on him, his burning sense of a gentleman foully wronged —it could only be he who could have had the combination of wish

256

and opportunity to square accounts he had always felt so detestably out of balance. Mr. Blandings framed a brief mental apology to Lorbet Neen for having momentarily confused him with the true villain.

For a long time Mr. Blandings gazed out the window and watched the countryside fly darkly by. He could think of nothing so detestable as apostasy. There was such a thing as taking the king's shilling, and the taking of it need not stanch a flow of soldierly bitterness. But it did set upon the soul of the man who took it the solemn obligation to be square with *something*. What that something was, Mr. Blandings, far adrift in the middle of some Sargasso Sea, did not know. He only knew that Communists turned Republicans, British scientists working for the Kremlin, American turncoats involved in betrayals so complex that the full hue and cry of the screaming American press could not bring the true facts clear, all filled him with a nauseous loathing. Pick something, and believe in it and stick to it, said Mr. Blandings, with silent vehemence.

Who is speaking? asked Mr. Blandings' daemon, in Mr. Blandings' ear.

The club car rumbled over the bridge that brought the railroad right-of-way from one bank of the Wintinock River to the other: the signal to Mr. Blandings to prepare for the Lansdale stop, two minutes ahead. He waited for the grade crossing signal the engine would sound as it began to reduce speed, and in a moment he heard it drifting back. But the railroad was switching its motive power from steam to diesel, and instead of the wild, elegiac howl that used to echo in the hills, the engine obliged only with an ear-filling monotonic noseblow. Then the train was in.

Mrs. Blandings was on the platform, looking fair indeed in a yellow dress. Husband and wife put their arms around one another as they walked up the platform to the station wagon. "I can see you're tired," said Mrs. Blandings, "but wait until I get you up the mountain and you hear what I have to tell you."

And when she got him up the mountain, comfortably in an armchair and surrounded by her love, she told him something incredible.

257

· 31 ·

W<small>HEN</small> <small>MR.</small> <small>BLANDINGS</small> awoke next morning he was sure it had been a dream. It certainly fitted in with dreamlike things more than with reality. He lay in bed and thought about it, and every few moments he cast a glance of loving admiration at his wife, still sleeping. It had been she who had caught the clue, and pursued it, and established the matter once and for all.

Sometimes—very seldom but sometimes—a man really felt in harmony with the universe. No cheap glee over a momentary success, but a feeling of true, placid, solid, unassailable oneness with the rest of creation, achieved out of a struggle for lofty ends, not mere ambition. That was how Mr. Blandings felt this morning. He felt like Walt Whitman. He felt like Henry Thoreau. He felt like Monsignor Fulton J. Sheen and the Reverend Norman Vincent Peale. Best of all he felt like himself.

Mrs. Blandings stirred and stretched beside him, and opened a happy eye. "Hello, my darling native son," she said. "How does it feel to know that all by accident you wandered home?"

Mr. Blandings grinned. "Do you remember," he said, "how after that square dance at Henry Simms' barn last winter I had that unearthly sense that I'd been there before, a feeling of *history* about the whole business?"

Mrs. Blandings nodded. "I think it was that that gave me the idea of following up old Jonathan Benjamin Lendicks in the first place," she said. "The minute I heard Daisy Fay utter his name it rang some sort of bell in my mind, and I'm sure that's why."

"You've no idea," she said, "how absolutely tedious genealogical research can be. And how absolutely confusing. If that archives

258

man at the State Library hadn't checked over everything I wouldn't feel nearly so sure of myself."

"I wish you'd read me his little one-page summary again," said Mr. Blandings. "I was so flabbergasted last night I'm not sure I took it all in."

Mrs. Blandings rose from her bed and donned a negligee. She picked up a piece of paper, and settled herself back comfortably on the bed, and began:

"Jonathan Benjamin Lendicks, Anglican divine, was born in the Hartford Colony, first seeing the light of day in the Connecticut River Valley in 1690. In 1711 he married Sarah Dolliver and—"

"Good God," said Mr. Blandings; "it isn't possible."

"Just relax," said Mrs. Blandings, and continued.

"—married Sarah Dolliver and became one of the leaders of the party of some thirty souls, among them Jared Dolliver, Abel Alders, and Crideon Eldridge, which founded the town of Lansdale (originally Lendicksville, and taking its present name subsequent to the American Revolution) in 1719. Always outspoken, sometimes to the point of extreme tactlessness, the Reverend Mr. Lendicks and his family found themselves in the late 1770's occupying a situation of steadily increasing unpopularity. Preponderant sentiment in most of the western Connecticut towns was extremely conservative, but despite that a respect for the Cloth was also an outstanding characteristic, the position of the Lendicks family became such that in 1777 it was forced to take refuge in New York."

"By God," said Mr. Blandings, slapping his knee under the bedclothes, "this is really rich. Go on."

"The original Reverend Mr. Lendicks," Mrs. Blandings continued, "died two years later in advanced old age. Following the conclusion of the Revolutionary War, his eldest son, also Jonathan Benjamin Lendicks, petitioned for permission to return to his family's home, and for the restoration of the considerable property that had been confiscated at the time of his father's hasty departure. In one of the comparatively rare cases on record among the thousand-odd families that left Connecticut for divers reasons between 1775 and 1783, amnesty was consistently refused. In the face of this unusually harsh treatment, the fortunes of the once prosperous family steadily declined. Most of its branches died out but

259

eventually one, its name corrupted by variant spellings and a fusion of the initial B (for Benjamin) with the surname, found its way to Ohio and settled on the Western Reserve lands, once regarded by Connecticut as a legitimate extension of its western area. The appearance, in early Ohio land records, of a deed recorded in the name of the Reverend John P. Blandings, an Episcopalian clergyman, taken together with documents from the ecclesiastical records of the Diocese of Connecticut, New York, and Ohio, offers more than conjectural proof that the names of the Blandings and (as corrupted) Blendicks families had their common origin in Jonathan Benjamin Lendicks, originally of Hartford, Connecticut, and a founder of the Lansdale colony."

That was all. Mr. and Mrs. Blandings said nothing for a little while, and the sun poured in the windows, and in the country silence they could hear the murmur of bees in the clover. Mr. Blandings spoke first. "If old Jonathan Benjamin married a Dolliver, in 1711, and she was a sister of the Founding Dolliver, what relation does that make me to our friend at the First National Bank?"

He answered his own question. "Still too close for comfort," he said; "too close for comfort on both sides."

"Was John P. Blandings of Cleveland your grandfather or your great-grandfather?" Mrs. Blandings asked. "I keep forgetting."

"Great-grandfather," said Mr. Blandings. "He was as far back as I ever knew anything about my family until last night." A transport of glee rocked him. "To think of it," he said. "To think that I have as much right to say I belong here as Anson Dolliver or any of his bunch. Of course there's the little matter of having been away on business for the greater part of two centuries, but that's a technicality."

"Purely a technicality," said Mrs. Blandings, happily. "Now you can really see what I meant when I told you I'd discovered something that changes our whole relationship up here. We aren't outlanders any more. We aren't strangers."

"Think of it," said Mr. Blandings. "If they hadn't confiscated Jonathan Benjamin's property it might turn out we really owned half the township."

Husband and wife joined in one another's merriment.

"You know," said Mr. Blandings, "I'm really proud of the old boy. He sacrificed everything for what he believed in. The trouble with people today is that they confuse what's best for them with what's best for everybody. Old Jonathan Benjamin didn't make that mistake."

While Mrs. Blandings mused, her husband sprang out of bed and began doing setting-up exercises. "You know," he said, after he had touched his toes five times and regained his breath, "the only trouble with that little account you read me is that it's too dry. It tells what happened without telling what *really* happened."

Mrs. Blandings laughed. "Well as to that," she said, "it wasn't hard for me to gather between the lines that Jonathan Benjamin and his family were practically tarred and feathered and ridden out of town on a rail."

"Marvelous," said Mr. Blandings. "That's having the courage of your convictions, never mind the consequences. I can see the old boy standing up there in his pulpit and preaching the gospel of the American Revolution to his precious Tory congregation. What a bunch *they* must have been!"

Mrs. Blandings, about to say something, hesitated and looked troubled. "Jim," she said. "Wait a minute. You've got the point wrong."

"What point?" said Mr. Blandings.

"The whole point," said Mrs. Blandings. "You've got it exactly reversed. Jonathan Benjamin wasn't too *radical* for Lansdale; he was too *conservative.*"

Mr. Blandings stopped his setting-up exercises and arched his eyebrows at his wife in an all-encompassing question mark.

"Certainly," said Mrs. Blandings. "What else would a well-to-do eighteenth-century Anglican clergyman be except a Tory?"

Mr. Blandings sat down on the edge of the bed, and for a moment he said nothing. It was disconcerting to have been discovered running toward the wrong goal post. A question was formed in his mind that he did not want to ask, but had to.

"And the Founding Dolliver, and his bunch?" he said. "I suppose they were—"

"They belonged to the Sons of Liberty," said Mrs. Blandings.

261

"Well," said Mr. Blandings after another pause. "That rather takes the fun out of it, doesn't it?"

"I don't see why," said Mrs. Blandings. "It all happened close to two centuries ago. It hasn't any bearing at all on today."

"I don't like having a Tory ancestor," said Mr. Blandings. "It makes me feel foolish."

"For heaven's sake," said Mrs. Blandings. "Why be upset over anything like that? What you said about a man sticking by his convictions is still just as true. He was loyal to his King and his Church, and he *did* sacrifice everything for what he believed. He spoke and wrote exactly what he felt and nobody could stop him."

"Why did they throw him out?" said Mr. Blandings. "And why were they so vindictive that they never let his family back?"

"Well," said Mrs. Blandings, "it must have been quite a thing at the time. They threw him out in 1777, which was the year the British sacked Danbury. He hid some British soldiers in his cellar, just like in the history books, and what with that and one thing and another, he got himself accused of treason."

To the very top of his upland, Mr. Blandings walked alone. There was a great oak tree there, and under its shade he sat slowly down. It was rather mean to leave Mrs. Blandings alone with the breakfast dishes, but he needed to be by himself.

He looked at the vast gap in the hills that was the valley of the hidden river. Across it the land rose up again in ranks and tiers much like the ones that descended below where he sat. The air was as unflawed as a weightless gem and only a high blue mountain range blocked him off from Ohio, from California, from Indo-China, from Ceylon. So long as he looked at the infinite distance everything within five miles was foreground. He dropped his gaze, and the foreground became fields full of wildflowers of yellow, orange, red, blue, and purple, all bowing and dancing before him, grave and beautiful on their tufted stalks. But they were not flowers to him: they were the adulterants of a hay crop. The time was again here when his fields must be shorn, yet in the year that had passed he seemed to have made no progress at all toward the solution of this elementary problem.

Nor any problem. His mind was buzzing with the brand-new

question of what to do with his and his wife's knowledge of Jonathan Benjamin Lendicks. For a while last night it had all seemed so incredible, so fantastic, so delightful. The god of coincidence that ruled his life had for once done him a good turn; in the first flush of the discovery he had known at last that he belonged in the country, *this* country; that instinct, so blind but so knowing, had led him here, and that all was at last well. For a little while his fantasies had been perfect.

But he had no sooner slept on them once, and awakened into a world in which he had at last felt at home, than it was revealed to him that his authentic ancestor, his claim to belonging to the soil in which he had been trying to hack out a bed for himself, was a high-binding snob; an aristocracy-worshipper whose ideas were so outmoded as to be cast out even before the eighteenth century had run its course—and cast out on the extremely unfrivolous accusation of treason to the new American Republic that, with the utmost hindrance from him, was trying to be born.

It was a hell of a fix for a man to be in—and it was a hell of a note that his wife, to whom belonged all the credit for the strange discovery, did not even see there was any particular fix at all.

But there was. There was not only a fix, but it was a twitching fix; he could not get it pegged down long enough to have one long clear look at it and see its form and outline. Here he was, as he saw himself, a man of good will; a disciple of progress; an open-hearted liberal, trying to fight out small battles on the side of the common folk and against the forces of entrenched privilege. But no one had really been on his side at all, except a few eccentrics here and there. Mr. Nellus had been on his side but had decamped; Mr. Silber was on his side and could not declare himself. Mr. Simms seemed to be on his side but offered him nothing. Everyone else seemed to be his enemy—and there was some mysterious X, that he had never been able to identify, that had him ticketed as someone subversive, someone about whom the word *Communist* was whispered by ignorant, toothless people. What did his wishes for progress in Lansdale *really* suggest to him? They suggested to him a sort of weak and watered-down homeopathic brand of the politics of Theodore Roosevelt, locally applied. Could he invoke Theodore Roosevelt as a character witness? He thought of the time

263

when once he had mentioned Theodore Roosevelt to Betsy. "I guess I've never heard of *him*," Betsy had said.

All of this had been complex and difficult enough. Now, this morning, as he looked backward, he could discover nowhere any line of true perspective. Whereas the liberal Mr. Blandings was descended from a hidebound, traitorous Tory, the reactionary Mr. Dolliver stemmed from "the people"—the brave and independent American pioneers, the Sons of Liberty, who successfully threw off the yoke of tyranny that Jonathan Benjamin Lendicks had done his best to keep on their necks. Here was the fix, and a pretty fix it was. His espousal of a sort of cambric-tea, 1906 liberalism had him ticketed as a Communist; now history had him ticketed as the modern-dress descendant of a Tory traitor. He knew better than to think these two accusations could be made to cancel one another out; perverse and preposterous though both of them were, they would somehow be made to reinforce each other in the minds of his enemies. The worst of it was, every day seemed to make him wonder more and more who he *really* was, what he *really* stood for. A man could see all sides of a question just so long—then, if modern instances were any guide, he ran shrieking into the arms of some sheltering dogma: where Argument was official, where Error was labeled, where Authority soothed the wearied mind and assured it that at last it could give up the burden of thinking for itself.

Mr. Blandings didn't want that, either.

He had thought he was just a harmless, middle-class American. In the rough, snarling city, that indeed was what he was; according to its simple customs, he pushed a voting machine lever once every two or four years and thus had done with all personal involvement in the political world until the next time. But in the quiet, leafy countryside complexities everywhere hemmed him in; as if his own attempts to act out his political beliefs did not have him sufficiently entrapped, the discovery of Jonathan Benjamin Lendicks now compounded everything. The enigma presented itself: although in the intervening centuries the Dollivers and the Blandings had changed sides, they were still on opposite sides. Mr. Dolliver's side had won once, and it looked as if it were fully destined to win again.

From where he sat this morning, as the sun rose higher and higher in its summer arc, the plights of Lendicks-ancestor and Blandings-posterity seemed much the same, and the solution forced on one seemed to be the same solution soon to be forced on the other: flight. For Mr. Blandings could never win. Suddenly, in the bright sunlight, he knew that once and for all; knew he had no basis for winning; that winning implied not only achieving an objective but holding it. Sometimes a man or a cause won some objective by a succession of crazy accidents, but holding what you won was done only by design. When you won something, you said to yourself this is for keeps; this is how things will be, and ought to be, from now henceforth. Winning something was the first step toward absolutes and certitudes. The reason Mr. Blandings had never won anything, it became clear to him, was that he didn't like to win, he didn't know what to do with winning if he won, he was unprepared for victory, he had no plan and never would have; only little scraps of disrelated ideas here and there.

When he got up from under the oak tree he discovered that his left leg had gone to sleep from thigh to toes; he tacked in a drunken circle for several minutes, slamming his dead foot on the ground, before he was able to set his course back to the house, back to his living room, back to his wife and daughters, descendants both of a vile, thunderous, apoplectic, rectitudinous, self-righteous Tory, died in shameful exile in New York, A.D. 1779.

"BUT MY DEAR FELLOW," said Auster Millowy, "I'm not saying a word against your motives in this thing. I have not reached the point of discussing your motives."

"There's always a gap between theory and practice," said Joseph Chasuble-Horn, with a smile of good reason and good nature.

Mr. Blandings listened glumly.

"The idea," said Auster Millowy, "of a state park in the Lake Shamalaug area rests on the mistaken assumption that it would be for the general good. If it were for the general good it goes without saying that I would be for it."

"The reason," said Joseph Chasuble-Horn, "that the idea never got any place when it was new fifteen years ago was because the people didn't want it."

"No," said Mr. Blandings. "I think I have to contradict you there. None of us lived here then but the evidence is pretty clear that the idea got killed before anybody among the public could say whether they were for it or not."

This much Mr. Blandings knew from the devoted researches of his wife.

"It seems to me," he went on, "that it would be a good, sound, fair idea to take a referendum or a poll or whatever and see what the people do want."

"Ah," said Auster Millowy, "but *which* people are to have the say in the matter?"

Nothing in Auster Millowy's published writings had prepared Mr. Blandings for this. "Why," he said gropingly, "the people who are concerned. The—well, what about the Town Meeting?"

"My dear fellow," said Auster Millowy, "a Town Meeting vote

would be entirely beside the point. *We* are the ones really affected by this idea—our whole little group here in Art Hollow—because we would be the property owners directly concerned. This very handsome map you've published"—he picked up the current issue of the *Blade* and rattled it for a moment—"shows this whole area all cut up with approach roads for the park. If you don't mind my pointing it out, one of them blasts a path a hundred feet wide right through the middle of my property."

"On the other hand," said Joseph Chasuble-Horn, "one must admit that there is nothing wrong with the theory of a Town Meeting discussion and vote. It doesn't—"

"Your detachment is very becoming, Joseph," said Auster Millowy. "Just because your own property isn't cut to pieces doesn't mean you'd like to find yourself living beside an express highway." He returned his attention to Mr. Blandings. "You see," he said, with elaborate quiet, "this is a very large township, and the people who come from the districts to the north and east of here neither know nor care about issues that center in *our* vicinity. Asking them to vote is just inviting ignorance to have an equal say with knowledge, which is clearly wrong."

"I think Auster is a little overwrought about this," said Joseph Chasuble-Horn.

"I am not overwrought," said Auster Millowy. "Things are going from bad to worse in Lansdale, but I don't see why we ourselves should hurry the process. When I first came here this was a community utterly unspoiled. I said to my wife at the time, I wonder how long this can last. I wonder how long it will be before all this beauty is *discovered*."

"That's true," said Joseph Chasuble-Horn. "Unimproved roads, very few telephones—"

"We were here before you," said Auster Millowy. "When we came we were in the vanguard of a small artistic colony, and we formed a compact, congenial, like-thinking group. Now, in the last five years, there's been an *influx*."

"An influx of what?" said Mr. Blandings.

"An influx of people from the city," said Auster Millowy.

"But you're from the city," said Mr. Blandings.

Auster Millowy looked at him pityingly.

267

"We came here to escape the city," he said. "Not to bring it and its whole atmosphere with us. The one thing we've hoped and prayed against was that anyone with ideas for *improvement* would begin to agitate this wonderful, peaceful, backward part of the country."

"And yet, Auster," said Joseph Chasuble-Horn, "we've all known it would end. Change must be faced. There's no state in the Union that's pressed the park idea harder than this one. It's a matter of historical record."

"I don't know what's got into you," said Auster Millowy. "This is not the way you were talking last week."

"I've been thinking," said Joseph Chasuble-Horn, with a smile at everyone.

"I for one will speak frankly," said Auster Millowy, staring at Mr. Blandings. "You are proposing something that will bring hordes of new people into this area. You want to see a great park set up here that will act as a magnet for thousands and doubtless tens of thousands of people from the most congested areas of New York. Your apparent idea is to invite them straight up here in their broken-down jalopies for a day's outing—littering the countryside with refuse they will be too innocent of taste or manners to pick up. And where will the overwhelming majority of them come from, geography being what it is? They'll come from the *Bronx.*"

"Well," said Mr. Blandings, "I suppose a lot of them will come from the Bronx. What's the matter with the Bronx?"

"In the broad sense," said Auster Millowy, "nothing is the matter with the Bronx, of course. If I wanted to live in the Bronx I would live in the Bronx without a moment's hesitation. I don't happen to want to. I happen to want to live here. In peaceful possession."

"All right," said Mr. Blandings, "so do I. But there's a great natural resource in our back yards that could be developed and made available to people generally. I thought this was the sort of thing you and your friends were in favor of."

"We are," said Joseph Chasuble-Horn, bringing gentleness into a situation that seemed on the verge of going rowdy.

"Of course we are," said Auster Millowy. "Surely you must be pretending that you don't see the *real* point. The real point is that

268

there are plenty of places for people from the Bronx to go without coming here. It's a question of appropriateness. It comes down to a matter of feeling. I suppose one either has feeling about things like this or else"—he gave a little shrug—"one hasn't." He smiled a compassionate smile, in which Joseph Chasuble-Horn joined.

"But only a month ago," said Mr. Blandings, "you were all for this. You said so. Both of you."

"That," said Auster Millowy, "was before it became evident that anyone was contemplating the entire project planted in our back yards, to quote an expression used just a moment ago. I've already said I think the whole matter turns on the question of appropriateness."

"Of course," said Joseph Chasuble-Horn, "the taxpayer—"

"I'm glad you brought him up," said Mr. Blandings. "The idea would be to make the whole project self-sustaining. There'd be a dime toll on the roads."

"Excellent," said Joseph Chasuble-Horn.

"Ah," said Auster Millowy. "Perhaps now we reach our point of really fundamental divergence. I seem to be alone in my argument today, but I am not in favor of *commercializing* this part of the country, no matter by whom. I think perhaps the advertising mind —quite naturally—examines everything with an eye to its commercial possibilities. It asks itself, What can be exploited here? What can be exploited to sell newspapers, which are in turn vehicles with which to exploit whiskies or depilatories or the rest of the claptrap on which a money economy depends."

A whole cluster of shell-less eggs collided point-on in Mr. Blandings' stomach. "Look here," he said, angrily; "just a few minutes ago you said you were not questioning my motives. What else are you doing now?"

Auster Millowy checked himself; his noble face took on a look of proud contrition. "Forgive me," he said. "I had no right to say that. It slipped out. But . . . since it did, should I venture a forbidden step further and ask if there is *really* no thought of exploitation in your mind here? Is there *no* connection between this park idea and the necessity for a circulation stimulant to the Lansdale *Blade*? If the question is improper, ignore it."

"Suppose there is?" said Mr. Blandings, uncomfortably. "Does that make the project a bad project?"

"Perhaps not," said Auster Millowy, "but it does not help it to be good. I am afraid nothing can do that. I am afraid that although I must apologize for raising the question of motive, my slip does not alter my fundamentals. My record is clear. Everything I have written for the last fifteen years places me unassailably on the side of the People in their battle against Privilege, but in choosing the underdog's side in this historic conflict I would do my most inviolable principles an irreparable wrong were I for a moment to sacrifice my sense of individuality to placate the Mob."

Mr. Blandings tried to let that sink in but it would not; it wabbled around on the surface of his mind like a mercury globule. "It seems to me you're going two ways at once," he said. "Isn't the Mob just an impolite name for the People?"

"I fail to see," said Auster Millowy, "that there is anything to be served at this time by involving ourselves in a discussion of semantics."

"Don't let them get you down," said Harry Silber.

"They have got me down," said Mr. Blandings. "They're doing just what you said they would."

"Intellectuals I don't trust," said Harry Silber. "Some ways I would rather deal with Mr. Dolliver and his bunch than I would with that crowd in Art Hollow. At least Mr. Dolliver never changes his ideas."

"Is that an advantage?" said Mr. Blandings.

"In some ways," said Harry Silber.

"Don't let them get you down," said Henry Simms.

Mr. Blandings said nothing.

"Are you getting any favorable reaction from your subscribers?" Mr. Simms asked.

Mr. Blandings shook his head.

"We need to stir things up," said Mr. Simms. "When the Town Meeting comes along next week I'm going to introduce a resolution in favor of the park idea. I'll spread the word around a little. I don't know what will happen, but that's the way to begin finding out."

Mr. Blandings, having suggested this to Auster Millowy, now found himself reluctant to confront his own idea.

"The farmers will be against it," he said.

"No question," said Mr. Simms.

"And the Catholic Poles."

"Not necessarily," said Mr. Simms.

"Yes," said Mr. Blandings, "necessarily. I had six letters of Catholic protest this week. Father MacDonald must have sounded off last Sunday."

"News to me," said Mr. Simms. "What about your aesthetes?"

Mr. Blandings expanded on his conversation with Auster Millowy and Joseph Chasuble-Horn; the latter had ended by telling Mr. Blandings, to the fury of his poet-colleague, that he would come out on the side of the park project.

"Well," said Mr. Simms, "at least you'll have a divided camp there. They can't stick together on anything. Main thing to hope for is they won't talk too much, for *or* against. It makes the natives mad."

"None of this sounds very promising," said Mr. Blandings.

"Now wait," said Henry Simms. "Take the commuters. I think they'll have a pretty good reaction. They want to see improvements."

Mr. Blandings emerged from a bog of thought. "Henry," he said, "let's not bring this thing up at all."

"Why not?" said Henry Simms. "Suppose it gets shouted down. The Town Meeting hasn't got the last word on it, you know. But it's a place to make a start. You don't win on things like this in the first round, anyway; it takes a lot of time and a lot of maneuvering, and you never can tell when you're going to be surprised."

"I know," said Mr. Blandings; "but when I come right up to it I'm not sure I'm in favor of this blasted park idea myself."

Henry Simms looked incredulous. "Now look," he said; "if there's one person who can't say that, it's you. You can't drop an idea you've sponsored when somebody offers to give it a fair shake for you. Why should you say such a thing?"

"Well," said Mr. Blandings, "I've been examining my conscience.

271

What does this whole project mean to me anyway? Auster Millowy up and told me I was just exploiting the idea to give the *Blade* a shot in the arm. He was a fine one to tell me, but I've been thinking about it and there's not much use pretending it isn't true."

"Suppose it is," said Henry Simms. "The park is still a good idea."

"That's what I said to him," said Mr. Blandings. "But then I caught myself wondering if I believed it. This business of being able to see both sides of the question—"

"Wait for the Town Meeting," said Henry Simms, "and you'll be able to see twenty-seven sides of the question. Very instructive."

Well, thought Mr. Blandings, here it comes. He and Mrs. Blandings were sitting well in the back of the Town Hall, longing to be as inconspicuous as possible. Henry Simms had carried out his idea —his threat, as Mr. Blandings had come to think of it—and moved that the Lansdale Town Meeting voice its approval of the Shamalaug State Park idea. Mr. Blandings had sat tense, waiting for a roar of disapproval to drown the very suggestion. His first surprise was when there was no roar of anything at all.

Henry Simms was a smart and skillful man in the politics of his native town and county; in bringing his resolution to the floor he had been careful, almost painfully careful, to say nothing about the Lansdale *Blade.* To hear his introduction you would have thought the park idea had been reborn quite independent of the *Blade;* that the paper had done no more than give advance notice of what was to be discussed in normal routine. This wasn't very flattering, thought Mr. Blandings, but it was probably the best way.

The first man on his feet for discussion was frail, benign Dr. Outcleff. There was a bit of prearrangement here, Mr. Blandings remembered; Mr. Simms had said he was going to ask Dr. Outcleff to get things off to a good start by a quiet endorsement. There was some merit in such a park idea, said Dr. Outcleff; if the idea were to be coupled with a wildlife sanctuary there would be a great deal of merit. This community didn't realize the terrible rapidity with which it was losing its fauna. It wasn't just a lax enforcement of the game laws, either: the automobile had become a deadlier killer than the gun. Dr. Outcleff paused, uncertain

272

where his thoughts were leading him. He began a damnation of automobile drivers as destroyers of all forms of animal life, and ended with a denunciation of anything that would bring any more of them a mile closer to the community where he had been born and raised. "Poor Doc," whispered Henry Simms to Mr. Blandings; "he got confused."

Following Dr. Outcleff's professional lead, Lansdale's three physicians then rose one after another, equated the park idea to socialized medicine, and attacked socialized medicine in a manner that brought to the evening its first touch of fury. What was the matter with the medical profession in America these days? Mr. Blandings wondered. The stereotype of the country physician was "old Doc"; stooped, white-haired, a little out-of-date clinically but a fount of human wisdom; counseling love, patience, nature's way. Now the man of healing was likely to be the leading political blackguard wherever you found him—full of bile, gall, and sputum.

When Auster Millowy arose it was as if there was tranquillity restored. In his beautiful voice, the paragraphs falling behind him like mowed wheat, he denounced the park idea. He did it with care; twice he emitted a phrase about exploitation by selfish interests, but he did not elaborate it.

There was an angry scrabbling for the floor when Auster Millowy sat down. Mr. Simms winked at Mr. Blandings as two local businessmen began talking at once, each of them sure he had just been personally insulted. Mr. Frapeer, optometry, having the louder voice, got the first recognition. He, too, attacked an enemy he did not name. "Some people don't realize how hard it is to make a dollar in a town where half the people never buy anything and the other half go to buy it in New York." Murmurs greeted this veiled complaint. Mr. Dobert, who had the town's Buick agency, went so far as to suggest that Lansdale might reflect that perhaps times were changing. He could remember the time when there was no such thing as a paved road in the whole county, and he wouldn't want to go back to those days. He was just as much against a planned economy as anybody else, but things ought to be considered from the standpoint of whether they would contribute to *prosperity*, and if they would, they were good, never mind pinning labels on them. He wasn't committing himself to the idea yet, but it sounded to him as if there was some new business and new money in it for folks who made their living by rendering a legitimate service to the public, and if so, it was likely to be a good thing. He glared in the general direction of Auster Millowy, and when he sat down he was seconded by Mr. Norb Rocklett, who used only slightly different words for the same thoughts.

What, thought Mr. Blandings, is going on here? The opposition is coming, on high pseudo-idealistic grounds, from precisely where I used to think there would be support—and there is support, on frank, unashamed levels of self-interest and aggrandizement, from the sources where I expected the opposition. He felt confused but easier in his mind. Henry Simms looked pleased, too. "See?" he whispered. "You never can tell how one of these things will come out."

Of course the farmers were yet to be heard from. Not that it would be what they said that counted; only what they felt. And Mr. Blandings could feel their enmity like a solid thing.

Mr. Joseph Chasuble-Horn was on his feet. He was an easy speaker. He'd been a Deputy Administrator for this and that during the war. He'd had his times with congressional subcommittees. His manner was so exactly right—relaxed but earnest—that it was hard to imagine anybody in the hall remembering he had once been a member of that widely despised thing, the government of the United States of America.

"I think," he said, "that we have here the beginnings of a tremendous idea. State parks are nothing new, but to me there is perhaps a broader design in this proposal than any of which its sponsors or seconders are thus far aware. So if you'll bear with me for just three minutes I want to consider its bearing on the possible future not only of our own town and county, or even of our own state, but of all New England."

Fair enough, thought Mr. Blandings: Joseph Chasuble-Horn was apparently big enough to take honest opposite sides from his friend Auster Millowy. He wondered why Mr. Simms had so abruptly ceased smiling.

New England, Joseph Chasuble-Horn observed, had been a

civilization while most of the rest of the continent had been a howling wilderness. It made him proud he could himself claim a New England ancestry. Until less than a hundred years ago, New England men, methods, money, thoughts, philosophy, had dominated the whole United States. It had once looked as if nothing could ever bring that domination to an end. But of course Salisbury Iron had had to give way to the richer resources surrounding the Great Lakes, and the drift of agriculture to the Middle West and the Great Plains was another example of something determined by forces stronger than man's will. Now then: some of the spirit of adventure had left New England in the general westward drift, too. Let's face that, friends. We hear a great deal about risk capital and venture money, but these days we hear rather more than we see. And this had been true for some time: for example, New England could have been the center of the automotive industry if its bankers had seen any future for the horseless carriage. But they had not. Well, others might deplore these as lost opportunities, but not he. To him, New England's true destiny lay in another direction altogether. It came from those assets of physical beauty that could never be dissipated and that took a minimum of brains to manage: beauty of seacoast, beauty of mountains, of rocks and rills. That was why, ladies and gentlemen, he welcomed the idea of the Shamalaug State Park. It might be a small step, but it was a significant step in a direction which, far from being resisted, ought to be encouraged in every way possible: looking to the future day when *all* New England, from the northeastern tip of Maine to the western valley of Connecticut, should become one great National Park!

The bastard, said Mr. Blandings; the utter, absolute bastard. He thought he had said it to himself, but a low, sibilant *"hush"* from his wife told him he must have spoken partially aloud. He exchanged hot glances with Henry Simms. Mr. Chasuble-Horn had seated himself with a pleased expression while the hall hummed with high-tension anger. Mr. Chasuble-Horn had been much more clever than Auster Millowy. He had carried out the letter of his promise to speak in favor of the project. Loathing it, he had put his endorsement of it squarely upon the most insulting grounds that could be thought of; grounds that were a guaranteed outrage and horror to everyone present.

There was no more use for Mr. Blandings to think that the park crusade was going to do anything for the Lansdale *Blade*. He even abandoned listening to the denunciations of the idea that now rose up from every side. The thing was done for. So was he.

In his blur of anger and humiliation he was conscious of only one surprise: a moment before the motion to reject was to have been voted there arose Mr. Anson Dolliver, looking very bland, with a substitute motion that the resolution be not rejected but merely tabled. There was no use, he said, acting too hotly; tabling the motion was better than putting something on the record that might look intemperate. It was so voted.

As the remnants of the meeting poured out the big front doors of Town Hall, Mr. Blandings found himself for a moment side-by-side with Mr. Joseph Chasuble-Horn, who offered him a smile of condolence.

"Stick-in-the-muds, aren't they?" said Mr. Horn.

· 33 ·

"THAT IS THE END," said Mr. Blandings, from the depths of his arm-chair.

"No," said Henry Simms. "It was a smart dirty trick, but it isn't the end."

"It's the end so far as I'm concerned," said Mr. Blandings. "Why shouldn't it be? If those two sons of bitches"—it was manifest he was discussing Auster Millowy and Joseph Chasuble-Horn—"if *they're* liberals, then I'm operating under the wrong label. I don't belong with their crowd at all. I never did. I've always been uneasy about them and with them, but at least I thought they might be square. Isn't there anybody on my side at all?"

"Of course there is, darling," said Mrs. Blandings. "Henry's on your side, and I'm on your side . . ."

"A fat lot of good that does me," said Mr. Blandings.

"I'm sorry," he said quickly. "I didn't mean that the way it sounded. It's just—"

Nobody said anything, but by the way Henry Simms kept knocking the ashes off a dead cigarette and taking quick little sips from a drink Mrs. Blandings had made him, it was obvious he was hunting for something diversionary.

"Anse Dolliver was in a good mood this evening," he said brightly, at last.

"Yes he was," said Mr. Blandings. "When he had the idea tabled instead of rejected I thought I was hearing things. God knows I don't like him or trust him but I guess Harry Silber's right that at least you always know where a man like that stands."

Mr. Simms lighted a new cigarette.

"Anyway," said Mr. Blandings, "I'd rather have a man against me on principle than for me because he thought it was fashionable."

"Maybe," said Mr. Simms. "I'll admit I was surprised the way he greeted you tonight."

"What did he do?" said Mrs. Blandings.

"Didn't you see?" said Henry Simms. "He walked up to Jim and took him by the arm and said 'Hello, old-timer.' And then he turned to me and said 'Why don't you bring your friend around to the Needlework Society for a quiet game some Saturday evening?' "

Mr. Blandings looked and felt stupid, and when his wife changed the subject he was just as glad.

"I want an extra-dry Martini and I don't want any olive in it," said Mrs. Blandings.

"Make that two," said Bill Cole to the waiter. "What do you hear from the children? Do they like going off to that godforsaken camp summer after summer?"

"How can you tell how your children feel about anything?" said Mrs. Blandings.

She took a substantial sip from her stemmed glass the moment it arrived. "This is Betsy's last year at camp," she said. "She's almost eighteen, you know; after this year I've no idea what we'll do about her. In fact, I've no idea what we'll do about anything."

Bill Cole ate a stale peanut from the dish in front of him at the little table in the Hotel Marbury's cocktail lounge, and said, idly, "How's Jim?"

"I don't want to talk about Jim," said Mrs. Blandings. "Yes I do, too. Would it be very unladylike of me to ask you to stop dawdling over your drink and order both of us another?"

"Just what is up?" said Bill Cole when the second round arrived.

"I am in a terrifying situation," said Mrs. Blandings.

Bill Cole waited patiently.

"Entirely for Jim's benefit," said Mrs. Blandings, "I did something that now I simply cannot tell him about."

"As soon as you give me something to go on I'll try to make a comment," said Bill Cole.

"Well," said Mrs. Blandings, "you know about Jim and the farmers. You know that not one of them will ever forgive or forget that oleomargarine editorial."

Bill Cole nodded.

"And you know about the state-park idea and how that was all messed up and betrayed, and you know about—"

"Muriel," said Bill Cole, "indeed I do know about all those things. When Jim and I had lunch together in this same hotel back whenever it was, I gave him a solemn warning. I told him to keep out of anything to do with dairying, even in thought; I told him never to sponsor a zoning ordinance—and I told him never to try to be the country-gentleman publisher of a small newspaper. Those seemed to me the three most infallible ways of getting into the deepest trouble in the country. But one by one Jim has done precisely those things. I must confess that when I talked about a zoning ordinance I never thought about anything quite so fancy as a state park."

"I know," said Mrs. Blandings.

"So now it isn't surprising," said Bill Cole, "if Jim is pretty completely boxed in. I don't wonder that there isn't any place for him to go from here."

"Oh but there *is* some place for him to go," said Mrs. Blandings. "That brings me right to my point. There's some place for him to go, but I know he won't go there, and he'll kill me when he finds out that I arranged it."

"You?" said Bill Cole. "You've got an out for him?"

"I have an out for him," said Mrs. Blandings. "Mr. Anson Dolliver is now claiming him as a long-lost brother."

Bill Cole replaced in the dish the peanut he had been about to eat.

"This is why I asked you to invite me to cocktails," said Mrs. Blandings. "You're going to have to tell me what to do now."

"First of all," said Bill Cole, "you're going to have to tell me what you've done so far."

"Well," said Mrs. Blandings, "just sit back and imagine that you're Mr. Dolliver, and this is your office, and I've just come in to see you . . ."

279

"This is quite a surprise," said Mr. Dolliver. He rose conscientiously, and arranged a chair for Mrs. Blandings, who looked very smart and pretty in a white linen suit and small straw hat.

"Mr. Dolliver," said Mrs. Blandings, "things are getting a little too ridiculous, and that's why I thought I'd pay a call on you. I am taking advantage of my husband's absence today in New York to visit you in your office."

It was a matter of long-standing pride with Mr. Dolliver that he could be cordial to anyone, if he thought it a good idea.

"Very pleased to see you," he said.

"I thought you ought to know," said Mrs. Blandings, "that I have just come back from Hartford, where I heard you called a Communist."

The cigar Mr. Dolliver was lighting fell to the floor, and he went after it in a hard scramble.

"Ordinarily," said Mrs. Blandings, smoothing her white gloves with womanly calm, "I would not have cared what names I heard you called, whether I thought them true or ridiculous. But in this particular case I felt I had a reason for pausing to inquire further."

Mr. Dolliver's attempts to relight his cigar were not meeting with success.

"By whom you were called a Communist I shall naturally not reveal," said Mrs. Blandings, "but I am violating no confidence when I tell you that this epithet was applied to you in the hearing of Mr. Eldo Fay, whom it affected most adversely."

Mr. Dolliver's cigar leaped afresh from his grasp.

"You know Mr. Fay?" he asked.

"Frankly," said Mrs. Blandings, "I had never met him until last week, and I was unaware that he was so powerful in the councils of your political party in this state. But his wife and I have been friends since childhood, and were roommates in college together."

"It would not be necessary to answer such a preposterous charge," said Mr. Dolliver.

"Oh yes it would, Mr. Dolliver," said Mrs. Blandings. "In fact it was. And I answered it on your behalf—or caused it to be answered. I hope I did right."

Mr. Dolliver stared.

"I thought it was generous of me," said Mrs. Blandings, "par-

280

ticularly since I know you have applied the same libel to my own husband."

"Now my dear lady—" said Mr. Dolliver.

"Never mind that," said Mrs. Blandings. "It's getting to be a deep-rooted American custom to call anyone with whom one disagrees by some abhorrent political name. I just happened to know at first hand the circumstances that had you branded as a Communist, since they were entangled with my younger daughter's essay on the atom, so I thought simple fairness demanded that I speak out."

"Mrs. Blandings," said Mr. Dolliver, hoarsely.

"If you really believe my husband *is* a Communist," said Mrs. Blandings, "then you will be wondering right now whether *my* assurances that *you* were not could have any persuasiveness with Mr. and Mrs. Fay."

Mr. Dolliver seemed to be looking at a mathematical point on the orbit of Halley's comet.

"But they did, Mr. Dolliver," said Mrs. Blandings. "Isn't it curious? Mrs. Fay and I had a third roommate at college whose name was Shibby Smith. I had utterly lost track of her, but from Mrs. Fay I discovered that she is the third and present wife of Andros Poonce. Isn't that ridiculous, Mr. Dolliver. Do you know him?"

Mr. Dolliver shook his head.

"Good," said Mrs. Blandings. "That checks. But you know who he *is*, of course?"

Mr. Dolliver nodded.

"Well," said Mrs. Blandings, "as one of the country's most authoritative ex-Communists, and as the author, successively, of *Russia Is Right!* and *Gird, Republicans!*, it is not surprising that Andros Poonce is at present Mr. Fay's most trusted political adviser and is in charge of the loyalty check on Republican party members now going on in this state. The question of your Communism had never been verified with Mr. Poonce, and it was my simple suggestion that he should be specifically asked if your name was in his files."

Mr. Dolliver waited.

"After a little delay," said Mrs. Blandings, "Mr. Poonce was able to give Mr. Fay an A-1-A clearance on you. He really went to a lot of trouble. He went through his alias cards three times. There was nothing."

"May I ask—" said Mr. Dolliver.

"I wouldn't say *all* the danger is past," said Mrs. Blandings, "because unless a man can claim actual friendship with an ex-Communist he never knows what may happen to him next. But at least Mr. Fay is now straightened out on your case, and I think your standing as a delegate to the next Republican National Convention is markedly improved."

"My dear lady—" said Mr. Dolliver.

"There is one more thing, Mr. Dolliver," said Mrs. Blandings. "Since you are not a Communist, I want you to cease promoting a cabal against my husband. Since you are not a collectivist I want you to cease directing a silent conspiracy against the newspaper my husband is trying to publish here. The reasons for your ill-will seem to hinge on your feeling that my husband is an outsider in this community of which you feel yourself the proprietor. I have one more bit of news for you. My husband has as much claim on being a native of this community as you have, and if you are surprised at this assertion, I have the documents to back it up. Mr. Fay's wife was instrumental in their coming into my hands."

Then she told Mr. Dolliver about Jonathan Benjamin Lendicks and how, through the further interests of Daisy Fay, she had discovered him and his posterity.

Bill Cole had sat silent during Mrs. Blandings' fifteen-minute monologue. "You certainly gave old man Dolliver a lot to think about," he said. "How did you leave it with him?"

"I said to him," said Mrs. Blandings, " 'There are two ways, Mr. Dolliver, in which you can take this turn of affairs. You can either decide that you and my husband are the authentic proprietors of a sort of New England McCoy-Hatfield feud all the way back to Lansdale's founding—or you can think that you are intertwined by something more important.' "

"And what did he say?" Bill Cole asked.

"He said, after he'd thought for a moment, 'The latter is the only view I'd be disposed to hold.' "

"You sort of clubbed the old boy," said Bill Cole.

"I thought I was being very smart at the time," said Mrs. Blandings.

"Weren't you?" said Bill Cole.

"Apparently not," said Mrs. Blandings. "I didn't count on Jim's reaction."

"You've told him about Dolliver?"

"Certainly not," said Mrs. Blandings. "I told you in the beginning—I haven't dared. Because he's spoiled everything. He was all happy and delighted about Jonathan Benjamin Lendicks until he found out the old gentleman was a Tory. Then he went into a mope. He seemed to think it was a blot on his own personal record as a—as whatever he thinks he is politically. He spoiled it utterly, and I can scarcely remember when I've been so hurt and disappointed. I put all my love and devotion into bringing him this incredible fact, thinking and praying it would make a deep, permanent difference in his whole, tortured, tangled life up there in the country—"

The waiter was near, and it was obviously time for the final pair of extra-dry Martinis.

"What will happen," said Bill Cole, "when Jim discovers that Mr. Dolliver is electing him to membership in the present-day Tories?"

"I just don't know," said Mrs. Blandings. "The way things are going I think it will be the last straw."

"Then let it be," said Bill Cole.

He looked Mrs. Blandings square in the eye.

"Listen, Muriel," said Bill, "there isn't any use trying to salvage Jim's life in the country. He's not the type for Lansdale County. Jim could be happy in the country if he had a professional interest he could practice there—like architecture, or veterinary medicine or counterpoint or sculpture—like Henry Simms and his friends. They're all fine people, but they don't care very much what happens to anything outside their own spheres of interest. They've learned to be indifferent to stupidity, to get along just as well with a knave as with an honest man. They're all for the right as they see the right, but if wrong triumphs, they're very relaxed about it. They were born to a different tempo than Jim or than you. They're quite willing to wait ten or twenty years, or forever, for something good to happen, and if it doesn't, they shrug their shoulders."

"I wish you'd say all this to Jim directly," said Mrs. Blandings.

"The difference between the country and the city," Bill Cole went on, "is that in the city everything's blurred, and in the country it's so terribly sharp. Jim can be neutral in the city because it costs him no effort; it never occurs to him that he has to fix Harlem or enlarge Van Cortlandt Park, or clean up the subways. He's lived among bad things so long he doesn't notice them. In the country, Henry Simms is like that—but because the country was new to Jim he saw all its faults with a fresh, sensitive new eye, and he thought to himself he had to fix them. But he was wrong. In the country the human defects are so terribly evident: the stupid are stupid and the brilliant are liars. Jim is neither. He has no place there. Let him come back to New York."

"And advertising?" said Mrs. Blandings.

"Certainly," said Bill Cole. "To what else? What else is he good at?"

"Now Bill," said Mrs. Blandings.

"All right," said Bill Cole; "that was blunter than I meant. All I really mean is that he's got a particular talent for a curious type of creation, and the economic world in which he lives seems willing to pay him a lot of money for it, so that his wife can wear clothes of expensive simplicity, and his two daughters can have the best of everything. What is wrong with that?"

"The only thing wrong with it," said Mrs. Blandings, "is that Jim doesn't like it."

"He should have decided that twenty years ago," said Bill Cole. "When he was at the age of that what's-his-name assistant of his."

"Dward Wayburn," said Mrs. Blandings.

"Yes," said Bill Cole. "Youth is the time for martyrdom. Middle-aged martyrs simply cannot stand the gaff. Can you sell your house?"

"I suppose so," said Mrs. Blandings.

"Would *you* like to come back to the city?"

"Oh God," said Mrs. Blandings. She gazed blissfully heavenward, as she finished the last of her last Martini.

"LUNCH IS READY," said Mrs. Blandings. "What are you doing reading the Bible?"

"Looking for something," said Mr. Blandings. "I don't think I want any lunch."

"The last time you had that Bible out was when Joanie was born," said Mrs. Blandings. "Come on; I've made us a corn soufflé, and I don't want it to collapse."

Mr. Blandings brought himself slowly to the lunch table and sat down at it with an air of suffering concealed.

"Are you still brooding over Auster Millowy and his friends?" said Mrs. Blandings. "I think you could afford to forget them by now: it's almost a month ago."

"I assure you," said Mr. Blandings, "they couldn't be further from my thoughts."

"Those are our own beans," said Mrs. Blandings. "If you don't want them just leave them alone and don't push them around on your plate."

Mr. Blandings gazed out the window. "I met Mr. Dolliver in front of the bank when I was on my way to the drugstore," he said.

"Oh?" said Mrs. Blandings.

"It really *is* the last straw," said Mr. Blandings. "He told me he was completely in favor of the park project. He told me he thought we'd done a very constructive thing."

"That's certainly news," said Mrs. Blandings.

"He ended up by offering to lend me some money for the *Blade*," said Mr. Blandings. "When I told him I didn't want to put the paper in hock do you know what he did? He said, 'In that case take some money from me personally, and issue a few shares of stock.'"

"That certainly makes it seem you've won your battle," said Mrs. Blandings. "I think you ought to be very gratified."

"Gratified?" said Mr. Blandings. "Gratified that in some incredible way I've gone all out for a project that has Anson Dolliver's endorsement? All I want to know is how in God's name I ever got onto the same side with him about anything. There's something in the Bible about 'What have I done that my enemies should praise me,' and I want to find who said it."

"I never heard it," said Mrs. Blandings. "Maybe you're just an unconscious conservative."

Mr. Blandings put his fork down heavily. "I am not," he said.

Mrs. Blandings also put down her fork. "Look, Jim," she said. 'You're being very disagreeable to everybody. Don't you *want* Anson Dolliver's good will? If you don't, what else could you ever have had in mind by asking to be accepted in this town? What other terms of acceptance are there? Was it your idea that you would someday *depose* Mr. Dolliver?"

Mr. Blandings felt a shock-wave in his duodenum. "Certainly not," he said. Saying it, he was aware it was a lie. His fantasies about what he would someday achieve in Lansdale had always been in a distinguished soft focus, but somewhere among them he had always been raised to the high places at somebody else's expense, and at whose expense could it have really been except Mr. Dolliver's? "Certainly not," Mr. Blandings repeated.

"Well then," said Mrs. Blandings. "This brings me to something important that I've got to tell you. I went and *bought* Mr. Dolliver's good will for you. Or at least I bought *off* his enmity. I did it in what I thought were your interests."

If Mr. Blandings' eyebrows had been singed off by a thunderbolt he could not have looked more blank.

"You may remember," said Mrs. Blandings, "that I got home from Hartford the day you were in New York, and all mixed up in

286

that nasty business about the piece in Vascal's column. So I went to Anson Dolliver that afternoon, and told him the whole story about Jonathan Benjamin Lendicks. I thought we—you—needed a haven somewhere, and this might supply it."

Mr. Blandings said nothing.

"I didn't know how he would take it," said Mrs. Blandings. "I ran that chance. I said to him, 'Mr. Dolliver, there are two ways you can take this. You can either decide that you and my husband are the McCoys and Hatfields of New England, or else you can think that you're intertwined by something more important.'"

"What did he say?" said Mr. Blandings, weakly.

"For a few moments he said nothing at all," said Mrs. Blandings. "But I had previously mentioned something else to him that I'm not going to discuss with you, and he was obviously weighing things in his mind. And finally he began to laugh, and at last he said, 'Well, I'm not sure who the joke's on, but tell your husband I'll buy him a drink any time.'"

Mr. Blandings found the energy for a long, shuddering sigh.

"All of this," said Mrs. Blandings, "I was quite prepared to tell you the very day after it happened, but you got so impossible when you found out your stiff-necked ancestor wasn't a starry-eyed Whig that since that moment there hasn't been a pleasant occasion on which to say anything to you at all."

"Muriel," said Mr. Blandings, "don't you see—"

"I know what I see," said Mrs. Blandings. "I see a man who's determined not to get along with other people on any rational basis."

"Don't you see," said Mr. Blandings, "that the one basis on which I can't possibly let myself be accepted by this town is the basis that's being offered to me right now? That you helped arrange?"

"I'd like to know why not," said Mrs. Blandings.

"If there was one thing I wanted to do," said her husband, "it was work out some of the frustrations in my own damned life in terms of doing something for this community. *That's* where I wanted some acceptance. I wanted some sort of triumph—I guess

287

it didn't matter very much what—that people would have linked up with me and said, 'Well, we have to thank Jim Blandings for that: if it hadn't been for him we'd still be doing whatever-it-was in the same old way.' Well, I can see that nothing like that's going to happen; I'm not so stupid but that I've seen that for some time. But *this*—this business of all of a sudden getting teamed up with the wrong side—it's just too much to take."

He got up from the lunch table. His wife sat still. He paused and put an arm around her shoulder. "Please don't think I'm crazy," he said. "And please don't think I'm ungrateful. I can see perfectly well why you did what you did, and why you thought it was the right thing to do."

This did not have the adequacy he meant for it. "Darling," he said, "I mean I think you're wonderful, and I'm much luckier to have you than I deserve to be."

But this did not serve the purpose, either. "All right," said Mrs. Blandings; "you go back to your study while I do the dishes."

"I'll help," said Mr. Blandings

"No thank you," said his wife. "I can really do them quicker by myself."

In the kitchen, while all the most modern appliances of modern housekeeping splashed and span, Mrs. Blandings reflected upon men, the male sex, the masculine characteristics. Above the essential primitive levels she could find very little to commend. Males were dedicated to the impossible. They achieved it just often enough—the luckiest ones, that is—to keep all the rest of the sex in a perpetual dither; perpetually sailing off in rockets to be vaporized out of existence; perpetually seeking the Absolute; perpetually falling into vats of boiling acid or perishing by falling two miles out of the sky. The death march of the lemmings into the sea was no more strange than the male's hurling of himself endlessly against the rock in the path until he should batter himself into oblivion, and the rock remain serene.

In his study, Mr. Blandings was concerned with an entirely different complex of ideas. He had resumed a determined search of the Bible, turning the exquisitely impressed pages backward and forward, restlessly and at random. After an hour or more he bent closer over the fine type. He had not found what he was looking

288

for but his eye had chanced upon the thirty-sixth verse of the tenth chapter of the Gospel according to St. Matthew:

A man's foes shall be they of his own household.

He got up and went looking for his wife.

"It feels to me," said Bill Cole, "as if I'd arrived here at the tag end of a family brawl."

"How ridiculous," said Mrs. Blandings.

"What would give you that idea?" said Mr. Blandings.

"First you forgot you'd invited me," said Bill Cole, "and I had to telephone you from the Lansdale station—"

"I just couldn't be more embarrassed," said Mr. Blandings.

"—and now it's way past the cocktail hour but nobody's doing anything but sitting around and moping."

Mr. Blandings rose forthwith.

"As soon as we've had a drink I'll bring up something interesting," Bill Cole said. "I've had a letter from an old friend."

Mr. Blandings made the drinks with an apothecary's precision.

"You know," said Bill Cole, "you can still sell the *Blade* to the Fassett people. And I'll tell you something remarkable: despite all it's been through, you can still get the same three thousand for it that you could have had in the beginning."

"Of course," he went on, biting a small piece of ice with his front teeth, "it wouldn't come out quite the same, for then it would have been a 100 per cent profit on an investment, whereas now it would be a recovery of a couple of cents on the dollars you've put into it."

Nobody contradicted him.

"Who's the old friend you had the letter from?" said Mrs. Blandings.

Bill Cole drew from an inner pocket a long white envelope. "Urmot Nellus," he said.

Inwardly, Mr. Blandings said a prayer. It was that Mr. Nellus had written to say that he was coming back to Lansdale, would resume all charge and control of the *Blade*, put it back on its singsong track, and let it go on that way until the type wore out. That would be it; that was about the only reason the old man would be writing Bill Cole.

"We've seen our last of *him*, all right," said Bill Cole. "He says he wouldn't come back to this part of the country again if they gave him the New York *Times* on the same terms he gave you the *Blade*."

All right; that's the way prayers were answered. The hell with it. "What's he got to say for himself?" said Mr. Blandings.

" 'Dear Mr. Cole,' " said Bill, reading; " 'I hope this finds you in good shape, and everything progressing well for our friends in Lansdale and on Bald Mountain.' "

He interrupted himself. "It's plain the old man wanted to write to you," said Bill, "but I guess some point of conscience wouldn't quite let him."

He resumed: " 'The climate here in Santa Barbara could not be more different, and we have day after day of unbroken——' "

"Skip the weather report," said Mr. Blandings. "What's on his mind?"

Bill Cole turned a page over and hunted for a new paragraph. " 'The *Blade* looks a whole lot handsomer with its new type and make-up than it ever did in my day,' " he read, " 'which is all the more reason why I'm sorry to see it so thin. The decline in advertising has certainly been heavy and there does not seem to have been the usual seasonal pickup. That oleomargarine editorial was a wonderful piece of work and hit the nail on the head, but when I read it and thought of what would happen I was glad I was safe on the other side of the continental divide. Here in Santa Barbara the temperature rarely—' "

"Is that all?" said Mr. Blandings.

"Keep your shirt on," said Bill Cole. "He has a couple of paragraphs here about his orange grove but he gets back to the *Blade* in a minute. Here it is:

" 'I suppose it was an attempt to get back on the right side of the fence that made my good friend Blandings throw in that series on the Shamalaug State Park. Well, it will certainly be a pleaser to Anson Dolliver. Personally, I was always able to hold him off when he tried to make me go to bat for it, but I guess I knew he was bound to get his way sometime. It first came up in the Roosevelt days as a WPA proposal, so all the town bigshots were against it, and got it all comfortably dead and buried. But it must have given them an idea, for Anse and his pals began buying up all the land around the lake they could get their hands on, and last I heard they had quite a few hundred acres between them; with a Republican legislature like they have now they would certainly get more for the land from state condemnation tnan they would from selling it off piecemeal to individuals. It's mighty funny how an idea depends so much more on *who has it* than *what it is*. In a general way—' "

Mrs. Blandings interrupted.

"Don't read any more just now, Bill," she said. "This all gives Jim and me quite a lot to take in."

"WE ARE ROUNDING out a good year," said Mr. Dascomb. "Some disappointments, some good luck that I hope was not wholly undeserved, but above everything a very steady and competent performance by the men and women of this agency. By all indications, next year will be better still."

"That's splendid, Mr. Dascomb," said Mr. Blandings. He had come to the city in answer to an extremely polite note from the head of the agency. The appointment had been for four o'clock, but Mr. Dascomb had been delayed, and now, as the two men talked, the autumn shadows grew and lent a still darker cast to the smoke-drenched New York sky. In a few minutes the Knapp Laxative sign would spring alight. Mr. Blandings sat poised, ready to wince.

"It's none too early to be thinking about next spring's schedules," said Mr. Dascomb. "The Arf people are getting ready to spend some really important money on Catchow next year, and Old Supine is pretty nearly doubling its schedules."

Mr. Blandings listened with a ringing counterfeit of eagerness.

"We have a new account that is going to bear some nursing along," said Mr. Dascomb. "The American Society of Exterminators is getting ready to go national."

"That sounds logical," said Mr. Blandings.

"It *is* logical," said Mr. Dascomb.

Mr. Dascomb shot his cuffs; Mr. Blandings shifted his weight from one buttock to the other.

"There are going to be a few changes, too," said Mr. Dascomb, in a gentle voice. "Suggerd Banton came East for the last directors'

292

meeting and made the definite decision that he wanted to sell his stock and retire from the agency to devote himself entirely to his pottery business. That raised the question as to who was in a position to buy him out, and to make a long story short Lorbet seemed to be in the best position of anyone outside myself."

Mr. Blandings listened carefully.

"I should not have any more stock than I do have," said Mr. Dascomb, "so the upshot was that we're returning about half of Suggerd's stock to the treasury to be made gradually available to a few members of Top Creative—and Lorbet is taking the other half. This is confidential, Jim."

"I understand," said Mr. Blandings.

"And so," said Mr. Dascomb, "around the first of the year, the name of the agency is going to change to Dascomb and Neen, to give a truer reflection of the actual situation."

"That's splendid," said Mr. Blandings.

"So I'd say we were in a very constructive situation," said Mr. Dascomb.

"Indeed it would seem so," said Mr. Blandings.

"Frankly, however," said Mr. Dascomb, "one thing troubles me."

Here comes something, thought Mr. Blandings.

"Our laxative situation is not good," said Mr. Dascomb.

On cue, the enormous Knapp sign flashed alive, and lighted up all midtown.

"I'll confess it's beyond me to explain," said Mr. Dascomb. "George Stout has been handling the account, and I hope I don't hurt your feelings when I say that I really can't myself see any difference in the copy. But sales are off. There's the test. It's all the more serious because we know that Knapp's percentage of the total field is declining. And last week the client said very frankly that unless we could guarantee you back on the account in pretty short order, he would have to think what other arrangements he might make. Now I could scarcely be franker than that, could I, Jim?"

"No, Mr. Dascomb," said Mr. Blandings; "I don't see how you could."

"And now that you've sold your newspaper," said Mr. Dascomb, "there really isn't very much to keep you up there in the country, is there? Particularly with a cold, hard winter coming on."

Mr. Blandings seated himself in the smoker of the train for Lansdale and stared fixedly at a pillar that helped support the Grand Central Station. It had been a month ago that Bill Cole had completed the transactions whereby the Fassett Newspaper Enterprises had paid three thousand dollars to Mr. Blandings and acquired the Lansdale Printing and Publishing Company intact. A brisk young man from Poughkeepsie had taken over with no fuss whatever; had scarcely needed to ask Mr. Blandings any questions. Whatever sadness Mr. Blandings felt at the time he felt no longer. "We live in an era of consolidations," the Fassett announcement of purchase had said on the *Blade*'s page one. "Economies of centralized purchase and production will enable us to offer an improved service to this community." Nothing was said about editorial practices or policies and indeed as Mr. Blandings looked at the changed paper he realized there were none: the Fassett "package" made them unnecessary. Six comic strips had instantly made their appearance; they were incomprehensible to Mr. Blandings but they seemed to be exactly what Lansdale wanted. It was as simple as that, if you knew how. Journalism? Crusades? How silly of me, Mr. Blandings thought; how old-fashioned.

"This seat taken?"

Mr. Blandings jumped, and began to make way beside him for an unwelcome stranger. Then he looked up and saw it was Henry Simms, a long tube of tracing paper clutched in one hand. "I thought that looked like the back of your head," said Henry Simms.

The train got under way. Mr. Blandings could not find much to discuss but Henry Simms did not seem to mind. "Going to the ceremonies on Saturday?" he said.

"Ceremonies?" said Mr. Blandings. "For what?"

"Why the steam shovel is taking the first bite of earth for the park project," said Henry Simms. "It's just a sort of token ceremony, of course; they can't really get going for a year, but I hear the Lieutenant-Governor is showing up to make a speech. You'd better be there."

"I don't think I can make it," said Mr. Blandings.

294

"Anse Dolliver will be there," said Henry Simms, "with bells on. You ought at least to make a showing, seeing you started it."

Mr. Blandings looked at his companion. "I didn't start it, Henry," he said. "You started it. You started it the day you told Muriel and me about how you ran the survey for it back in the Depression."

"No, *I* didn't start it," said Henry Simms. "Must have been Harry Hopkins or F.D.R. or somebody. And look who's running with it now."

"Yes, look," said Mr. Blandings.

There was a moment of silence.

"Henry," said Mr. Blandings," when you told us about the project that day, you must have known that in the intervening years Anse Dolliver had bought up an awful lot of the land that the State's taking off his hands now at a very good figure. You get around a lot; you must have known that."

"Why yes," said Henry Simms. "I knew that. Why?"

So Henry Simms wanted to know why. He was a good man, and an honorable man, but he wanted to know why.

"It just seems to me," said Mr. Blandings slowly, "that you might have let me know."

"Well I would have if I'd thought of it," said Henry Simms, "but great Scott, what difference does it make? The park's a good project, isn't it? What else matters?"

Mr. Blandings had once used that argument himself; he could not very well attack it now.

"It's just that I found myself in a very peculiar position," he said. "I can't say I liked being the accidental means of stirring up a lot of enthusiasm that anybody could make a profit on out of public funds, at the same time he goes around damning all governments and demanding more freedom of enterprise and less restraint by the State."

Henry Simms offered a mild chuckle. "I can't answer for anybody's inconsistencies except my own," he said, "but you're not suggesting there was anything *wrong* there, are you?"

The train came to such a palsied stop that Mr. Blandings' answer was lost.

"*Certainly* not wrong," said Henry Simms. "Just smart. If I'd

295

had that sort of sense, and some money, I'd probably have done the very same thing."

"No you wouldn't," said Mr. Blandings.

"I probably would," said Henry Simms. "You can't prove I wouldn't."

Nothing was in the open. What people said and what people did were two independent phenomena. And nobody cared much. *That* was the point: nobody cared. Learn that, Blandings.

The conversation became desultory. "Ever see anything of Joseph Horn and Auster Millowy these days?" asked Henry Simms. Mr. Blandings shook his head. He did not want to discuss with Henry Simms his last conversation with Auster Millowy; the one in which the poet had denounced him as a tool of the interests.

Henry Simms tried a new topic. "I've canceled my subscription to the *Blade* under the new management, I hope you'll be pleased to know," he said. "I didn't want my kids seeing those comics. My God!"

Mr. Blandings thought this over for a moment. "I'm putting my house on the market," he said. His sentence had so exactly the quality of a retort that he had to add, "Did you know?" in a milder voice.

Mr. Simms turned to look at him in amazement. "No!" he said. It was disbelief.

Mr. Blandings nodded.

"But I saw Muriel no later than yesterday, and she never said a word about it," said Henry Simms.

"On the market just the same," said Mr. Blandings.

"But I'm shocked," said Henry Simms. "I built that house for you and your kids to live in for—well, for a quarter of a century anyway."

Mr. Blandings smiled. He was getting a faintly malicious pleasure out of shocking Henry Simms; he felt he almost knew why he liked doing it, and that if he dared to pry at his mind for a minute the true reason would come clear. He did not think he wanted to know it, because it would be petty, and inconsistent with goodness of heart and generosity. So he did not probe himself, but instead made a small ceremony of lighting a cigarette.

"Yes," he said. "I think it's back to the city for Muriel and the kids and me."

He offered no elaborations, and Henry Simms, feeling a curtain fall between himself and his companion, ceased in a moment his efforts to brush it aside. It is not a lie I have told, Mr. Blandings said to himself; it is merely a premature truth. Having said what I have said I must now discuss with Muriel the matter of selling the house and see how she feels.

It was one thing to offer a house for sale; it was another thing to sell it. Whereas in the years the Blandings had not wanted to sell their house scarcely a week went by without a brusque offer, now no one came to look at the house at all, no one could be persuaded near it, it was shunned. Mr. Blandings had listed it with all the local brokers; the same gentry that had brought him the prospects he had not wanted earlier. Until the moment he had listed the house the market had been very active, yes sir, very active indeed, I don't know when I seen it so active. Then suddenly there was no market at all. Why where have you been keeping yourself that you don't know that things are deader than a doornail, particularly for anything over $18,000? I don't know when I've seen it as dull since maybe the Depression. It began to seem to Mr. Blandings that Lansdale was now to inflict upon him the living death; he was free to leave it, he was indeed silently urged to leave it, but no one would show his house to anyone who might relieve him of it and thus make it possible for him to go.

This was bad.

This was not Mr. Blandings' only shock. The other one was the instantaneous unanimity with which his first proposal to sell the house and return to the city was greeted by the three women of his family. There was no argument, no discussion. Within five minutes it was apparent to him that his wife and daughters had, for more time than they would even faintly confess, been yearning with all their hearts to return to the city. It was all very well to have the family so quickly and perfectly agreed on a point so important, and God knew it was rare, but something about the agreement haunted Mr. Blandings. He had always regarded himself as a father-in-the-cartoons: the unappreciated, hard-working provider that kept rapacious American womanhood beminked and bejeweled, and was made the butt of every family joke for his pains. Something very different from this was now emerging: a conspiracy among his wife and daughters, formed to keep him happy; a pact between them that no matter how hard things went for them they would not reveal to him one scintilla of their troubles. But on one word from him that he was ready to bring the experiment of country living to an end, the dam had burst: teary joy surrounded and drenched him.

"But Muriel," said Mr. Blandings, as his wife got into bed after a long evening, "Muriel darling; why haven't you ever *said* anything? If you're this eager to go back to New York that means that you've been unhappy here for a long, long time. You should have told me."

Mrs. Blandings looked at him in fond surprise. "After all these years, don't you know anything about what makes a woman want to be a wife?" she asked him. "Don't you know I'd do *anything* to make you happy? Anything, always?"

From sitting up, the covers drawn about her knees, she suddenly lay down, and with her arms she beckoned her husband. "But some things with more joy than others," she said, and snapped out the light.

"How do you think this reads?" Mr. Blandings asked the next morning at breakfast: "'Country dwelling, four modern bathrooms, completely electrical kitchen, superb view, oak grove, apple orchard, fruit trees, trout stream, hayfields, barns, seclusion, 31½ acres, paved highways, commuting distance.'"

"That's wonderful," said Mrs. Blandings. "You *do* write so well."

"I'm going to put it in the Sunday *Times*," said Mr. Blandings. "I'm tired of waiting for these local pirates to dig up a prospect."

"Do you think you ought to add 'Will sacrifice'?" said Mrs. Blandings. "It seems usual."

"Definitely not," said Mr. Blandings. On his way into the city on the train he added "Will sacrifice," and Miss Willersley immediately phoned his composition to the classified ad department of the *Times*. When it appeared it produced an instantaneous reaction.

"Mr. Blandings," said Harry Silber over the telephone on Sunday, before Mr. Blandings himself had seen the New York papers, "it was news to me you're going to sell your house until now I look at the *Times* classified under Lansdale."

"Why Harry," said Mr. Blandings, "it's been listed with every broker in town for I don't know how long. I put the ad in myself because I'm getting tired of waiting."

"You won't have to wait long now," said Harry Silber. "Listen; I just sent a husband and wife name of Kirker to your place two minutes ago. They were looking for it and got lost practically in my back yard. Don't let them get away."

"Prospects?" said Mr. Blandings.

"Hot," said Harry Silber. "I made up a price. I said I'd heard you might let it go for sixty-five thousand, but I didn't know."

"My God, Harry," said Mr. Blandings. "I wasn't going to ask—"

"Don't tell me," said Harry Silber. "They ought to be there now if they don't blow all their tires first. I told them I thought they might be too late."

"But I haven't—"

"Yes you have," said Harry Silber. "I have an uncle would buy your place if you'd sell to him."

When Mr. and Mrs. Kirker arrived at the top of Bald Mountain they were poised, casual, and controlled. Mr. Blandings had tried to act that way once himself, under the selfsame maple trees. . . . It seemed so long ago.

Mrs. Kirker was well stocked with sensible questions about the efficiency of the town snowplows in winter, and how often the electric current failed. Then she began to approach more intimate topics. Mrs. Blandings gave her husband the signal for silence and took on the inquiries herself.

"How about the neighbors?" said Mrs. Kirker.

Mrs. Blandings smiled gently. "Typically lovable Nutmeg Yankees," she said. "Of course, you've got to *know* them."

"Naturally, naturally," said Mr. Kirker with an impatient glance at his wife.

"We have two daughters," said Mrs. Kirker, beginning again. "How—"

"How interesting, so have we," said Mrs. Blandings.

"How would you describe the schools?" said Mrs. Kirker.

"Solidly rooted," said Mrs. Blandings. "My husband is too modest to say so, but he has been a member of the Board of Education."

"Is *that* so," said Mr. Kirker. "Must have been a thankless job." Mr. Blandings smiled strongly.

"No nonsense about progressive education, I take it," said Mr. Kirker.

Mr. Blandings felt that his wife would entrust him with one word. "None," he said.

"In these small towns," said Mrs. Kirker, whose voice struck Mr. Blandings as pleasant but a little insistent, "there's sometimes a certain amount of feeling against new people."

Mrs. Blandings' eyes took on a faraway look. "I think," she said, "the word 'tolerant' describes Lansdale remarkably well."

I got something out of Bryn Mawr, said Mrs. Blandings to herself, even if it was only knowing that the Latin *tolerare* means to endure, to put up with, to suffer, to bear. After all, there has never been a lynching in Lansdale County.

"Yes," she repeated, "tolerant is a very fair description."

Mr. Kirker cut politely through these feminine delicacies with a man's question.

"Any mortgage, may I ask?"

Mr. Blandings repeated his previous success. "None," he said.

"But I'm sure," said Mrs. Blandings, "that Mr. Dolliver at the First National Bank would be more than eager to extend an accommodation to any new purchaser up here."

Mrs. Kirker returned to a topic from which she had been deflected. "I'm not too crazy about living in the midst of a lot of hicks," she said.

"There is quite an art colony up here," said Mrs. Blandings decisively. "You can see why."

She had been leading her prospects up, up the hill; to the orchard and the upland beyond. When she reached her strategic point, where she knew the flaming glory of the Indian summer foliage was made almost insupportable by contrast with a tiny silver thread of river, she whirled about. With her right arm she made a Grecian gesture she had once admired in Jane Cowl.

300

Mr. Kirker stared. His compressed lips were trembling. "God," he said. He had tears in his eyes.

"Tell me," said Mrs. Kirker; "why are you people giving up this place?"

Mr. Blandings cleared his throat. "To be perfectly frank," he said, "it is somewhat more than our needs dictate now that our daughters—"

"I see," said Mr. Kirker.

Mrs. Blandings gave her husband a covert glance of admiration before she turned back to Mr. Kirker.

"Would you commute?" she asked him deferentially.

"Yes he would," said Mrs. Kirker. "And I'm not at all sure it isn't too far out. He has to be in the office every day. He's a hard-working advertising man."

There was a tiny pause, which Mrs. Blandings broke. "How *int*eresting," she said. "Jim, I think we should be absolutely frank with Mr. and Mrs. Kirker. If they're interested I don't think it would be fair to let them get their hopes up *too* high."

As if bolted on platforms geared together, Mr. and Mrs. Kirker turned to Mrs. Blandings.

"I don't know anything about the ethics or etiquette of these situations," said Mrs. Blandings, "but the fact is we're considering a prior offer."

The house brought a good price; a very good price indeed. Even after Mr. Blandings paid off every country debt there would still be quite a lot left over. He had made Harry Silber accept a five per cent brokerage commission for getting Mr. and Mrs. Kirker back on the proper road, and still there was quite a lot left over. Mr. Blandings didn't care whether this was inflation or not; it felt fine. But of course there was one problem that was very difficult.

One day Mrs. Blandings came home radiant from a trip to the city.

"What do you suppose," she said. "Emily and Alex are going to get a divorce."

"Your cousin Emily?" said Mr. Blandings. "What's such good news about that? I thought you were crazy about her. I thought she and Alex were supposed to be the perfect love match."

"I am," said Mrs. Blandings. "They were. But it's all gone to smash and there's no use crying over spilt milk and don't you *see*? Emily says we can have their apartment."

Mr. Blandings perked up.

"It's as if it had been built for us," said Mrs. Blandings. "It's on East 83rd Street, and it's on the eleventh floor, and just think—out of a side bedroom window you can catch a little glimpse of Central Park."

"Say," said Mr. Blandings; "that sounds mighty attractive. It would be wonderful to have a little greenery to look at."

He rose, and kissed his wife with warm affection. "Gee," he said, "you're adroit at finding things. You've got a knack."

· 36 ·

W<small>HEN</small> <small>MR.</small> <small>BLANDINGS</small> got to the office one morning he found Miss Willersley in a state of high emotion. "Oh Mr. *Blandings,*" she said. "Wait till you look on your *desk.*"

For whatever significance it might be to Dr. Abraham Udderweld, the eminent psychiatrist he was determined to begin visiting next week, Mr. Blandings' instant mental image was of a coiled king cobra.

"I'm so *happy,*" said Miss Willersley. "I'm so thrilled and happy I just don't know what to do." Her eyes, Mr. Blandings noticed, were filled with tears.

He struggled to get off his rubbers, covered with snow that was already beginning to make a pool on the carpet. The windows were plastered with wet, hard-driven flakes, and although it was ten in the morning the lights were on all over.

"Don't be so slow," said Miss Willersley in an agony. "I can't bear it. Mr. Blandings, *you've won the Mahoffey Award.*"

Everybody knew about the Mahoffey Awards. Mr. Blandings felt some unidentifiable emotion which was perhaps curiosity. "Judith," he said, "you know there isn't *a* Mahoffey Award: there are thirty or thirty-five at least, every year."

"Yes I do know," said Miss Willersley, her words coming fast and excited. "I just spoke that way. Actually, Mr. Blandings, you've won *three.* A gold medal, a bronze medal, and an honorable mention. *Look*—why won't you *look?*"

She snatched the top letter from his desk and thrust it in front of him: "Class Seventeen: Weekly Newspapers of 2500 Circulation or Under: Series of Articles Deemed Most in the Public Service; Gold Medal. Editorial Best Exemplifying Independence

303

of Thought; Bronze Medal. Excellence of Typographic Design; Honorable Mention."

"Wait a minute," said Mr. Blandings. "Let me get this sorted out."

"The Gold Medal is for the Shamalaug State Park series," said Miss Willersley.

"That belongs to my wife," said Mr. Blandings.

"The Bronze Medal is for the oleomargarine editorial," said Miss Willersley.

"I wrote that when I was a little tight," said Mr. Blandings.

"And the Honorable Mention for Typography—well, that explains itself," said Miss Willersley. "The Award Dinner's at the Waldorf three weeks from Thursday. Mr. Blandings, it'll all be in the papers, won't it? Could I go? It says you can have eight tickets."

Here was this girl, thought Mr. Blandings, who had been his secretary now for almost seven years, if you left out the time he himself had been away. She thought he was somebody. He was quite sure that she had already found some pretext for telling every secretary on the floor that morning that her employer was a thrice-crowned Mahoffey Medalist, and a man of substance and distinction far above the other bosses of less fortunate girls. He owed her something in return for her faith; he could not tell her that her faith was foolish.

"Well, Judith," he said, "that's gratifying. Yes, it really is. Particularly the typography one; I've always fancied myself as a typographer."

"I should think you'd be so proud," said Miss Willersley. "*I* am. You're always winning something or other; you and the whole family."

Yes, thought Mr. Blandings, that is so. Before these bestowals this morning there had been Joanie's spectacular award from *Nubile Girlhood Magazine,* so long ago. Years before that there was, too, the Gold Medal from the Harvard Advertising Awards that had first crowned Mr. Blandings as a young copywriter and said that no one in the world had written more beautiful and powerful words than he in the service of a chocolate-covered laxative. And some time before that, he now reflected, oh a long

304

time before that, he had been an occasional gold and silver badge winner from that dear, dead giver of gifts, *St. Nicholas.* There was no question, the Blandings family could win prizes.

"Yes," said Mr. Blandings, answering Miss Willersley, "both the children seem to have the same sort of ability, too. There was Joanie's prize from *Nubile Girlhood;* very gratifying. And now Betsy—"

"Betsy?" said Miss Willersley; "how wonderful; what's Betsy done?"

"Just the other evening," said Mr. Blandings, "Betsy came home with a blue ribbon she'd won at cooking school."

"Cooking school," said Miss Willersley. "How wonderful. I didn't know she was going to cooking school. That sounds as if— don't let me ask a fresh question, but is there going to be some good news about Betsy soon?"

Mr. Blandings looked startled. "Why I don't think so," he said. "She's always loved to cook; she's an extremely feminine type, you know, and she's just been using her spare time to take some lessons at the Cordon Bleu."

"Still," said Miss Willersley, "I suppose a father is often the last to learn."

"I suppose he is," said Mr. Blandings.

He sat down at his typewriter. What was he going to do about the Mahoffey Awards, he wondered. Decline them, on the grounds that he wasn't the paper's proprietor any longer? No, he couldn't exactly do that. But he didn't see how he could accept them either, without making himself a part of a conspiracy for which he had no stomach at all. Well, fortunately or unfortunately, he couldn't even acknowledge them today; he had a couple of pieces of copy to bang out that he should have had finished two days ago. He typed out his name at the top of the copy paper and fell into a bemused staring. Just for experiment he tapped out two lines of iambs with a spondee at the end. Then, without even crossing out the words, he tore the whole sheet from his machine. He'd have to do a thousand times better than that, but one thing was immutable: the words had to fit the theme of the Bach Passacaglia. Hank Rivvuld had been a long time gone from the radio department of Dascomb & Neen and whether he would ever again be a well man was unhappily doubtful. His discovery of the theme's adaptability to the uses of the American Tobacco Company— which had been what his psychiatrist had called the "precipitating factor" in his unfortunate illness—had never got anyplace, but it had found its uses just the same: rewritten into triplets and re-scored for flutes, brass, and percussion it made a tune that had taken the fancy of The Makers of Queeze. It was up to Mr. Bland-ings to provide something that would go appropriately with Bach.

The buzzer sounded under Mr. Blandings' desk. "Mr. Neen's office is on the line," said Miss Willersley. "He wants to drop in for a minute." It was being a delightful day for Miss Willersley: that Mr. Neen should come to Mr. Blandings' office was the way things should be appointed.

"Jim," said Lorbet Neen, closing the door on Miss Willersley, "this is about my boy Nadwell."

Mr. Blandings' last notions of how to collaborate with Johann Sebastian Bach left him.

"He doesn't want to go back to college," said Lorbet Neen. "God damn it, you try to plan so your children will have the advantages you missed, but it doesn't work out the way you plan."

The thought of Lorbet Neen as the victim of a frustration gave momentary balm to Mr. Blandings.

"He wants to start earning his own living right away," said Lor-bet Neen. "He wants to learn something *practical*. So he wants to go into the agency business."

"Not surprising," said Mr. Blandings.

"I told him," said Lorbet Neen, "that I wouldn't lift a finger to help him get a job in this agency. If he could sell himself to Mr. Dascomb, I told him, that would be another matter. But I told him he couldn't work in my department no matter what happened. I don't believe in favoritism."

Mr. Blandings sat in deathly quiet.

"Well," said Lorbet Neen, "to make a long story short he sold himself to Mr. Dascomb."

There was some hitch in the talk; Mr. Blandings felt impelled against his will to help it out.

"What sort of work does he want to do?" he asked.

"He wants to write," said Lorbet Neen, heavily. "He takes after his mother."

Could there be coming what Mr. Blandings thought was coming?

"Mr. Dascomb," said Lorbet Neen, "has had an idea that he thinks is a very good one."

"What's that?" said Mr. Blandings.

"Since you need a new assistant," said Lorbet Neen, "Mr. Dascomb thinks that it would be just the thing if you would take Nadwell on and sort of break him in to the copy end of the business."

It was important not to say the wrong thing. Mr. Blandings made a lightning search among a wide assortment of responses.

"What does anybody else think about this idea?" he said. "Nadwell, for instance?"

Lorbet Neen cleared his throat. "He's all for it," he said, throwing his cigar violently out the window.

"Lorbet," said Mr. Blandings, "we should all remember that my last assistant didn't turn out to reflect much credit on me, or the agency or anybody."

"If you don't like the idea of taking Nadwell over just say so," said Lorbet Neen.

"It isn't that," said Mr. Blandings.

"I'll tell you how *I* feel about it," said Lorbet Neen. "I feel that if you would teach him how to write good copy, it would be a very good thing. And I'll go a step further, and say I think you have something here in the nature of a *responsibility*."

"A responsibility?" said Mr. Blandings.

"A responsibility," said Lorbet Neen. "Why the hell should the kid want to quit college and start supporting himself if he weren't so crazy about your daughter?"

It was in the wind, it would happen, the time was coming, it would not be put aside. Mrs. Blandings confirmed these fears when her husband faced her in the bedroom that night.

"But she's too young," said Mr. Blandings in despair.

"She won't be in six months," said Mrs. Blandings.

"Why didn't you *tell* me something?" said Mr. Blandings.

307

"I didn't want to add to your worries," said Mrs. Blandings. "And there really isn't very much to tell. They just see one another all the time, that's all, and there's no question they have what used to be called an understanding. I don't know what they call it now. If Nadwell does well in the agency I imagine it will be sooner rather than later that—"

Fathers were the last to know after all, just as Miss Willersley had said. Mr. Blandings' shoulders bowed in the knowledge that as he taught young Nadwell Neen the rudiments of copywriting, so he prepared a marriage bed for his daughter. That night, two pellets of phenobarbital were insufficient to bring him sleep. A series of endlessly repeating visions tramped roughshod through his mind. Himself and Lorbet Neen in cutaways and gray-striped trousers on opposite sides of a chancel. Himself and Lorbet Neen relaying to one another the latest messages from the obstetrical floor of Doctors' Hospital. Himself and Lorbet Neen standing before a baptismal font. Himself and Lorbet Neen genetically combined, once and for all, forever.

"The poor little bastard," murmured Mr. Blandings. He was offering sympathy for life's rough journey to a child yet unconceived. "As far as I know," he thought to himself, and twitched.

MR. BLANDINGS sat in the Chart Room and on the large yellow pad in front of him doodled with a soft pencil. "We need," he heard Mr. Dascomb saying to the Plans Board, "a new approach."

Ah, another new approach. To what? Mr. Dascomb had been talking for fifteen minutes; Mr. Blandings had heard the sounds without taking in any of the substance.

Mr. Dascomb diligently continued. "I'm satisfied, and yet I'm not. It's too bad we have to go to the client so quickly, because to be wholly frank I don't believe our own thinking has jelled. The copy's good, but to me it has a quality of, well, I don't know quite how to put it, that lacks a sort of—"

For Mr. Dascomb, this was unusually precise criticism.

George Stout, who had been wrestling with the copy, looked troubled. "There are so many of these effervescent hangover cures on the market, Mr. Dascomb," he said, "that trying to find a new approach—"

This recalled to Mr. Blandings the topic now before the Plans Board.

"Very true, George," said Mr. Dascomb. "But on more than one occasion this agency has taken a product into what seemed like a hopelessly crowded competitive situation and forced it into a commanding position. I don't want to think we've done that for the last time. And forgive me for saying I don't like the phrase 'hangover cure' very much, either; I don't think we should let it creep into our thinking."

Like a child's chant, three rhyming words came into Mr. Blandings' head. One of them was the product's name. The three words made up a sentence that could be punctuated in three different ways. Before he knew what he was doing he had uttered them aloud in a trance-like voice.

Silence fell. God, thought Mr. Blandings, why can I not keep my more vacuous thoughts to myself? Is it asking too much that I should be given the power of discrimination whereby I should utter the merely preposterous and be able to suppress the abysmal?

The pause lengthened until Mr. Blandings wished he were dead.

Mr. Dascomb was silently intent upon his yellow pad, following the point of his pencil very closely with his eyes, a tiny tip of his tongue thrust between his beautifully fitted teeth. He was trying to draw a rectangle.

"Lorbet," he said, "will you call the Art Department and ask Joe to step around for just a moment?"

The silence became awesome. Whenever Mr. Dascomb summoned the Art Department, the act was portentous. The silence continued until a haggard, collarless man, his face green with fatigue, opened the Chart Room door and made a pathetic attempt to come to attention in the presence of the full high brass of the Dascomb & Neen agency. "Yes, Mr. Dascomb?" he said.

"Joe," said Mr. Dascomb with the quiet deference he reserved particularly for speaking to the noncommissioned personnel, "are the Klink layouts finished?"

"In another hour, Mr. Dascomb," said Joe. "In another hour or maybe an hour and a quarter at the outside."

"I didn't call to hurry you," said Mr. Dascomb, in gentle reproach.

"They'd be finished now except I'm alone," said Joe. "I kept most of the crew until around three this morning, so I told them to take their time about coming back in."

"What time did you get home, Joe?" asked Mr. Dascomb.

"I haven't been home," said Joe, "but that's all right, Mr. Dascomb."

"You're too conscientious, Joe," said Mr. Dascomb. "We can't afford to let you have another breakdown. Relax on those layouts right now. I don't think we're going to use them, so there's no more cause for hurry."

Joe swayed slightly.

310

"Not use them," he said, spacing his words oddly, not even making a question of them.

"I'm afraid they've become obsolete," said Mr. Dascomb. "Mr. Blandings has just come up with an idea that I believe revolutionizes our entire approach to this type of account. The layouts will need complete rethinking."

In wild alarm, his heart pounding, Mr. Blandings stared first at Mr. Dascomb, then at Joe. He had done something again. In three months there would be a new electric spectacular on Broadway. In four months someone from the Columbia faculty would be called in to render his chant into Arabic. But until this instant he had not known, so help him God, he had not known. . . .

"Could you," Mr. Dascomb said to Joe, "in the hour that now need not be spent on finishing the old layouts, make us half-a-dozen tissue roughs along this line?" He thrust the empty, unsquare rectangle at Joe, and repeated to him, in a voice of deep Eastern mysticism, Mr. Blandings' three words.

Joe, with eyes like underexposed film, moved toward Mr. Dascomb. His gaze was circling the table, hunting for Mr. Blandings. It was obvious that his brain and retina were by now all but disconnected, and Mr. Blandings had plenty of time to make of his hands a tent over his face before the gaze should rest on him. He waited, and when he felt a sensation as of a heavy photoflash lamp roasting his exposed forehead for an instant, he knew the gaze had found him out.

"Jim," said George Stout, "you're a wonder. You're a master of the advertising form."

There was nothing ungenerous about George Stout. He sat on a window sill in Mr. Blandings' office, his face aglow with pleasure. "Here I've batted my head against the wall for six weeks on that damn copy and then you come along, never having heard about it before, and take the ball on the first play. And with just three words. It's a good thing I haven't got a jealous disposition."

Mr. Blandings stared out the window. Once Mr. Dascomb had announced that Mr. Blandings, who had only thought that he had mumbled a singsong aloud, had in fact contributed a revolutionary idea to the marketing of fizzing pick-me-ups, a new apprecia-

311

tion of his talent had swept the Chart Room like a flash fire. But a man who does something without knowing he has done it seldom finds in his inner soul that calm sense of achievement often credited to him by those not in on his secret.

"Come on out to lunch," said George Stout; "it'll be like old times."

"I wish I could, George," said Mr. Blandings, "but I have a date."

It was a lie; he had no date.

George Stout looked disappointed. "I had something I wanted to talk over with you," he said. "Could we take a minute now?"

Mr. Blandings nodded.

"I have a piece of news," he said. "It's very gratifying, and yet at the same time it's kind of exasperating, too."

He paused.

"Mr. Dascomb really ought to be telling you this," he said, "but you know how he manages to slide out of things he doesn't want to do. I can't help admiring—"

"What's up?" said Mr. Blandings.

"Well," said George Stout, "do you remember that $50,000 contest the Hair Removal Institute was getting under way about the time you went away?"

"Yes," said Mr. Blandings. "It was after I'd gone but I followed it, sort of."

"Nobody can say we didn't have the most illustrious set of judges, from the medical world and the literary world, that anybody could have picked," said George Stout. "Well, they finished their work, and night before last they opened the sealed envelopes with the code numbers corresponding to the code numbers on the entries. And you could have knocked me over with a crowbar when I saw who'd written the winner."

Mr. Blandings' mouth had gone dry, but his lips were able, just able, to form the conventional questioning word.

"Yes," said George Stout; "your daughter Joan."

"Fifty thousand dollars?" said Mr. Blandings in a whisper.

George Stout nodded. "Now the exasperating part is this," he went on, speaking quickly. "Either Joan wasn't interested in the money, or else she didn't read the small type, but in either event, of course, she can't compete, because naturally any employee of the Institute, or of its agency, or any member of the family of any such employee, is disqualified under Rule XIV."

"Naturally," said Mr. Blandings.

"But entirely apart from the money," said George Stout, "what amazes me is the gift of expression that child has. If she can do that well at fifteen, what won't she be able to do when she has a little more maturity? Did you"—George Stout found a moment's difficulty in going on— "you didn't know about this in any shape or way, obviously, did you, Jim?"

Mr. Blandings shook his head. "If I did," he said, "do you think I'd have disqualified her by coming back to work here?"

George Stout laughed; a hearty, healthy, good-natured laugh. "Well look," he said. "Even though the first prize will have to go to somebody from South Bend, we've got to do something handsome for Joan. And *Mrs.* Dascomb, if you please, has sold her husband on what may turn out to be a whale of a powerful idea. She makes the very good point that since advertising is appealing to people with younger and younger minds, so to speak, an alert agency ought to have what she calls a Junior Advisory Executive Committee, to examine all copy, and express their opinions. She got the idea from the radio, but it's still a good idea. She wants Joan to be on it—for a real cash retainer. She thinks Joan is the sort of girl who could have a big future in advertising, really big."

"No," said Mr. Blandings. "My kid doesn't want that sort of thing. My kid wants to be a scientist; she wants to be a second Madame Curie." He did not think he had ever called Joan "my kid" before in his life; a sort of encircling, protective instinct made him do it now.

George Stout smiled. "I know," he said. "When my daughter was Joanie's age and even before, she played the piano like a streak; really brilliant. And do you know who her heroine was? Myra Hess. Yes sir, Myra Hess's pictures were all over our house when we were living on that campus up at Oliensis. And then one summer when she needed some money she got a job in a department store, and that's the last we've heard of Myra Hess. She's a perfume demonstrator now."

"Myra Hess?" said Mr. Blandings. He felt numb.

313

"My daughter," said George Stout. "And if she isn't on her way straight to the top in department-store merchandising, I miss my guess. You can't stand in your children's way, Jim."

Left alone, Mr. Blandings realized he must have some lunch. He had said he had a date, when he had none. Now he must be careful not to be seen lunching by himself. The crowded elevator brought him to the lobby. He walked slowly from Madison Avenue to Lexington and went into a hamburger counter. He stood quietly behind a stool occupied by a stooped man who looked like the head bookkeeper for a dishonest firm of religious book publishers. In ten minutes, he had his seat.

"One rare," he said to the Negro counterman.

The counterman turned a handsome dark face toward the chef in the window. "Blood and sand!" he sang in a rich baritone.

When his hamburger came Mr. Blandings munched on it, and drank the coffee he had not ordered, and had a piece of shriveled pie for dessert. Perhaps, he reflected, perhaps I should take a hint. The hints are indeed rather broad that there is one particular world in which my instincts least often lead me astray, I prosper best. Not only that, but one of my daughters seems to have committed herself to this world, and of the other it has been said just this morning that she is showing talents for it. I do believe that every man has his destiny, but perhaps in asking that my destiny should give me pleasure I have asked too much. Perhaps, then, if I narrow my focus to include only that for which I have a demonstrated capacity I may find my existence more easily endured. If I spent the rest of my days devoted to what I do best; if I eschew, from now on, any distraction of ideas or activities that are not in this ken, there is every good likelihood that I shall be able to scale my peak, three words at a time, three words at a time, until at last I achieve my summit; and looking about me discover there is no longer anything visible at all.

314